Praise for Doug Peterson's Historical Novels

The Disappearing Man

Doug Peterson takes us into the story of Henry "Box" Brown, a slave in Richmond, Virginia, who makes a daring escape attempt by allowing himself to be shipped north in a wooden box. I got hooked on the storyline in the past—the abuses, the romance, the friendships—only to find myself hooked again on the harrowing portions dealing with Henry's imprisonment in the box. It is more than just fast-paced entertainment; it is an eye-opening and educational reminder of the importance of grace, acceptance, and equality. Even as the lives of many slaves blew away like windswept leaves, those leaves spread seeds and life that continue on into today.

—Eric Wilson, *New York Times* Best-Selling Author

What a wonderfully inspiring story! The way the novel is written, I could see the scenes playing as if I was watching a film. It would make a terrific movie. This book is full of great historical details, has moments that will choke you up, and others that will make you laugh out loud. One of the most unique and fascinating novels I've read in a long time!

—Deborah Raney, Award-Winning Novelist

The Puzzle People

Peterson is a master at combining intriguing fiction with historical events. I highly recommend *The Puzzle People*.

—Dave Trouten, Division Chair, Kingswood University

The Berlin Wall forms an almost literal backdrop to *The Puzzle People*. The story follows the lives of a handful of people whose lives have been ripped apart, sometimes brutally, by the totalitarian East German government, and the lure of freedom only yards away on the other side of the Wall. The story has many elements of a Cold War thriller. There are spies, soldiers, government agents, and more than one shoot-out. But ultimately this book is about findi͏ng ͏ith ͏ often very painful past. The characters mu͏st ͏me successfully, others not so much. ͏ight of East Germany does not mean th͏at ͏ "normal." Overall, an excellent read. I ͏book!

—Chuck Payne, Amazon Reviewer

THE
VANISHING
WOMAN

THE VANISHING WOMAN

Based on a True Story

Doug Peterson

BAY
FOREST

Cover Illustration by Mona Roman Advertising
Interior Design by Bookmasters

Published by Bay Forest Books
An Imprint of Kingstone Media Group
P.O. Box 491600
Leesburg, FL 34749-1600
www.bayforestbooks.com

Printed in the United States of America by
Bay Forest Books

Library of Congress Cataloging-in-Publication information is on file.
ISBN 978-1-61328-081-2

To Willis and Irene,
loving parents.
Thank you for knowing
what it is all for.

Also by Doug Peterson

The Disappearing Man
The Puzzle People: A Berlin Mystery

Find Doug at *www.bydougpeterson.com*
Also, follow him on Facebook at **Doug Peterson Author**

Acknowledgments

Thank you, Macon.

When my wife and I visited Ellen Craft's hometown of Macon, Georgia, in the spring of 2012, we found a welcoming city dedicated to preserving the memory of the past, including the difficult, painful history of the peculiar institution of slavery.

Thank you, Andy Ambrose, director of the Tubman African American Museum in Macon, for taking the time to show us the museum. Ellen Craft has a special place in this museum, which overflows with art and history. Also, a special thanks to the guides at the Sidney Lanier Cottage, the Hay House, and the Cannonball House, who did a sensational job bringing the Macon past to light. Macon was the epitome of southern hospitality, including the fine staff at the 1842 Inn, a superb bed and breakfast that operates from a house that Ellen and William Craft would have passed by regularly in their time.

In addition to visiting Macon, we went to Savannah, Georgia, and Charleston, South Carolina—two stops along the way for Ellen and William Craft. I would be remiss if I didn't highlight our tour guide, Ed Grimball, a 12th-generation Charlestonian, whose love for his city and for preservation is strong.

My wife, Nancy, continues to be the greatest support; thank you for walking the chalk-line with me for more than 35 years of marriage, bringing balance and brightness to my life. And thanks to our children, Michael and Jason, who show me every day what life is really all about.

I also acknowledge the usual suspects—people who are always there to help me along and save me from doing anything too ridiculous:

- My enthusiastic publishers, Steve Blount and Art Ayris at Bay Forest Books.
- My steadfast agent, Jonathan Clements, of Wheelhouse Literary Group.
- Tom Hanlon, a wonderful writer and editor whose guidance is golden.
- My manuscript readers, Heath Morber, Dave Evensen, Kathy Gullang, Ric Peterson, Michael and Jason Peterson, Bill and Jane Sutton, my mother Irene Bland, and my wife Nancy.
- Shannon Morber and my wife Nancy, for their insights on the birth experience.
- My prayer partner, Scott Irwin.
- Pat East, for combining creativity with technical excellence in Web design.
- Bob Starnes, Jeff Trubey, and the gang at Brentwood Studios.
- Mona Roman Advertising and Bookmasters, for giving the book its form and look.
- The University of Illinois librarians, who make my historical research so much easier. It's handy living in a community with one of the best libraries in the world.
- Macon historian Conie Mac Darnell for taking the time to answer my questions.

Finally, I thank Jason and Kristen Peterson for being living proof that love transcends color, for we are all One Blood. One drop of His blood has made it so.

"I appear this evening as a thief and robber.
I stole this head, these limbs, this body
from my master. Ran off with them."

—Frederick Douglass, escaped slave

PROLOGUE

ELLEN CRAFT DASHED ALONG THE COBBLESTONE STREETS, USING the gas streetlights as markers and running as fast as possible in a long skirt. She had been told to stay put and stay hidden, but she had to see William, had to talk to him. So in the dead of night, when everyone in Reverend Parker's house was sound asleep, she changed into her dress, put on her cloak, and slipped out the back door without rousing the house.

Ellen knew the danger was real. Reverend Parker stored a loaded gun in his desk drawer and kept a sword nearby for good reason. Still, she was so weary of all the hiding and all the disguises. Her husband, William, was determined to face the slave catchers head on, and she was just as determined to be by his side.

She maintained her speed—a dangerous thing to do in women's clothing in the pitch black, when there were so many obstacles all around. As she turned the corner at full speed, her foot caught in the hem of her dress, her right ankle twisted, and she let out a cry as she slipped and crashed to the cobblestones, her right shoulder taking the brunt of the fall. The breath was knocked out of her, and she groaned softly as she rolled onto her back. She pushed up into a sitting position, hoping to get back on her feet before she was discovered.

She wasn't quick enough.

"Who's there?" came a voice from above.

Peering up, she saw the silhouette of a man's head peek out of a second-floor window. He looked from side to side and then she thought he looked straight down, directly at her. It was hard to tell for sure where he was looking, for his face was completely wrapped in shadow, as if he had a black hood pulled over his entire head. She didn't move, didn't make a sound.

Her ankle throbbed, and she breathed through her nose, trying to will away the mounting pain. Then she saw him pull his head back inside. At any moment, the man might be down the stairs and outside, looking for signs of intruders. He might turn out to be a friend, but with slave catchers on the prowl she couldn't take any chances. Her only consolation was that the color of her skin might protect her from suspicion. Her skin was white—not what you would expect for a fugitive slave.

Getting up on her knees and then to her feet, Ellen tested her ankle. Pain flared, but not so much that she couldn't hobble along. She kept going, turning onto Southac Street. It was only a short distance now. She knew where she was headed, but it was difficult to distinguish the correct building in the dark. She lost her bearing for a moment and wondered if she had even gone down the right street.

"Stop!"

The voice came from a figure, barely visible in the halo of a gaslight, moving toward her from the front stoop of a brick row house. Ellen obeyed; she stood perfectly still, praying that the person was friendly. The man emerged from shadow, and she saw that he was a Negro. That brought some relief, although free blacks had been known to aid slave catchers.

"Sister Ellen?"

Ellen could see him clearly now—a small, trim man, with bushy eyebrows and a thick black beard. It was Lewis Hayden, owner of the house on Southac Street where William was holed up.

"Yes, it's me."

"Sister Ellen, what're you doing out on the streets?" Lewis didn't wait for an answer, but took her by the arm and directed her toward the front door of the narrow brick home. "Hurry, follow me."

Ellen and Lewis slipped up the short set of stairs and entered. As she moved through the dimly lit foyer, she nearly stumbled over a hulking barrel at her feet.

"Careful," he said, catching her before she fell.

"What's that?"

"You don't want to know."

Ellen stopped and stared. There were two barrels, barely discernible in the light spilling out from the nearby parlor. The odor was familiar.

"Brother Lewis, what is gunpowder doin' in your foyer?"

"You don't want to know."

Lewis tried to pull her away from the kegs, but she wouldn't be moved. "You can't be thinkin' of takin' this house down with gunpowder."

He released his grip and stared her in the eyes. "If they come, we won't be captured."

"Does William know about this?"

"I do," came a voice from the staircase. "What I don't know is why you're here."

As William came down the stairs and moved into the candlelight, she noticed a gun jammed into a holster, and on the other side was a knife in a sheath on his belt. He was slim, close to 6 feet tall, and he had a medium-length beard, thick eyebrows, and hair that sloped across his head. His skin was considerably darker than Ellen's.

Still limping, she hurried across the foyer and walked into his embrace. He kissed the top of her head.

"Why're you here? It's too dangerous. And what happened to your foot?"

"It's nothing."

Ellen pulled back and looked up at William. The presence of explosives, so near, terrified her. "But why gunpowder?"

"We need to be ready for anything. And that's why it's too dangerous for you to be here. Brother Lewis, we need someone to escort her back to Reverend Parker's."

Ellen held on to William even tighter. Lewis moved to her side and put a hand on her shoulder, but he didn't try to force them apart. Neither did William.

"I'm sorry, Ellen," William said.

"I'd rather die at your side than…" Her throat constricted, choking off her words.

"You need to go, Ellen. It's not safe here."

"Then come with me."

"I can't. This needs to be settled, needs to be faced."

"Then let me face it with you."

"You need to be safe."

They had gone through so much to get this far; it didn't make sense that they couldn't face this new threat together. But before Ellen could put up any more argument, the front door swung open. William moved her to the side, putting his body between her and the door. She noticed his hand go to his gun, and Lewis also pulled out a revolver.

Entering the door was a black man, breathing like he had just run a race; he had his gun out as well.

"Trouble," the man said. "They're coming."

Ellen felt the stab of the words. She hobbled over to the stairs, sat down, and put her face in her hands. Had she been followed? Had she brought death to this house?

"Ellen, you gotta go out the back," William said, taking her by the arm and pulling her to her feet.

As she rose, her eyes returned to the two kegs of gunpowder just inside the front door. She realized that this day had an air of inevitability. She realized that they had been sitting on a powder keg for a long time now, and it had been just waiting to go off ever since that day in Macon, Georgia, when it all began.

1

Macon, Georgia
Thursday, December 21, 1848

ELLEN'S TEETH CHATTERED, AND SHE PULLED THE THIN BLANKET around her shoulders. She was cold, and she was terrified. In the dim glow of a single candle, she sat on a stool and watched her husband William emerge from the darkness with a pair of scissors in his right hand. They were the scissors that she had used for so many years as a seamstress. Now they were being turned against her, like so many things.

"Are you sure?" William asked.

Ellen ran a hand through her long, black hair. Her hair was her glory, her pride, and without it she would wear shame upon her head. But she had no choice. It had to be done. The Lord would understand.

"I'm sure."

She felt William's hand, a gentle tugging as he took up her hair, which cascaded down her neck to the middle of her back. Then he paused, and she heard the wind pick up, rattling the branches of the trees surrounding their cabin behind the Big House.

"The first cut," he warned.

Ellen heard the metallic snip and felt another tug, like a fish on the end of a line. Already, her head felt lighter—so strange, so foreign. She tried to hold back the tears. Her hair would grow back, of course it would. But how long would it take? A year? Only one other time had her head felt so bare, and she tried not to think of that day.

Sister Tillie said you had to cut your hair on a full moon if you wanted it to grow back, and tonight a quarter moon hung in the night sky. Ellen didn't believe such nonsense, but sometimes she wondered. Sometimes she worried.

Ellen's skin set her apart from other slaves on the Collins estate, for she was as white as her master, but that was not surprising. Her master was her father, while her mother was a light-skinned slave who also had a white father. Ellen's hair was long and softly curled; it was not as dry as other African women's hair, but she still had to regularly treat it with bacon fat and goose grease. Working inside the Big House as a maid and seamstress, she was allowed time to make herself presentable every day, something never allotted to field slaves. So she would carefully curl her hair with a butter knife, heated in a can.

Ellen was 22 years old, three years younger than William, and she had a small, round face with delicate features—thin eyebrows, thin lips, soft eyes. Only her nose seemed a little long for her face—a trait she always felt self-conscious about—but that feature would work to her advantage, helping to disguise her femininity. She stood 5 feet, 6 inches, which was tall enough to pass as a man without raising any suspicions.

Now her hair was gone, dropping noiselessly to the dirt floor of the cabin. Ellen wiped away a tear. Then she felt the gentle brush of her husband's thick beard against her ear as he leaned down and kissed the side of her head.

"Next. The clothes," he said.

Looking over her shoulder, she watched William disappear into the darkness, his skin blending into the shadows, and she heard him unlocking the bottom drawer of their dresser. A master cabinetmaker, he had constructed the dresser himself. He stepped back into the light, holding out a pair of gray trousers and a white shirt that Ellen had sewn in secret. Was it right to do this? She had asked the Lord many times if this was permissible, but there was no other way. She couldn't pass herself off as a white woman, because a woman could not travel north with a male slave. She had to pass herself off as a man. *A white man.* The Lord would understand. He carried the Israelites to freedom, and she had the same Israelite audacity.

She took the trousers from her husband, and he turned away. He probably knew she would feel even more humiliated than she already felt if he watched her step into a man's clothing. So he turned his back as she slid on the trousers.

So this was what it felt like to be a man. The material felt so constricting around her legs. Her body felt so strange, so foreign, like it wasn't hers any longer. Next came the shirt, and then the dark black boots.

"I'm ugly," she said as William tied a cravat around her neck.

"You can't never be ugly."

"But my hair..."

"It'll grow back."

William bent over and scooped up the pile of hair on the floor, and his eyes caught hers. He had a guilty look, as though he'd been caught committing a crime. "I best get rid of this."

Ellen nodded, and William ducked out the low cabin door, where she heard him moving off through the woods. The wind kicked up again, and she knew the gusts were taking her hair and scattering it across the land. When he returned, he helped to tie a sling around her neck and nestle her right arm in the cloth. The sling had been her idea. They knew that at some point she would be required to sign her name—an impossible feat since she could not read or write. So she suggested her right arm be put in a sling, and then she could pretend that she couldn't write with an arm ravaged by arthritis.

"Almost there, now," he said, as he began to tie another bandage, this one wrapped around her chin—like a toothache bandage. It would hide much of the smooth skin of her face.

Next, Ellen slipped on a bulky black coat, which hid her womanly features. In her pocket was a pair of green spectacles, too dark to wear at night like this. But come daylight, the tinted glasses would do the job of hiding her feminine eyes. The finishing touch was the top hat, a poor substitute for her hair.

She felt like such an imposter. Deep down, she still felt like herself, like a woman, and she was sure that people would see through her in an instant. She hated the pants, the bandages, the hat—these new forms of bondage.

"You make a most respectable-looking gentleman," William said with a grin.

He was trying to lighten the mood, but the words hurt, like touching a bruise. She didn't want to look like a gentleman. She hated the very idea, but what else could she do?

"Do you really think people will believe what they see?" she asked.

"Try a deeper voice."

"But I feel so foolish."

"Say that in a deeper voice."

"But I feel so foolish," Ellen said, this time lowering her voice. It sounded ridiculous.

William stared at her and scratched the side of his face. "Try not to speak if at all possible."

After years of working so closely with Miss Eliza, Ellen knew exactly how to speak like a proper southern white woman. But a white *man*? That was another thing entirely. She was doomed.

"Let's pray," William said, and all that Ellen could think was that they would need a lot more than a single prayer to pull this off. They needed a real Spirit-breathed miracle. They settled down on their knees, and William recited a Psalm he had memorized, his favorite.

"In God I put my trust; I'll not be afraid of what man can do to me. Thy vows are upon me, O God. I give praises unto thee. Thou hast delivered my soul from death, so deliver my feet from falling, so I can walk before God in the light of the living."

"Amen," said Ellen, taking a deep breath. "You have your pass?"

William slipped a hand into his coat pocket, just to make sure. William's master, Ira Taylor, was good about giving passes at Christmas to visit relatives in Macon, and so was Ellen's master, Dr. Collins. They had permission to be away for a few days, although Dr. Collins would explode if he knew just how far they planned to go. A thousand miles was a long way from Macon.

William blew out the candle, plunging them into darkness, and they stepped out into the cold morning air. The ground crunched beneath Ellen's black boots. William and Ellen's lodging was just behind the Big House, which was dark and quiet, with two roaming cats the only sign of life. The wind had died down, and everything was as still as death. Trees were silhouettes, and already the eastern horizon was beginning to lighten with a yellow smudge of dawn. In the harsh light of day, she would surely be seen for what she was—a woman. A slave.

She began to sob, and he wrapped his arms around her, removed her top hat, and kissed her hair—what was left of it.

"We'll do this, Ellen. The Lord'll carry us there."

She felt so foolish. She knew she couldn't break down when she got out in public or she'd be seen as an imposter.

"I'm sorry," she said.

"I'll meet you at the train."

They had decided to take different routes to the train station because they didn't want to be spotted together by neighbors. People would know something was amiss if they saw William walking with a strange white man. So William slipped away, and Ellen watched him head toward Walnut Street, which would take him down to Fifth Street and the city bridge across the Ocmulgee River. Her husband was a confident man, sure they could do this. But Ellen...she just didn't know.

She began to make her way to the station, alone and terrified of crossing the path of anyone—especially someone she knew. She tried to walk like a man: firm, strong strides; confident strides. No swaying of the hips. She had practiced it, but now she was confused, almost clueless about how to walk. They had a thousand miles ahead of them, and things were already going wrong in the first few steps.

The Collins' house stood on Mulberry, and she decided to take Wharf Street down to the city bridge and the Ocmulgee River, where pole boats carried cotton to downriver markets. Located close to the center of Georgia, Macon was the heart of the Cotton Kingdom.

The city was quiet at this time of day, and she tried not to hurry, not wanting to raise suspicions. However, as she turned right onto Wharf Street, she heard the jangle of a bridle and rattle of wagon wheels; to her horror she spotted a dray rolling in her direction. A man sat up front, and there appeared to be a boy sitting in the back of the wagon, keeping company with several large sacks and a big black dog.

The glasses! She had almost forgotten! It was now light enough that wearing green-tinted glasses would not seem odd. She fumbled through her coat pocket and put them on. The wagon was almost upon her.

Confident strides. Strong strides.

What's her name if they ask? Her mind had suddenly gone blank, and she licked her dry lips. Her heart was racing. Mister William Johnson! That's it. She wasn't Ellen Craft any longer. She was Mister William Johnson.

The man steering the wagon was unfamiliar, which was a good thing. They were not yet upon her, but she could tell that the man was staring at her intently, and so was the young boy in the back of the wagon. It wasn't every morning that they saw someone strolling down the street with one arm in a sling and a bandage around the face. This stranger could see right through her, she was sure. The dog barked, as if it too knew her secret.

All of a sudden the man broke into a smile and tipped his hat. "Good morning, sir. Fine day ahead of us."

The boy also tipped his hat, and the dog barked again. Ellen gave them an awkward smile, an artificial grin, and tipped her hat. She didn't dare speak. If she did, her voice would crack.

Then just like that, the wagon was gone, rolling off to meet the day. The man had looked straight at Ellen, but he didn't see her. He saw only William Johnson. Ellen Craft had disappeared—vanished into thin air.

2

Clinton, Georgia
May 1836: Twelve Years Earlier

"Now you pay attention, Ellen. Don't you be dreamin' of bein' outside none."

The voice of Ellen's mama snapped her back to attention. She had been gazing out the window at the children playing outside—the master's children—and he had plenty of them with his wife. But the master had a few "yard children," too—children whose skin was varying shades of brown.

Ellen would know. She was one of his yard children, although her skin was white, with barely a hint of brown, and her hair was straight, except for some gentle curls. But that still didn't give her the right to be playing outside with the full-blood children when there was work to be done. Still, at least she didn't have to work in the fields, picking cotton until her hands cracked and bled.

"You can't be dreamin' when we got so many chores," Mama said.

At 10 years old, Ellen still had to stand on a stool to see into the bowl where her mama was mixing up a concoction for Miss Eliza's hair. Ellen took one more glance outside on a day that was about as fine a spring day as they had seen in Clinton this year. The kitchen curtains fluttered in a gentle breeze that carried the scent of flowers.

"Pay attention, I said. Now tell me, Ellen, what did I just put into this here mixture?"

Ellen stared into the bowl and drew a blank. She could see that there were yolks swimming in there.

"Eggs, Mama."

"How many eggs?"

"Three."

"*Two.* And what did I add with it?"

Ellen had absolutely no idea. "Hog's lard?"

"Lordy, Ellen, why would I be puttin' in hog's lard for gettin' rid of scurf?"

With a shrug of her shoulders, Ellen said, "Sorry, Mama."

"I mixed in the juice of a lemon and beat it all together. Now you remember that 'cause ya'll be in charge of these things someday."

"Yes, Mama."

"Now take this on up to Miss Eliza. I gotta run outdoors and beat the daylights outta two rugs, so don't you spill none."

"Yes, Mama."

Mama carefully placed the porcelain bowl in her hands. Mama's skin was light brown, much lighter than any of the other women working in the house or in the fields, but not nearly as light as Ellen's. It was all so confusing, all these different shades and all the different rules that went with them. Just outside she could see the master's son, Elliott, who had been born the same year as Ellen. They had the same father, but his mother was Missus Smith, so he was outside playing.

Singing to herself, she went up the stairs, careful not to spill a drop of the egg mixture. The home of Major James P. Smith was not a piddling thing; it was large, for he owned this plantation, a hotel, land in nearby Macon, and close to 100 slaves. Ellen had not been in the homes of very many other white folks in Clinton, but just comparing them from the outside she knew the Smith house was larger. It was what people called a mansion. Upstairs was a passel of rooms, and down at the end of the hall was Miss Eliza's room. Ellen knocked.

"Miss Eliza, I got you your hair concoction," she called through the door.

She could hear Miss Eliza sigh all the way through several inches of wood. "C'mon in then."

After Ellen entered, Miss Eliza said, "I don't know why my mama thinks I need this. I don't have the scurf as bad as all that."

Actually, Miss Eliza's hair did sometimes have flecks of dry skin caught in it like little pieces of plaster, but Ellen didn't contradict her. Miss Eliza Cromwell Smith, 17 years old, sat at the mirror in her shift and corset. Ellen thought she was pretty, although maybe a little too thin. Her dark black hair came down in ringlets on the sides of her head, and her plucked dark eyebrows arched above piercing eyes.

"Set that down over there, and run this brush through my hair, Ellen."

"Yes, Miss Eliza," she said to her half-sister, no different in skin color or curl of the hair.

Miss Eliza put on airs now and then, but she was a lot nicer to her than Elliott or the other four Smith boys. Maybe it was Miss Eliza's desire for female companionship in a house overrun with males that did it, but she seemed to enjoy sharing secrets with Ellen. Miss Eliza wasn't about to let down her hair with her mama, who could be as cold as December, even in July.

"Did you hear about the company coming this evening?" Miss Eliza asked.

"Yes, ma'am. Some pretty important folks, I hear." But that was nothing new. Important politicians were always parading through on Saturdays and Sundays for meals fit for King Solomon. Ellen loved these days because there were always leftovers for Mama and her and the other house workers.

Ellen ran the brush through her half-sister's long hair. The brush had wide bristles so Ellen could get down to the scalp. Sure enough, she could see little specks of skin coming off like snow.

"I think there may be some young men among the party," Miss Eliza said, oblivious to the blizzard on her head. "That's what Mama says."

Missus Smith was working hard to find a match for her only daughter.

"Here, let me run the brush through *your* hair," Miss Eliza said, swinging around on her stool.

Ellen stood motionless, mouth open like a fish.

"C'mon, Ellen, don't you look so shocked. You have the finest hair I've ever seen, and I just love to give it a brushing so I can see it shine."

Ellen looked toward the open door and bit her lip.

"Don't you be so scared now. You have nothing to be afraid of." Miss Eliza slipped the brush out of Ellen's hand and went to work on her hair. It felt good, the brush working through her long strands, like a plow through soft soil. Ellen caught a look at herself in the mirror and smiled. Miss Eliza was right. Her black hair glistened like the sun on the river.

"I should let you use some of my oil of behn," Miss Eliza said.

"But Miss Eliza..."

"Your hair should smell as nice as it looks."

Oil of behn was a perfume that carried the scent of flowers, giving your hair the smell of spring.

"I don't know, Miss Eliza."

"Stop your worrying, Ellen. Just as soon as I'm done running this brush through your hair, I'll have you fetch it."

Ellen had always known that Miss Eliza wanted to have a sister, but this was playing with fire. Years ago she used to play with Ellen like she was another one of her dolls, dressing her up. But Missus Smith didn't like it none, and she hated it even more when Miss Eliza treated her like a little sister—once even letting her share the bed during a bad storm.

"But shouldn't I be doin' *your* hair, Miss Eliza?"

"In time, in time."

"But what about the hair concoction?"

Miss Eliza ignored the fear in her voice. She just kept chattering about the big to-do in the evening.

"I hear Dr. Collins of Macon will be among the guests. I sure hope he brings along his two sons."

"Mmm, yes." Ellen closed her eyes, savoring the feel of the bristles through her hair. She was beginning to enjoy this, and her worries were carried off in the breeze.

"Have you ever set eyes on Abner Collins?" Miss Eliza asked.

"No, ma'am."

"He's as handsome as they come."

Ellen smiled and opened her eyes to catch another look at herself in the mirror.

She nearly let out a scream.

In the reflection, she saw Missus Smith standing in the doorway, looking in and glowering at the scene in front of her—her only daughter brushing the hair of a slave. Missus Smith was a short woman, a little plump and pasty, but she could be as dangerous as a rabid dog—and twice as mean.

Missus Smith pounced.

"Eliza Smith, what in the world do you think you're doing! Do you think you're a slave girl or something?"

Dropping the brush to the floor with a clunk, Miss Eliza spun around, her face changing from a dreamy grin to an instant look of horror.

"No, Mama, I just—"

"And you have a lot of nerve askin' my daughter to brush your hair!" Missus Smith stormed, whirling around to confront Ellen.

Missus Smith lunged at Ellen. Ellen tried to duck and run, but the woman was quick for such a stout lady. Missus Smith's arm shot out as quick as a whip and snatched Ellen by the hair and yanked her back. Ellen yelped in pain as Missus Smith twisted her long hair, sending a flare across her scalp, like fire.

"I'll put you in your place, you little wench!"

Ellen saw Missus Smith reach for a pair of scissors with her other hand. She was sure the woman was going to kill her right there on the spot.

Miss Eliza screamed, "Mama, what are you doing?" Then she melted into tears.

Letting out a scream of her own, Ellen tried to take off, but Missus Smith still had a tight hold on her hair, like it was a leash. Any moment now, she expected the scissors to sink into her back, so Ellen reached for the bowl of hair concoction, thinking maybe she could throw it on her mistress and break loose. But as she grabbed the rim of the bowl, Missus Smith gave another tug on her hair, and the bowl came crashing down on the floor, egg splattering yellow everywhere.

"Now look what you've done!"

In the shock of the shattering pottery, Missus Smith let loose of Ellen's hair for just a moment, and that was all Ellen needed. She broke away and went sprinting through the door—and ran straight into the waist of the master, Major Smith. She tried to squirm around the master's legs, but he slapped an arm around her waist and lifted her off the floor like a sack of potatoes.

"What in heaven's name is going on in here?"

The room was in chaos. Miss Eliza was still in tears—big, heaving sobs—and Missus Smith was standing amidst the fragments of the bowl, with a wide splatter of egg at her feet. She looked angry, dog-kicking angry.

"Lordy, what's happened?" came another voice. It was Ellen's mama, come to rescue her. "I heard a commotion from outside. Sound like someone dyin' in here."

Mama caught sight of Ellen in Major Smith's arms, the shattered remains of the bowl, and the mess of eggs. "Ellen, did you break that bowl? I told you to—"

"Maria, you best stay downstairs and let me sort this out," said Major Smith.

Ellen's mama looked at the major, then at Missus Smith, and then finally at Ellen, and her eyes filled with fright. Ellen didn't often see fear in her mama's eyes. But there it was, plain as day.

"But if my girl done—"

"I said I will handle this, Maria."

Mama nodded, backing up slowly before turning and retreating down the staircase.

"That *thing* had our Eliza brushing her hair!" Missus Smith snapped, pointing at Ellen. "Who does she think she is? I think we—"

"Quiet!"

The major was about the only one who could silence Missus Smith with a single word—even a single glance. He carried Ellen to the edge of Miss Eliza's bed and sat down. He carried her gently, like a real father.

"But Papa—" Miss Eliza started to say, but one look from the major silenced her, too. He was a large man, well over 6 feet tall, broad-shouldered but also a little wide in the waist. His hands were huge, and his voice deep. He had a ruddy face and could shake a windowpane with his laughter. But he could also be as stern as a schoolteacher.

"Did you break the bowl?" he asked Ellen. He spoke calmly, quietly.

Tears streaming, Ellen nodded. "I thought she was gonna kill me." She wiped her eyes with the back of her hand.

The major's eyes moved from Ellen to the gold scissors, still clutched tightly in his wife's hands.

"She's out of her mind," Missus Smith said. She gripped the scissors so hard that her knuckles were white.

"But Papa..." Miss Eliza said.

Ellen thought that Miss Eliza was going to explain it all, tell him it was *her* idea that she brush Ellen's hair. But Miss Eliza broke down again and couldn't get any more words out.

Major Smith motioned toward his wife. "The scissors."

Missus Smith looked down at the scissors, as if she had forgotten they were in her hands.

"Hand me the scissors."

Ellen stared at the scissors, terrified that the major was going to do something awful with them. She thought about running, but the major had a tight hold on her, and she knew it would only make things worse.

But could things really get any worse than being stabbed to death?

Major Smith held out his right hand, an enormous hand, and his wife slowly stepped forward. She handed him the scissors, like a surrendering general giving up his sword.

"Is it true, Eliza? Were you brushing Ellen's hair?"

"Yes, Papa, but it wasn't—"

"That's all I need to know."

Miss Eliza went stone quiet, her face twisted from crying.

"Then we best make sure that doesn't happen again."

Ellen kept her eyes on the scissors, terrified, disbelieving.

The major set her down on the floor and took hold of her long hair in his large fingers. If Ellen was going to run, this was the time, but she was petrified. She couldn't move.

Then she heard the metallic snip. The major began to cut her hair, snipping it off close to her scalp, and Ellen began to sob and shake. She wondered if it would have been better for the major to kill her with the scissors than to take away her hair, her beautiful hair. She watched large clumps of it drop to the floor, and the silk-thin strands didn't make a sound. Her glory was gone.

3

Macon
Thursday, December 21, 1848

ELLEN CROSSED THE BRIDGE AND APPROACHED THE MACON station, where a scattering of people were waiting to board the Central of Georgia train. All eyes seemed to move in her direction, as if automatically drawn to her. She was sure they were looking right through her disguise, but if that was true, wouldn't somebody be saying something? Raising a ruckus? Calling the authorities down on her?

As Ellen slipped in among the crowd, she realized that the gazes were sympathetic stares directed at an ailing man. A little boy pointed at her—this strange young man with a sling and a bandage wrapped around his face. Ellen smiled back shyly, not accustomed to so much attention. As a house slave, she was part of the background, like just another chair pushed up against the wall.

The train station, a modest wood structure lined with rows of plain wooden benches, was clouded by cigar smoke. The place was a forest of top hats, as men shuffled about or stood guard by their large square traveling trunks with their oversized initials emblazoned on the side. Ellen bumped up against the hoop skirt of a young woman with a bonnet tied by a pink ribbon.

"Pardon me, sir," the woman said, her eyes flitting to Ellen's sling.

Ellen realized that a response was required on her part, so she said, in as deep a voice as possible, "My apologies, ma'am."

The woman smiled back and turned away, and Ellen let out a sigh of relief. Those were her first words spoken as a man, but now an even bigger test awaited: the station master.

"Please, sir, you may go ahead of me," said a middle-aged gentleman in a gray coat and top hat—another sympathetic soul. He tipped his hat and stepped aside for Ellen.

"Thank you, sir." She moved past and stepped up to the station master's counter, which was occupied by a friendly sort, all grins and teeth. "Two tickets, please. One for me and one for..."

She almost said "my husband" but caught herself just in time.

"...and one for my slave."

My slave. The words sounded so unnatural.

"How far you travelin', sir?"

"Savannah. Two tickets for Savannah, please."

"Just keep an eye on that slave of yours. Might try to take advantage of a gentleman in your condition and skedaddle on you."

Still grinning, the station master slid two tickets across to her, and Ellen plucked them from the counter. "He's an obedient one, sir, but thank you for the warning."

Every sentence that came out of Ellen's mouth was an agony. She had to concentrate on every word, making sure that her voice was as low as possible. Even on a frosty December day, she was beginning to sweat under the strain as she exited the depot and slipped out onto the platform. When two boys approached her, selling rocks that they had heated by a fire, Ellen shook her head and moved on. The last thing she needed was more heat.

"Train a comin'!" came a shout from above, and Ellen looked up to see a young boy perched on a tall pole, staring off down the tracks. He scrambled down, like a sailor on a mast, and the crowd became agitated and excited. Relatives began to make their final farewells all along the platform.

Then Ellen saw it coming—a big, black iron locomotive pouring out smoke like a house on fire. The smokestack was narrow at the bottom and wide at the top, and the train's bell clanged its approach. The train was just another reason to be scared. Ellen had never been on one. In fact, the railroad was still new to Macon, with the tracks from Savannah reaching the outskirts of the city just 5 years ago. Dr. Collins had taken the train many times, and she'd heard him telling folks that the train could reach 30 miles per hour. It was a terrifying thought. Horses could run that fast, but she could trust a horse. The Good Lord made horses, but ordinary mortals made trains.

"Master Johnson! Master Johnson!"

It took a few seconds for Ellen to realize that *she* was Master Johnson. She whirled around and saw her husband, William, approaching her through the crowd. He lowered his eyes, the "down look" of a slave deferring to his master. His wife.

How do you speak to a slave?

"Your ticket, boy," said Ellen coldly, holding out the piece of paper.

William looked up and grinned, as if amused by her act. Ellen maintained her stern look; she didn't crack.

"Thank you, sir. The trunk is all stowed in the baggage car, sir."

"Good work, William."

Their eyes met. Ellen knew it wasn't proper for William to be holding eye contact, slave to master. But she liked it, and she looked for some reassurance in her husband's eyes, some indication that they weren't making the biggest mistake of their lives. Their masters weren't awful, as masters go—not the kind who whipped you in the sugar house until you fainted away or screamed for mercy. But if they got caught, there's no telling where they might be sold and with whom they might wind up.

William nodded, letting his eyes linger on her much too long. "I best be goin' to the colored car," he said.

"You do that..."

Ellen could see that William was amused by every word coming out of her mouth. He cast a conspiratorial smile over his shoulder, and he made his way toward the baggage car, where slaves and free blacks had to travel. When he disappeared into the crowd, she turned on her heels and climbed into one of the cars trailing behind the engine like a colorful snake.

The inside of the car bustled with activity as people found seats on each side of the center aisle. The car was pretty, with fine red curtains hanging above every window and wooden seats with red-cushioned backs. She really didn't want to sit next to anyone, afraid of conversation, so she decided to sit on an empty bench farthest away from the potbellied stove. She figured that most travelers would want to be close to the heat, so if she hoped to avoid companionship she would have to deal with the cold and sit farthest from the stove.

Ellen slid next to the window and leaned against the cold glass, hoping to sleep—until it occurred to her that if she muttered or talked in her sleep, she would do so in a female voice. She couldn't take the chance. She would just pretend to sleep.

After a few moments, she opened her eyes, which were still concealed behind her green-tinted glasses, and she saw that the car was filling up fast. It was beginning to look like she was going to be stuck with company after all, because at this rate people were going to be forced to fill all of the seats, even the cold ones.

Ellen's heart nearly stopped. Moving down the center aisle, looking for a seat, was Mister Cray. *Mister Cray*, her master's friend. He had just dined at the house a day earlier! He had known Ellen since she was a little girl, and he had come to bring her home. Ellen was sure of it. Their escape was crashing to an end even before it began.

*****

William couldn't have been more proud of his wife. She was going to pull this off for certain if she kept up the act. Her voice was still a little high for a gentleman, but not out of the ordinary. If he hadn't already known who she was, he would have been taken in by her disguise the same as everyone.

After checking his coat pockets to make sure he had his ticket, William walked along the station platform, heading for the baggage car. It wasn't going to be much in the way of accommodations, but he didn't care, as long as it was taking them away from Macon. The first leg of the journey was east, not north, heading to Savannah near the Atlantic Coast. But from there they would take a steamboat north.

William was almost to the colored car when he spotted him: John Knight, a man employed in the same cabinet shop where he worked. Alarmed, William ducked for cover behind a wagon loaded with boxes of whiskey. A young white man in his late 20s, Knight didn't own the cabinet shop, but he acted like he did most days. It was obvious that Knight resented working beside a slave; as a white man, Knight thought he had the God-given authority to order William around. There was bad blood between them.

Knight glanced in William's direction, and for a moment William thought he had been caught, but Knight didn't act as if he had seen him lurking behind the whiskey wagon. He kept on asking questions of a train official. Knight knew that William's master, Mister Ira Taylor, had given him permission to be away from the shop for Christmas, so why would he be suspicious? Perhaps he had come to the station on entirely different business.

When Knight proceeded to climb into the baggage car, William's fears went up a notch. Not too many white gentlemen would go into the colored quarters like that. They would send someone else in to check on the baggage—unless he had other reasons for going inside.

"Hey, boy, what you think you're doin' there?"

This challenge came from directly behind, and William spun around to see an enormous white man, more fat than muscle, striding toward him, a cane in one hand.

"Sorry, sir, just needin' a place to lean against for rest."

"Well, lean somewheres else. Say, you have a pass to even be here?"

"I'm with my master, sir."

"Can you prove it? Did he give you any papers indicating that you're traveling together?"

The man glared at William. He had wide-set eyes and thick eyebrows that nearly touched above his nose, like two caterpillars crawling toward each other.

"C'mon now, let's have it."

William looked over his shoulder. The train was filling up fast and would be leaving the station at any time; he needed to be aboard. He had a pass, given to him by Mister Taylor, but it only gave him permission to visit Ellen's relatives on the outskirts of Macon for several days. It said nothing about a train.

"You could ask my master, sir. He's on board the train."

"Your pass. Surely you have a pass!"

William shifted from one foot to the other and kept shooting looks at the train, as the last people boarded.

"Please, sir, the train's gettin' set to leave."

"You better produce a pass right now or I'm gonna—"

The man looked like he was making a move to crack William in the side of the head with his cane when a much younger man came running up. "Mister Hawkins, come quick, Thomas run off with several bottles a' whiskey!"

"What?" The man swung around, shifting his fury from William to the bearer of bad news. "Are you sure?"

"He couldn't a' got far. He didn't think I'd notice, but I seen him lifting out two bottles. When I seen him, he made a run for it."

The big man let out a string of expletives not fit for a railway station, where children hovered nearby, and he took off running, a heavy, lumbering stride. William didn't hesitate. He dashed for the train, which was getting set to leave.

He paused at the entrance to the baggage car.

During the confrontation with the man, William had lost all track of John Knight. The last he had seen of the man, he was getting on board the baggage car. If Knight was still in there, William would be caught dead to rights. He'd be a fool to climb on board, but if he didn't act soon, the train—and Ellen—would leave without him.

"You have a ticket there, boy?" came a voice to William's left.

It was the conductor, holding out his hand.

"Yes, sir, I do." William produced the ticket, which the conductor studied carefully. He handed it back to William and sniffed. "Where's your master?"

"Already on the train, sir. He's the gentleman with the sling and bandage on his face."

"Oh, yes. Hard to miss. You take care of him then. Hear?"

"Yes, sir."

William stared at the door of the baggage car, still afraid of what he was going to find waiting for him inside.

"Well go on then," the conductor said.

William nodded, took a breath, and climbed aboard the train as the bell rang out its final warning.

4

Clinton, Georgia
August 1836: Twelve Years Earlier

IT WASN'T FAIR, ELLEN THOUGHT. HERE SHE WAS, LUGGING THREE buckets filled to the brim with water fetched from the well—two in her hands and one balanced on her head. And there was her cousin Frank, kneeling in the dirt and playing marbles with one of the Smith boys. Her other three cousins, Mary and the twins, Antoinette and Emma, were off to the side, sitting on the grass and playing with their dolls. Mary's blue dress spread out around her like a pretty picnic blanket.

Frank made his own marbles out of balls of clay, baked in the sun. He leaned close to the ground, one eye shut, tongue sticking out, as he flicked a marble toward the cluster of clay spheres in the dirt. Then he sat up straight and smiled, satisfied with the result.

"Careful not to spill," said Frank, leaning over, reaching out, and giving Ellen's bucket a gentle push as she passed by. Some of the water sloshed out.

"Stop it, Frank!"

Ellen tried to give him a swift kick to the back, but her foot missed, caught nothing but air, and she nearly fell on her backside. The bucket on Ellen's head crashed to the ground, splashing her legs, and this set the boys to laughing so hard that Frank fell onto his back.

Cousin Frank was 13, three years older than Ellen, and his sister Mary was 11, while the twins were 6 years old. They lived in Clinton with one of the wealthiest white men in the area, a bachelor by the name of Terrence Slator. Many years ago Mister Slator had bought a slave girl to work in his house—a girl named Molly, who just happened to be Ellen's aunt—her mama's sister. The story going around was that he started treating Aunt Molly like she was his new wife. Marrying out of your race was illegal in Georgia, so they weren't wed, but some said he treated Aunt Molly with a fondness reserved for a spouse. He also pampered Frank, Mary, and the twins—Aunt Molly's children—giving them the freedom of full-blood white children. Most people guessed why. Frank showed a strong resemblance to Mister Slator—with skin almost as white as Ellen's. Mary also looked white, while the twins displayed more African traits.

For most people, the stories about Mister Slator and Aunt Molly were stitched together from many different rumors, a crazy quilt of speculation; Ellen, though, knew for a fact that Mister Slator and Aunt Molly were like husband and wife. She had been visiting her cousins' house on a Saturday night almost a year ago—with permission from the master, of course—when she witnessed a most incredible sight.

*****

"You awake?" Mary asked.

"Wide awake," Ellen said. She didn't even want to go to sleep; she was happy getting to lie on a real feather mattress, and she didn't want to miss the experience by dozing the entire time. On the Smith estate, she slept on a bundle of blankets, curled up on a pallet just outside Miss Eliza's door, in case her half-sister needed something during the night. So sleeping side by side in cousin Mary's bed was heaven to her. No hard surface caused her to ache and wake up all night. She was floating. It was a hot summer night, and the air was still, so no breeze came in through the open window to give relief. But

who cared about the heat, as long as she could drift on top of feathers?

Evidently, Mary cared. "Wanna go outside, where it's cooler?" she asked.

"In the night?" Ellen was spooked by the darkness.

"The moon is pretty near full."

"I don't know. I like it too much just layin' here." Ellen had heard that a full moon brought out evil in the night.

"C'mon, Ellen."

Ellen heard Mary's bare feet hit the wooden floor. She didn't want to move, so she shifted to her side and closed her eyes, but Mary came around to her side of the bed and shook her by the shoulder. "Please, Ellen. The grass feels cool to the toes."

Groaning and pushing up from the mattress, Ellen decided she'd better do as her cousin asked. The only reason she was even allowed to visit was because Mary had begged for permission, again and again and again, from her mama, Aunt Molly. And Aunt Molly had gotten Ellen's mama to get permission from the master. She'd better do as Mary asked if she ever wanted to repeat this experience.

Ellen was wearing one of Mary's cotton nightdresses—much nicer than anything she owned—and they crept out the bedroom door. The Slator home was large, and it creaked at night like a big ship.

"This way," Mary whispered, and they moved through the hallway, past several rooms, one where Frank slept and the other where Emma and Antoinette dozed. Then they moved down the staircase, which curled around before reaching the landing. And that's when they saw candlelight flickering on the first floor. Someone was still awake.

Mary put a finger to her lips, and they peered down from the landing. They could see light seeping out from the ladies' parlor, where Ellen's Aunt Molly sat on a chair facing her master—Mister Slator.

"We should go back," Ellen said, but Mary put her finger to her mouth again. Then she crept down several more stairs, moving slowly, not making a sound with her bare feet on wood.

Ellen nearly gasped when she saw the knife in Mister Slator's hands. Mary must have been startled as well, because she grabbed Ellen's left hand and squeezed with all her might. What was going on? Mary pulled her down three more steps—as close to the parlor as they dare go. The full moon had brought out evil, just as Ellen feared.

Then they saw Molly—Ellen's aunt—hold out her right hand, and Mister Slator placed the knife against her palm and drew it across the skin, as if he were cutting fabric. Mary squeezed Ellen's hand even harder. Then Mister Slator did the most bizarre thing that Ellen had ever witnessed. He leaned over and put his mouth on Aunt Molly's palm, where he had just drawn blood. Was he kissing her hand?

No. He was tasting her blood!

Ellen's own blood went cold. She wanted to run back upstairs and hide under the covers. She had heard of friends cutting their fingers and merging their blood—making them sisters in blood or brothers in blood. But a grown man and woman? This was different. This was strange.

Then they heard Mister Slator speak. "Now I have African blood. One drop of African blood."

Mister Slator kissed Mary's mother, and Mary immediately turned and moved back up the stairs. She had seen enough. She had seen too much. They didn't say a word, as Mary pulled Ellen back down the long corridor and they climbed into the big featherbed.

Ellen didn't say a word. She lay on her back, side by side with Mary; when she turned her head, she noticed that Mary was just staring up at the ceiling, her eyes wide.

"Mister Slator has African blood," Mary finally said. "One drop is all it takes."

*Ellen knew she was right. A single drop of African blood made
you black, even if your skin was as white as the coldest snow.
"I know," Ellen said. "Mister Slator's just like us now."*

*****

Ellen and Mary never spoke about that night again, and Ellen hadn't
slept on a real mattress since. She still slept on the pallet outside Miss
Eliza's room, and she still worked much of the day, while her cousins
played like free children. She often dreamed of having a father who
put her on his knee and brushed her hair and told her stories—as
she supposed Mister Slator did with her cousins Mary, Emma, and
Antoinette. She dreamed so hard, it was almost painful. But her papa
was Major Smith, and most of the time he acted as if she was just
invisible. She could walk right by him in the house, and he wouldn't
even bat an eye at her—unless he wanted her to do some chore or
other. It wasn't fair. Sometimes, she imagined that her real father
lived in a far-off city, and he would come swooping in like a knight
to rescue her and her mama from this life.

"Ignore Frank," said cousin Mary, a girl tall for her age, with
knobby knees but the prettiest face Ellen had ever seen. Her long
hair was softly curled; it was as pretty as Ellen's hair, which had grown
back some since the day it had been snipped away. Mary got up from
the ground, stepped alongside Ellen, and they walked together down
the path leading toward the Big House.

"You need some help luggin' the water?" Mary asked.

"That's kind of you, but Mama wouldn't like me tryin' to shift my
chores onto someone else."

They trudged along, and Ellen noticed Mary smoothing the long,
straight hair of her white doll. Ellen wished her father would give her
a gift like that.

"I hear Dr. Collins is payin' a lot of attention to Miss Eliza these
days," said Mary, throwing in a skip as she walked.

Ellen laughed. "The wrong Mister Collins, though."

"You mean she don't like the older Mister Collins?"

« 30 »

Ellen set down the buckets to rest her thin arms, which were getting weary. "Miss Eliza had her eyes on the son, Abner. Imagine her surprise when old man Dr. Collins turned out to be the one smitten with her. He's old enough to be her daddy!"

Mary looked down and twisted her doll's hair in her finger. "Nothing wrong with havin' an old husband, 'specially if he's rich." Mary was never one to get angry, but there was a hint of irritation in her voice. Mister Slator, her father, was much older than her mother.

Ellen felt bad about what she'd said, so she touched Mary on the arm and said, "You're probably right. Miss Eliza, she's already warmed up to the idea of catchin' the fancy of such a man."

"I bet her mama likes the arrangement, too."

"Missus Smith, she's in heaven at the just the idea of them bein' hitched someday."

"You think it'll come to that?"

"Lookin' that way." Ellen took a breath and picked up the buckets once again. Miss Eliza had talked to her several times about her reservations marrying an older man when she had her heart set on the son. But as Dr. Collins lavished gifts on her—jewelry, painted miniatures, and flowers—she became accustomed to the idea of being courted by him. Besides, there was no hope of snagging the son if the father had his eyes on her; Missus Smith wasn't about to let her only daughter pass up marrying such a wealthy, powerful man.

"You sure you don't need help?" Mary asked again.

Ellen stared toward the cluster of trees just beyond the quarters of the field slaves; on the other side of the trees was the Big House. "I better not take the chance of gettin' caught shirkin' my duties."

Ellen continued on, Mary skipping alongside. But as they approached the slave quarters, Ellen noticed that the chickens were out of the poultry yard. Somebody had opened the wooden gate, and a mob of chickens that the field slaves tended were bobbing along, pecking at bugs on the ground.

"Oh heavens now, who done let out the chickens?" Ellen set down the buckets and started herding the birds back to the poultry yard. Mary jumped into action and tried to be helpful—too helpful. Doll in hand, she made a run for the chickens, scattering them in all directions, a flurry of flapping wings and darting birds. Exasperated, Ellen decided she had to settle Mary down before she stood any chance of settling down the chickens and shepherding them back to the enclosure.

Then Mary let out a scream, and not the playful squawk of a child trying to snag elusive poultry. This was genuine fear. Emerging from the poultry yard was Ellen's half-brother, the white boy Elliott. He carried a chicken upside down by its legs, and the bird's head dangled loosely like it was attached by a string. The neck had been snapped.

"You put that down, chicken thief!" Ellen went after Elliott, oblivious to the fact that he stood a head taller than she, and she tried to yank the bird out of his hands.

She felt his hand smash her in the chest, a stiff-armed shot that sent her sprawling backward into the dirt. Mary screamed again, and Elliott took off in the opposite direction, away from the Big House. The chickens, meanwhile, shot off into the trees, their skinny legs moving at top speed as they scurried in spurts toward the house.

"You all right?" Mary got behind Ellen and tried to help her up from the ground, but Ellen waved her off. Her pride hurt more than anything.

"You stay here. I gotta get those chickens before they run beneath the porch of the house!" Ellen didn't want Mary to help because she would just make things worse. Ellen took off through the narrow belt of trees and burst out onto the other side, seeing four of the chickens making straight for the porch. Once they got under the porch, it would take some doing to get them out.

She was so focused on the fleeing birds that she didn't even see the people at first. When she finally did, she came to a sudden stop. Gathered there on the house's big wraparound front porch were Major and Missus Smith, Miss Eliza, and Dr. Collins. In an instant, she knew she had made a major mistake.

Missus Smith had always told her to stay out of sight whenever Dr. Collins was around courting Miss Eliza, so she should have known better. Ellen was aware that Dr. Collins was visiting this afternoon, which was why she had planned to circle around to the back of the house and stay out of view. In all of the excitement with the chickens, however, it hadn't occurred to her that they might be out on the porch.

Ellen's eyes immediately went to Missus Smith, who was staring at her like she was the devil in a dress. Missus Smith looked like she was ready to leap out of her chair and snap her neck like Elliott did to the chicken.

Major Smith showed no emotion—just the thin, straight line of his mouth. His hand had stopped midway from drawing a cup of tea to his mouth. He stared.

Miss Eliza looked as scared as a rabbit, but Dr. Collins just smiled back at Ellen. He was an older gentleman, clearly over 50, but he was handsome with his brown hair flowing back from his head, friendly eyes, and a bushy moustache that merged with his big sideburns. He set down his teacup and leaned forward, for he had never before laid eyes on Ellen.

"Why, Major and Missus Smith, I knew you had yourself a whole army of boys, but I didn't know you had another daughter. And a pretty one too. Looks just like her sister."

He winked at Miss Eliza.

No one said a word in response.

What could they say? It was obvious that Dr. Collins thought Ellen was a white child, not a yard child. He had no idea that she was a living reminder to Missus Smith of her husband's indiscretions.

Ellen wasn't sure what to do. She knew that Missus Smith wanted her gone, out of sight, but it would be rude to just turn and run. Her eyes went from Missus Smith to Miss Eliza, who stared back at her, open-mouthed.

Still grinning and oblivious to the tension boiling around him, Dr. Collins turned to Miss Eliza and said, "Your sister has hair almost as beautiful as yours, Miss Eliza."

Ellen felt her skin go hot.

Miss Eliza cracked an awkward, sick-looking smile, and then she looked over at her mother for help. Her mother appeared so angry that the tea in her cup was sure to start boiling. Poor Dr. Collins glanced over at Major and Missus Smith and finally picked up that something was wrong. Ellen saw a blush cross his face, as he glanced from the Major to Missus Smith and back to Ellen. Then he studied Ellen from head to foot, his mind working away on what was making everyone so uncomfortable. Ellen could almost see the exact moment when he put it all together. His eyes widened just a little, and his mouth puckered slightly, but no words came out.

"Ellen, go along and play with the others," Major Smith finally said, breaking the awful silence. "Forget the chickens. You can round them up later."

Major Smith spoke in calm, even tones, as if nothing out of the ordinary had just happened.

"Yes, sir," said Ellen. She turned and went sprinting back the way she had come, her feet carrying her faster than she had ever run. She knew she was in big trouble. Come evening, Missus Smith was sure to smack the tar out of her for having the audacity to show herself in front of Dr. Collins. But even worse, what if Dr. Collins decided not to marry Miss Eliza because she had a yard child for a half-sister? If that happened, Missus Smith would do more than smack her around. This time she really would kill her. Tonight Ellen would have a hard time sleeping knowing that her mistress might sneak down the hall in the middle of the night and drive scissors into her back.

Ellen ran until she was out of sight. If she could have hidden under the porch with the rest of the chickens, she would have.

5

Macon
Thursday, December 21, 1848

MISTER CRAY SAT DOWN NEXT TO ELLEN.

She didn't look at him, wouldn't look at him. She kept her eyes out the train window, her heart clicking as quickly as a telegraph. But Mister Cray didn't slap a hand on her shoulder, didn't try to drag her out of her seat with threats to have her whipped within an inch of her life. Perhaps he didn't recognize her after all, but she could feel his eyes boring in on her. Was he studying her? Was he thinking that something about this odd gentleman behind the green glasses struck him as familiar? Only one day earlier, Ellen had served him a meal in the Collins dining room.

The man said nothing, did nothing, and Ellen continued to look out the window, feeling a sick twist in her stomach. She could hear Mister Cray getting himself situated. He didn't speak, but she knew enough about the man to realize that he wasn't one to just sit and think or sit and read. He liked to talk—and talk. Just last night he had nearly put the entire Collins household to sleep with his chatter about the weather and land prices and banking and cotton planting and more weather.

She knew it was coming.

"It's a fine morning, sir," he said to Ellen.

What do I say? He'll know it's me the moment I open my mouth.

Ellen continued to stare out the window. She didn't turn, didn't move. She prayed for him to just go quiet.

"I said it's a very fine morning, sir."

On cramped horse-drawn coaches, conversation among passengers was customary, so Mister Cray probably had the same expectations for train travel. He wouldn't give up easily. Ellen wondered if she was making a bigger scene by *not* answering, but if she gave him any encouragement, even a single word, he would launch into a conversation that stretched on and on like the never-ending tracks of the railroad.

"Sir! It's a very fine morning!" he said, volume rising.

Probably the entire coach heard those words. Ellen noticed a man in the row directly in front of them laugh, and she could sense growing agitation in Mister Cray.

"You're wasting your breath, mister," said the man in the next row. "I think the poor guy's mostly deaf."

Deaf? That's not a bad idea, Ellen thought. If she pretended she couldn't hear, even Mister Cray was bound to leave her alone.

Then again...

Ellen felt the gentle tap on her shoulder, and she knew she had to respond in some way. It would not be natural to ignore the tap, so she turned and looked directly at him. Mister Cray was a stern-looking gentleman, with dark, deep-set eyes, a long, narrow face, a shock of gray hair, and a billy-goat beard on the tip of his chin. He was deadly serious about everything in life, especially the weather.

"It's a fine morning, isn't it, sir?" By this time, Mister Cray was talking so loudly that he had drawn the attention of the entire car. Necks craned, faces turned in her direction. When she answered, everyone would be listening, but she *had* to answer. She had no choice.

"Yes, it is!" Ellen spoke as loudly as she could while still maintaining a deep voice. Then she turned back to the window and stared out. She wiped away a bead of perspiration that had slipped down her forehead.

"It's no use, sir," said the gentleman in the row in front of them. "Bein' hard a' hearin', he's not gonna be much of a conversationalist."

Ellen could hear Mister Cray harrumph. "If he's hard of hearing, then where's his ear trumpet?"

"Don't know," said the other man. "Maybe he's got one of those newfangled ear trumpets that you wear above the ear."

She sensed their eyes on her, probably trying to look at the reflection in the window to see if she had an ear trumpet perched on the opposite ear.

"Or maybe he left his ear trumpet in his luggage," whispered the other man.

"Maybe so."

*****

William stepped into the baggage car, bracing himself for the smack of John Knight's cane across his face, but all he saw were two black men on the opposite side of the baggage car, hunched over a game board. No sign of John Knight, praise the Lord.

The front end of the car was partitioned off by a screen and packed with luggage of all sizes. The back end, what little space existed there, was for free blacks and slaves who had permission from their masters to travel with them. The baggage car/colored car had only a few rough benches, no heat, and a window on each side; it was hitched directly behind the engine and coal tender, because the first car in line ran the greatest risk in the event of a crash. Also, if you cracked open a window, most of the smoke from the engine would come pouring into the colored car instead of the passenger car. William didn't really care. He was just excited the train was taking him out of Macon.

"Where ya headed, mister?" came a voice from the midst of the baggage, and William noticed two young boys perched on top of the stack, kicking their dangling feet against the trunks and bags.

William wanted to say "none of your business," but there was no sense in causing a fuss one minute after stepping aboard the train.

"Savannah."

"Wanna join in?" said one of the men playing the game. William noticed that the two men were playing mancala, an African game that involved moving seeds from hole to hole in a board. It required counting, and although William couldn't read, he could certainly tally in his head. Counting was necessary in cabinetmaking, with all of the measuring required.

"Sure," William said.

"You can play the winner."

William dropped down onto the splintery seat and watched the two men take turns moving seeds from hole to hole to hole, with the object of getting the most seeds to one of the two large holes at each end of the board. One man was slim and grinning and having a grand time, while the other one sat there studying the game board so seriously that you'd think the outcome was going to decide whether he lived or died.

"The name's Johnny," said the thinner man. He looked to be about age 30—clean shaven with thick eyebrows and an easy grin. He had slicked-down hair and wore a vest and coat—pretty nice hand-me-downs. Most strange, though, was the slight indentation, shaped like a horseshoe, in his forehead.

Johnny must have noticed where William was staring.

"Got kicked by a horse 5 years back," he explained, almost as if the indentation was a badge of honor. "Your master up front?"

"Yes, my master...he's traveling to see a doctor."

"That so? He the one I saw all bandaged up?"

William nodded. He didn't want to elaborate. A complicated story might be hard to remember and square with Ellen's story.

"What's he ailin' from?"

"Joint pain real bad."

"He ever try willow bark?"

"Sure has, but it ain't enough to get rid a' the pain."

"Stop your squawkin' and take your turn," groused the other man playing the game. He had just been sitting there, staring and scowling and waiting for Johnny to shut up and move.

"What's your hurry? We got all the time in the world." Johnny gave a wink to William and added, "Jimmy here is just mad 'cause I whipped him three games in a row."

"Two games," muttered the gloomy one. "And the name's Jim, not Jimmy."

"Make that *three* games, Jimmy." Johnny made his final move to seal another victory, and Jim growled out a few curses before stalking to the other side of the baggage car to sulk.

*****

Ellen felt a lurch, the train suddenly began to inch forward, and as the locomotive left the station Mister Cray mercifully decided to leave her alone. But Ellen felt a new fear creep beneath her skin: train wrecks. She didn't understand how something so big and so strong could stay positioned on two rails as narrow as pieces of lumber. When the tracks turned, wouldn't this monstrous piece of iron keep going straight ahead into a ditch? She also couldn't figure how two trains, going opposite directions, could share the same stretch of track. Wouldn't they smash head on? She'd heard stories from a slave once who said he'd been given the job of collecting body parts after two trains had crashed into each other.

The locomotive slowly picked up speed, and Ellen noticed that her hands were clenched so tightly that her knuckles had gone white. The train gave a sudden, sideways jolt, and she nearly screamed. She thought for sure it was coming off the rails. Within a few minutes, the train was moving faster than a stagecoach, much faster. Ellen closed her eyes, and she wondered if she would have been better off shooting herself out of a cannon than riding this death trap. She felt so helpless, and she wanted to cry, but tears would give her away. So she prayed, and when she opened her eyes again, she saw a farmhouse near the tracks go flying by, as if it was powered by steam and flying away on its own strength. The colors of the fallow winter fields became a blur, and it made her dizzy, so she closed her eyes again. But that just intensified every motion, every jerk, and every sound of the locomotive until it seemed as if the whole mass of metal was about to come apart.

"Looks to me like a nervous rider," said Mister Cray to the other man, assuming she couldn't hear.

"Maybe he hasn't ridden before."

"Could be. But some people never get used to train travel. My aunt has to down two brandies before she'll even step on a train."

Ellen felt Mister Cray's hand on her shoulder again, and she slowly turned to look at him. She breathed hard and tried to hide her fear behind a smile. He was trying to be kind, but his serious face conjured up imminent doom.

"Don't you worry, sir. I have ridden this train many a time, and it's as safe as can be!" He spoke loudly, for all the car to hear.

Ellen nodded and smiled. Then she turned back to the window and watched the land race by. She was trapped.

*****

The train gave a sudden lurch, like a horse bolting from its stall, and it threw William forward off the bench, setting Johnny off on a laughing fit. This was William's first time on a train, and he was thrilled at the idea of tearing down the countryside inside the most powerful vehicle ever created by the hands of man. He got up and stood at one of the windows, watching the land begin to roll by like a panorama show as the train picked up speed.

"C'mon back here and help me set up the game board," Johnny said to William. "You act like you ain't been on a train before."

It occurred to William that behaving like a first-time passenger might raise suspicions. Would the slave of a well-to-do gentleman have plenty of locomotive experience? It's possible, so William pulled away from the window and sat back down.

"I always love it when the train pulls out, that's all."

Johnny smiled. "You play much?"

"I made me my own game board."

Johnny slapped his knee. "Well you must be a big-timer then."

"No. Just like makin' things."

As they reset the game board, Johnny looked up and said nonchalantly, "What doctor your master gonna see?"

He sure liked asking nosey questions, and that worried William. Some slaves acted as the eyes and ears of their master or other authorities, and Johnny seemed unnaturally curious about his master's ailment. William wasn't about to let out that they were heading all the way to Philadelphia.

"Don't know," he said, shrugging. "Just some Savannah doctor."

"You don't even know?"

"It's my master's business, not mine to know."

"If you're his personal servant, I'd a' thought it would be your business to know."

"Mister Johnson, he's a private man."

"Quit your gum flappin' and get to playin' another game!" came a bellow from Jim on the other side of the car. "I'm playin' winner, and I don't wanna wait until my teeth fall out 'fore I can play again."

"Hold your horses!" Johnny shot back at the grumpy man. He shook his head in disgust and continued to rearrange the seeds into the correct piles. But William was grateful to Jim for shutting up this jabberer.

Suddenly, there was a loud bang, like a gunshot, and William's heart did a little jump in his chest. He twisted around to see what had happened.

"Beat that!" shouted one of the two boys, dashing to the open floor of the car where a sizable trunk had just landed. The sound was one of the boys hurling the trunk across the car, and it must be carrying something substantial, for it had hit the floor so hard that William was afraid it might have broken a floorboard.

"That ain't much to beat!" challenged the second boy, while his friend used a piece of chalk to mark the spot where the trunk had landed. "I can top it easy."

"This I have to see," said Johnny, stopping to watch the two boys compete. "I've done some baggage flingin' of my own. It's a fine art."

The second boy, taller than the other one, dragged the trunk back to the other side of the car and stood in the midst of the baggage piled up on both sides. The object was to fling the trunk through the opening in the partition, as far as possible across the baggage car. There wasn't a lot of room to wind up before letting the luggage loose, so the boy positioned himself, set his left foot, spit on his hands, and then stared across the room.

"Stay behind the line," warned the shorter boy.

The tall boy swung the trunk back and forth like a pendulum, testing its weight, and then he stepped into the hurl, letting loose when the trunk was at the apex of his swing. The trunk soared across the train car, and it hit the floor with a crack, like a breaking tree limb.

William shook his head. It's a wonder anything arrived at its destination in one piece.

"Beat ya by a mile!" yelled the tall boy.

"You cheated," said the other. "You stepped over the line."

"Did not."

"Liar!"

Johnny was up on his feet, stepping between the boys in an instant. "It looked fair and square to my eyes," he told the short boy, who glared back at him but didn't dare speak his mind. "But try it again, both of you, and this time I'll be the judge."

Taken in by the unfolding competition, William didn't even see the grumpy man, Jim, crossing the baggage car until he heard a thud. The man sat down at the game board.

"You move first," Jim scowled. "If that idjit ain't gonna play, then I am."

"Sure, sure," said William, feeling some relief. His new opponent might be an irritable old badger, but at least he didn't ask questions.

Macon

When John Knight had hunches, he was right more often than not. He had gone straight to the station come morning and checked the train because he had another one of those gut feelings, but he found no sign of William Craft in the colored car—just two black men playing a game of some sort. Still, something about William going off for Christmas didn't set right. If he had slaves of his own, he wouldn't be letting them off just because it was Christmas, but some masters were absolute fools, and William's master, Mister Taylor, was the king of fools.

Still uneasy that William might be making tracks for parts unknown, Knight decided to pay a visit to Willis Hughes, the Macon jailer who was just as disgusted by masters who pampered their property. The Macon jail was a one-story building built out of hewn logs and consisting of four cells looking out on the jailer's office.

He found Hughes polishing his gun—a 6-bore pepperbox gun that the man treasured. The jailer was a fastidious man and kept a clean office and even cleaner weapons. In the center of the room, he sat behind his desk in a light brown vest with the gold chain of his pocket watch draped across his waist. His hat tilted jauntily off to one side of his head, and he spoke with a cigar clenched in the corner of his mouth.

"You come to make a reservation in my jail, Mister Knight?" Hughes asked. "With all the drinkin' and carousin' come Christmas and New Year's, I think I'll have a full house. So you better save yourself a spot now."

Hughes motioned for him to take a seat, and Knight slid into a wooden chair.

"I'm here about William Craft."

Hughes immediately stopped his cleaning and stared at Knight. "He ain't run, has he?"

"No...well, *maybe*. I have this feelin' he's up to somethin'. The way he's been actin' at the woodshop."

Hughes set down his gun and neatly folded his polishing cloth, taking as much care as if he was folding the American flag. "How's he been actin'?"

"I have a suspicion he's been buyin' all manner of things on the side."

"What manner of things?"

"Green spectacles and a pair a boots that looked too small for him...things of that sort. Not sure why he'd have need of spectacles."

"At what shops? I'll make them think twice 'bout sellin' to slaves. We don't tolerate black market dealings."

"I ain't got proof, just a suspicion he got these materials from Macon proprietors."

"So you ain't got any names of shops for me?"

Knight shook his head. "I was worried William might run, so I also checked the colored car on the train out of town. Nothing."

"So you have no evidence at all. I presume William was given a pass from Mister Taylor to visit relatives for Christmas."

"Afraid so. He also got permission to take off from my boss at the woodshop, but I told Mister Cubbins it's risky givin' away free days like that. He's givin' William a mighty big temptation to run. But Cubbins don't listen."

Mister Cubbins, owner of the cabinet shop, shouldn't have hired William to work there in the first place, Knight thought. It saved him money on white labor, but it was humiliating for Knight to work alongside a slave every day, as if they were equals. It wasn't right, wasn't natural. Knight had figured he would own his own business in Macon by this time, but things just hadn't worked out the way he planned, and he was trapped working next to a slave. He figured if he could catch William on the run, then William Craft would end up where he belonged. On a plantation. In a cotton field. Or at the end of a rope.

"But William wouldn't run far without his girl."

"I know. But Ellen got a pass too. I was worried she might be runnin' with him."

Snorting, Hughes adjusted the gun on his desk so it was perfectly parallel with the edge of his folded polishing cloth. "Ellen's master's one of the worst, always preaching about the proper treatment of slaves. He's about as bad as abolitionist scum."

"I think we need to check their whereabouts," Knight said.

"With Christmas comin'? Like I said, I'm expectin' a lot of drunken traffic through here. Don't got the time to spare on your hunches."

"But I'm talkin' slave escape here. It's a little more serious than people who imbibe too heavily."

Noticing a smudge on his pepperbox gun, Hughes picked it up and rubbed the barrels until they shimmered. Colt revolvers were becoming more popular, but Hughes liked the old technology—six separate barrels mounted around a central rod, making the weapon look like a deadly form of a peppermill.

Finally, Hughes spoke. "Tell you what, Knight. Check on their whereabouts—both William and Ellen. If you can't locate 'em, come back to me."

"Then you'll help?"

"I always love a good hunt, even on Christmas. Gets me in the spirit a' things."

6

Clinton, Georgia
April 27, 1837: Eleven Years Earlier

MISS ELIZA FACED ELLEN STRAIGHT ON AND TOOK BOTH OF her hands.

"I'm going to miss you, Ellen," she said. "You're like a sister to me."

I am your sister, Ellen thought. Half-sister at least, but she wasn't about to remind her of that. Not on Miss Eliza's wedding day. Not ever, actually.

Miss Eliza looked beautiful in her white wedding dress, with flounces cascading down, each one 6 to 8 inches wide. It looked like she was immersed waist-deep in white frosting. She wore a bertha, a lacey cape-like collar that hung down almost to her waist. A line of pink flowers trailed down her gown, as if they had been planted in the material.

Ellen was clothed in her best dress, a hand-me-down from Miss Eliza—light blue with a white collar and dark blue sash around the waist. She was always proud to be seen in it, but she looked like a pauper in comparison to her half-sister.

"I'm gonna miss you too, Miss Eliza," said Ellen, and she really meant it. Sometimes, Miss Eliza acted as a buffer between her and Missus Smith. When Missus Smith was getting ready to thrash Ellen for allowing herself to be seen in front of Dr. Collins a full 8 months ago, Miss Eliza had begged her mama to go easy on Ellen. Missus Smith had wound up whacking her a few times with the hairbrush, but it would have been much worse if not for Miss Eliza. Now, with her half-sister married off and living in Macon, there was going to be nothing between Ellen and the lady of the house's hurricane personality. She was fully exposed to the storm.

When the door to the room suddenly swung open without warning, Miss Eliza dropped Ellen's hands, as if they were hot pokers. Ever since the hair-brushing fiasco, Miss Eliza had been careful not to cross any social barriers in front of her mama.

As it turned out, Ellen's mama was the one entering the room. They could breathe easily.

"You sure lookin' fine, Miss Eliza," said Mama, holding the veil in one hand. "The guests is all ready, and it's almost time."

Ellen helped Mama put the veil in place, and then they escorted Miss Eliza down the stairs and outside. The wedding was set up in the flower garden, and although there had to be well over a hundred guests, Ellen saw no trace of Mister Slator, her aunt's "master." He had been scratched from most invitation lists in the county because of the rumors going around about him and Aunt Molly.

The day began cloudy and muggy, which had put Missus Smith in a particularly foul mood. As the clouds cleared, though, so did her attitude. She smacked Ellen in the back of the head for dawdling when asked to carry flowers for the tables, but for Missus Smith that was good behavior on such a high-stress day.

Ellen wished she knew how to paint, for she would have loved to capture all the colors out in the garden, both the flowers and the dresses of all the women. The groom was dressed in a black swallow-tail coat, with a white vest, white necktie, and white gloves. He looked handsome and trim for an older man, but it sure seemed odd seeing Miss Eliza's papa giving away his daughter to a man close to his own age. Ellen could have sworn that she saw Miss Eliza throw a couple of glances in the direction of Dr. Collins' oldest son. Miss Eliza was probably wondering what this day might have been like if Abner had been the one receiving her as his wife, and Ellen couldn't really blame her. She wasn't sure she would want to be given away to some old widower.

After the "I do's," the party streamed over to the tables, which overflowed with pound cake and West Indian fruits, sliced turkey, smoked tongue, pickles, breads, and jellies. Old Widow Johnson played the harp, and then there was dancing to fiddle music. Ellen worked through most of it, fetching and hauling things for her mama, but every time she moved through the crowd she tried to imagine she was one of the guests. Missus Smith must have noticed her drifting along in her own personal fantasyland because she gave Ellen a nasty look. She would never give her ear a twist in front of the guests, but she would probably do it when the day was over. Ellen tried not to think about that as she brought out another platter of tropical fruit.

The party stretched into the night, when the pine-pitch torches were lit. Many of the guests had climbed back in their buggies and driven off, but some of the diehards remained behind. People usually didn't give wedding gifts, but a few had lavished the new couple with quilts, silver, tea sets, and such. Ellen was in the kitchen, sitting on a chair and munching on some bread left over from the feast, when Mama came through the back door, biting her lower lip. She did that when she worried.

"Ellen, set that food down. The missus wants ya. Whatcha do now?"

Ellen's mouth hung open, and she just stared.

"Close your mouth, I don't want to be lookin' at what you been chewin'. But just tell me. Whatcha do now? You break somethin'?"

"No, Mama."

Ellen was afraid of what kind of punishment awaited her. She didn't think Missus Smith would smack her in front of the guests, but with it being dark maybe she was planning on dragging her off into the shadows to give her a wallop.

"Now get movin'. Don't keep her waitin' now!"

Mama pulled Ellen to her feet and gave her a little smack in the behind, sending her off into the night. It was a pleasant night as long as you stayed near the lights. Ellen didn't believe in ghosts and such, but the Smith boys were always trying to scare her with spirit stories, and they knew how to make her skin crawl.

As she approached the gathering, she noticed something odd. Missus Smith was actually smiling at her. Now why in the world would she do that? Ellen couldn't remember her ever sending a smile in her direction.

"Come on over here, Ellen. Don't be shy."

Missus Smith stood in a circle of torchlight, with a scattering of guests gathered all around, some munching on the remains of cake. Most everyone was smiling, so it appeared that Ellen wasn't going to get a smack after all. But it seemed so odd, Missus Smith smiling and acting nice. It was almost as unsettling as getting slapped.

Missus Smith reached out and pulled Ellen closer. Then she put her hand on Ellen's shoulder. The movement was almost motherly, and Ellen felt herself tighten up inside. This just wasn't normal.

"Dr. Collins, I know you're going to take good care of our Eliza," Missus Smith said, her hand still resting on Ellen's shoulder. "The major and I couldn't be more proud of our daughter marrying such a fine man and setting up a house in a fine place like Macon."

"Here, here!" came a voice from the darkness.

Suddenly, Ellen felt Missus Smith's fingers dig into her shoulder, and she had to keep from yelling "ouch."

"Ellen here has been a hardworking girl for Eliza for many a year."

I have been? This was shocking news coming from Missus Smith.

"I'm afraid Eliza might be lost without her services, so I am giving ya'll an extra special wedding gift. I'm giving ya'll *Ellen* as a gift."

Eliza's face lit up at the news and she clapped, and Dr. Collins smiled back and nodded appreciatively. But Ellen? She felt like Missus Smith had just reached into her chest and given her heart a nasty twist, instead of twisting her ears as she normally did. Ellen had never been away from Clinton, never been away from her mama. She almost burst into tears right then and there.

"Won't that be wonderful?" Miss Eliza said, beaming back at Ellen. "We'll be together *forever*!"

Ellen looked down at her feet and dug the toe of her shoe in the grass. "Yes, ma'am."

Missus Smith's chubby fingers continued to dig into her shoulder, a not-so-subtle way of telling her to raise her head and smile. But Ellen couldn't do it. She wanted to cry. She started breathing rapidly and her shoulder was hurting, her heart was hurting, and she felt the tears coming. She knew she wouldn't be able to keep them down much longer, so Ellen broke away from Missus Smith's grasp, and bolted into the dark.

She found her mama standing not too far away, dabbing at her eyes with a handkerchief. She had obviously heard. Ellen hurled herself at her mama, and the tears came gushing out.

"I ain't gonna leave ya, Mama. I ain't."

Ellen didn't have a father, a real father at least, and now they were taking her away from her mama. She wanted to scream.

Mama got down on her knees and wrapped her in a big hug. Ellen could smell all of the food prepared during the day, a mixture of odors that had settled into the creases of her mama's clothes. She buried her face on Mama's shoulder, her chest heaving; she had a hard time catching her breath as she sucked in air and sobbed uncontrollably.

"It gonna be all right," Mama said, but Ellen didn't believe a word. Then she whispered into Ellen's ear, "You gonna be far from Missus Smith, and that's a good thing, little one."

"But I don't wanna be far from you."

"I know, child, I know. But you gonna be safer there."

Safe? Without her mama? And so far away! Macon was a little over 12 miles away.

"Can't you talk to Missus Smith? Tell her I'll behave better?"

Ellen felt a presence, the kind of presence the Smith boys talked about whenever they tried to spook her in the night. Then she felt a hand reach under her arm and yank her away from Mama. Ellen looked up and over her shoulder, and she saw Missus Smith leaning down on her, a shadow in the torchlight.

"Who do you think you are, running away like that?" Missus Smith kept her voice down so the guests couldn't hear.

"She don't mean nothin', ma'am," said Mama. "She just come to say goodbye."

"Rather than saying goodbye, Maria, I suggest you get her things all packed up. She'll be leaving with my Eliza in the morning."

Mama didn't respond. She didn't move.

"You heard me, Maria. Pack her things."

Ellen saw her mama dabbing her eyes again, her white handkerchief standing out in the dark. She remained kneeling. She didn't move.

Ellen had never seen Missus Smith smack Mama. She was afraid it was coming, and she couldn't bear to see something like that. So she decided to draw Missus Smith away, as quickly as possible before the woman could strike.

"Can you take me back to talk to Miss Eliza now, Missus Smith?" Ellen said, trying to talk without her voice cracking. "I wanna tell her how excited I am."

"That's what you should've been doing right from the start." Missus Smith gave her arm a shake and dragged her away.

Ellen looked back and saw her mama, still kneeling on the ground, still dabbing at her eyes. She wasn't moving. She knelt there and stared back at her little girl as they got farther and farther apart, and then Mama just merged with the darkness.

7

Macon
Thursday, December 21, 1848

JOHN KNIGHT TOOK IN THE ROOM—THE LADIES' PARLOR OF
Dr. Collins' house—and felt a twinge of envy as he waited. He was
afraid to take a seat, for fear of smudging the immaculate, light-
gold upholstery, so he wandered up to get a close look at the three
gold-framed portraits on the walls. Passing by the fireplace, he noticed that perched on the mantle was a tea caddy, a blatant reminder
that the Collinses were wealthy enough to own highly prized tea.
They might as well post a sign that says, "We are rich. You are not."

"I am sorry, Mister Knight, but Dr. Collins is not home at present," came a woman's voice, and he turned to see Eliza Collins sweep
into the room in a cloud of perfume. Knight bowed and tried not to
inhale too deeply, for fear of coughing. He still couldn't get over the
fact that Dr. Collins, at age 65, could be married to someone so young
and attractive. But money can buy just about anything.

Missus Collins' waist was pinched so tightly that he was shocked
she could breathe, and she wore a light pink dress with a white collar.
Knight didn't usually notice eye color, but her eyes were so blue they
looked like they had been hand-painted.

If she wasn't already married...

"Could I inform my husband that you called on him?"

"You may, but you too might be able to answer my inquiry."

"Oh?"

"It's about one of your household servants. I wanted to know if your maid, Ellen, has been given permission to visit relatives for the holiday."

Eliza Collins' eyebrows rose, and she became guarded at the mention of Ellen. "What business is this of yours? Has something happened?"

"No, ma'am, I was just askin' because William, her husband William, is gone and—"

"Gone? He hasn't run, has he? The two of them were supposed to be with her aunt until Christmas."

Knight rubbed the back of his head and then ran his hand down his neck. "He ain't run that I know of. But I've been wonderin'... William has been actin' strange at the shop this past few weeks. I was wonderin' if you noticed anything different about Ellen."

Eliza walked over to the grand piano, set against the wall. She placed one gloved hand on the polished piano, as if posing for a painting.

"It sounds to me like you think they have run off, Mister Knight."

"I really cannot say that. I have no evidence, just a feelin' that not everything was right with William."

"That's not much to go on, Mister Knight."

"I realize that, Missus Collins, but I have a way of sensing these things, if I must say so myself."

"Sensing things? You weren't so good sensing things when you first came to Macon."

Knight had known she would probably remind him of that embarrassing day. She always dug under his skin whenever she had the chance.

"Did William receive a pass to travel with Ellen? I was informed that he had," Eliza said.

"Yes, he did receive a pass. But that would be expected if he ran off."

"But it's also to be expected if he *didn't* run off, Mister Knight."

"I realize that, ma'am."

Eliza suddenly straightened herself, as if she was firming up both her posture and her opinion.

"Ellen is visitin' her mother and aunt, as she does every Christmas. And she would never leave me, if that is what you're thinkin'. We are like sisters, the two of us."

Knight nodded. He knew many southern women who took a slave's loyalty for granted, only to be stabbed in the back. Sometimes literally. His mind flashed back to the memory of Missus Matilda Jenkins, who was murdered in her sleep by her maid.

"So you have not noticed anything unusual about Ellen these past weeks?"

"Mister Knight, I think you should talk to my husband. You are upsetting me with this line of questioning, which I think is not warranted. Ellen is visiting her aunt, and she will be back here on Christmas day. We've never spent a Christmas day apart."

Knight averted his eyes. "I'm sorry, Missus Collins, if I have raised any unwarranted concerns. I didn't mean to do so. My concern is more about William. I am sure you are a good judge of Ellen."

Knight didn't believe his last sentence for a moment.

"Of course I am a good judge of her. Ellen and I grew up together."

If she says, "We're like sisters" again...

"I will inform Dr. Collins that you paid a visit. But I am afraid he will not be available to speak with you for several days."

By then, William and Ellen might be long gone. But Knight didn't speak those thoughts. He bowed once again, took one last look into her eyes, just for the pleasure of it, and departed. Even as he stepped back into the brisk December air, he could tell that some of her perfume had latched onto his clothes. He breathed it in, for the hint of perfume was just the right concentration—just enough to keep the image of Eliza Collins alive in his mind.

On the Train to Savannah, Georgia

Mister Cray got off at Gordon, an early stop along the way, and Ellen felt a lot of the tension leave with him. No one else on the train had the gumption to try to draw her into a conversation, believing that she was hard of hearing. So she kept to herself and stared out the window.

The train rolled on at breakneck speeds close to 30 miles per hour, but at least her pulse was no longer racing. She had become accustomed to the train's speed and the rattling and creaking. Many of the men in the car had snapped open their newspapers; Ellen listened to the rustle of papers, and she wondered if she could ever learn how to read once they reached the North. Miss Eliza once taught her to recite the alphabet when she was very young, but Missus Smith put a quick end to that.

Conversations sprouted up throughout the train, punctuated by "pitooeys" and the clang of spittoons. She was thankful that it wouldn't be her job to empty the spittoons in this train, as it had been back at the Collins mansion.

"Look-ee here," came a voice, two rows behind her. "Fanny Kemble is back in America!"

"The Brit?" chimed in another.

"The very one."

"She should stay on the other side of the ocean where she belongs and stop her meddlin' in our affairs."

"If she steps back on Georgia soil, I'd have her arrested."

Ellen had heard Dr. Collins complain about a woman named Fanny Kemble, but she didn't really know what the fuss was all about. She just got the sense that this woman was kin to the devil.

"She should take her abolitionist ways all the way back to England," arose another voice.

Abolitionists. That had to be the most common topic of talk among southern men, next to cotton and slaves. From what Ellen was told, abolitionists were vile villains who only pretended to look out for the well-being of black folk. She was told that once slaves reached the free North, their lives were a constant misery—a stream of abuse from northern whites. Ellen and William had heard it all, but they were willing to take their chances.

"Pierce Butler filed for divorce earlier this year, but Kemble has come back from England to defend her honor."

The word *honor* ignited a chorus of scoffs.

"How a southern gentleman could be taken in by an abolitionist woman in the first place was always a puzzle to me."

"Did you ever see her in real life? I saw her perform on stage, and I can see how she could turn someone inside out. A real beauty."

"That's right. I think Pierce Butler thought he could make her see the truth about our way of life."

The passengers spent a little longer complaining about abolitionists before they reached another stop along the way. Many got off to purchase food from vendors, but Ellen didn't dare. She was safer staying by herself, by the window, isolated from the crowd.

Ellen felt a gentle nudge, and she turned to find herself being addressed by a tall, thin man, bending low to address her. His mouth was buried beneath a large bushy moustache, much too large for his narrow face. "Excuse me, sir, but I could obtain some food for you if you'd like." The man spoke loudly because, like everyone else on the train, he thought she was hard of hearing.

Smiling, Ellen shook her head and tried to match his volume. "Thank you, sir, but I don't have much of an appetite."

The man paused, and Ellen wondered if he was analyzing the timbre of her voice. Did she speak deeply enough?

"You are so kind to ask, though," she added, trying to deepen her tone.

"I understand. I hope you feel better."

The tall man tipped his hat and headed for the exit. The gentleman seemed to be all legs—not much from the waist up, but the longest legs Ellen had ever seen on a human being, as skinny as a snake on stilts.

When the train took off again a short time later, Ellen felt herself getting drowsy, and for a moment she drifted off to sleep. When she jolted back awake, she didn't know how long she had been asleep, and she was afraid she might have talked in her sleep—*in a woman's voice.* She looked around, but no one seemed to have taken any notice, a good sign. Her mouth was dry, and her stomach ached for food. She had been told that the trip from Macon to

Savannah took 12 hours, but it felt like 24 hours instead. The train stops rolled by, Bostwick and Heradon and Cushingville, and on and on, and darkness set in with early evening. Ellen ventured off of the train only once—in Eden, Georgia, to pay a very necessary visit to an outhouse.

Two stops later, she heard the word that she both craved and feared: *Savannah.* She craved the word because it meant she would be able to escape the confines of the train at last, but she also was afraid because she knew that the second leg of their journey—the steamboat—would pose a whole new set of challenges and dangers.

Ellen remained in her seat with her eyes closed, pretending to sleep, hoping she could leave the train after everyone else had departed. But she felt another nudge, a hand on the shoulder.

"Wake up, sir, wake up. We have arrived in Savannah."

Ellen did her best to mimic the groggy confusion of someone struggling back to consciousness. "Savannah? We're here?"

Her neck ached from leaning against the window, and she sat up straight and adjusted her cravat. She was being awakened by the same fellow with the incredibly long legs. He bent over her like some huge, spindly insect, and he smiled graciously.

"We're here. Time to disembark!" He very nearly shouted his news.

"Thank you! You're so kind."

"Do you have anything that I can carry for you?"

"Pardon me?" Ellen cupped her ear.

"I said do you have anything that I can carry for you?"

"No, no, everything is in the baggage car. My boy will take care of it."

My boy? My husband.

The tall man took her by the elbow and helped her down the aisle, and she worried that he could tell it was a woman's thin arm beneath the fabric. She wished he would just leave her alone. The disadvantage of her bandages was that they drew out the best in people, who just wanted to help when she wanted nothing more than solitude. Solitude meant safety.

When they were off the train and immersed in the platform crowd, the tall man turned to face her and spoke so loudly that he nearly blasted the hat from her head. "Are you sure I can't do anything to help you?"

Ellen shouted back amid the hum of the crowd. "You are so kind. But my husband..."

Ellen stopped. Terror took hold. She had spoken the word: *husband*. She was so used to saying the word that she had been afraid it might slip out if she wasn't careful. Now it had happened, and she wasn't sure what to do. Laugh? Make a joke about it? She felt flush, and a river of shock flowed up her arms. Her knees went weak.

The tall man's genial expression vaporized. His jaw clenched. "What did you just say?"

Ellen didn't answer. Her mind was a jumble. She was tempted to run, lose herself in the crowd on the platform. Everyone who passed by on the platform shot a look at Ellen and her bandages.

To buy time, she acted as if she didn't hear him. "What's that?"

"I was asking what you just said!"

"What?"

"What did you say to me?"

He leaned down to hear her response, and she bellowed into his ear. "I said...I said my hatband is pinching me. If you are a milliner, you might be able to help me. But I am fine in all other respects, thank you."

The tall man stared directly into Ellen's eyes. *He knew. He knew.*

Then he broke into a grin. "Hatband?" He laughed and slapped her on the back. "In all this noise, a fellow's ears can play tricks! Have a safe journey from here, Mister..."

Ellen held out her one good hand—her left hand. "The name is Johnson!" she shouted.

"Prendergast!" boomed the tall man. "Leroy Prendergast!"

They shook hands. *Firm handshake, firm handshake,* Ellen told herself, and she squeezed so hard and pumped his arm so fiercely that she was afraid she had pulled it out of its socket.

"Good evening, Mister Johnson! Safe travels!" Mister Prendergast tipped his hat.

"The same to you, Mister Prendergast!" Ellen tipped her hat.

"But get that hat fixed!"

"I will, Mister Prendergast!"

The tall man turned and merged with the crowd, but with his height he stood head and shoulders above everyone else. Ellen spotted a bench and wobbled over. She had to take a seat before she fainted, and she wished William would get to her side before she went completely insane with fear.

*****

William was happy to be free of Johnny and Jim. He had trounced both of them in mancala, again and again, and he thought Jim was going to slug him in the jaw after every game they played. Even happy-go-lucky Johnny started to get irritated about losing, but at least the defeats shut him up for the last 2 hours of the trip. Before that, Johnny was a question machine, asking William about everything under the sun. Where was he born? How long had he been with his master? What kind of work did he do? Was he married? William had not been prepared for such a barrage, and he hoped he didn't slip up in his stories.

With a heavy trunk in hand, he worked his way along the platform and found Ellen sitting on a bench, looking as white as a cemetery statue. She looked like she was about to be sick.

"You feelin' all right, sir?"

Ellen looked up at him with frightened eyes, and William could tell she wanted nothing more than to hug him. It wasn't the kind of look a master gave his slave.

"I'm fine, boy, just fine," Ellen lied. She got hold of herself and stood up, a little wobbly on her feet. William took her by the elbow until she was steady.

"Did you have a fine trip, sir?"

"It was an experience."

"Yes, sir."

Diverting his eyes like a good slave, William set down the trunk and went about locating a carriage, an omnibus drawn by two white horses. William helped Ellen climb aboard the packed coach, and then he scrambled to the roof where the other Negroes rode. For once, he found that the colored accommodations were much nicer. It was a bit nippy sitting on top of the coach on a December evening, but it was still better than being jammed inside the stifling coach, with bodies squished so close together, you couldn't slide a piece of paper between them.

The coach ride was a short one, down West Broad Street to the wharfs along the Savannah riverfront. Everywhere was movement: people rushing, slaves lugging baggage and sacks, roustabouts loading freight, barrels being rolled along and rumbling like thunder. Two roustabouts, huge white men, used hooks to grapple with massive bales of cotton, each bale weighing 400 pounds or more, he would guess. Another roustabout was twisting the tail of a cow to get it moving up and onto the ship. From all appearances, a steamboat was a floating zoo, with pigs and chickens and cattle and ducks and who knew what.

William and Ellen had never been on a steamboat, and it looked like it was going to be close quarters on board—especially for passengers booked on the lowest deck, where William would be. He was glad they had saved up enough money for Ellen to ride on the second deck, the boiler deck, so she could get her own room. Privacy was going to be critical to their success, and there would be no privacy on the lower deck.

The steamship, the *General Clinch*, was magnificent—like a Georgia mansion floating on water. The railings were ornate, with gingerbread trimmings, and the row of posts holding up the second-level boiler deck reminded William of the columns he saw on so many Macon mansions. Two enormous, black smokestacks sprung out of the steamboat just in front of the pilothouse. This was a massive side-wheel steamboat, and people streamed aboard on stage planks.

"Make way for Lord Lowsley! Make way for Lord Lowsley!"

Startled by the sudden command, William wheeled around and saw two tall men creating a pathway through the crowd. People stepped aside for the man trailing behind the two tall servants—a middle-aged man with a red coat, a black sash from shoulder to waist, and a gold-trimmed high collar. He had a trim white beard, and he walked chin up with a gold-topped cane, not making eye contact with the people on all sides.

"Make way for Lord Lowsley! Make way for Lord Lowsley!"

Was royalty traveling on this boat? Incredible!

William stepped out of the way and watched the man parade by in splendor, followed by a line of porters carrying so much baggage that it was mind-boggling. How could one person have need for that much clothing?

When the parade had passed, William looked around for Ellen, who had gone off to purchase two tickets for Charleston. He warmed his hands beneath his armpits and stamped some life back into his feet. With the sun down, it was chilly, especially with the wind blowing.

"Hey Willie! Willie!"

It couldn't be. For the better part of half of the train ride to Savannah, Johnny had insisted on calling him "Willie." And now it sure sounded like Johnny's voice cutting through the commotion. William closed his eyes and prayed that it wasn't Johnny.

It was. Dear Lord.

"Hey, Willie, what you doin' here? Did you just see that royal personage go walkin' on by as if he owned half the world itself?"

The voice was right behind him, and William rolled his eyes to heaven. He slowly turned, and there he was, Johnny in all his glory. Johnny smiled and clapped a hand on his shoulder.

"What you doin' here at the wharf? I thought you told me you was stoppin' in Savannah to get your master's ailments treated."

William cast a nervous glance toward the ticket station, where he could see Ellen still waiting in line. "No, you musta heard wrong. We're headin' on up to Charleston to see a doctor."

Johnny shook his head. "No, no, no, I remember clear as a bell. You said you're goin' on to Savannah. I asked you what doctor he seein' and you didn't know."

"Maybe I misspoke then." William gave a shrug. "My master, he's seein' a specialist in Charleston. I musta been meanin' to say we're just passin' through Savannah on the way to Charleston."

"That's a long way to be goin' to see a doctor," Johnny said. "Ain't there a doctor closer to home? Maybe there's a good one here in Savannah."

"Why you askin' me? I just go where my master tells me to go." William hoped a touch of irritation would send him on his way.

Another quick glance at the ticket booth. Ellen was in the process of paying for their tickets. *Please Lord, don't let her come within 10 feet of this fountain of questions.*

"Where's your master, Willie? I have some treatment ideas of mine own he might like to know about."

William groaned inwardly. "Just off tendin' to something."

"What kind a' something?"

He never stopped with the questions. Time to change the focus. "You ain't goin' to Charleston, are you?"

"'Course I am! Why else would I be standin' here? My master don't just let me roam where I want. That's him comin' right there."

Johnny motioned toward a tall man moving through the crowd, head and shoulders above everyone else.

"You got the tickets, Mister Prendergast?"

The tall man ignored the question. With Johnny as his servant, he had probably learned long ago to block out the constant queries. "Grab my bags, Johnny, and hurry along. And quit your dawdlin'!"

Rolling his eyes at William, Johnny grabbed two heavy suitcases. "Yes, sir."

After William watched them wander off and merge into the crowd, he pivoted to see Ellen moving through the mass of people and turning heads at every step. People moved aside to make room for the invalid; it was like she was parting the waters as she passed by.

When she reached William, her eyes were on the crowd, where the tall man rose above everyone else.

"What were you doin' talkin' to that white man?"

William followed her gaze. "You know him?"

"He kept tryin' to help me along on the train. But how do you know him?"

"I don't. But I know his servant, a curious one. He was askin' me ev'ry question under the sun while we were on the train."

Ellen adjusted her sling. "Don't like the sound of that."

"No, sir. Me neither." William couldn't keep from smiling every time he called her "sir."

William watched Ellen's face as she stared toward the plank leading into the steamboat. She looked a little frightened, as if the plank was on a pirate ship and she was being forced to walk it. He wished so much he could put an arm around her.

"We better get moving before the boat leaves without us," she eventually said, breaking away from her thoughts. "Could you get the trunk?"

Leaning in close, William said as softly as he could, "Don't ask me. *Tell* me."

Ellen stared at him, as if she didn't know what he was saying. Then it seemed to dawn on her, and she hardened her face and snapped, "Well...what ya waiting for? Take hold of my trunk, boy, and let's board!"

William was a little startled by her sudden blast of words, but that was much better. "Yes, sir."

Trunk in hand and smiling, William led the way, clearing a path to the stage plank. Then they crossed over and entered the *General Clinch* steamboat, as a deep-voiced Negro bellowed, "All ashore that goin' ashore!"

"C'mon now! Don't dally!" Ellen snapped, and William had to stifle another smile and mutter, "Yes, sir."

Ellen was starting to get a hang of this master business.

8

Macon
April 28, 1837: Eleven Years Earlier

LLEN FIGURED THAT MISS ELIZA WAS AS SCARED AS SHE WAS.

Miss Eliza was Missus Collins now, but in the fine southern tradition she would remain "Miss Eliza" in Ellen's mind. She had not yet been married for a full day, and she was unnaturally quiet on the coach ride to Macon, about 12 miles from Clinton. She had a captured-animal look in her eyes, even though on the outside she still looked every bit the beautiful newlywed. Her new bonnet was as blue as her eyes, and she wore a low-cut dress, made more modest by a lace chemisette.

"Unnaturally quiet" was not how Ellen would describe Dr. Collins. He was a genial man, but he spent most of the time talking about his business dealings and cotton and railroads, things that meant little to Miss Eliza or Ellen. Dr. Collins, a physician and businessman, said he was working to bring a train line between Savannah and Macon, and he was also a trustee for the Georgia Female College. Whatever a trustee might be, Ellen had no idea, but Dr. Collins made it sound important.

He also liked talking about slaves, and he had more than 60 of them, but his ideas were a bit different than anything she had ever heard.

"Good water is indispensable for my Negroes," he said, staring so hard at Ellen that she felt his eyes boring into the side of her head as she watched the land scroll by the window. He sat opposite Ellen and Miss Eliza in the coach. "I try to get all of the water from fresh springs, and I have a system for catching rainwater from the roofs."

He paused, as if waiting for Ellen and his new bride to applaud.

"I also try to shade the servants' cabins with china or mulberry trees, and I provide field hands with plenty of food—5 pounds of good clean bacon and 1 quart of molasses per week for each hand—men, women, boys, and girls, the ones large enough to go into the field to work. Also, as much good bread as they require. And strong coffee, sweetened with sugar, every morning before they go to work during the fall or sickly seasons of the year."

Another pause. Was he aiming to impress Ellen or Miss Eliza—or both? Miss Eliza gave him a strained smile. "You run an efficient operation, Dr. Collins."

He grinned. "An efficient and *modern* operation. The only thing missing has been a woman to run the house...until yesterday."

Dr. Collins put a hand on Miss Eliza's white-gloved hand. Her eyes grew wide at those words, and Ellen noticed her breathing speed up. Dr. Collins probably thought it was the touch of his hand that excited her, but Ellen knew better. Miss Eliza was scared, and Ellen could guess why. She had never run a household before, and her mama hadn't done much to prepare her.

The coach rattled across the city bridge over the Ocmulgee River, where Ellen saw a couple of boats churning the water, and then they rolled into Macon. She was struck by the orderliness of the city. No twisting, meandering streets were in this part of town—just straight lines. The houses were so neat and pretty. The coach made a right turn and worked its way up a hill, and Dr. Collins was beaming.

"I'm taking the long route to our new home because I want to show you the Georgia Female College. The same architect built our house, dear."

Miss Eliza flinched at the words "our new home" as they turned onto what Dr. Collins said was College Street, and then she leaned across Ellen to get a good look. Ellen had never seen such a glorious building—the reddest of bricks with a row of columns soaring three stories high across the front of the school and a castle-like tower rising from the middle. The people of Macon sure liked their white pillars.

Dr. Collins started in on the city and its history, and Miss Eliza just kept nodding and trying to smile. She looked like someone caught in swamp quicksand and trying to look happy about it.

They turned left off of College Street, and the carriage moved downhill along Mulberry—their street. The Collins' house stood out like an enormous Greek temple along a street lined with magnolia trees. The Collins Estate. More columns. More grandeur. Six enormous white pillars rose two stories high to form the mansion's porch, but the house was actually three stories—with a wing on either side and a third-floor balcony perched on each wing. Most women would jump at the chance to be in charge of such an imposing place, but not Miss Eliza, not from the look on her face. Dr. Collins didn't seem to notice. He was too busy talking.

Two Negro servants came out and carried the trunks, and they all paraded into the mansion. A row of servants stood at the base of a long, long staircase, which was flanked by an equally long pier mirror that the ladies used while walking downstairs to make sure their white petticoats were not peeking out from beneath their dresses. "Make sure it's not snowing down south," Miss Eliza's mama always told her.

Dr. Collins introduced his bride to the servants, one by one, and they all smiled at her like she was the Queen of England. Then Ellen followed Miss Eliza and the servant carrying her trunk up the staircase, and the heat intensified as they rose higher. It was only April, but the second and third floors would probably be stifling at the peak of summer. At the top of the staircase was a red-upholstered fainting couch, which was useful in the heat, especially for ladies who kept their corsets too tightly cinched.

Ellen's mistress held her composure the entire way up, but when they reached the second-floor hallway, Miss Eliza seemed to sag in spirit. She stared at the paintings in the hallway, one by one. Collins ancestors, bearded men most of them, watched her go by, as if sizing her up. One of the paintings featured a stern-looking old woman, who seemed particularly judgmental of Miss Eliza as she passed. Dr. Collins was still downstairs, talking to the help, so Miss Eliza no longer tried to hide her fear.

"This here's your room," said the servant, opening the door to a palatial bedroom. "Your lady's maid will help you unpack."

Her lady's maid: That was Ellen.

"Thank you..."

"Moses, ma'am."

"Thank you, Moses."

Moses? From the look of the bedroom, this Moses had just led Miss Eliza to the Promised Land, but from the expression on her face you would think they were still wandering in the desert. After depositing the trunk in the room, Moses excused himself politely and disappeared down the stairs. Ellen's eyes were on the 4-poster bed with a mattress so thick and rich that Ellen couldn't imagine how many geese had given their feathers so Miss Eliza could sleep in heaven. Miss Eliza put a hand on one of the bed's posts and her chin started quivering. Ellen didn't understand how someone could be so sad when she had just been handed the keys to the kingdom.

Miss Eliza stared Ellen directly in the eyes. She looked so much as if she wanted to throw her arms around Ellen and give her a hug for comfort, but she knew she shouldn't. She *couldn't*. Ellen knew full well that what Miss Eliza wanted was a *full* sister, not a half-sister, not a black sister, not even a black sister who looked white.

Ellen also knew she couldn't initiate a hug or even give her a soothing touch on the arm, but maybe Miss Eliza would do it. She had done it in the past—when they were younger and Missus Smith wasn't looking. Missus Smith wasn't looking today, and wouldn't be from now on, being miles away. Tears welled up in Miss Eliza's eyes, and Ellen could feel them starting to pool in her own eyes. They both wanted their mamas, so badly.

At last, Miss Eliza stood up straight and wiped the corner of her eyes with her handkerchief.

"That will be all for now, Ellen," she said.

"Yes, ma'am."

Ellen walked out the bedroom door, and then she paused and turned, just in case Miss Eliza wanted to say something more. Miss Eliza stared back at her, looking so sad, but she didn't say a word. Then Miss Eliza tried to bring rigidity to her expression, a stoic coldness that her mother was so good at displaying. It didn't work no matter how much she tried. She just looked like she was playacting.

The door closed in Ellen's face. That was all for now.

9

JOHNNY WAS AT IT AGAIN, FLAPPING HIS GUMS AND ASKING questions.

"You mean your master's already gone to his room?" he said to William. "That seems mighty odd. The men are all gathering to play some cards and talk business in the saloon."

"He's just not feelin' right."

"You bring him to me, Willie, and I'll set him straight on some good home remedies."

William didn't answer. Standing at the railing of the lower deck, he looked out on the dark water, which had terrified him since he was a young one. He had fallen out of a boat once, and it still spooked him to think about the few moments before his papa had hauled him back in. He still wasn't a strong swimmer, so he backed away from the railing.

"Where is Mister Johnson?" came another voice, off to his right. It was the tall man—Johnny's master. Mister Prendergast.

"He's not feelin' well, sir. So he's off to his room to sleep."

"So early in the evening? That's a shame. He's a fine man. You take care of him, now." Mister Prendergast said the words like they were a threat.

"I will, sir. In fact, I need to be gettin' the flannels and opodeldoc prepared for him, sir."

"Then what are you standing there talking to this fool for?" Mister Prendergast barked, pointing a finger at Johnny. "Get to work."

"Yes, sir."

If Ellen wanted to learn how to pass herself off as a master, she should take lessons from Mister Prendergast. William felt a little sorry for Johnny, even as annoying as he could be. Mister Prendergast was not an easy man.

Needing to escape all of the questions, he headed for Ellen's cabin on the boiler deck above. As he moved along the outer promenade railing with his head down, he couldn't help but hear raised voices down at the end. It appeared to be Lord Lowsley, and he was shouting at one of the crewmen.

"You call that the finest room on the boat?" Lord Lowsley boomed.

"I'm sorry, sir, but it is the finest," said the crewman, a scrawny fellow with his hat in his hands. "It's three times the size of any other berth. And it has its own water closet, sir!"

"If that's three times as big as the other berths, then you must be fitting people in with shoehorns! I demand to talk to the captain about this!"

Lord Lowsley turned and shot a fierce gaze in William's direction, so William quickly located Ellen's cabin, knocked, and ducked inside. Looking around the cabin, he wondered if perhaps Lord Lowsley was right. The ordinary cabins were more like closets. Most horrifying, though, William noticed that the cabin contained two small berths.

"You're sharing this cabin?" he said to Ellen.

"Appears that way. Good thing there's two beds."

"Still..."

William didn't like it one bit, but Ellen was right. Sharing a bed with a perfect stranger was not unusual in hotels and guesthouses, so he should be grateful that the berths in this cramped cabin were barely wide enough to fit one person. The room was about 6 feet by 6 feet and had two doors, one leading to the exterior promenade and the other to the interior saloon, where most of the social activity took place. The two berths were attached to a wall, and there was also a mirror, stool, and spittoon. That was all that could fit in the cramped quarters.

"Which berth you think I should take?"

"Upper," William said without hesitation. "If your cabinmate comes in late, stinkin' of drink, he'll be floppin' in the lower bunk. You don't want to be flopped on."

Ellen nodded and stared into space, as if picturing such a horrifying thing.

"I'll be heatin' these up and be right back," William said. He started to reach for the bag that held the bandages and ointment, which sat on the upper berth, when Ellen suddenly moved in on him and wrapped her arms around him tightly.

"I don't know if I can do this any longer." She buried her head on his shoulder.

"You're doin' fine. The Lord, he'll deliver your feet from fallin'. Keep rememberin' that, and you'll be fine."

Ellen clung to him for dear life, but all that William could think was what would happen if her berthmate walked in on them at this very moment and saw them embracing. He fixed his eyes on the door in front of him, the one leading into the saloon, but he was highly conscious of the second door, the one directly behind him, which he couldn't see. William gently pulled away and gave Ellen a quick kiss on the forehead.

"You climb into bed now and pull those covers over you, and you won't be disturbed by no one. I'll be back with these bandages all medicated."

After another kiss on the forehead, William exited onto the promenade and made his way to the kitchen, a cramped room on the boiler deck. The kitchen was quiet at this time of night, except for two men. One was a cook, a black man who kept the huge stove stoked with wood, and the other was an unshaven lanky white man, who looked to be in his 20s, with his feet propped up on a chair. The skinny man's cheek bulged with tobacco—like a tumor—and his face was odd: large ears, wide-set eyes, and brown teeth, the shade of burlap. Keeping his back to the man, William spread out the flannels on the stove and went to work. The warmth of the oven felt nice on a December night.

"What's that you got there, buck?" came the voice from behind, followed by the sound of spitting.

William turned and smiled. "Liniment for my master, sir."

"Oh, I seen him on board. The one with all the bandages?"

"Yes, sir."

William went to work, mixing up the ingredients—powdered soap, camphor, oil of rosemary, and spirit of ammonia. Powerful stuff. When he applied the mixture to the flannels and it got to heating, the kitchen filled with a pungent, potent odor. William hated this chore, but he had no choice but to go through the motions of preparing poultices for his master. It added credibility to their story, for this preparation was standard for people suffering from rheumatism. The cook took one whiff of the mixture and went rushing out of the room for fresh air.

"Boy, what's that called that you're mixin' there?" asked the lanky man, who wasn't as eager to leave. He probably didn't want to give up his comfortable seat. "Smells bad enough to knock a dog off a gut wagon!"

"It's opodeldoc, sir."

"I should think it's opo-*devil*! It stinks enough to kill or cure 20 men!"

"I'm sorry, sir."

"Not as sorry as I am. Now away with it or I reckon I'll throw it overboard—along with you!"

William hoped he was joking about throwing him overboard, but you never knew; he had heard that steamboats carried some rough characters. The thought of tumbling into dark waters filled him with dread, so he gathered up the medicated flannels, which felt so nice and warm, even though they stank to high heaven. As he left, the skinny man looked like he was going to gag on his tobacco. He waved the air in front of his nose and made the most awful faces.

When William arrived back at the cabin, he laid out the bandages at the foot of Ellen's bed. "Maybe the smell will drive away your berthmate."

"Glad I don't really have rheumatism and have to smell this every day," she said.

William didn't linger too long in the cabin, for fear of raising suspicions—and truth be told, he wanted to get away from the odor. There were no sleeping quarters for Negroes on the steamboat, so he made his way down to the cargo deck, where he encountered Johnny, of course.

Johnny took one whiff of William's clothes and scrunched up his nose. "Did you just hug a dead man, Willie?"

"Just opodeldoc."

"Whooo! Steer clear of me for a few hours, Willie boy."

William smiled and was happy to oblige. He wanted to be alone, although that wasn't going to be easy on the cramped lower deck. No wonder booking passage as a "decker" was so cheap. He passed by a large group of Irishmen, singing and passing the bottle; another cluster of men, all speaking German he thought, smoked pipes and played cards. He peeked inside the freight room, where deckers tried to find space to sleep away from the December wind, but a short white man rushed up to him, snarling like a guard dog.

"Boy, what you think you're doin'? You ain't allowed in here!"

William backpedaled quickly. "Where am I supposed to sleep, sir?"

"On another ship, if I had my way! Now scat! And take that smell with you!"

The day's strain had finally caught up with him, and he felt bone weary. His lifeline, his optimism, was fraying like an old rope. He paced the deck, looking for a good place to catch some winks, and finally found warmth not far from one of the funnels. He climbed up on a huge bale of cotton that hadn't yet been claimed—a soft bed fit for a king. With the radiating heat from the funnel, he couldn't help but think that his bed was probably considerably more comfortable than Ellen's. He stared up at the stars and listened to the creaks and splashes all around him, until he drifted away like a branch being swept off into dark waters.

*****

"Who's strangled a skunk in here?"

Ellen didn't say a word—just kept her eyes squeezed shut. She wasn't sure if she had slept at all for the past 4 hours, but she was definitely wide awake now as she heard the door to the cabin squeak open, and she sensed the presence of a man in the room. She also *smelled* his presence. The man had nothing to complain about when it came to odors because he reeked of liquor and sweat, and Ellen wondered if he had taken a bath in the past decade.

He groaned and sputtered, "Don't think I'm gonna be able to breathe in here."

Ellen faced the cabin wall, keeping her back to the man. She didn't move, didn't say a word.

"Are you awake, or did the smell kill you?" the man asked Ellen, but she still didn't answer. She thought about snoring to signal she was sound asleep, but that would be laying it on too thick.

She heard the man pulling off his shoes and clothes and could picture him standing there in his dirty long johns, which he had probably been wearing for so long that it had become another layer of skin. She felt like the time she was sleeping out under the stars and a bear came sniffing around, snorting and growling. She had kept perfectly still until the bear left, and she kept perfectly still now, waiting for this hulking presence to collapse in his bed and begin his hibernation.

The man continued to bang around for a few minutes. What he was doing Ellen had no idea. But then she heard him grunting and felt him just behind her, the alcohol odor wafting from him in waves. From the sound of it, the man seemed to be standing on the stool and attempting to climb into the upper berth! *Her berth!*

"Oh, God, the smell, the smell," he kept muttering to himself with the slurred sentences of a drunk.

Ellen kept her eyes closed. At some point the guy had to notice that there was already a person underneath the covers in the upper berth. She prayed he would spot her before he hurled his body into the bed, right on top of her. It was difficult to tell which was worse—the smell of the opodeldoc, the smell of his alcohol-soaked breath, or the smell of his sweat. The three mighty odors battled it out in the air all around Ellen.

Ellen thought that the man was just getting ready to heave himself onto the upper berth when his hand landed on one of the medicated bandages, laid out at the edge of her bed. All of a sudden, she heard him roar, as if he had stuck his nose in a beehive.

"Oh, God!"

The man tumbled backward and crashed to the floor, and all went quiet; Ellen began to wonder if he had died. Still, she didn't move, didn't even shift around to check what happened. She didn't want to take the chance of him noticing she was awake. *Please Lord, let him live*, she prayed, knowing that a coroner's inquiry would be her undoing, but she was being ridiculous. Who had ever died from falling backward off a stool?

Things like that happened.

Then Ellen heard the sweetest sound: snoring. She didn't dare look, but she was pretty sure that the man had fallen asleep on the floor of the cabin. He smacked his lips a few times, muttered a few unintelligible words, and then started snoring and snorting, like a hog rooting away in a pile of potatoes.

To Ellen's ears, it was the sweetest sound in the world.

10

Macon
Autumn 1845: Three Years Earlier

LLEN WAS A YOUNG WOMAN NOW, 19 YEARS OLD. SHE HAD DARK black hair and the same dark, piercing eyes of her half-sister, and her once gangly frame had filled out over the past 8 years since she had arrived in Macon with Dr. Collins and Miss Eliza. The family resemblance to Eliza had increased with every year.

It was corn-shucking time, and Ellen felt the pull of excitement as she helped with food preparations. It was one of her favorite nights of the year, but she warned herself not to get her hopes up too high. Since she had arrived on the Collins estate, she had become a seamstress, but she did all manner of work, and on corn-shucking nights, everyone pitched in on food.

With preparations done, she rode in a wagon just behind the coach of Dr. Collins, Miss Eliza, and the doctor's aunt, who was visiting for a couple of months. She could smell the chicken and dumplings and pumpkin custard and apple pie that had been placed in the back, directly behind her, driving her wild with hunger. They were headed for the Whitaker farm on the outskirts of Macon, and as they approached the plantation, she marveled at all of the lights from pine-knot torches, and savored the sound of laughter drifting across the dark lawn.

Corn shucking was a fine time to assess the men from the various estates, particularly the new faces. She was about the same age that Miss Eliza had been when she got married 8 years ago, and it was high time she snagged herself a man, her mama told her.

Her mama.

Ellen and her mama were back in the same town, thank God, and had been for almost 7 years now. A little over a year after Ellen had been taken to Macon by Miss Eliza and Dr. Collins, Major Smith had moved to Macon, bringing along his entire household, Mama included. Of course, that meant Miss Eliza's mother was also back in the same community, and it was no picnic seeing Missus Smith from time to time. But it was worth the grief if it meant having her own mama back in her life.

The Whitaker home was massive, with four huge pillars in front. They disembarked in the circular drive and then carried everything around back where three long tables stretched all the way to tomorrow, already loaded down with victuals. As Ellen unloaded the food, her eyes drifted back toward the corncrib, where the cornerstone of the night's activities would take place. She could see the men already choosing up sides, moving about in the torchlight and horsing around.

"I'll take this, honey," came Mama's voice from the side, swooping in to lift the apple pie from Ellen's hands. "You and Mary go on now, the shuckin's about to begin."

"Thank you, Mama." Ellen planted a kiss on her mother's cheek. She knew perfectly well that her mama didn't care a whit whether she missed the corn shucking; what Mama didn't want her to miss was the socializing with young men ahead of the contest.

Ellen greeted cousin Mary with a kiss on the cheek. Mister Terrence Slator owned property in Macon, and he had moved his family to town 3 years back, bringing along Ellen's Aunt Molly and the four cousins, Mary, Frank, and the twins. Even today, no one outside the family knew the true nature of Mister Slator's relationship with Aunt Molly, a slave woman, but the rumor mill continued to churn out stories as quickly as a gristmill pounded out flour. And Mary still had the kinds of freedoms no daughter of a slave typically experienced. The one time that Ellen had broached the subject, Mary didn't talk to her for a day. (That was as long as Mary could stay angry.)

Tonight, Mary was bubbling over, and she hooked Ellen by the arm. "C'mon. I think the captains have already been chosen."

They hurried across the yard to the corncrib, just west of the stables, where several horses nosed around at the grass. Beyond the corncrib was an orchard, with rows upon rows of trees bearing apples and peaches. But Ellen's attention was drawn to the ears of corn, which had been piled into two huge equal-sized mounds. Mary was right. The two teams had already been chosen, and they totaled about 80 Negro men from plantations all around. The autumn air smelled fresh, and temperatures were warm for this time of year. Ellen scanned the gathering, looking for new faces—new *male* faces.

"I think that one's looking your way, Ellen," Mary whispered in her ear.

"Which one you talkin' about?"

"The one with the beard. With the team on the left."

"How do you know he ain't lookin' *your* way?"

"Believe me, I know."

Ellen knew exactly which one Mary was talking about, and he diverted his eyes as soon as she caught sight of him. She also knew that if he was looking her way, chances were it had nothing to do with physical attraction. He was probably wondering what a white woman was doing amid all of the Negro women. By this time, Ellen was used to the stares of black men, puzzled by her presence and her shade of skin. Light-skinned Negroes were not unusual, but Ellen looked more like a plantation owner's daughter. It was difficult being caught in the twilight world between black and white; she felt separated by her white skin and black blood—almost leprous in her isolation.

"You know his name?" Ellen asked.

"William Craft, I heard. He's new to Macon."

Ellen caught him looking in her direction once again, so she turned away, swinging around to find herself facing another man—Joshua Hamm.

"Why good evenin', Miss Ellen," said Joshua, one of the field hands from Dr. Collins' plantation. Dr. Collins had purchased him 4 years ago, when Ellen was only 15 and he was 16. At that time, Joshua had taken one look at the color of her skin and assumed that she put on airs. He had been merciless, having fun at her expense, always trying to bring her down a peg; in the past year, though, she had noticed a change in his attitude.

"Good evenin', Mister Hamm," Ellen said.

"Did you notice that I'm captain a' one of the teams?"

"I thought as much by your hat." His large, floppy hat was adorned with corn shucks—a badge of honor.

"That's right." Joshua looked at her so hard that she thought he was trying to melt her with his stare.

Unsure what to say or do, she laughed uncomfortably and stammered, "Miss Mary and me, we just arrived." Ellen motioned toward the spot where Mary had been standing, but when she turned toward her cousin, she noticed that she was waving toward an empty patch of grass.

"Mary? She your invisible friend?" Joshua asked.

Scanning the grounds, Ellen spotted Mary a ways off, already talking it up with Emil Carpenter. No surprise there.

Ellen smiled. "More like a magician. She just up and disappeared."

"And I'm gonna make certain that this here pile a' corn disappears so fast you'll think I got magic in my fingers." He held his fingers to his mouth and blew out a breath of air. "Poof!"

Joshua moved in closer. He stood a head taller than Ellen, he was trim and muscular, and he smelled of wood smoke. He also had a powerful singing voice—an important quality in a captain. "Will ya cheer me on, Miss Ellen?"

"I will."

Ellen had to admit: She really liked the new Joshua Hamm.

Beaming, he jogged back to the pile of corn, where the overseer was getting ready to start the contest. Joshua climbed to the top of the enormous heap of corn and took his place, like a king with a pine-knot torch planted at his feet. The rest of his team formed a circle at the base of the pile, and Ellen noticed that the bearded man who had gazed in her direction—William Craft—was on Joshua's team. This night was looking good, with the attention of two men already coming her way. People often told Ellen she was pretty, but she never really believed them.

The overseer, Mister Peters, stood between the two corn-shucking teams and asked if they were ready. The team that shucked through the corn with the greatest speed came away with an extra dram of whiskey for each member. But that was not the only incentive. Buried at the bottom of each pile was a full bottle of whiskey. And then there was the prospect of uncovering a red ear of corn.

The overseer snapped his handkerchief, and the two teams dug into the pile of corn, hands flying, shucks ripping. Then the singing began, and Ellen heard Joshua's voice ring out, clear as a bell.

"Old master shot a wild goose," Joshua sang, and the men in the circle answered back with a loud "Ju-ran-zie, hoi ho!"

> *It was seven years fallin'.*
> *Ju-ran-zie, hoi ho!*
> *It was seven years cookin'.*
> *Ju-ran-zie, hoi ho!*

Fueled by music, the men worked double time. But Ellen noticed the strangest thing. While most of the men stripped the ears with a speed to save their lives, one of them moved slowly, methodically, in no particular hurry. It was the bearded man she had seen earlier— the one named William Craft. Joshua seemed to have noticed his slow pace as well, because he cast a hot glare in William's direction and almost lost the rhythm of the song for a moment. William just stared back and smiled, stripping off a husk with a methodical tear, like someone who had all the time in the world. Ellen could tell that Joshua would have liked nothing better than to pick up his torch, climb on down from his throne, and crack William Craft in the side of the head. And she couldn't blame him. It didn't seem fair that William was moving so slow when the rest of the team worked like men on fire.

A knife couldn't cut it.
Ju-ran-zie, hoi ho!
A fork couldn't stick it.
Ju-ran-zie, hoi ho!

Ellen was mesmerized. In the early goings, it was hard to tell which team was ahead, but the more intriguing contest in her mind was the one developing between Joshua and William. Several other men also noticed what was going on, and one of them appeared to be shouting at William, while another cast red-hot glares at him— branding-iron hot. William just smiled back, calm as can be. Then, as he pulled back slowly on another husk, he looked over his shoulder and stared straight at Ellen—and smiled.

She averted her eyes.

I got a rock.
You got a rock.
Rock is death,
O my Lordy,
O my Lord.
Well, well, well,
Run here, Jeremiah.
Run here, Jeremiah.
I must go
On my way.
On my way.
On my way.
On my way.
Who's that ridin' the chariot?
Who's that ridin' the chariot?

Joshua would sing each line, and his team answered in a rhythm that matched the ripping. By this time, the two piles of corncobs had been chiseled away to one-third their original size, and it was becoming clear just how close the contest had become. Joshua cast a glance at the opposing team's stack and switched to a song with an even faster pace, trying to fuel the frenzy with a rush of music.

As the two teams worked their fingers to the bone, Ellen grew to resent William Craft and his slow ways. It didn't seem fair to the other men.

Then all of a sudden, one of the men from the other team shouted out, "Red cob!" and everyone came to an abrupt stop. The contest paused as the man who uncovered the red cob marched into the crowd, picked out a suitable young woman, and planted a big kiss on her lips. The people applauded and hooted, and the man bounded back to the pile of corn, still holding the red cob high. On the overseer's signal, the contest resumed—at least until the next red cob was uncovered and the man kissed the woman of his choosing.

The two teams continued to move at breakneck speed, and the rhythmic singing picked up the pace.

Old number 12
Comin' down the track.
Comin' down the track.
Comin' down the track.
See that black smoke.
See that old engineer.
See that engineer.

Joshua was leading his team down the final stretch, pouring out the words; the lyrics became the fire that drove his team forward. Hands moved in a blur—all except the hands of William Craft, who still hadn't picked up his pace.

Told that fireman
Ring his old bell
With his hand.

Ring his engine bell.
Ring his engine bell.
Well, well, well.
Well, well, well.
Jesus tell the man,
Say, I got your life
In My Hand;
I got your life
In My Hand.

"Red cob!"

Another worker had peeled back a red ear, and the two teams took another break. It was a welcome respite, for most of the men were breathing hard and had worked up a good sweat. The fortunate fellow who had found the red cob was William Craft, and the crowd erupted in applause, although Ellen noticed that Joshua and a few members of his own team were not clapping, not smiling. The fact that William had uncovered a red ear must have infuriated them. It infuriated *her*. It didn't seem fair that the team member shirking his duty had been so rewarded.

"Who ya gonna kiss?"

"Pick out a lady!"

"C'mon now!"

Holding the red ear of corn high above his head, William turned and scanned the crowd of spectators, searching, searching, searching...finding.

His gaze had landed on Ellen.

She stared in horror as this man, this perfect stranger, approached in the torchlight. She noticed that Joshua had stood up on top of the pile—what was left of it—and he glared in their direction. Joshua had a temper, she knew that for a fact, and she could sense his anger burning as bright as pine pitch. It was an anger that could keep these torches burning for weeks.

Out of the corner of her eye, Ellen also noticed Mary smiling in her direction when it became obvious where William Craft was heading. Ellen wasn't smiling. She was terrified by what might happen if this stranger chose her.

William was now standing only a foot away from her. He gave her a grin, but not the kind of smile he had been sending in Joshua's direction. This was not an aggressive smile. It was almost shy. This man, who had been exchanging glares with Joshua all night, couldn't even keep his eyes fixed on her. He looked down at the ground, and then he moved one step closer. He raised his head. In the torchlight, she noticed a small scar on his right cheek, and she wondered if he had grown the beard to hide even worse scars.

Then he leaned forward and kissed her. He didn't take advantage of the moment, didn't give her a long kiss or a hard kiss. Just a soft touch on the lips and a wink, and then he turned back to the pile of corncobs.

Ellen was embarrassed by the smiles coming at her from all sides, but worst of all was the glare coming from one person. The eyes of Joshua moved from her to William and back to her again, and she knew right then that this night was not going to end well.

11

*On the Steamboat to Charleston
Friday, December 22, 1848*

T HE CLANGING OF A BELL BROKE INTO ELLEN'S DREAM, UNTIL the sound seemed to lodge in her ear. Someone was ringing a bell and shouting something about breakfast, but Ellen just wanted more sleep. She wasn't sure how long she had been asleep, but it hadn't been nearly enough. The night had been one long torment, with worries pestering her like flies inside her head. The steamboat made so many sounds that it was unnerving—animals on the deck below, drunken deckers hooting and hollering, wood creaking, clangs, clanks, and bangs, and most persistent of all, the steady throb of the steam engine.

And now someone was ringing the bell for breakfast.

Peering over the edge of her berth, she noticed that her cabinmate was still sprawled out on the floor like a dead man. Just as she suspected, he was wearing long johns that from all appearances hadn't been washed since Moses strolled the earth. She spotted his clothes piled up in a corner, but what caught her eyes was the flash of gold spilling out from one of the pockets of his discarded pants. The man's pocket was stuffed with jewelry—gold and gleaming. The thought crossed her mind that the man might be a thief, so she was glad that William was keeping track of their money; no one would think of lifting valuables from a slave. She wondered if she should report this theft to the captain, but doing so would raise a ruckus, and it was vital she keep a low profile.

Realizing that it would be wise to get out of the room before the man woke up, she quietly, carefully climbed down from the berth. But when her feet hit the floor, she accidentally stepped on the man's ankle, and he muttered and groaned and rolled over, curling into a ball. Ellen held still until his movements subsided.

Her cabinmate blocked access to the inner door, leading into the saloon where breakfast would be served. She had to go out the other door and onto the promenade, where she was hit with a refreshing blast of morning air. It was a fine day, with only wisps of cloud against a blue sky. Nature was calling, and one of her fears all along the route was how she was going to meet her needs without giving herself away. Fortunately, accommodations on the boiler deck included access to one toilet with a bolt on the door, offering Ellen the privacy she needed.

Moving back out onto the promenade, she felt oddly alert after such a fitful night.

"Master Johnson! Master Johnson!" It was William's voice, coming from below. She peered over the railing, down onto the lower deck, and there, hat in hand, stood her husband, beaming up at her.

"Yes, boy?"

"Will you be needin' someone to cut up your food for you?"

Good point. Dining was going to be difficult with her right arm in a sling. "Yes, boy. Come on up, and don't dawdle! Meet me at the doors to the saloon."

"Yes, sir!"

Ellen wished she could ride out the remainder of the trip here on the promenade, away from others, but she was famished. She met William at the back of the boiler deck, and they entered the saloon together—William two steps behind, of course. The only black faces she had seen on the boiler deck were cooks and stewards and such, but she hoped that a personal slave would be permitted inside the saloon in her situation.

As they entered the back of the spacious saloon, she immediately realized that she had made an awful mistake in bringing William with her. She passed by a table of women, and they stared back as if she was carrying cholera in with her. Ellen smiled and tipped her hat. None of the women smiled back. She saw only horrified expressions.

Mister Prendergast swooped in, took her by the arm, and whispered into her ear, "Mister Johnson, don't you realize what you just done?"

Ellen was dumbstruck. She realized her mistake, but it was too late now. She had brought a slave into the saloon, and they were in deep trouble, from the looks on people's faces.

"You're in the *ladies'* cabin," Mister Prendergast whispered.

Ladies' cabin? But this saloon was all one big room!

Mister Prendergast's eyes went to the floor. "The carpeting, Mister Johnson, the carpeting."

Ellen noticed that the back one-third of the saloon was carpeted, while the other two-thirds was a plain wooden floor. The back one-third was also furnished with greater refinement: lace curtains on the windows; ornate mirrors on the wall; a chandelier hanging from the ceiling like something she had seen in a Georgian mansion.

"Our apologies, ladies," said Mister Prendergast, "but Mister Johnson here is probably more accustomed to high-end boats, where the ladies' cabin is partitioned from the gentlemen by walls."

That sounded like a good excuse, and Ellen went with it. "Yes, yes, I never been on a boat where the ladies' cabin was marked off by carpet. I am so sorry."

Most of the women accepted her apology with polite smiles, although one elderly woman still looked like she would have liked nothing better than to have had Ellen tossed into the water. Ellen and William hurried off of the carpet, as if it were a bed of hot coals. The ladies and men shared the same saloon space, but just stepping off the carpet still felt like she was entering an entirely different world—the world of men. The saloon was a long room, stretching nearly 200 feet, but it was also narrow, barely 25 feet wide. This was the locus of activity for the above-deck passengers—the place where men played cards and passengers of both sexes read books and newspapers and sometimes even danced. The woodwork was intricately carved in steamboat gothic style, the doorknobs were glass, and there was even a piano at one end. Ellen and William approached a round dining table—for men only.

"C'mon and join us for breakfast," Mister Prendergast said, raising a glass of water clouded with enough sediment to grow corn in it, as the old saying went.

Ellen took a seat at the men's table, and she was nearly thrown off her feet when the steamboat jolted; it was docking on shore, probably to take on more freight and people—although she wasn't sure how they could jam any more passengers on the crowded lower deck.

Seated at the table was Mister Prendergast, a young southern military man wearing his Army blue, the steamboat captain, and—to Ellen's horror—the man with whom she had shared the cabin all night. He had covered his dirty long johns with a shirt, jacket, and trousers, but his face looked just as bedraggled—bristly beard and long, wiry hair. Leaning his elbows on the table, he glanced up from his chicken and broke into a greasy smile when his eyes landed on Ellen's sling.

"Ooo-eee, mister! You must be the one I shared a bunk with last night. You nearly knocked me unconscious with that medicated bandage a' yours!"

"It can't be helped, Ichabod. Mister Johnson here has enough to handle with his rheumatism without you complainin'," said the captain, who wore a smart blue jacket with a gold pocket-watch chain draped across his vest. He had a long, thick gray beard, with patches of black hair in his moustache.

"I meant no disrespect, captain. I'm only sayin' that I feel for Mister Johnson 'cause his cure seems as bad as the ailment."

Ellen worked up a smile but said nothing. The last time she had sat at a dinner table with white folk was when she and Miss Eliza used to have tea parties together—in secret, hidden from Missus Smith. Now she was dining at a table of white men in wide-open spaces, with the captain—*the captain*—sitting only two people away!

"Where you bound for, Mister Johnson?" asked the young Army man. He was a handsome man—broad-shouldered, long brown hair, trim moustache, kind smile.

"Philadelphia," said Ellen.

Mister Prendergast set down his fork with a clank and gave her a hard look. "Philadelphia? My colored boy, Johnny, told me you were stoppin' at Charleston to seek medical care."

"I'm not sure where he got that notion," said Ellen, her panic rising.

"Why, he got the notion from your boy here." Mister Prendergast waved in the direction of William, who stood directly behind Ellen, two steps back, eyes averted. "Johnny said your boy told him you were headed to Savannah, and then he changed his tune and said Charleston. Now you're sayin' your destination is Philadelphia?"

Why didn't William tell me he had said such things?

"Don't pay no heed to what my boy says. He wouldn't know the difference between Bostwick, Georgia, and Paris, France. We're headed to Philadelphia."

Mister Prendergast nodded and cast a disapproving look at William, who kept his eyes on his feet. As the captain mercifully changed the subject and talked about the scheduled time of arrival in Charleston, a Negro servant swooped in to slide a plate of chicken and potatoes in front of Ellen.

"Let me, sir," said William, coming to her side, picking up her silverware and beginning to cut up her chicken. Ellen could see the hunger in his eyes, and she wished she could allow him even one bite of her breakfast.

"You have a very attentive boy, but you better watch him like a hawk when you get to the North," said the captain after William had stepped away to retrieve a cup of coffee for Ellen. "I know several gentlemen who have lost valuable slaves among those blasted abolitionists."

Abolitionists again. Did they talk of anything else?

Ellen nodded and smiled. But before she could answer, the man she shared the cabin with—Ichabod—leaned back in his chair and said, "Sound doctrine, captain, sound doctrine." Then he jammed his thumbs in the armholes of his vest. "I wouldn't take a slave north, no way. I never saw a one who ever had his heel on free soil that was worth anything."

William returned, finished cutting Ellen's chicken, and stepped back from the table, eyes not making contact with anyone.

"Thank you, William," Ellen said.

Complete silence. From the looks on their faces, you would think that Ellen had just announced that she had placed a keg of gunpowder beneath the dining table. Ellen had done something wrong again, but for the life of her she didn't know what. The young officer made all things clear.

"Excuse me, sir, for saying, but you're likely to spoil your boy by saying 'thank you' to him," the Army officer said. "Nothing spoils a slave so soon as a 'thank you' or 'if you please.'"

"That's true," added Mister Prendergast. "If you want to keep him in his place, then storm at him like thunder and keep him tremblin' like a leaf."

She nodded, trying to look appreciative for the advice, but she was the one trembling like a leaf. She couldn't seem to do anything right at this breakfast, and she feared that at the rate things were going she would be completely exposed before she could even get halfway through her main course.

Things only got worse.

"Say, Mister Johnson, if you make up your mind to sell your boy, just mention your price," said Ichabod. "I'll pay for him with hard silver dollars."

Ellen suddenly realized that she had just shared the night with a slave trader. If this man ever discovered her true identity, he would murder her on the spot.

"I'm sorry, sir, but I do not wish to sell. I cannot get on without him."

"And I think we have all bothered Mister Johnson enough for one morning," said the Army officer, rescuing Ellen from her interrogator. He seemed particularly protective of her and shot a warning look at Ichabod.

The men changed subjects, to Ellen's relief, but Mister Prendergast kept throwing suspicious glances at her. She focused her eyes on friendlier faces, as the captain and the Army officer discussed the speed of various steamboats and the wisdom of racing when an overheated boiler could explode—and *had* exploded during many river races.

"If I was captain, I'd hang a weight on the safety valve and feed pine knots in the furnace to get my fire good and hot and the boat movin' faster than a bat outta hell," said Ichabod.

"Then it's a good thing you're not the captain," said Mister Prendergast. "You'd explode your boat and kill half of us on board."

"I don't care, long as I'm among the livin' half."

The change in conversation gave Ellen a chance to wolf down her food; as she did, she slipped a piece of chicken into her sling, intending to give it to William when she had a chance. Mister Prendergast gave her a sidelong look, and she wondered if he had noticed her subterfuge; he seemed on the verge of saying something, when his eyes suddenly darted to the doors of the saloon. Everyone turned, including Ellen, and she saw the most startling sight. A tall, portly man dressed in a red uniform, decked out in medals, stood just inside the saloon door, flanked on either side by two tall butlers in black coats. It was Lord Lowsley, the one they had seen parading onto the boat.

"Captain, may I have a word?" asked Lord Lowsley, speaking in a formal British accent.

"Good morning to you as well, Lord Lowsley," said the captain without a trace of a smile. "How may I help you? You can speak openly."

The dignitary strode across the room with regal authority, and his eyes scanned the men gathered around the table; it was the same look he might have given to something on the bottom of his boot.

"Sir, I would like to dine at table on land."

The captain dabbed at his mouth with his napkin and took a sip of water before answering. "On land?"

"That is right, captain. The boat is docked, so it is not unreasonable for me to insist that I dine off of this vessel."

All eyes moved in the captain's direction to see how he would respond. Ichabod jammed a wad of tobacco in his cheek and offered the pouch to Lord Lowsley, knowing full well he would be ignored.

"I am sorry, sir, but all passengers must dine on the boat. We have the saloon and we have the lower deck. Which would you prefer?"

Lord Lowsley spoke evenly, without emotion. "I choose land."

The captain motioned toward the one open chair left at his table. "We have a chair right here. Would you care to join us?"

Lord Lowsley's eyes landed on the empty chair, but he was not about to be seated next to Ichabod. He would probably sooner dine with a skunk. "Captain, I did not pay extra for this passage to be insulted."

"Oh. I see." The captain folded his napkin carefully and set it back on the table, not saying a word. He set his palms down on the table and sighed. Ichabod grinned up at Lord Lowsley, his teeth brown with tobacco.

"Very well, then," the captain said, and Ellen could tell that the other men were visibly disappointed by his tone of defeat. It was as if General Washington had just surrendered at Yorktown. "If you must eat on land, away from the rest of us, then you must."

"I must," said Lord Lowsley.

Ichabod's grin was gone, and Ellen could see that Mister Prendergast wanted to say something but held his fire.

"Very well, sir. I will have a porter bring your meal to a place of your choosing."

"I will be waiting on shore."

As soon as Lord Lowsley was out of the saloon, the other men cut loose.

"How could you agree to such a thing, captain?"

"If he's too good to eat with us, then he's too good to *travel* with us."

"I'd force him to eat with the deckers, if I was you."

The captain didn't answer any of their questions. He only said, "Lord Lowsley paid good money to be treated with respect," and he left it at that. After the captain ordered a porter to prepare a table for Lord Lowsley on land, several of the men dogged his heels, trying to convince him not to cave in to this blasted Brit. The captain did a good job ignoring them as he informed the ship's four cooks of the arrangements.

"Just don't use one of our finest sets of china," he said to the head cook.

"That's it? That's the extent of your response?" said Ichabod. "Don't give him our finest china? Oh, I bet he'll be tremblin' in his boots when he hears that!"

Ellen knew she should probably return to her cabin and hide from sight, but she couldn't resist the theatrics of what happened next. People massed at the railings of all three decks—the lower deck, the boiler deck, and the uppermost hurricane deck for crew members. Two Negro porters carried a table down the plank, onto land, and then found a nice scenic spot in a grassy area near the edge of the water. With the temperature comfortable, Lord Lowsley didn't have to wear a coat over his brilliant red uniform. He paraded down the plank like a colorfully plumed bird, followed by his butlers, one carrying a tray of food and the other carrying a tray with a glass and pitcher of lemonade. Irishmen in the lower deck bowed and hooted and made catcalls, and Lord Lowsley showed no emotion—just a dignified stride, chin up.

"I almost forgot," Ellen whispered to William as they stood side by side at the railing of the boiler deck. She slid her left hand into her sling, plucked out a piece of chicken, and slipped it to her husband. William pretended to cough as he consumed the juicy morsel.

By this time, Lord Lowsley was seated at the table along the bank, and the white tablecloth and plates were set before him. He began to dine.

The next moment, the steamboat came alive. The engine roared like a beast, and the two butlers snapped their heads in the boat's direction. The bell clanged, but Lord Lowsley did not move a muscle, did not even turn his head to look at the boat. He continued to eat, one small piece at a time. Dignified, always dignified.

As the steamboat began to edge away from shore, one of the butlers started to make a run for the ship, but he stopped and returned to the table—probably on the command of Lord Lowsley. Finally, the royal dabbed at his mouth and turned to stare at the steamboat one last time. From what Ellen could see, it was a look of contained disdain. Then he turned back to his meal, picked up his glass, and took a long drink. The two poor butlers stared in horror as the boat pulled away from shore. They had been marooned in the midst of American savages.

The lower deck erupted in applause, and hats were thrown into the air. Several Irishmen started doing a jig and one of them nearly tumbled in the water.

"Three cheers for the captain!"

"Huzzah! Huzzah! Huzzah!"

Even William was shouting, but Ellen didn't dare. If she tried to yell, her voice would come out high-pitched. In the excitement of the moment, Mister Prendergast slapped her on the right shoulder and exclaimed, "Good riddance to Louse Lowsley!" Then he quickly added in almost a whisper, "So sorry, Mister Johnson. I forgot about your ailment."

"That is all right," said Ellen, realizing she had neglected to wince when he slapped her on the shoulder. She eventually cringed, several seconds too late, and she wondered if he had done it on purpose—as a test of some sorts. Mister Prendergast gave her a squinty-eyed stare.

"Your hearing seems to have improved," he then said, adding to her mounting panic. On the steamboat, she had dropped her hard-of-hearing ruse, completely forgetting that Mister Prendergast had witnessed her act on the train.

She tried to make light of it. "When a fellow doesn't feel like talking about the weather with a stranger on a train, he will do just about anything."

Mister Prendergast gave her a piercing stare before breaking into a smile. "You are more sly than you seem on the surface, Mister Johnson."

She smiled back, but she was dying inside. She abruptly excused herself, ordered William to the lower deck, and retreated to her cabin, where she prayed she could be alone for the rest of the day.

Macon

John Knight was bound and determined. He strode up the steps leading to the porch of the Slator estate and pounded on the front door. When he didn't get a response, he knocked again.

Just as he was getting ready to pound his clenched fist against the wood a third time, the door opened, and standing before him was the infamous Molly. A Negro woman. A mulatto slave. But she was so much more than that, if the stories he heard were true. Molly was a nice-looking woman with high cheekbones and a fine figure, and he couldn't blame Mister Slator if he had taken a fancy to her. What he couldn't accept was Slator's treating her as his wife.

"Where's Mister Slator?" Knight demanded, stepping into the house without so much as an invitation. He removed his hat and looked around the grand foyer.

"Mister Slator is in town," said Molly. "Can I help you, Mister Knight?"

Knight paused, unsure whether to broach the subject with a slave. "I'm lookin' for William Craft and your niece, Ellen."

Molly didn't answer right away. Knight could tell that his words had taken her by surprise. There was a widening of the eyes, and her mouth opened just slightly. She spoke with the tone of cultured southern society, which irritated Knight to no end. "What reason do you have for seeking William and Ellen?" she asked.

"None of your business. I take it that they haven't visited you then."

Another pause. He was sure of it now. He had taken her by surprise, that much was certain. "Yes, they are spending time with us for Christmas," she said tentatively. "They just aren't here at the moment."

She was lying, but Knight played along. "When did they come to visit then?"

"Why are you so interested in my niece's whereabouts?"

"As you might know, I work with William at the cabinet shop, and I have information for him from our boss."

"Could I pass on the information when they return to the house, sir?" This time, Molly spoke with a little more conviction, which simply meant she was becoming more confident in her lies. The initial surprise that he saw in her eyes told him so much more. William and Ellen Craft hadn't come for a visit. He was sure of it.

"No, but thank you. I need to talk with William directly, so can you let him know?"

"I will, Mister Knight."

Knight stood only a few feet from her, and he could catch the scent of her perfume. She was dressed in as fine a gown as he'd ever seen on a plantation woman—certainly better than anything he had ever seen a slave wear.

"Thank you, Miss Molly." Knight popped his hat back on his head and took two steps at a time down the front porch. As he approached his horse, he noticed a wagon heading for the house, carrying four people—Molly's children, from the looks of it. The twins sat in the back, while the two older children sat up front, with the oldest boy driving. Frank was his name, if he recalled correctly. Frank and the older sister looked to be close to the same age as Ellen and William— in their early or mid-20s.

Knight decided he might get more information out of the children than he had from the mother, but as he waited for the wagon to come to a halt, he noticed Miss Molly bang open the front door, hold up the hem of her dress, and come hurrying across the lawn— probably hoping to intercept them before he got to them.

"Good morning!" Knight called out to the children jauntily, tipping his hat.

"Good morning," said Frank, warily. He tipped his hat as well. "It's Mister Knight, isn't it?"

Knight noticed that all of the children were dressed as finely as their mother. He moved in quickly, hoping to fire off a question before their mother could intercept them.

"I was lookin' for your cousin, Ellen. Any idea where she might be?"

The children stared back at him—blank looks from all of them. *Just answer*, Knight thought. *Just answer before your mother tries to put words in your mouth.*

"Frank and Mary, Antoinette and Emma, I'm so glad you're back home!" exclaimed their mother as she neared. "Mister Knight here is looking for your cousin Ellen, and I was wondering if you saw her and William in town. Are they still there with Mister Slator?"

Knight scowled. The children looked puzzled and said nothing, their eyes moving from their mother to Knight. The oldest, Frank, spoke up first.

"Oh, yes, the last we saw of Ellen, she was with Mister Slator. But they ain't comin' back home for some time."

The boy knew how to lie, just like his mother.

"Shall we tell her you want to see her when they return?" Frank said to Knight, as cool as a cucumber.

"It's actually William he wants to see," Molly explained.

"Oh. I see. Then we'll tell William you were looking for him," said Frank.

Knight shook his head in disgust. He was wrong. This boy wasn't as good a liar as his mother. He was *better*. He should enter politics.

"Thank you," said Knight, as he unhitched his horse and put his foot in the stirrups. "Good day, then," he added, with a final tip of the hat.

"Good day, Mister Knight." The boy smiled, tipped his hat, and pulled the wagon onto the drive leading back to the barn.

Knight watched them go. *Liars all of them.*

But they weren't going to keep him from getting the information he needed. He was going to head into town, where he would track down Slator and find some answers, come hell or high water. Then he would act.

12

Macon
Autumn 1845: Three Years Earlier

ELLEN HAD SO FAR MANAGED TO STEER CLEAR OF WILLIAM CRAFT throughout the night after the corn shucking was over. Besides, he wouldn't dare approach with Joshua staying so close to her side all evening. Joshua's team had won the corn shucking despite William's best efforts to slow them down, so he was riding on top of the world.

After the food came dancing and music. Brother Emmitt brought out the fiddle and everyone danced hack-back, where couples lined up facing each other and danced forward and backward, meeting and retreating. Joshua was always paired with Ellen. He made sure of it.

She caught William watching her from afar several times, but she figured she would be safe from his attentions as long as she stayed near Joshua. But Joshua, whose team had won the jug of whiskey, had taken more than his share of spirits, and he was getting a little out of control, dragging her to do the various dances with him—no longer asking.

He didn't settle down until the music took a more spiritual turn with a ring shout. Women broke apart into several groups to dance in a counterclockwise circle, while Brother John sang out the call, and all of the other voices responded. With his powerful voice, Joshua joined the men up front singing, leaving Ellen as an observer, and the music must have carried for miles through the darkness. The women moved in a single-file circle, elbows bent, knees bent, dipping and moving and calling back. The ring shout was pure Spirit worship, with some women clapping in rhythm, some singing the tune in response, some singing in harmony. It was a living, moving prayer, with no crossing of the legs and no stiff-limbed dancing; only corpses had stiff limbs, and these dancers were far from dead.

I want to be my Father's children,
I want to be my Father's children,
I want to be my Father's children,
Roll, Jordon, roll.
O say, ain't you done with the trouble of the world?
Ah! Trouble of the world.
Ah! Say ain't you done with the trouble of the world?
Ah! Roll, Jordon, roll.

"How 'bout you, Sister? You done with the trouble of the world?"

Ellen inhaled sharply. William Craft had slipped up beside her in the darkness. She considered walking away, but she stood her ground, not responding.

"You still mad 'bout that kiss, Sister Ellen? It's Sister Ellen, ain't it?"

Ellen continued to stare at the women dancing in a circle, holding out their long, brown dresses and swishing them from side to side as they danced in rhythm, singing in response to Brother John's lead.

My sins so heavy I can't get along,
My sins so heavy I can't get along,
My sins so heavy I can't get along,
Roll, Jordon, roll.
O say, ain't you done with the trouble of the world?
Ah! Trouble of the world.
Ah! Say ain't you done with the trouble of the world?
Ah! Roll, Jordon, roll.

"I chose you for the kiss 'cause you're the finest woman here," said William. "That so wrong?"

Finally, Ellen turned to face him. The torchlight cast a harsh light on his features. He was smiling at her, but she didn't smile back.

"Why am I the finest woman here? 'Cause a' my skin?"

He laughed. "No ma'am, that ain't it. Your skin could be green as grass, and you'd still be the finest woman for miles around."

She showed the hint of a smile. "Green? I don't think you'd a' given me that kiss if my face was green."

"I sure would. Go paint your face up green and I'll show you."

"You'd sure like that, wouldn't you?"

"I would."

Ellen stared at the row of singers and noticed that Joshua had his eyes on her. Joshua gave a slight shake of his head, and she took it to be a warning sign: Stay away from William.

I cast my sins in the middle of the sea,
I cast my sins in the middle of the sea,
I cast my sins in the middle of the sea,
Roll, Jordan, roll.
O say, ain't you done with the trouble of the world?
Ah! Trouble of the world.
Ah! Say ain't you done with the trouble of the world?
Ah! Roll, Jordan, roll.

"I'm sorry if you didn't like me kissin' you, Sister Ellen, but I'd do it again in a heartbeat if I found me another red cob."

She folded her arms across her chest. "That ain't why I'm mad, Brother William."

"Ah! So you know my name. Then tell me: Why ya'll mad at me?"

"Cause you're a shirker. Sorry I have to say it, but you're a *shirker*!"

William leaned back and laughed again.

"What's so funny? It ain't funny you bein' a shirker."

"I'm sorry, but I thought you were all mad 'bout the kiss, and you're just mad 'cause I didn't shuck the corn as fast as the overseers wanted us to."

"This ain't 'bout the overseers. It's 'bout you not bein' loyal to the team and shuckin' as fast as you can. You looked like a fool."

William's grin vanished. "Listen, Sister Ellen, the ones lookin' the fool were the men workin' through that pile like madmen just to reach a jug a' whiskey. The master and the overseers, they're the ones playin' them for fools. Put a jug in the corn, make a big contest out of corn shuckin' and he gets 'em workin' double speed. They're the ones playin' the game on us, and I didn't want no part of it. I'm a lot of things, Sister Ellen, but I ain't no fool."

She was struck speechless for a moment. She had never looked at it that way.

"I think you were just bein' ornery to the other men on your team."

"I was bein' ornery to the overseers standin' around watching us workin' our fingers to the bone—just for a jug a' whiskey—and them laughin' inside. I think we all shoulda been slowin' things down, the entire team. That woulda showed the overseers."

"That woulda also got ya'll whipped."

William just shrugged. By this time, the song had moved on to another spiritual, and the women kept moving in a circle, improvising their dance steps.

Don't be weary, traveler,
Come along home to Jesus;
Don't be weary traveler,
Come along home to Jesus.
My head got wet with the midnight dew,
Come along home to Jesus;
Angels bear me witness too,
Come along home to Jesus.

"Tell ya what, Sister Ellen," William said. "If the prize for corn-shuckin' woulda been *you* instead a' whiskey, you woulda seen me workin' like a crazy fool. I'd a' shucked the whole pile myself in less than 10 minutes."

Ellen turned away, trying to hide her smile. This William was a bold one.

"Which plantation you from?" she asked.

"Don't work on no plantation."

"You ain't free are you?" There weren't many free blacks in Macon, not like she heard could be found in places like Charleston or Richmond.

"I wish I was, ma'am. My master is Mister Ira Taylor, but he hires me out at the cabinet shop run by Mordecai Cubbins."

"You're a carpenter?"

"Just like Jesus and Joseph."

Where to go I did not know,
Come along home to Jesus;
Ever since he freed my soul,
Come along home to Jesus.
I look at the world and the world look new,
Come along home to Jesus;
I look at the world and the world look new,
Come along home to Jesus.

"Workin' on furniture is the best work in the world. Only thing that could make it better was if I was a free man doin' it."

Ellen nodded her head. William Craft must have some real talent to be put to work in a white man's woodshop, instead of sweating in the cotton fields.

"I also wait on tables at the hotel across the street from the cabinet shop, and I get to keep some of my money," he added. "I suppose I work close to a hundred hours a week."

Ellen gave him a sidelong look. "Hundred hours? I take it back, Brother William. You ain't no shirker."

He let out a big laugh and grabbed her by the hand. "C'mon, Sister Ellen, you wanna do a chalk-line walk with me?"

Pure panic. He had taken her by the hand! She considered yanking her hand back, but she didn't; instead, she shot a look across the way to the line of singers. By this time, Joshua was doing some quill blowing, which he was quite proud of. But while he played, he stared straight at her, making his anger obvious with his eyes.

"I don't know if we should," she said to William, but inside, she felt a desire to buck against the wishes of Joshua. He didn't own her, and he needed to learn that as soon as possible. One master was already one too many.

"You sure, Sister Ellen? Then how 'bout we take a stroll around and you can tell me 'bout your seamstress work."

Going on a stroll together would be even worse, she thought. If Joshua saw them wander off into the night, there would be blood.

"No, no, a chalk-line walk would be just the thing. I hear there's a plum cake for the winners."

"Now that's something I'll work for. If the master's givin' away prizes for strollin' with a beautiful woman, that I can do—much better than workin' my fingers to the bone for a jug a' whiskey."

William had to sense her ambivalence and fear, but if he did, he didn't seem to care. He still had her by the hand, and he tugged her along to where several couples were getting ready. They picked up their buckets of water and took a spot in the line.

One quick glance and Ellen could see that Joshua's eyes had become menacing in the torchlight. Being filled to the gills with whiskey probably didn't help his mood, but he still hadn't made a move. He continued to play the quills—a row of pipes made from canes of all different lengths, each producing a different tone. Joshua could play 10 quills, a rare feat, and he never gave up the chance to show off his skills.

A dozen couples were set to go, all of them balancing pails on top of their heads. A piece of cloth, coiled in a circle, sat on each of their heads, cushioning the scalp and providing a nest for the bottom of the bucket. The music started up, and the first couple paraded arm in arm, not a drop spilling from the carefully balanced pails on top of their heads. The second couple didn't fare as well. They marched one direction fine as can be, but when they turned to make the return trip, the woman's bucket went sliding off her head, sending a wave of cold water onto the poor man's side. The crowd roared with laughter, and the drenched man joined in; then he put an arm around his gal and drew her away. They were eliminated.

When it came Ellen and William's turn, they were steady. Ellen had done a lot of water fetching as a girl, and she knew how to balance a pail on her head. It was all a matter of a perfectly aligned back and an even gait—no bouncing up and down. But Ellen wasn't sure if William was up to the challenge. A little water sloshed from his bucket when they made the turn, but they came back without disaster. She was impressed. Walking side by side like that, with every eye upon them, Ellen almost felt like they were bride and groom, walking up a dirt aisle. It felt strange, arm in arm with a man she had despised only an hour ago.

The music picked up momentum, and so did the chalk-line walkers. Couples moved along the imaginary line with greater speed, and several more met with big spills—but not William and Ellen. Not a drop had spilled from Ellen's bucket, and a little had sloshed from William's, but they were still in the running. All of the couples that didn't spill their buckets would be judged at the end.

"Where'd you learn to balance a bucket like that?" William asked as they waited for their next turn.

"Sister Tabitha taught me. She's not alive no more. Born in Africa and lived to almost a hundred."

"She taught you good."

The texture of the music had changed since the dance began, and Ellen suddenly realized why. The quills weren't sounding any longer. Ellen's eyes went immediately to the row of men singing, and she saw that Joshua was no longer sitting among them. She spun around, looking for any sign of him, but he was nowhere. That's a good thing, she told herself. Maybe he up and left.

Moments later, the plum cake suddenly looked to be in William and Ellen's reach. The flawless couple, the ones who hadn't spilled a drop, had been making their way back, smooth as silk, when the man tripped; his gal, with her arm linked with his, was yanked forward as well, and both of their buckets came crashing to the ground. They were out of the running, just like that.

It was William and Ellen's turn. Buckets back in place, they went arm in arm to the end of the line and smoothly turned. She heard William go "Woaah," and for a split second it looked as if his bucket was going to slip-slide off the side of his head. But he put out two arms, like a tightrope walker, and he bent at the knees and managed to keep the pail upright. Not a drop spilled out.

They made it back without catastrophe, and the judges were quick in their final decision after lining up all of the remaining couples. William and Ellen had won the chalk-line walk—together. And just like that, the plum cake was theirs.

The music became rousing, and the crowd formed a large circle around a space where two torches were jammed in the ground; in the center of the circle, men and women took turns doing jigs, one or two at a time. Ellen and William stood side by side in the circle, clapping to the beat, stomping their feet, and she wondered if she had ever had such a good time in her life. She felt lifted up.

She looked over at William and caught him staring at her; embarrassed, she quickly drew her eyes away, but she felt his eyes remain on her. It was awkward but exciting. A cabinetmaker? That was really something. She made clothes, and he made furniture. The perfect fit, she thought. And he had a strange sort of courage. He had stood up to the overseers in his own odd way, and it suddenly seemed heroic in her eyes. It couldn't have been an easy thing to do, especially with his teammates judging him so harshly—especially with people like *her* judging him so harshly.

Ellen didn't even think through what happened next. She just did it. She reached out with her right hand, took him around the neck, and drew him down to her level. Then she planted a kiss on his cheek, just above his thick black beard.

There was that laugh again. "Why, Sister Ellen, you gotta have the red cob to be doin' a thing like that! I need to see—"

Several women screamed, and Ellen turned. It all happened so fast. She saw movement, swift movement, and a ball of flame coming straight toward them.

Joshua had attacked with fire.

13

Charleston
Friday, December 22, 1848

T HE *GENERAL CLINCH* ARRIVED IN CHARLESTON BY LATE
morning, but Ellen remained inside her cabin, where she had
been cooped up since breakfast. She heard the other passengers
bustling and bumping about, laughing and chattering as they all
disembarked, but she stayed in hiding.

"Time to go," said William, who went up to the boiler deck to
fetch her.

Ellen sat on the edge of the lower berth and stared into space,
too scared to move. "What if there's slave catchers waitin' for us on
the dock?"

It was a realistic fear. If someone back in Macon had noticed they
were gone, telegrams would be flying in all directions by now, alert-
ing train stations and port towns of their disappearance. Her mind
had become obsessed with the possibility.

William took a seat beside her. "We can wait before disembarkin'.
I don't think any slave catchers are out there; but if they are, they'd a'
seen everyone get off the boat and be on their way."

Ellen nodded solemnly. The strain was getting to her. Her head
had begun to ache, a slight throbbing behind the eyes, as steady as
the steamboat engine. She leaned her head on his shoulder, and William put his arm around her, although she could tell by his jittery

movements that he was afraid someone would walk into the cabin without warning.

Ellen was so weary, and they had so far to go. They waited for as long as they could, until they heard movement nearby, someone shuffling along the deck, opening and closing cabin doors. William leaped to his feet and so did Ellen. She slapped her top hat back on and slipped on her green-tinted glasses just as the cabin door opened.

"Oh! Pardon me!" said one of the white deckhands. "I thought everyone was off the boat, Mister Johnson."

"I'm sorry," Ellen said. "I was feeling poorly, that's all. But I think I'm fine now."

The deckhand stepped aside and let Ellen pass; she hobbled through the door and onto the promenade, steadying herself on the railing.

"Don't just stand there, as useless as a no-legged dog!" the deckhand barked at William. "Give your master a hand. Do it!"

"Yes, sir."

William held out an arm, Ellen latched on, and they made their way slowly off the ship, where they were relieved to see that all of the passengers had cleared off. All that were left were workers unloading cotton and miscellaneous freight, and no slave catchers were waiting to pounce. All along Charleston Harbor were rows of tall-mast ships. Ellen had never seen anything like it: a forest of masts and a jungle of rigging. They made a left turn and came upon another astounding sight: three parallel rows of cotton bales stretching far into the distance. So much cotton all in one place!

William and Ellen found a carriage, and she asked to be taken to the nearest hotel, where she hoped to grab something to eat. She was famished, and she could only imagine how William felt because he hadn't been fed nearly as well. The carriage rolled past rows of palmetto trees and some magnificent homes, even larger than the Collins estate, lined up overlooking the water.

"Too bad you're here in December or I would recommend the saltwater bathing house," said an elderly gentleman with pure white hair, who was sharing the carriage with Ellen. He leaned forward on his cane. "It might do wonders for what ails you. What is it—rheumatism?"

Ellen nodded. "Got it bad."

The man tapped his cane against the carriage floor. "Then come in summer. Nothing better than floating in saltwater."

"Thanks, but I'm heading to Philadelphia and hoping the doctors there will find a way to ease my rheumatism long before next summer."

"I hope you're right, I hope you're right."

Silence descended, but she could tell that the old gentleman preferred conversation. He fidgeted, glanced out the window a couple of times, and then settled on a new line of conversation. "Yes, it's just too bad you're here in winter. Other times of year you could have taken a boat straight to Philadelphia."

Ellen's heart dropped. "Excuse me, sir, but are you saying that no steamboats go directly from Charleston to Philadelphia?"

The man pounded his walking stick against the floor again. "Of course I'm saying that! Don't you know? You'll have to take a steamer to Wilmington, then a train from there."

Ellen leaned back and groaned inwardly. She had thought that the next steamboat would be the last transport they would have to take.

"Sorry to be the bearer of bad tidings," said the gentleman. "But you'll make your way to Philadelphia by and by. Mark my word."

"I pray you're right."

The carriage rolled past more rows of palmetto trees, pulled onto Church Street, and rolled to a stop in front of the Planter's Hotel, a three-story building with a beautiful, dark-turquoise, wrought-iron balcony on the second level. Ellen found a table in the hotel's elegant dining room, and she asked if William could remain by the table to cut up her food. The Negro waiter looked horrified at just the suggestion.

"Oh, no, sir, you know that ain't allowed. But don't you worry none. I'll cut up your food into good and small pieces for ya'll."

"Thank you, boy," Ellen said, and then she immediately realized that she had just said "thank you," again, to a slave. It was a good thing no one else heard her.

*****

William stared down at his dinner plate, which was stained black by who knows what and chipped in three places. The fork they handed him carried so much rust that it looked like it had been painted orange. The cook, a tall, thin black man, worked wonders with the victuals going out to the dining room, arranging the food with as much care as a mother tucking in her child. But William's food? The cook slopped some cold, greasy leftovers on his plate and motioned him to a small table in the corner, where another Negro was polishing boots.

The man doing the polishing smiled at William as he brushed the boots to a fine shine. He was a short man, thin as a stick. His hair was greased up slick, and from the smell of it, he had probably used the kind of axle grease typically smeared on wagon wheels. It had done the trick, though, smoothing out the hair. If he wanted to hide his African hair, William wondered why he didn't just shave his head, as many male slaves did. It was a lot less bother.

"Say, brother, where you from?" the man said with a thick African accent. William had noticed that many of the slaves on the seacoast had strong accents.

"Macon." William washed down his first bite with a gulp of cloudy water.

"And which way you goin' with that done-up buckra?"

"Philadelphia."

"By squash, I wish I was goin' with you! I hear 'em say that there's no slaves way over in them parts. That so?"

"That's what I hear," William said. He didn't really feel like talking.

The man tossed down the boots and rose to his feet. "Then those are the parts for Pompey! I hope when you get there you'll *stay* there and never have to follow that buckra 'round no more!"

This wasn't the kind of talk that William wanted to be associated with—not if he wanted to avoid attention. He forced the last mouthful down his throat, said, "Thank you," and headed for the door. But before he could exit, Pompey grabbed his right hand and started shaking it, as fierce as shaking a rug.

"God bless you, brother, and may the Lord be with ya. When you gets to freedom, and you're sittin' under your own vine and fig tree, don't forget to pray for poor Pompey."

Pompey had tears gathering in his eyes, and William couldn't ignore his passion. He wheeled around to face Pompey squarely and put his hands on both of the man's shoulders. It just about brought tears to William's eyes, seeing this man so emotional in front of a perfect stranger.

"I won't forget you, Pompey. May the Lord deliver your feet from falling, so you can walk before God in the light of the living."

Pompey beamed. "*Walk*? What's this 'bout walkin'? If I get free, I'm gonna *leap* before the Lord in the light a' the living!"

William gave his hand a final shake and returned to the dining room, where he was shocked to find three Negro servants waiting on Ellen. One was clearing away the plate, another was brushing her top hat, and the third was staring at the money that Ellen had just put in his hands. In fact, all three seemed to be clutching coins as they worked.

"Your master is a big bug!" said the one who had been staring at the money—also speaking with an African accent. "He's the greatest gentleman that been this way for 6 months."

"Yes, he is some pumpkins," William said, as he took Ellen's arm and helped her across the dining room, past watching eyes.

Once outside the hotel, he leaned in and said under his breath, "You can't be drawin' attention to yourself like that."

"I had to give 'em somethin'," Ellen whispered back.

"But we don't have a lot a somethin's to give. We're gonna need every bit a' money we got."

She looked away and softly said, "I'm sorry."

William sighed and glanced around, afraid they were now making a scene on the street. They moved on. The afternoon avenues were crowded with mules pulling carts, people selling bread and sweet-grass baskets beneath canopies, Negroes sitting around and sharing a pipe, and small boys chasing a dog. William had never seen so many black people in one place. Half the city had to be the same color as him, and the other half the color of Ellen. They had just spotted a carriage to take back to the wharf to book a steamboat to Wilmington when a familiar voice penetrated the street noise.

"Willie! Willie boy!"

It was Johnny. *Again.* Could they never lose the man? William had successfully kept this one-man question generator away from Ellen, but not this time. Johnny came running up to them breathless; he took William by the arm and drew him off to the side of a nearby stable. Ellen looked on, standing about 10 feet away, but she didn't say or do a thing. William thought about how a real master would never let a slave yank his servant away without a good explanation.

"Somethin' wrong, Johnny?" William asked. Ellen moved in closer, and this made Johnny nervous. He kept looking from William to Ellen and licking his lips.

"It's all right," William assured him. "You can speak."

Johnny took a deep breath. Then he glanced around at the crowd before answering. "It's my master. Prendergast is after ya'll. He knows all 'bout what you done. What the *two* of ya done. And he's after ya'll, both of ya."

*****

Ellen stared at Johnny in stunned silence. Her first thought was actually a picture in her mind—a picture of her back in Macon and being yanked out of the back of a wagon with black iron shackles on her legs and a steel collar cinched around her neck. In her mind, she saw Miss Eliza's face—stone cold with rage and betrayal. She couldn't let herself be captured; she would rather throw herself in the deep water and let the chains drag her to the bottom.

Finally, William spoke. "What're you sayin', Johnny? What does Mister Prendergast know 'bout us? What is there to know, except that we're headin' on to Philadelphia?"

"Mister Prendergast says that Mister Johnson ain't who he says he is."

Oh, God, Ellen thought. *Oh, God, oh God.*

Johnny took off his hat and turned to Ellen. "Beggin' your pardon, Mister Johnson, but this is what my master thinks, not me. He thinks your arm ain't really in a bad way."

A pause.

"He's callin' ya'll con artists."

"Con artists?" William feigned outrage. "Where would he get such a notion?"

Johnny shot a nervous look at Ellen. "He saw Mister Johnson here hidin' things in his bandaged arm, saw him slippin' things to you, Willie. He thinks...I mean this is him thinkin', not me...but he thinks ya'll been stealin' jewelry on the steamboat."

He thinks we're thieves? Ellen thought.

"I'm sorry, Mister Johnson, but that's why I wanted to warn ya. I like ya'll, so ya'll better get outta town before he catches ya."

"*We're not thieves,*" William said.

"Then you better be able to prove it. I'm just warnin' ya'll, that's all."

Ellen worked to control her runaway emotions. Mister Prendergast thought she was a thief, a con artist, not a slave woman—and that was something to be thankful for. Less than a minute ago, she had thought her identity had been uncovered, but Prendergast's suspicion still put them in serious danger. If he brought the police down on them, and if they brought in a doctor to determine whether she really suffered from arthritis, their story would unravel fast. They would discover that she was worse than a thief. They would discover that she was a slave woman, trying to steal her master's property. Trying to steal *herself.*

"What makes him even think there was thieving going on in the steamboat?" Ellen asked.

"One of the women claimed to be missin' necklaces, watches, all manner of valuables."

"We didn't hear nothin' 'bout that on the boat," William said.

"The woman didn't notice till she got to the Charleston Hotel, where Mister Prendergast is stayin'. She started screamin' from her room, and announcin' to the world she'd been robbed on the boat."

Ellen's thoughts flashed back to the long night she had spent in the cabin with the slave trader. She remembered him lying sprawled out on the cabin floor, drunk as a skunk with jewelry spilling from his pocket. She wished now that she had said something, despite the danger of speaking up.

"I think I know the real thief," she said to Johnny.

Johnny's eyes flicked in her direction. "Sir?"

"The man named Ichabod. I think he's your real thief."

Johnny scratched his head, trying to work it out. "But how would you know this, sir?"

"A gut feeling, Johnny." Ellen couldn't say she had seen the stolen jewelry because questions would be raised about why she didn't report it at the time.

Johnny nodded his head and repeated the words as if he didn't quite believe them. "A gut feelin'..."

"We greatly appreciate you warning us like this, Johnny," said Ellen, speaking in cool, even tones, masking her terror.

"When you see Mister Prendergast, tell him we're stayin' at the Planter's Hotel," William said. "He'll look for us there and get thrown off the scent for a spell. And tell him Ichabod is his man!"

"I'll do that, Willie."

Ellen plucked a coin out of her pocket and handed it to Johnny, whose eyes lit up. "Thank you, Mr. Johnson, most kindly. But I best be runnin'. If my master catches me talkin' to you like this, we'll all be wearin' chains."

"We're forever grateful," said William, shaking hands with the man he had considered a pest—but who now appeared to be their savior.

After slapping William on the shoulder, Johnny disappeared into the crowd.

"So whata we do now?" Ellen asked.

William kneaded his forehead. "We get on that steamboat to Wilmington quick as we can."

William flagged down a fly, a two-wheeled carriage with a man perched on the back carrying a long whip in his hand, and they raced to the wharf, praying that Prendergast hadn't already sent the police there to intercept them. The Custom House office was packed with travelers waiting in a long line to purchase tickets. Women and servants remained with the luggage, while white men stood in a line that snaked outside the office door. Ellen wished she could push her way through, but when one man tried to cut a couple of spots in line, another man yanked him back by the collar, while a third one poked him in the ribs with his cane. She wisely waited her turn.

Ellen kept looking toward the end of the wharf, where she expected the police to appear at any moment. After 10 minutes of eternity, she moved up enough in line that she squeezed into the stuffy Custom House office. Cigar smoke hung over their heads like low-lying fog, and some men had the audacity to chew and spit, even in such cramped quarters. When one man splattered another gentleman's shoes, Ellen was sure a fistfight was going to break out. Some men began pushing from behind, and the room became so crowded that Ellen, for the first time, feared that she might be pushed up so close to the men around her that they might be able to notice her womanly features beneath her thick jacket.

Another 5 minutes passed, and no police pushed their way inside—no one came in looking for a man with a bandaged arm and face. If William had been taken, wouldn't they have at least checked inside the Custom House for any sign of her?

Finally, Ellen reached the ticket window, where the principal officer sat staring at her with the most tired eyes she had ever seen. They were bloodshot and puffy, with black circles beneath. The man had cheese-colored skin, heavy eyebrows, a small nose, a whiff of a moustache, and the most enormous forehead. It was as if he had been squeezed in the middle, forcing his most prominent feature to burst out at the top. The man did not crack a smile.

"C'mon, c'mon, speak up. Where ya'll headed?"

The man gave Ellen half a second to speak before rolling his eyes.

"Speak up, man! Where ya'll headed?"

"Two tickets to Wilmington, North Carolina, sir. One for me, and one for my slave."

The man shoved a ledger across the desk and slammed an ink pen on the countertop. "Register your slave and pay the dollar duty on him."

Ellen dug deeply into her pocket and put the dollar on the desk. Her left hand was shaking, and she couldn't control it. She motioned toward her sling.

"I'm sorry, sir, but as you can see I am not able to sign my name. Would you please sign for me?"

The principal officer stared back at her and folded his arms across his chest. Then all of a sudden he thumped the register with the flat of his hand. "Sign using your left hand, or you and your slave don't go nowhere."

Ellen cast a look over her shoulder at the impatient crowd. Her sling was no longer eliciting sympathy.

"Get a move on!" came a shout from the back.

"Just sign it!"

Ellen stared down at the register page, which already carried so many names in an indecipherable code. She fought to try to remember how to write the few letters she had learned so long ago. Maybe she could copy one of the names she saw in the list. But with her left hand?

The man slapped the register once again. "You can't take a slave outta the state without signing. *So sign!*"

Ellen wanted to cry. She had no idea what to do.

Macon

Macon was a beautiful city—as long as you didn't look at your feet, where you would discover an unpleasant reality. Manure. The streets were spotted with mounds of horse droppings like tiny, remote islands scattered in the dirt. The horse population was booming in Macon, and so was the population of hovering flies.

John Knight noticed that the street sweepers hadn't done a very good job clearing the manure on Mulberry Street this afternoon. His own horse made its own contribution to the mess as he tied it up and set off on foot. A single horse can produce 15 to 35 pounds of manure in a day, which made it a real chore for the slaves to keep the streets clean—especially on days like this when traffic was thick. Carts, drays, and coaches rattled up and down the street. Knight tried not to even think about the smell.

Molly said Slator was doing business in town, and he aimed to find him—and to find out whether William and Ellen Craft were really visiting them for Christmas. He passed by a grocery store run by a free black by the name of Solomon Humphries—an anomaly in these parts, where there were only a handful of free blacks. It irked Knight to see a black man running his own business, so he hurried on past.

"You seen Mister Terrence Slator?" Knight asked Jeb Thomas, a blacksmith friend coming out of the Harp and Eagle.

Thomas looked up and down the street, mouth hanging open, revealing a missing front tooth. "No, but I see his wench right there." He pointed, and Knight was shocked to see Molly bringing her wagon to a stop right in front of the bowling saloon.

"Or should I call that wench his wife?" Thomas said with a grin.

Knight cursed and sprinted down the street. The woman had come to warn Slator that he was asking questions about the Crafts, and Knight was intent on getting to the bowling saloon before her. He might have done it, too, if he had been watching his feet instead of glaring at the woman. His shoe hit a fresh pile of manure, and the next thing he knew his leg was shooting out in front of him, and his eyes were looking up into the blue afternoon sky as he fell squarely on his rump—landing in another fresh and steaming pile.

Back on his feet, he rushed toward the bowling saloon, using his handkerchief to brush the slop from his pants as he ran. He tossed aside the stinking handkerchief just before ducking into the establishment where men gathered for drinking and tenpins. The aroma from his coat drew stares and whistles and scrunched-up noses as he pushed through the crowd.

He spotted Mister Slator near the bar and let out a silent stream of obscenities. Molly had just reached the man, and she too was drawing her share of stares. With the stories going around about Slator and Molly, the two of them were not usually seen together in public, but today was an exception. Today, Molly had to warn him.

"Mister Slator!" Knight called out.

Slator and Molly turned to face him, and he rushed up, stinking to high heaven.

"What happened to you, Mister Knight? You smell like you've been sleepin' in a stable." Mister Slator smiled. He was a vibrant-looking gentleman, especially for his age, for he was probably 25 years older than Molly, who looked to be pushing 40. Slator had red hair, at least what was left on top of his head, and he had a pug nose and broad face. Rumor had it that he had fought bare knuckles when he was younger, and that was one reason people rarely challenged him openly about his relationship with Molly.

"I need to ask you something important, Mister Slator."

"But *we* need to talk first," said Molly, and Knight's hopes rose. It sounded like she hadn't already spoken to him, hadn't already warned him.

"It can wait, Molly," Slator said. "Let me first find out what Mister Knight wishes to speak to me about."

"But—" That was as far as Molly got in her protest before Mister Morris, the bowling saloon proprietor, emerged from the crowd. He was a large man with not a speck of hair, except for his massive beard, and he didn't look pleased. Even though Molly was mostly white on the surface, he knew what kind of blood coursed beneath her skin.

"Mister Slator, would you please escort..." Morris looked Molly up and down, as if wondering whether she deserved the title *lady*. "Would you please escort *her* off the premises."

The bowling saloon was no place for a lady or a Negro, and Molly was both. Knight grinned, taking pleasure in her rebuke.

"And I'd prefer it if you'd air yourself out on the street as well," Morris said, snapping a scowl at Knight and taking a whiff of his clothes.

The words slapped Knight's smile right off his face.

The three of them made for the door, and Knight saw his chance to fire off his question. "Mister Slator, I would like to know if William and Ellen Craft are stayin' with ya'll for the holiday."

Molly answered for him. "Of course they've been with us, like I told you earlier, Mister Knight."

"I wasn't askin' *you*." They stepped out into the bustling street, keeping near the edge, away from horse traffic.

"Easy, Mister Knight." Slator had an edge to his tone, a warning.

"I'm just sayin', Mr. Slator, that I am askin' you how long William and Ellen Craft will be stayin' with ya'll."

Molly jumped in. "And I told you—"

Slator cut her off. "And what business is it of yours, Mister Knight?"

"I need to know when William'll be comin' back to the cabinet shop."

"Doesn't your boss know? Ask Mister Cubbins."

"I haven't been able to talk to him."

"Why on earth not?"

Knight struggled for words. It was obvious that Mister Slator knew something strange was going on here, and he wasn't going to be forthright with any information about William and Ellen Craft.

"I need to know 'cause I work alongside William, and he's accountable to me," Knight said.

"William's accountable to Mister Cubbins and Mister Taylor, not you."

"Me being a white man, he's also accountable to me."

"You're not his master. You're more fool than master."

Taken aback, Knight began to stammer out a response when the door to the bowling saloon suddenly swung open. Mister Morris had a drunk by the scruff of the neck, and he tossed him through the door. The drunk stumbled into Molly's path, catching himself just before he would have knocked her over like a human bowling ball.

"Pardon me, miss," the drunk said, setting his eyes on Molly. He smiled and caught his balance, wobbly as that was. "My, my, what do we have here?" He tipped his top hat and adjusted his tie. "You sure look fine, ma'am. You need company for the afternoon?"

The drunk obviously figured Molly was fair game, as most Negro women were in the eyes of white men. He was oblivious to the presence of Mister Slator, standing just behind him.

"Take it easy, mister," said Slator, putting a hand on the drunk's shoulder.

The drunk, a heavyset man with stubble for a beard and disheveled appearance, stumbled around to get a good look at Slator.

"And who are you?" he demanded, trying to focus his eyes.

That was a good question, one that Knight would like to hear answered. Would Slator describe himself as Molly's master or husband—or both? Knight moved in closer.

"That's none of your business."

"Well, if you ain't her master, then what I propose to do with this wench is none of *your* business."

The drunk wheeled back around toward Molly and put his paws on her shoulders, as if he aimed to force a kiss on her right there in the street. Molly screamed, and Slator acted. He ripped the drunk off Molly, and the man stumbled backward to the ground, crashing against the soil like a huge, unwieldy barrel. The drunk came up spitting and swinging. Slator was trim for his age, and he was already in boxing position. He dodged the drunk's first clumsy swing, and then popped the man in the nose. It was obvious he could have hit the man harder; his punch was a warning shot, just barely enough to draw blood.

The drunk reached for his nose, moaned, and stared at his hand, which was splotched with fresh red blood.

"I don't want trouble, mister, so just go on your way," Slator said, still in boxing position.

The drunk swung again. Another easy dodge, another miss. The momentum of his swing nearly carried the drunk to the ground. He caught his balance.

Then he pulled a gun from his waistband.

Molly screamed, and someone shouted, "Gun!" People scattered, and Slator held out a warning hand.

"You put that away now. I don't want trouble. And *you* don't want trouble."

Knight backed away about 10 feet, but not so far that he didn't have a good look at what was unfolding. The gun was pointed at Slator, so he didn't feel as if he was in any imminent danger.

"Hand over the gun," Slator said, taking a step closer to the drunk.

"Stay back or I'll blow that smirk off your face!"

The drunk's hand shook, but he stood so close that even a shaky aim would probably take off a big piece of Slator's body if he pulled the trigger.

Slator slowly stepped to his right, and the barrel of the gun followed. Knight noticed another man, Mister Morris, moving in from the right, looking for a chance to disarm the drunk. Slator kept moving until the drunk was positioned with his back to Morris, who continued to advance from behind. Then Slator stopped.

"Think this through, mister. You don't want to shoot," he said.

"I will if I have to."

Morris pounced from behind, but he failed to get a good grip on the drunk's gun hand, and the weapon went off with a pop. Two pops. A small cloud of smoke rose from the gap between the drunk and Slator. Molly screamed, and Morris and another man wrestled the drunk to the ground. The gun went off a third time, and Knight moved in closer once it looked safe to do so. Slator was down but struggling to sit upright. He was covered in blood. He had been shot in the neck, and blood was spurting out like an oil gusher. Molly was also covered in his blood, as she pressed her hand against his neck, and Mister Morris pulled her off and tried to control the bleeding with a handkerchief. Knight was mesmerized. He had seen men die before, but mostly at public hangings. He had never seen a man bleed to death right before his eyes. Blood also leaked from Slator's chest, where he had been hit by a second shot.

Molly broke loose and began to kiss Slator's face—until a man from the crowd pulled her away again. Her shrieks sounded like a dog caught in a bear trap, and she fought the man holding her, thrashing and kicking like a wild woman.

Knight had heard of slaves mourning their master's death in dramatic fashion, but not like this. Her display of rage and sorrow didn't seem natural for a slave and a master. If anyone had ever doubted that there was something between Slator and his slave, they would have changed their mind after seeing this unfold.

Finally, Morris stood up, and he too was covered in the man's blood, like a butcher after a day's work. He shook his head, and the man holding Molly released her. She threw herself onto the lifeless body of Terrence Slator, wrapped her arms around him, and wailed. The lady had gone insane, and Knight backed away from the scene. He had seen enough.

14

Macon
Autumn 1845: Three Years Earlier

LLEN SPUN AROUND AND SAW WILLIAM THROW UP AN ARM TO block the flaming torch that Joshua had swung at him. The torch clubbed him in the forearm with a sickening crack, sparks flying, and the loose fabric of his clothing caught the flame, but William either didn't see it ignite or simply ignored it. With his head down, he drove his body into Joshua's, taking him thudding to the ground. William was on top, his sleeve still in flames, and Joshua, flat on his back, still had the torch in his right hand. Joshua reached around and placed the flame against William's back, and the fire took hold. The back of his clothes burst bright.

Screaming William's name, Ellen ripped Sister Harriet's good shawl right off her shoulders, and wrapped it around his burning back, attempting to put out the flames. As she did, Joshua shoved William off him, knocking him backward into Ellen. William lost his balance, and so did Ellen, and he fell on top of her. From her position pinned beneath William, she slapped at his sleeve, which was still smoldering. Joshua was infuriated, seeing them tangled up on the ground, even though it was his doing. William scrambled back to his feet, the flames on his back now doused, and he reached out to help Ellen to her feet.

Her eyes went wide. "Watch out!"

William spun around just in time to see the flaming pine-tar torch whooshing through the air, coming straight for his face. He ducked, and the hot club went sizzling only inches above his hair. All of this happened so fast that no one stepped into the middle to stop the fight; from the look on the overseers' faces, they were having a grand time watching two slaves nearly kill each other over a woman. One of them leaned up against a tree and watched, arms crossed.

As Joshua prepared for another charge with his torch cocked back, Miles Johnson, an elderly church deacon, stepped in front of him.

"Now, you put that down, Joshua, or I aim to take it out of your hands my own self."

Deacon Miles was 40 years older than Joshua, and he walked with a cane, so the notion of him snatching away the torch was comical. But what the deacon lacked in size and strength, he made up for with moral authority. It was Deacon Miles who had gotten Joshua's little brother out of jail a year ago when authorities wanted to string him up for sassing a white woman.

Chest heaving, eyes blazing, Joshua glared at William and Ellen. His eyes then moved to the deacon and the crowd of people encircling him on all sides. When Deacon Miles took one step toward him, Joshua cocked the torch back, as if intending to swing, as if daring the old man to come one step closer. His nostrils flared, he breathed hard, and beads of sweat stood out on his face in the glare of the torch.

Finally, Joshua turned on his heels, and the crowd stepped aside to let him pass as he marched toward the Big House. He passed by the table of food, spied the plum cake that William and Ellen had won in the chalk-line walk, and he jammed the torch, flame first, into the sweet reward. He kept on moving, into the darkness.

"You all right, son? Your back pretty near became bacon," said Deacon Miles, putting his hands on William's shoulders and turning him around to inspect his back. The fire had turned the fabric black in spots and burned a couple of holes.

"I'm fine. I think Sister Ellen here may have saved my skin."

"You better get someone to look at your back right away. You might need to be puttin' wheat flour on that burn."

Ellen thought about asking if she could help, but she wasn't foolish enough to suggest something so bold as to tend the wounds on his bare back.

"I think I'm all right," William said.

"Ya'll still better come inside and have one of my boys look you over," came the voice of Mister Whitaker, master of the estate, who had just appeared from the house. "Mister Taylor sure wouldn't like it if I let you get injured during our corn shucking."

Nodding, William consented to having his burns treated, and he made his way with Mister Whitaker to the house. Ellen watched, her heart still racing and her hand tightly clutching the burnt shawl.

"You all right?" asked Mary, coming up from behind.

"Yes, yes."

Ellen looked around and saw a large crowd staring at her.

"I'm all right," she announced, and she told the fiddler to strike up the music again. "Go on now. I said I'm all right."

As the music brought the festivities back to life, Mary put an arm around Ellen's shoulder. "You sure?"

Ellen wasn't sure. Her hand still shook, and her mouth was bone dry. She looked down at her hands and realized how tightly she was clutching Sister Harriet's scorched shawl, which hung in her hands like a burned battle flag. Sister Harriet, with her hot temper, was the wrong person to snatch a shawl from, but the whole situation was so absurd that Ellen burst out laughing.

"Don't know what's so funny!" Sister Harriet yanked the shawl out of Ellen's hand. "Took me a long time to make this, I'll have you know."

As she stormed off, she tried to put the shawl back on, but a piece of it flaked off, and Sister Harriet didn't notice.

"I'm sorry, Sister Harriet. I'll sew you a new one," Ellen called out to her.

Sister Harriet, with her back to Ellen, flung up a hand. "You bet ya'll gonna do that!"

Ellen sighed and looked around for a place to sit because she was suddenly dizzy. She staggered over to a bench and sat down. Mary followed and dropped down beside her, and they sat in silence for about a minute, listening to the music.

"So what do you think of him?" Mary finally asked.

"You mean William Craft?"

Mary nodded eagerly. "Who else?"

"He has his charms."

"And what about Joshua?"

"What about him?"

"Do you still fancy him—after what he done tonight?"

"Would you?"

Mary shook her head and stared into the darkness, where Joshua had disappeared in an unholy fury.

"I don't suppose Joshua is gonna let this go between you," Mary said.

"'Fraid you're right."

"This is the best we could do with it," said Sister Charity, an elderly woman, the mother of 10 children—eight of whom had been sold away from her over the years. Moving slowly across the grass, she carried what could be salvaged of the plum cake—about one-third of it.

"Thank you, Sister Charity," said Ellen, rising to her feet to lift the cake from her hands.

Sister Charity leaned in close. "That man a' yours, Mister William, he takes the cake, you know."

Ellen smiled. "I discovered that tonight."

"Well, then, what you waitin' for? Get on up to the Big House and share some of this reward with him."

Ellen glanced back at Mary, who smiled and said, "Go on now."

Ellen looked off across the yard to the Big House, lit up in almost every window. She stuck in her finger and tried a taste of the plum cake before heading in the direction of the house, before heading in the direction of William Craft.

Three Days Later

Armed with her broom, Ellen swept the room where Dr. Collins' aunt had been staying for the past 2 months. She was a stern old lady, closing in on 90 years old, and she made it clear that she didn't approve of her nephew's "soft ways" with slaves. She preferred the whip, so Ellen felt nervous just being in the lady's room; if she broke anything, she didn't know what might happen.

By the fireplace, her heart dropped when she knocked over a face shield—a kind of metal half-moon fan used to keep the lady's face from melting. Dr. Collins' aunt had battled the pox many years back, and her face was scarred with pockmarks. So she did what many fine women did—fill the pockmarks with wax and powder over them. She used the metal shield to cover her face when sitting in front of a fireplace so her waxy face didn't slide down her cheeks.

The face shield clattered to the floor, and Ellen was thankful she hadn't knocked over a breakable object. After checking for dents (there were none), she carefully put the shield back on the fireplace mantle.

"Ellen." A woman's voice suddenly sounded directly behind her, and a startled Ellen spun around, nearly knocking into an end table that held a fragile vase. Standing in the doorway was her cousin.

"Mary, don't do that, you gave me such a fright," Ellen said with a slight smile.

Her smile vanished when she saw Mary's distressed expression and realized that something had happened. Mary hurried across the room and wrapped Ellen in her arms. The news couldn't be good.

"Oh, Ellen, he's been caught. He's been caught."

Ellen felt prickles of panic, and she held on to her cousin for support, not saying anything at first. Then she pulled away and searched her cousin's eyes. "Has he been hurt? Tell me the truth."

Mary took out her handkerchief and wiped her eyes. "Oh Ellen..."

"*Has he been hurt?*"

She nodded. "He's been hurt real bad. Dogs done it."

Ellen felt the panic grow and spread, for this was this worst possible news. Why did that man have to run? Deep down, she knew the answer, but she pushed the thoughts away. Deep down, she believed it was her fault.

"Where is he, Mary?"

"They're bringin' him into the house, puttin' him in a back room till the doctor can come. But don't worry. Dr. Collins is fetchin' his own family doctor."

Ellen made for the door, but Mary snagged her by the arm. "You don't want to go down there. Stay here, please."

"I can't. This is all my fault."

"It ain't your fault he went runnin'. Please don't go down."

Breaking away, Ellen rushed down the hallway, and she heard the babble of many voices downstairs as she took the steps two at a time. The front door burst open, and chaos entered. Three Negro servants were hauling a man—what was left of a man. All she saw was torn clothing, blood, and mangled flesh. She stopped in her tracks and dropped down onto one of the steps.

"Cover your eyes," said Mary, settling down beside her on the stairs.

She wouldn't cover her eyes. She had to see what she had done. It was like watching a nightmare parade as the Negro servants lugged the half-dead man right in front of them through the foyer and toward a back room. Behind the bloody mess came Dr. Collins and Mister Franks, a professional slave catcher. And two steps behind them were Dr. Collins' aunt and Miss Eliza. Miss Eliza looked horrified, but old lady Collins' face was stiff and emotionless—as if the wax on her face had turned to stone.

"I'm not paying you a cent!" Dr. Collins told the slave catcher. Dr. Collins' face was red and his voice booming.

"I got mileage and a reward comin', and I'll see that you pay!" shouted Mister Franks, a muscular man of 30 or so, with close-cropped hair and a bushy red moustache. This slave catcher wasn't one to be easily intimidated.

"But I told you not to use dogs and you didn't listen! So why should I pay you? You're gonna pay *me* for what you did!"

"No dogs? Whatya talkin' about, no dogs?"

"You heard me! And you heard me 2 days ago when I said to hunt him down *without* dogs! I wanted him back unharmed! What good is he to me this way?"

"Yeah, but I was also told you changed your mind."

Dr. Collins stopped and faced the slave catcher squarely. "What?"

"Your aunt done told me you changed your mind and wanted me to hunt with dogs."

A tense silence. Dr. Collins looked thunderstruck by the slave catcher's words. Slowly, he turned to face his aunt.

"Is this true?"

The woman, draped in heavy brown clothes and her face powdered pure white, glared at her nephew. "If one of them gets a little torn up by dogs, you should not worry so much. It will send a message to them all."

Old lady Collins looked past her nephew and stared directly at Ellen. "And what are *those two* doing here?" she added.

For the first time, the two white men became aware of Ellen and Mary sitting nearby on the stairs. Ellen knew they should move out of earshot, so she rose to her feet and rushed toward the back room.

"Don't go in, Ellen, don't do it," said Mary.

"I gotta."

When Ellen edged open the door, she found the three Negro servants on their knees, praying for the bloody man on the bed. Praying for Joshua Hamm. Joshua had run away 2 days ago, and Ellen knew it was all her fault. Broken by what had happened at the corn shucking, Joshua had run for his life; he had run to get away from her, and now here he was, torn apart by the slave catcher's Cuban bloodhounds, with barely any life left.

Ellen dropped to her knees and Mary was right beside her, hands on her shoulders. One of the servants raised his hands and called on the Lord's ministering angels to fill the room.

Ellen forced herself to look, as punishment for what she had done. She had ripped Joshua from the inside, and the dogs had done it from the outside. His face was mostly blood and raw flesh. His eyes were open, and he seemed to be aware of her presence. Their eyes locked.

"I'm so sorry," she said. "I'm so very sorry."

Ellen looked for some reaction in Joshua's eyes, but she saw nothing. He just stared back at her like a mute judge, and she felt her heart melting inside, sliding away like it too was made of wax.

15

Charleston
Friday, December 22, 1848

LLEN STARED AT THE PRINCIPAL MAN, AND HE STARED BACK, tapping his fingers on the desk and waiting for her to put her signature on the register. She and William had run into a brick wall. She had been sure they wouldn't require her to sign her name if her arm was in a sling. She couldn't have been more wrong.

"C'mon, mister, sign the blasted thing with your left hand!" someone shouted from the back of the Custom House at Charleston Harbor.

"Just do what ya can. We ain't got all day!"

Ellen didn't dare turn around and face all the people crowded into the stuffy building, but she could feel the heat of their anger, like standing with her back to a bonfire.

"Sign!" The principal man suddenly slapped his hand, palm down, on the register opened in front of Ellen.

Ellen jumped at the sound and used her good hand to rub her brow. The principal man spit his tobacco and wiped the juice from his mouth. The grumbling built, and she heard men sighing and cursing behind her back.

Then a voice. A familiar voice. "What's the problem here? I know this man!"

The words came from the very back of the room, and Ellen finally worked up the courage to turn and face the mob. The crowd rippled with movement, as someone pushed toward the front, and Ellen saw, with surprise, that the voice belonged to the young Army officer from the steamboat. It was the same person who had tried to teach her how to address her slave properly. Another man, dressed like a ship's captain with a dark blue jacket and brass buttons, was at his side.

"I asked what the problem might be," the Army officer said to the principal man, as he and the captain stepped up beside Ellen. They made an intimidating pair.

"This gentleman here says he can't sign the Custom House register," the principal man groused, flinging his hand in Ellen's direction.

The Army officer folded his arms on his chest and stared at the principal man, as if daring the man to talk back to him. "You see his arm in a sling. You have eyes, don't you?"

"Yes, but—"

"Then sign for him!"

"But the rule—"

"Listen here, I can vouch for this gentleman!" the young officer snapped. "Or do you question my associations?" Ellen picked up the scent of liquor as he spoke.

"You mean you know this man?" the principal man asked, softening in the presence of the two officers.

The young Army officer looked Ellen directly in the eyes but didn't answer. He stared at her so hard that she was sure he could see behind her green-tinted glasses and tell that she had feminine eyes.

"He's Mister Johnson, of course! Mister *William* Johnson! I know his kin like I know a book!" he said. "So I suggest you let him through if you know what's good for you."

"I'm sorry, sir, but he still has to sign," the principal man insisted, using a polite tone with an Army man. "Everyone has to sign. I'm sorry, but them's the rules."

The steamboat captain, a handsome man of about 40, with blond hair, long sideburns, and a wide smile, stepped forward. "If Jenkins here says he knows this fellow, then I will register the gentleman's name myself."

The principal man looked flabbergasted. "Are you certain, captain?"

"Don't I sound certain or did you not hear what I said?" The captain's genial tone became sharper, and the man retreated quickly.

"Yes, yes you do, captain...I mean, yes I did."

Grinning broadly, the steamboat captain leaned over the register and shouted out Ellen's name as he wrote each word. "Mister! William! Johnson! And! Slave!"

The crowd burst into mock applause, and the captain spun around and bowed like a stage actor. Ellen smiled as best she could and thanked him profusely.

Back outside, she basked in the late afternoon breeze, glad to be away from the suffocating air inside the building, glad to see that William was waiting for her and hadn't been arrested. She looked around the wharf. No sign of Mister Prendergast. The captain headed for the steamboat, but the young Army officer, the one named Jenkins, lingered by her side.

"Thank you, kindly," Ellen said once again to Jenkins.

"Ah, nothing!" He waved off the compliment, like a fly in front of his face. "Those Custom House nitpickers need to be put in their place sometimes—just like you need to keep the coloreds in line. Promise me you'll remember the lesson I taught you on the steamboat."

The lesson about speaking fear into her slave? How could she forget?

"I'll remember, sir."

"Say, I'm heading to have myself a drink and a cigar! Care to join me, Mister Johnson?"

Ellen hated to turn him down after he had just rescued her. She didn't want to anger him, but there was no way that she was going to head back into town and risk being seen by Prendergast. She just wanted to get aboard the steamboat and hide.

"Thank you, sir, for the fine offer, but I am not feeling all that well."

"A drink will pick you up like nothing can," said Jenkins.

"I'm sorry, but I do appreciate all of your kindness."

"Happy to do it for a friend! Happy to do it!"

The young officer spoke so loudly that he drew stares from anyone within earshot. Then he strode off, belting out a sailing tune.

If buttercups buzz'd after the bee,
If boats were on land, churches on sea,
If ponies rode men and if grass ate the cows,
And cats should be chased into holes by the mouse,
If the mamas sold their babies
To the gypsies for half a crown;
If summer were spring and the other way round,
Then all the world would be upside down!

William sidled up to Ellen, and together they watched the officer stride down the wharf, his song fading.

"What was that about?" William asked, hat in hand and scratching his head.

"He's the man who just saved our skin. The Lord moves in mysterious ways."

"If that man just saved us, then the world really is upside down."

"Upside down and hanging by a thread."

William picked up the trunk and followed Mister William Johnson onto the steamboat. The boat couldn't leave soon enough, as far as Ellen was concerned.

Macon

Knight stared at the drunk, who slumped behind the bars, red-eyed from the booze and the weeping. The drunk had sobered some, and the realization of what he had done seemed to be crushing the life out of him.

"I didn't know what I was doin," he whimpered from the jail cell. "I didn't mean to kill him."

"Coulda fooled me," said the jailer, Willis Hughes. "Three shots, point blank from 3 feet away. If ya'll didn't know you could kill Mister Slator, then you're a bigger fool than I thought."

"But it was the whiskey actin'. It was the whiskey causin' me to shoot. It wasn't me."

"Well, then, I guess we're just gonna have to string up the whiskey for murder. And if the whiskey just happens to be sloshing around inside of you, that's your problem."

At the words "string up," the drunk hurried into the corner and threw up. It sounded like someone tossing slop to a bunch of hogs.

"Aw, for mercy's sake!" Hughes threw a pencil against the wall.

John Knight, who was at the office giving his statement about what had happened, smiled. "He's just airin' his pouch and gettin' the whiskey out of his system, so he won't have to be a part of the hangin'."

Hughes pushed away from his desk, stormed to the back room, and ordered a slave to get in the cell and clean the mess. Then he returned to his desk, slid into his chair, and rubbed his eyes with the palms of his hands.

"This is just the beginnin'. Come New Year's, we're gonna have so many men in that jail pukin' and stinkin' and makin' a mess. I hate messes."

"Well...?" said Knight, hoping to bring their conversation back to the subject that occupied his mind. "What do you think about William and Ellen Craft? I suspect, more than ever, that they ain't been visitin' Molly's family."

"Why don't ya'll just let it be Dr. Collins' problem what happened to Ellen, and let it be Mister Taylor's problem what happened to William?"

"You don't care that two slaves might be on the run?"

"What I don't care to do is roam the countryside with a posse, aimin' to snare us a runaway, only to find out that William and Ellen are still in Macon all along. I don't care to look a fool. I asked you to get some evidence, and so far you ain't done nothing but watch a man get shot."

"Molly was there to warn him about me askin' questions."

"Maybe. But maybe not. It's 3 days till Christmas, and I need some-thin' more solid before I go gallivantin' around lookin' for runaways."

Knight looked down and rubbed the palm of his left hand with his right thumb. He knew he was right about William and Ellen Craft. Why couldn't Hughes see it, plain as day?

"If you're so sure, go to Taylor and tell him your suspicions about William. He's his owner, not you."

"I know Taylor, and he's so naïve, it's...he won't believe my suspicions."

"You still haven't talked to Dr. Collins either. I hear he's back in town on Christmas Eve. Talk to him then."

Christmas Eve? But every hour takes the Crafts that much farther north. Knight heard sobbing, and he looked toward the cell, where the drunk was sitting on a stool, face in his hands, bawling like an overgrown infant.

"What's gonna happen to Molly and her children now that Slator is dead?" Knight asked.

Hughes shrugged. "Dunno. She might claim to be his wife and try to snag the property as her own."

"Don't Slator got any relatives to inherit?"

"Other than those four children?"

"He never claimed them as his own—not legally at least."

"True, true." Hughes got up and retrieved the pencil he had hurled against the wall. "There is a man named Simon who claims to be his nephew. Slator always insisted he had no relatives, but this man made some noise a ways back 'bout bein' related to him."

Knight perked up at this news. "Really? I ain't heard that. You think he really is a nephew?"

"Could be. I met him a coupla times when he took up residence here behind bars."

"What for?"

"Petty crimes. And I don't think I was ever more glad to get rid of a prisoner when his time was up. Drove me outta my mind with his gripin' and moanin'. I can understand why Slator denied this man bein' a relative."

Knight glanced over at the cell where the drunk was still blubbering. He couldn't imagine how the nephew could be more annoying than this drunk.

"You know where the man lives?"

"The edge of town, I'm pretty sure. Why? What do you have in mind?"

"Nothin'. Just wonderin'."

Knight stood, put on his top hat, and made for the door.

"Why are you so single-minded 'bout Molly and her niece Ellen Craft anyway?" Hughes called out to him. "This ain't 'bout what happened several years ago, is it?"

Whirling around, Knight glared. Hughes just leaned back in his chair and gave him a defiant smile. Knight wanted to smack the smirk off the man's face, but he said nothing. What had happened two years ago was nobody's business but his own.

16

Macon
Spring 1846: Two Years Earlier

THE SUN ROSE ON ANOTHER SUNDAY MORNING, THE ONLY DAY OF rest for Ellen and most slaves, the only day in which folks had time enough to get gussied up. Sunday mornings in spring were fine, especially when the sky was clear and the breeze soft. Ellen passed among the cabins at the back of the Big House, where the smell of bacon fat brought her senses alive.

"Mornin', Sister Ellen."

"Mornin', Brother Edward."

Brother Edward puffed on a pipe and sat on a barrel, combing out the hair of his youngest son using a tool with strong steel teeth and a wooden handle. "Jim crows," they called them.

"You're lookin' sprucy, Sister Ellen."

"Thank you, Brother Edward."

"William passed this way earlier."

Ellen smiled and continued on her way to the field beside a wooded area where a traveling Methodist exhorter, a young free black man by the name of Brother James Wilson, was set to preach. Brother James had received his preacher's license at age 19, from what she heard, and he knew how to pull in the converts, even attracting some white folks to his revivals. In Macon, he drew on black folks from all kinds of churches—Presbyterian and Baptist, not just the Methodists. Today they were all coming together to hear this preacher rattle the heavens.

The women were looking fine in colorful dresses with sashes and hats and feathers and their hair fixed up and scented. Sunday was a day in which every hair on a woman's head was born again, for it was the only day when most black women were given the time to fix up their hair in style.

"You're lookin' as fine as flowers this mornin," said William, meeting her at the edge of town and extending an arm. She and William had been courting since the corn shucking last fall—something she still felt guilty about in light of what happened. Joshua Hamm had died of his wounds, and she never felt his forgiveness before he slipped away.

Several Negro men headed toward the revival field in gleaming vests, with black jackets and top hats—and bare feet. They slung their shoes over their shoulders, for fear of muddying them during the walk over; they didn't slip on the shoes until they reached the lush grass of the revival grounds. Sister Harriet emerged from the woods, wearing a bright green dress, all flounces and poofy sleeves. She carried her Sunday finest clothes with her from the plantation, and she changed in the woods, because her master would get furious if he saw her in fine clothes not befitting a slave. The Lord's Day could be complicated.

William and Ellen parted ways when they reached the gathering place, for the ladies collected on one side and the men on the other. People stood or sat on the ground, but within a short time Brother James had half of the crowd on their knees or falling prostrate. He was in fine form, standing on a wooden platform rising about 6 feet from the ground; he was slinging his words like David slinging stones, and striking people smack in the forehead with every syllable. For more than an hour, he worked over the same Scripture passage, as if he was attempting to drive the words deep.

He leaned far over the pulpit, each hand gripping the podium. "The voice of him cries in the wilderness, the voice cries out to say,

'Prepare ye the way of the Lord!' The Way I say! The Way I say! The Way of the Lord!"

"Prepare ye, prepare ye!" Sister Harriet shouted back.

"Come, Lord Jesus!" called another.

Brother James held up both hands, stared down at his feet, and shook his head. "The voice of him cries across Georgia! Prepare ye the way of the Lord! Make straight in the desert a highway for our God!"

"Amen!"

Arms shot into the air, and the worshippers were stirred to a boiling.

"Make straight through the *cotton fields* a highway for our God!"

"Amen!"

"Make straight through the *rice fields* a highway for our God!"

"Amen!"

"Make straight through *Savannah* a highway for our God!"

"Amen and Amen!"

"Make straight through *Macon* a highway for our God!"

"Amen and Amen!"

"Make straight through our *souls* a highway for our God! Make straight through our *cabins* a highway for our God! Make straight through our *hearts* a highway for our God! Make straight! Make straight! Make straight!"

Brother James held his hands up high and looked to heaven and stamped his feet.

"Amen, Amen, Amen!" shouted Sister Prudence. She was hopping up and down, and Brother Edward was running in place so fast that you'd think he'd wear a hole in the ground clear down to China.

"The blood of Jesus is a river running along that highway, a crimson river that leads us all the way to Jehovah God! One drop from this river is all it takes, my brothers and sisters. Dip yourself in this stream, and one drop of his blood is all it takes to make us—*to make us all*—children of the Mighty One, the Morning Star, the King of Kings, the Prince of Peace, the Alpha and the Omega, the Author and Finisher of our Faith, our Dayspring. One drop of our Savior's blood is all it takes! So come forth, throw yourselves on the horns of the altar, and become His child! Drink from the river, drink of His blood, drink of His forgiveness!"

"Yes, Brother James! Yes, yes, yes!"

"And the glory of the Lord, the glory of the Lord, the glory of the Lord shall be revealed, and all flesh, ALL flesh and blood shall see it together, for the mouth of the Lord hath spoken it!"

"Speak it, Lord, speak it, Lord!"

Brother James wiped his forehead with his handkerchief and continued. Ellen sought forgiveness to cleanse her from all that had happened with Joshua, for the image of him staring at her, judging her, had become deeply fixed in her mind. She looked across at William, and she saw a man standing in front of him suddenly flung backward, knocked off his feet by the Spirit, as if shot on the battlefield. He was hurled backward and William caught him, and the man lay on the ground like a corpse before rising back to his feet. Others streamed forward to the Anxious Seat to profess their new life.

Eventually, the preacher's voice gave way to some powerful singing, and by late afternoon the people finally began to disperse. The colors of the clothes streaming across the grass looked like a field of flowers on the move with reds and yellows and greens and blues. William took Ellen by the arm and drew her away, beneath a massive magnolia with a trunk as wide as any she had ever seen.

"William, what do you think you're doin', drawin' me away like this? You tryin' to start a scandal?"

"We're still in the eyesight of the preacher, so you got nothin' to worry 'bout." William smiled as he leaned his back against the tree and propped his right foot against the bark.

"Brother James was talkin' strong, wasn't he?" Ellen said.

"Yes, yes...prepare ye the way. That's a bit of what I had in mind to talk to *you* about." He stood up straight and took her by the hands.

"You wanna talk about the preacher's sermon?"

"Well...not exactly. But I wanna talk 'bout preparin' a way."

"A way for the Lord?"

"A way for the two of us."

Ellen caught her breath. She thought this might happen some day, but she was not prepared for it to happen today. She didn't respond. She was terrified. She hadn't decided exactly what she would say to him in response—but she had an idea.

"Would you prepare a way for me to come into your life, Ellen? Would you marry me?"

Ellen looked away. William's gaze was too intense for her to hold the connection. Her palms were becoming moist, and she shifted the weight from one foot to another. She looked back in his eyes and could tell that he was having a difficult time keeping his grin going, waiting for her answer. He probably expected a quick and easy "yes" followed by a long embrace.

She sighed. Just say it, she told herself, just say it.

"I can't, William."

Ellen felt the strength drain out of William's hands.

"You..."

"I can't."

"But I thought..."

"I do love you, William Craft."

"Then marry me."

"I can't."

"You keep sayin' that."

William let her hands drop. He took off his top hat and mopped his brow with his handkerchief.

"I've pondered this a long time," she said. "I can't marry till we're free."

William paused in the middle of wiping his forehead. He stared back at her, clearly confused.

"Till we be free? And how do you suppose that's gonna happen?"

"You're gettin' to keep some of what you make at the restaurant and cabinet shop, ain't ya?"

"Sure, but not enough to buy your freedom, let alone mine."

"Then we wait."

"That's a long wait."

"Jacob waited for Rachel for the longest time, and he had to keep workin' in the fields for her father for what seemed like forever and a year."

"But why...why wait?"

Ellen reached out and took William's right hand in hers. "I ain't gonna lose my children. And I ain't plannin' on ever losin' you. And there's only one way to do that. Be free. Then we'll marry."

Pulling her toward him, William wrapped his arms around her. "I won't let no one take you from my arms."

"If I get sold, how you plan on doin' that? And how do you plan on keepin' our children from bein' sold away?"

"We fight back."

"Then our children will be killed."

"Then we run."

"Like Joshua did?"

Ellen gently pushed out of his arms. She knew they were making a scene. People back at the church were staring in their direction, smiling and talking among themselves—probably assuming he was proposing and she was accepting.

"When I was split from my mama, I decided I never wanted to see that happen with my own children," she said. "Never again."

The tears came, and William embraced her.

*****

This day was not turning out anything like William thought it would. He assumed they would be announcing to the world their wedding, and friends would be slapping him on the back, and the women would be talking about whether Ellen could get a hand-me-down wedding gown from Miss Eliza.

He didn't understand why Ellen was doing this to them. It was like she was putting them into double bondage. If she feared being split apart by their masters, then why *choose* to be kept apart? Wasn't she just making the same choice that she was afraid the master might make? Just because it was her choice, and not the master's, didn't make it any easier to stomach.

But on another level, he understood. He did.

"I know what it's like to lose my mama when I got taken away," Ellen said. "It was horrifyin' and that was only for a year. I was fortunate. We might not be so lucky."

William didn't answer, and she pushed away from his embrace.

"Do you even hear what I'm sayin', William Craft? Do you *understand* what I'm sayin'?"

William rubbed his left shoulder and let out a sigh. "'Course I do, I know *exactly* what you're sayin'. I lost my family, so I know."

He had never told her. Ellen touched him on the cheek and held her hand there for a moment.

"Our master, Mister Craft, was needin' money bad, so he sold off my parents, two brothers, and a sister," he said. "Then, when Mister Craft found himself wantin' to speculate on cotton, he mortgaged me and my other sister to the bank to raise money. My sister Sarah was the only family I had left."

Ellen said nothing. She took hold of his hands once again.

"When our master couldn't make payments to the bank, Sarah and me, we were put up for sale by the bank. I was only 16 at the time."

*****

William was told to climb up onto the auction block. It was only three steps up, but they were the hardest steps he had ever taken. It felt like climbing a mountain. His eyes were on his 14-year-old sister Sarah, as she was led away by the arm and loaded into the back of a wagon.

The auction was being held out in the open under a sizzling sun and not a shred of cloud to block its blaze. Heat danced in the air, and a crowd of almost a hundred planters was standing all around, sizing him up like a prize cow. He was so thirsty, so tired.

The auctioneer stood just in front of William, talking about what a fine specimen he was and getting ready to start the bidding. The auctioneer was so close that William could have tapped him on the shoulder—or clubbed him in the back of the head, if he had a club.

William leaned over from the auction block and said, "Please, sir, can you hold off long 'nough for me to say goodbye to my sister?"

The auctioneer craned his neck around and gave William a snarly stare, as if daring him to speak again. William did anyway. "Please, sir, I need to say farewell to my sister Sarah." He motioned toward the wagon.

"You need to shut up is what you need to do."

The wagon began to pull away. Sarah was standing in the back, and her tears were coming, and she was staring at William, not taking her eyes off him for a moment. The wagon hit a rut, and she had to hold onto the sides to keep from tumbling out. But she kept her eyes on William even then.

"Please, sir, she's leavin', sir."

"Too late. You'd have to run to catch up with her, and we can't have ya runnin'."

"Sir..."

The auctioneer turned away from William and began to address the crowd, telling them again what a fine worker he would make. William felt so angry, like he had lightning in every vein. He wanted to jump down from the block and reach in and tear out the tongue of the auctioneer, who started spouting words and numbers. Anything to make him stop. Instead, he fell inside himself, like stepping off a cliff in the dark and just tumbling and falling and waiting to hit rock bottom. He watched Sarah disappear, the last remnant of his family gone, just like that.

*****

"I'm sorry," Ellen said.

William turned his head away and rubbed his right eye.

"But that's why we can't marry," she said gently. "Not yet at least. I ain't gonna watch my children be taken away like that. You understand? *You understand?*"

William nodded and shrugged. He understood. But that didn't make her decision sting any less. He felt like he had stepped off that cliff again and into the void.

*****

Three days passed, and Ellen was desperate to see William again, to make sure that everything was still fine between them. She saw her chance on the day Miss Eliza sent her into town to pick up material. After leaving the dress shop, she passed by the cabinet shop and found the door locked; no one answered her relentless knocks. She gave the door a final hard tug before she conceded defeat and headed down the street in the direction of home.

The central Georgia breeze was so strong that Ellen had to hold onto her hat as she stepped out into the street. She used her right hand to grip her hat—a flat, broad-brimmed straw hat with a blue ribbon tied around its shallow crown. Tucked under her left arm was a package of calico for the dresses she was making. She had built a reputation as an expert with the needle, and she made dresses for many women in Macon—not just for Miss Eliza. She was thrilled whenever she caught sight of a wealthy Macon matron on the streets wearing one of her dresses. Most of the women didn't acknowledge her work, but a few did—and Ellen was inordinately proud when it happened.

She felt sorry for William. Folks were talking, and they knew he had asked for her hand—and been turned down. He had to endure, in silence, the wild speculations about why she refused him. She wished she could tell people her reasons. She wished she could tell folks that she wanted to marry him so badly, wanted children more than anything, but it was a private matter.

A sudden gust very nearly knocked her down, and as she struggled to maintain her footing, the hold on her hat loosened for a split second, and the wind whipped it right off her head. Ellen let out a startled squeal, and the hat went end over end, flying down the dusty street at an incredible speed. An alert pedestrian saw the runaway hat and trapped it with the tip of his cane before an approaching wagon could trample it. The hat's rescuer was a man, a young white man she had never laid eyes on.

The young man plucked the hat from the end of his cane and approached, brushing dust from the wide brim with his gloved hand. He was a tall, thin man—clean-shaven with a thick head of brown hair, swept back from his forehead. He was handsome, and his clothing was impeccable—a vest that looked new and trousers without a speck of dirt, even around the cuffs.

He bowed and held out Ellen's hat.

"Thank you, sir," she said. Ellen curtsied, accepted the hat, and diverted her eyes with the usual down look of a slave. But in this social situation, between a man and a woman, the down look could also be the sign of a woman simply being shy and demure.

"I am new in town, so permit me to introduce myself. Mister John Knight at your service."

He bowed once again, and Ellen saw where this was going—and it could be nothing but trouble. The young white man, Mister Knight, obviously assumed that she was a white lady. It happened with strangers.

"But sir—"

"No need to thank me. The look on your face is all the thanks that I need."

What look? Ellen assumed that her face was plastered with fear, not gratitude. She had to inform this man that she was a slave before he went too far. She decided to show him her slave pass, which gave her permission to be out on daily errands in Macon. That would be the easiest, least awkward way of conveying her station in life. But as she reached for the pocket in her dress, the man intercepted her hand and drew it to his mouth.

He kissed her hand!

Ellen was petrified. In the blink of an eye, things had suddenly gone too far. Dangerously far. If she told the man what he had just done, how could she be certain that he wouldn't strike her in the face for letting him kiss the hand of a slave? How could she be certain he wouldn't beat her on the spot?

So Ellen said nothing. She just wanted to get away, to escape this situation.

"I am honored to have been your knight in shining armor."

Ellen stammered her answer. "Thank you kindly. I am most grateful, sir." Then she hurried away, and she sensed the man's eyes on her as she fled the scene. She prayed they wouldn't encounter each other ever again.

*****

Knight was a man of action. When he saw what he wanted, he went for it, and with his storehouse of charm, he found that he usually got it. As soon as he parted ways with the woman on the street, he approached the nearest stranger and inquired about her identity. The man said her name was Ellen, and that she was unmarried and lived in the home of Dr. Robert Collins. The stranger seemed slightly amused by his interest in Miss Ellen, but perhaps that was because she already had a beau courting her. With her features, he would have been surprised if she didn't already have a pack of men chasing her, but Knight didn't care. He was thrilled by the hunt.

Ellen Collins. That name made her the daughter of one of the wealthiest men in Macon—Dr. Robert Collins. This woman possessed the perfect pedigree: wealth, high social station, and beauty. He was so pleased that her hat had blown off at the very moment he was strolling by. He would never complain about a windy day again.

The day after their chance encounter, Knight cradled a bouquet of red roses in his arm as he rode his horse slowly down the streets. He was dressed in his finest formal coat, with his cravat tied to perfection, and a shimmering top hat perched on his head. It never failed with the ladies. He knew he was handsome, and he used it to his advantage with young ladies of wealth and standing. He may be a simple cabinetmaker, new to the job, but he had the bearing of a much wealthier man—which he planned on becoming in the future. He vowed he wouldn't leave Macon without making his fortune.

He admired the impressive homes along the tree-lined streets. Macon boosters liked to call their city the Athens of the South because of its stunning public buildings. Others said the city design was modeled after Babylon, but Knight preferred the Athens image because it conjured up images of pure white temples. He moved along College Avenue, past Mister Gresham's stunning home with its wide porch, great white pillars, and black shutters. Then he turned onto Mulberry, descending the steep street until he reached the Collins house.

Dismounting, he stared at the huge home and decided this was the kind of house he planned to own once he made his money. Pillars. He wanted pillars lining his front veranda, for they would reflect his own rise in the community; he planned to become a pillar of the city, every bit as imposing as the pillars holding up the porch of the Collins' house. He approached the front door, so white that it looked freshly painted, and he rapped on the door with the polished gold knocker.

"I am here to see Miss Ellen," he said to the young servant girl who answered the door.

The servant's eyes grew large and focused on the flowers in his hand.

"Miss Ellen, sir?"

"Yes, Miss Ellen Collins."

"Do you mean, Miss *Eliza* Collins, sir?"

Eliza? Knight was sure the man had said her name was *Ellen*. The servant girl seemed strangely agitated.

"Is Miss Eliza the name of Dr. Collins' daughter?"

"Oh, no, sir. Miss Eliza is Dr. Collins' *wife!*"

Knight felt a jolt to his gut. Had the man on the street been leading him on? Did he intentionally steer him in the direction of a married woman—what's worse, a woman married to one of the community's most prominent men? One of the pillars?

Knight felt as if his own internal pillar was beginning to teeter.

"May I help you, sir?" came the voice of a woman, who appeared from a back room. She was a beautiful, dark-haired woman, a little older than the girl he had met in the street. Knight wondered if this woman could be a sister of the girl on the street, for there was a family resemblance—although he thought the other girl had more striking hair.

The servant slipped away, disappearing into a back room, but she was probably still within earshot. Knight knew the eavesdropping ways of servants.

"Excuse me, ma'am, but permit me to introduce myself. I am John Knight, and I am new to Macon."

He bowed.

"I am glad to make your acquaintance, sir." The young lady's eyes shifted from his face to the flowers in his hands. "May I help you?"

His eyes flitted to his flowers, and he smiled awkwardly. "I am sorry, ma'am, but I was led to believe that a young lady by the name of Ellen lived in this residence. Your sister, perhaps?"

Miss Eliza's face paled, and Knight saw a tightening of the lips, a narrowing of the eyes. Had he said something wrong?

"Miss Ellen, sir, is a Negro servant," she said slowly, like she was speaking to a child.

Now it was Knight's turn to blanch. Blood drained from his face, and panic mixed with confusion.

"But ma'am, I met Miss Ellen on the street just yesterday, and I thought...are you sure we're talking about the same woman?"

"Prudence, fetch Ellen right quick," Miss Eliza called over her shoulder to the servant girl, who was still out of sight but just around the corner.

"Yes, ma'am," came the girl's response, a squeak of a voice, for she was obviously embarrassed about being caught lurking within earshot.

"I am sorry, ma'am, but I must surely be mistaken. I was led to believe..."

Knight vowed that if he saw the man who had directed him to this house, he would knock the hat off his head and give him such a thrashing.

"Did you want me, ma'am?" The voice was familiar. It was the voice of the woman he had met yesterday. She appeared in the doorway, wearing a simple green dress with a white apron. When she caught sight of Mister Knight, her mouth opened but no words came out. She took a step backward, and when she saw the flowers in his hands, she made a sudden intake of air.

"This is Mister John Knight," Miss Eliza said, smiling and savoring this awkward moment. She seemed to be taking great pleasure in Knight's discomfort. "I take it the two of you have already met."

"This woman is your servant?" Knight said. He had heard about white Negroes, but he had never met one that looked as white as Ellen. His embarrassment—and anger—grew. He tried to hide both emotions.

Miss Ellen curtsied. She didn't meet Knight's gaze, but averted her eyes. He wondered if she could be an indentured servant—a white girl. But no, Miss Eliza said she was her "Negro" servant.

"I beg your pardon, ma'am, but I appear to have made a serious error in judgment."

"I believe you have, Mister Knight," Miss Eliza said. "But you are new to Macon, and mistakes do happen." The words sounded kind, but Miss Eliza's smile seemed to be growing with every second. She was enjoying this moment immensely.

"Here. Shall I take these from you?" Miss Eliza said, reaching for the flowers.

Knight watched in stunned silence as the woman of the house lifted the flowers gently from his hands, as carefully as a mother lifting her child. She turned toward Ellen.

"Ellen, would you please put these beautiful flowers in water? They're for you, after all."

Ellen nodded, still keeping her eyes on anything but John Knight. She took the flowers from Miss Eliza and very nearly ran from the room.

"I apologize, once again, for my error," Knight said, backing up toward the door. He wanted to say more, to explain himself, but he was just digging a deeper hole. He kept running his hands around the brim of the hat in his hands—a nervous habit. He wanted to ask the mistress of the house to not breathe a word of this to a soul. If she did, he would become a laughingstock. But he didn't dare demand anything from a woman of her standing.

"Good day, ma'am." He turned to leave.

"Mister Knight, one more thing," said Miss Eliza.

He stopped and turned back.

"The flowers are beautiful." She spoke in an exaggerated singsong way, and she smiled once again. Was she mocking him?

"Thank you, ma'am."

Knight fitted his hat back on tightly and walked as fast as he could to his awaiting horse. He moved across the front porch quickly, for fear that the pillars themselves were about to topple over and crush him below their weight. It felt like they already had.

17

Friday, December 22, 1848

ELLEN SLEPT. SHE NEEDED A REPRIEVE FROM THE TENSION, AND she thanked the Lord that she got it. After she and William boarded the steamboat at Charleston, she hid in the cabin—just as compact as the one on the *General Clinch*—where she climbed into the upper bunk and dove into a deep and dreamless sleep. Exhaustion overpowered anxiety, and when she awoke, she was one day closer to Philadelphia.

The steamboat trip to Wilmington, North Carolina, was uneventful, and they arrived on Saturday morning, December 23. From there, they boarded the Wilmington and Raleigh Railroad, with William relegated to the baggage car and Ellen left to fend for herself—once again. The train rolled on throughout the afternoon and into the evening hours. The potbelly stove sat in the very center of the car, and she felt the radiating heat hit her as she leaned against the windowpane and pretended to sleep. A couple of times she actually dozed; she was terrified by the idea that she might call out in her sleep and give away her real voice. When night fell, the potbelly stove, which was stoked with coal, glowed like a devil's eye, and she listened to the steady creak of the kerosene lamp swinging above her head, tossing light from side to side. So much fire in this wooden box of a train! When trains derailed, especially in winter with the stoves in each car blazing, if the crash didn't get you, the fire would. She opened her eyes and stared out on the dark landscape, seeing sparks pour from the train's smokestack and scatter into the night like a brimstone storm.

At long last, the train pulled into Richmond, and Ellen tracked down William, who was pulling her trunk out of the baggage car.

"How did you fare, Master Johnson?" William said.

"Not well. And you?"

"The colored car was crowded and noisy, but I managed to sleep a few winks."

Ellen was envious. And weary. She was so tired of wearing uncomfortable clothing, so tired of the constant vigilance, so tired of being stared at because of her bandages.

"Chin up, Master Johnson. Only one more day."

It was Sunday in Richmond, the day before Christmas, but it was very early and most people were still in bed. The streets were quiet as they made their way to Broad Street, where the next rail line—the Richmond, Fredericksburg, and Potomac Railroad—left the city. The train was scheduled to leave Richmond at 8 o'clock, so they had plenty of time. They found a church on Broad Street—a beautiful white stone structure with a small dome and pillared entrance—and they passed through the church's portico, past a monument of some sort, and entered the sanctuary, which was empty at this time of day. Then they spent time in prayer—the closest they would get to a church service until they reached Philadelphia.

"We better get a move on," said William after their prayer, and they made their way down Broad Street. The only signs of life were other travelers and a group of Negroes gathered in front of a cake shop, talking and playing cards.

There was no depot in Richmond for this particular train line, so freight and passengers were loaded directly from Broad Street. William and Ellen parted ways again, and Ellen's legs ached with exhaustion. Her eyes felt heavy with sleep, and she wished she could be wearing her cotton dress, rather than these scratchy pants. How could men stand it? She was hungry and wanted to pick up a treat from the cake shop, but she doubted the owner was selling on a Sunday. Besides, it looked to be a black-run business, and she was white—for one more day, at least.

Suddenly: a scream.

A woman let out a shout just three cars up, near the baggage car. An elderly woman, as wide as she was short, was having a fit of some sort, and Ellen wondered if there was a doctor nearby. The woman's face was red, and her round cheeks seemed ready to burst the bonnet tied around her face.

While fluttering a fan in her left hand, the woman raised her right hand and pointed one fat finger. "Apprehend that slave! He's a fugitive! Grab him! Grab him! Grab him before he runs!"

Ellen lurched inside. Good Lord, the woman was pointing directly at William.

Macon

Mary's world had collapsed in on her. Mister Slator, her father, had been killed, shot down on the street, and the protection he provided was suddenly gone. His power, property, and presence had sheltered their family, but now he was dead, and she had no idea what that meant for them.

But she knew one thing: They had to flee.

Only one problem: Mama had made it clear that she wouldn't leave Macon without giving her husband—yes, he was her husband—a proper Christian burial. So here it was Sunday morning on Christmas Eve, and they were trapped in Macon when they should be running for their lives.

Frank had oiled his father's favorite gun, a shotgun, and he stayed on the porch most of the night, afraid that townsfolk might try taking the house from them, now that their father was gone. The body was still at the undertaker's, and Mama wanted to see him one last time before burial. But when could they have a decent funeral or even be able to obtain a respectable coffin? If William were around, he could construct a coffin for them, but Mama had no idea where he and cousin Ellen might be. Frank thought they had run.

Everyone was deserting Mary, and she felt so alone. Where was Ellen when she needed her most?

Mary sat in her bedroom, wearing her black mourning dress, black bonnet, black gloves, black crepe—clothes that made her invisible to Death, at least that's what they say. For most of her life, she had been living the life of a white girl, but now, with her father's death, she would suddenly and magically become black in the eyes of her neighbors.

"Have you packed your things yet?" came her brother's voice.

Sitting on the edge of her bed, her black dress blossoming out from around her waist, she craned her neck and saw her brother Frank peering into the room, the shotgun still in his hands. He had carried it everywhere since their papa's death.

"Why bother?" she said. "We're trapped here until we get Papa's body."

"But we have to be ready to flee at any moment. We have to be ready for anything."

"What good is being ready? We can't stop what's going to happen."

"Don't talk like that. We need to be strong for Mama."

Mary didn't want to think about how Mama had come bursting into the house covered in blood and wailing. How could she be strong with images like that stuck in her head? Mary wiped her eyes. She had cried so much in the past 2 days that she didn't know where these tears could even be coming from.

"Frank, are we being punished?"

"Punished? What're you talkin' about?"

"Am I being punished for my pride?"

Frank leaned the shotgun carefully against the wall and took a seat next to his sister. He put a hand on her shoulder.

"I sometimes thought we were better 'cause we lived...differently," Mary said. "We weren't like Ellen. We weren't...I thought of Ellen as a slave...I did..."

"We ain't bein' punished for that. Besides, you love Ellen, and you've always been so kind to her."

"But sometimes my thoughts...sometimes in my head I thought she was different...thought she was below me. And now I'm bein' punished, ain't I?"

"It's just evil comin' at us from all directions. It's not God punishin', it's the devil comin' after us."

Frank rubbed her shoulder and then got up and paced the room. He stopped at the window and stared out. A few moments passed before something caught his attention—something outside.

Mary noticed his body tense. "What's wrong, Frank?"

Her brother didn't answer. He moved closer to the window and stared out.

"What's happening, Frank? Whatya see?"

He still didn't answer. He sprang into action, snapped up his shotgun, and ran from the room.

*****

John Knight didn't even have to knock. As he and his two companions stepped up on the porch to the Slator house, the door opened before them. That was the first surprise. The second surprise was the gun. He hadn't expected to be greeted by the barrel of a shotgun. The family's only boy, Frank, the new man of the house, aimed a shotgun directly at Knight's face.

Knight and his two companions shuffled back a few steps.

"Whoa, whoa, Frank, I come in peace," Knight said, tensing like a cat.

"Frank! What on earth are you doin'?" Frank's mama, Molly, appeared from the background, along with the older daughter, Mary. Molly put a hand on Frank's shoulder, but her son kept the shotgun aimed. "We don't need no more bloodshed," she said. "Frank! Please! For me."

Slowly, Frank lowered the gun, and Knight felt his shoulders relax.

"We come on business," Knight said. "Nothing more. I need to talk to your mama, and so do these two gentlemen here." Knight cast a glance at the men standing next to him. One of them was Willis Hughes, the jailer, but the other man was his special surprise. This man stood about 5 feet, 8 inches tall, with a scraggly beard that had spread some unruly hairs across his cheek. He had short hair sticking out in little jagged tufts at the back, as if he had tried to cut his own hair with a dull knife. His hairline had receded, and his small eyes were intense.

"Permit me to introduce myself, ma'am," said the stranger. "My name is Simon Slator." He bowed slightly.

Just as Knight expected, Molly looked stunned. "Slator?"

"Yes, ma'am," said Slator. "I am a nephew of your...of the late master of this estate."

"But my master said he didn't have any livin' relations," said Molly.

"That's just it, ma'am, my uncle didn't like to recognize my existence. But as you can see with your own two eyes, I do exist."

"I don't believe you."

Slator smiled, revealing several gaps in his teeth. "What am I? A ghost?"

"No. A charlatan."

Slator sighed and smiled, seemingly amused by her accusation, rather than offended. Knight noticed that Molly had closed the door, but not all the way.

"May we please come inside and discuss this like civilized people, Miss Molly?" Knight asked.

"You can talk just as well standin' on the porch."

"But this is vitally important, Miss Molly."

"What is there to discuss? I'm buryin' my master, and I have much to prepare."

Slator moved one step closer. "That's just it, Molly. You may be buryin' one master, but you need to be welcomin' your new master."

"I don't have a new master."

Slator extended his arms and smiled. "You're lookin' at him. I'm your new master!"

It took a few moments for the words to sink in, but Knight could see the effect they had on all three of them—Molly, Mary, and Frank. Molly seemed to wilt right before his eyes and had to lean on the open door for support. Frank raised his shotgun once again, and this time his mama didn't tell him to lower it.

18

Macon
Spring 1846: Two Years Earlier

WHEN MISS ELIZA SENT ELLEN INTO TOWN TO PICK UP additional material for a dress she wanted made for an upcoming ball, Ellen saw her chance to see William. The chore brought her just down the street from the cabinet-maker's shop where William worked, which meant she didn't have to wait until Sunday church to speak with him.

What had happened with John Knight had unsettled her. She had done nothing wrong. She had tried to tell the man she was a Negro woman, but he hadn't given her a chance. The incident drove home just how dangerous it was to be a black woman with white skin. It also made her think how badly she wanted to be with William, regardless of the risk.

She found William alone at the shop, so the timing was perfect. She had heard that a new cabinetmaker had been hired to work alongside William, but there was no sign of him on this early Tuesday morning. William didn't even see her enter, for he was busy sliding a plane across a door, skimming off a curling skin of wood, and then running his hand across the surface and feeling for high and low spots. The scent of wood was strong, as if she had entered a forest. Tools hung all over the walls of the expansive room, and an enormous lathe wheel dominated one corner like a massive wagon wheel.

"Mornin', William."

William looked up and smiled. They didn't often get a chance to meet during the week, and he beamed. Setting aside the plane, he approached and lifted her off the floor in his embrace.

"I'm so happy to see you, Ellen."

"And I'm glad to catch you alone."

He set her down and gave her a kiss. "The new man is out for a spell."

"He a black man?"

"No."

William's vanishing smile was an obvious sign that the new employee was not a welcome addition. She decided to change the topic quickly, for she had better things on her mind, and she probably didn't have much time before the other man returned.

Running her hand across the smoothened surface of the door, she hooked her other arm into William's. "I been thinkin'."

He turned to face her. "A good thing to do every once and awhile."

"I been thinkin' 'bout the two of us."

William came to attention.

"You asked me an important question this past year," she began.

"Yes, I did."

"And I been thinkin'..."

He leaned in closer, ever so slightly.

"I just thought you might have that certain question still floatin' around in that head a' yours."

He still didn't respond, looking ever so serious. She shrugged and ran a finger in circles on the back of his hand.

"The question didn't go away, did it?" she asked.

At last, he smiled. "I got lots of questions stacked up in my head. Which one should I be takin' down from the shelf and showin' you?"

Now he was playing with her.

"This is a special question, so I believe it's probably sittin' there on that shelf in your head in the most honored position. You can't miss it."

"I see." William wiped some of the sawdust from his hands. "But what if that question disappeared somehow some way?"

"I don't think that happened. It's still there, gatherin' dust."

"You think so?"

For a moment, she wondered if he was being serious. Was the question gone? Her smile disappeared.

William must have realized he had teased her one step too far, for he took both of her hands. "You're right, the question is still there, and it's been collectin' plenty a' dust over the past few months, covered in cobwebs."

"I do a lot of dustin' at the Collins place, and I've cleaned out plenty a' cobwebs. I can deal with it."

"Well then..." William pushed a hair out of Ellen's eyes. "I guess I should do this proper, shouldn't I?" He went down on one knee, took Ellen's right hand, and ran his fingers across it. Then he looked up. "Ellen, would you do me the honor of bein' my wife?"

She put a hand to his cheek. "Of course I will."

William stood back up and they kissed and embraced, but Ellen realized the most difficult part of this talk still lay ahead. It was the second part of the conversation that had kept her awake last night.

"Like I said, I been thinkin' a lot 'bout this, William."

"I ain't been able to think of nothing else since I met you at the corn shuckin.'"

"I decided I had to be with you as man and wife, no matter the risk of us bein' split...but I still...I still can't be havin' children with you...not till we're free."

William pulled away and stared at her. He began to stroke his beard. "What did you just say?"

He had heard her, but she repeated it. "I said I don't want children, not till we're free."

"No children?"

"Not till we're free."

Lacing his fingers behind his head, William stared up at the ceiling and rubbed the back of his scalp, digging his fingers into his hair. He groaned. Then he lowered his gaze to meet her eyes, his smile completely gone.

"Then what's the point of us bein' married if we have to live like brother and sister, not husband and wife?"

"We *will* be husband and wife. But we just...we'll have to wait. We'll have to be patient. Like Jacob and Rachel."

Groaning, William swiped the wood shavings from the table and then walked to the far side of the room. He clenched and unclenched his fist. This was worse than Ellen imagined. She had hoped and prayed he would understand. She began to cry, but he didn't seem to notice or care.

"But we would still be together every day," she said.

"But we wouldn't...or would...?"

She knew what he was afraid to ask: Would they have relations as husband and wife?

"I don't know if we can risk it," she said.

"Then what's the point?" he shouted.

"We would be together!" Now Ellen was beginning to feel the fury. She thought that being together every day would be something. "I thought you'd be happy."

"Happy? You thought that would make me *happy*?"

"Yes, I thought it would! I wanna have children with you, but if we have children now, they'd belong to Dr. Collins, and I can't be havin' that. Can you?"

William stood there, not saying a word, just staring at her hard. Then he looked up at the ceiling and groaned; he walked out the back door, slamming it on the way out. Ellen was left standing in the middle of the shop, growing angrier by the moment. She waited, expecting William to come back and hash this out. But he didn't return.

Finally, she whirled around toward the front door, intending to do her own bit of door slamming, and she gave out a startled yelp. Striding through the doorway was John Knight—the very man who had mistaken her as white.

The moment he saw her face, he stopped and stared. He looked very confused. Then, even worse, he smiled and winked.

"Ah, I see ya'll found out where I work," he said.

Where he works? John Knight is the new man working in the wood-shop? Good Lord.

"You work here?"

Ellen edged backward to the worktable and leaned against it, wondering if she should just turn and run. Knight moved a few steps closer and placed his hand on the worktable, a few inches from hers.

"Don't play with me. You know I work here. You tracked me down." Another smile.

"No, I'm sorry...but...no..."

Ellen was afraid of insulting him, but just as terrified of leading him on. She didn't know what to say.

"I learned that you're Missus Collins' half-sister," he said, moving one step closer. "The prettier half, I'd say. I'm glad you sought me out."

"Mister Knight, you have this all wrong." Ellen knew how terrible these situations with white men could become. Her mother, after all, had been in a similar predicament with Major Smith. She looked around. Where in the world was William?

"I admit, I didn't know you were a servant girl at the time. But I have nothin' against servant girls."

Ellen took one step back, and Knight advanced.

"Mister Knight, I think you should understand something."

"I do understand."

Ellen looked around for something she could use as a weapon, and saw some knives on a table across the room. They were too far out of reach.

"I don't think you do."

"Then let me show you how much I understand."

Knight stepped even closer, just as the back door suddenly opened. Thank God. She looked over her shoulder and saw William entering; he stopped in his tracks when he saw John Knight standing so close to Ellen. William's face switched from confusion to anger, and he strode across the room, picking up a mallet when he reached the worktable.

Don't strike him, Ellen thought. *Don't.* She had already seen one man die because of her. She could see Knight's eyes going to the mallet in William's hand.

Knight, clearly intimidated, smiled and motioned toward Ellen. "Lookee here, Bill. We have a customer."

"She ain't a customer," said William, the anger showing through in his tone. "We're betrothed."

The word "betrothed" hung there in the silence. If Knight was embarrassed the first time he had approached Ellen, he was doubly devastated the second time. He looked at Ellen, and then at William. William's hand tightened around the mallet's handle, and Knight had to notice that.

Strangely, though, he smiled again. His grin was his only weapon.

"Bill, it's a dangerous thing leavin' a young woman alone in an empty shop," he said. "Mistakes can happen."

Shockingly, Ellen had to agree with the man. How could William have left her alone like that? Knight's smile broadened, for he could probably see that his words hit the mark. William looked down, embarrassed by what he had done.

"Mistakes can happen. Remember that, Bill," Knight said, driving the point home and heading into the back room to hang up his top hat.

William turned to Ellen and said softly, "Ellen, I'm sorry I walked out on you."

A fury came over her. "Well, I'm not sorry 'bout walkin' out."

And with those words, she turned and strode out the front door. She didn't forget to slam it on the way out.

19

Richmond, Virginia
Sunday, December 24, 1848

"BLESS MY SOUL! THAT THERE IS MY SLAVE, NED!"

A small crowd began to gather as the woman in the green dress continued to point at William. She was convinced that William belonged to her! Ellen stared in shock as William, who had his back to the lady, kept on walking for the baggage car. He hurried his steps.

"Grab him! Someone take hold of him!"

A nearby conductor did as commanded, and he latched onto William's arm. If William fought back, this could be their undoing. Ellen had to act quickly, and she had to put on her best performance yet.

"Unhand him!" she said, trying to raise her voice and still maintain a deep tone. "How dare you lay claim to my property, ma'am!"

Ellen tried to be intimidating, but she felt too slight, too weak, especially in the face of this large steamship of a lady.

"Your property, sir?" The woman didn't back down. She was an ample woman, dressed as if she was going to the opera, and she had the loud, almost melodious voice of an opera singer, even when angered. "This, sir, is my slave, Ned, who ran away from me!"

"That is not possible, ma'am. This man's name is William, and he's been my property since he was a small boy."

"Well, I don't know how that—"

"Madam, the two of us grew up together. William's been owned by our family and given to me on my 21st birthday."

If the woman demanded to see written proof of Ellen's ownership of William, they were undone. So she decided to pull out the trump card.

"Ma'am, this boy is also providing me invaluable assistance in getting me to medical help. He is my property, he is my servant, he is my help. Without him, I'll never manage it to Philadelphia to see my doctor."

That silenced the woman. She looked Ellen up and down, as if for the first time she was noticing that the young man standing before her had his arm in a sling and a bandage around his face. She stammered.

"But, sir..."

"Ma'am, take a good hard look. Do you really think my William is your Ned?"

The conductor let go of William's arm. The lady came up close to William and studied him front and back, up and down, as if he were a statue in an art museum.

"Well..." She began to falter and blush, a sign that Ellen may have won the day. At last the woman surrendered. "I beg your pardon, sir, but I was certain this was my runaway slave. I never in my life saw two black pigs more alike than your boy and my Ned."

"Mistakes happen, ma'am." Ellen turned her anger on William. "Now, boy, get to the baggage car! And hurry! If you hadn't dawdled in the first place, you wouldn't have inconvenienced this fine woman here. Go!"

"Yes, sir," said William sullenly. Ellen could tell he was seething from the woman's characterization of him as a pig.

Ellen boarded the train, eager to flee this scene and this woman, but the large lady followed closely behind her. To Ellen's dismay, the woman took a seat directly across from her, while the gentleman in the seat next to Ellen stood and tipped his hat to the large lady. He was one of the men who had observed the confrontation outside the train.

The woman reached out, put a hand on Ellen's arm, and said, "Oh! I hope, sir, your boy is not as worthless as my Ned was. Oh! I was kind to him, like a mother to him. And it grieves me very much to think that after all I did for him, he should go off without any cause whatever."

Ellen noticed the man sitting next to her smile to himself. He had reddish cheeks, high cheekbones, and dancing eyes, and he seemed entertained by the woman's words.

"When did your Ned leave you?" Ellen asked.

"About 18 months ago, and I have never seen hair nor hide of him since."

"Did he have a wife?" asked the man next to Ellen, suddenly injecting himself into their conversation.

"I beg your pardon?"

"Did Ned have a wife?"

"Yes, he did. Her name was July, but the poor thing was so ill that she was unable to do much work. I had no choice but to sell her to a man who took her to New Orleans, where the climate is nice and warm."

The woman drew a finely embroidered handkerchief from her small handbag and dabbed at her eyes, as if the thought of her ailing slave was enough to bring tears.

"Was she *glad* to go to the South to restore her health?" the man asked.

"Of course not! She was not happy, but slaves never know what's best for them!"

Ellen looked over to the man sitting beside her, hoping he would continue to keep the woman occupied. He obliged in a most surprising way.

"If your July was such a good girl, ma'am, and had served you so faithfully, wouldn't it have been better to emancipate her?"

Ellen was almost as shocked as the woman. This was the first time she had ever heard such an opinion voiced in public by a white person. Sympathy for a slave!

The woman squeezed her embroidered handkerchief into a ball in her fist. She spoke loudly, firmly. "I do not think I should have emancipated her, sir. It would have been the worst thing to do! It would have been positively unkind!"

Ellen jumped in, displaying a reflexive flash of irritation. "Do you mean it would have been unkind to your slave—or unkind to yourself?" Immediately, she regretted being so blunt, for it was just the kind of thing to draw attention.

The woman stared in blank astonishment, probably in shock that she was being challenged by two different white men.

"It's cruel to turn slaves loose to shift for themselves when there are so many good masters to take care of them!" she countered. "In fact, I do not believe there are any white laboring people in the world as well off as the slaves!"

"I'm not sure about that, ma'am," the gentleman said. "Before my widowed mother died, she emancipated all her slaves and sent them to Ohio, where they are getting along well. I saw several of them last summer myself."

"Well, a plague on them! We have had 10 slaves run off on us, and I am convinced they all are finding life intolerable! That's my final word with the bark on it!"

The man laughed, obviously taking great pleasure in riling the woman. If there were a hornet's nest nearby, he would probably jam a stick in it just to see what happened.

"Well, ma'am," he said, "then I have no doubt that Ned and your other nine Negroes will discover their mistake and come running back to your home in no time."

The woman, as touchy as a teased snake, could take no more sarcasm. She jammed her handkerchief into her bag and leaped to her feet with unusual speed for such a large woman. She shifted seats to the back of the car where she didn't have to hear another word from this man.

Ellen couldn't suppress her smile. The man in the seat next to her caught sight of her smile, tipped his hat, and grinned back.

"Samuel Smith, at your service, sir."

Ellen nearly laughed out loud.

Macon

Mary looked on with growing dread as Frank continued to aim his gun at Simon Slator, the man who claimed to be their father's nephew. Frank had stepped out onto the porch and blocked the doorway to their home, while Slator, Knight, and Hughes stood a few feet away, not daring to move any closer. No one said a word as a stray black cat wandered across the porch, pausing to rub its side against John Knight's leg. Knight, afraid to cause a stir by kicking the cat away, could only look down at his leg in helpless bafflement. The cat eventually slunk away and hopped off the porch.

Mama, standing to the left of Frank, began to weep, and Mary put her arms around her. Frank's face was contorted by suppressed rage, and she could tell that he wanted nothing more than to see Simon Slator's face go up in an explosion of gunpowder, blood, and bone. She wanted it, too, but she knew that Frank would be a dead man if he fired. Her father was gone, and she couldn't lose her brother.

"Frank, no," she said. "There's another way."

"Listen to your sister," said Slator. "I won't be takin' you away this morning to be my servants. You'll have time to bury your...your old master. But I aim to claim what's rightfully mine. So put down the gun."

"Think it through, Frank. You can't shoot all three of us, can you?" Hughes added, and Frank shifted his aim to the jailer.

"But I can send *one* of you straight to hell," said Frank.

No one said a word, as if they feared that the wrong statement would trigger a gun blast. Knight shuffled back two steps, and Frank noticed. He shifted his aim to Knight.

"Now, boy, think this through," said Knight, flinching and holding out a hand, as if he expected to deflect the gunshot with his palm. His voice cracked under the strain.

"I won't shoot none of you if you get off our property. *Now.*" Frank moved the gun from face to face, seeing each of them flinch—except Hughes.

"That's just it, Frank. You know it's not your property," Hughes said.

"It is. Mister Slator was our father."

Hughes turned to Mama. "Tell him, Molly. Tell your boy that Mister Slator didn't leave a will. Tell him this property ain't rightfully yours."

Frank cast a look at his mother, as if imploring her to deny this. But Mama remained silent. She looked dazed and disoriented, a deathbed look, like she was ready to just give it all up.

"I told you, Frank, bury your father," said Slator. "Comfort your mother. Then I plan to return with the authorities, and I *will* take you to live with me. Mark my words."

Biting his lip, Frank breathed heavily through his nose, and he shifted his aim back to Slator. Mary was beginning to think he might actually pull the trigger.

"Please don't, Frank," she said.

"We will return," said Hughes, taking two steps back. "And don't attempt to leave Macon, 'cause we will treat it as a slave escape, and the dogs will bring you down in no time."

"And I don't want the dogs ruinin' that pretty face of yours," said Simon Slator, eyeing Mary. He licked his dry, cracked lips.

Frank took careful aim.

"Easy, Frank," said Hughes. "We're leaving for now, so don't do anything your mother will regret. But we will be back, so you might have to sleep with that gun in your paws." At the bottom of the steps, the three men turned their backs and left the house, as if daring Frank to shoot.

Mama finally broke her silence. "Don't," she said, as if she could read Frank's mind.

Frank didn't. He lowered his shotgun and stared at the three departing figures. He put his right arm around his mama, and Mary buried her face on his left shoulder and cried. Their old life was dead and buried.

20

Macon
Spring 1846: Two Years Earlier

LLEN SAT AT HER SPINNING WHEEL, DRAWING BACK ON THE cotton as it twisted into tightly spun thread. It was like playing an instrument, with her feet working the pedals that turned the wheel, while the fingers of both hands played on the thread, feeding it into the machine. For accompaniment, she could hear the chattering squeaks of a goldfinch just outside her window.

Miss Eliza had set Ellen up with her own cabin, not far from the Big House, at the edge of the woods. It was a small brick structure, and she even had her own bedroom for the first time in her life. Ellen tried to be grateful she wasn't a field hand out hoeing the soil in teams under the hot sun, but comparing her life to theirs didn't make a stitch of difference. Not this week. She was still angry about what had happened with William and John Knight at the woodshop, and she didn't even try to maintain the mask of happiness that Dr. Collins and Miss Eliza expected to see from all their slaves, but especially from Ellen. Miss Eliza commented on her moodiness, and Ellen didn't try to deny it or explain it.

"Cheer up, Ellen," Miss Eliza had told her the day before—as if she could command happiness. "*Smile.*"

Ellen had resisted rewarding her half-sister with an artificial smile. All she could think was that if she gave birth, her child would belong to Dr. Collins and Miss Eliza.

Ellen kept on spinning. It had a calming effect, although she was going to have to work through enough thread to clothe all of Georgia before she reached the point where she didn't want to murder her master in his sleep.

Ellen had dyed the cotton brown using walnut bark, transforming white to brown. Mulatto thread, she called it. It made her think of the tales she heard of white children being captured and dunked in large vats of brown dye made from walnut bark, and transformed into slave material. She wondered if it was really possible.

"Ellen?"

Mary called to her from the cabin door. It didn't make her feel any better to see her cousin, who gallivanted around living the life of a white woman. Ellen had often been jealous of Mary, but never more so than this week.

"What is it?" She spoke harshly, and she didn't apologize for it.

"Can I come in?"

Ellen cast a glance over her shoulder and noticed that Mary had already taken two steps inside. "Looks like you're already in." She kept on spinning.

"Can we talk a spell?"

Letting out an exasperated sigh, Ellen brought her spinning wheel to a halt and turned to face her cousin. She quickly assessed her clothing, as she always did. Yellow calico dress. Yoke neck. Ruffle on the wrist. Heel shoes. The dress looked brand new, finer than anything Ellen had ever worn.

Mary took three steps closer and tried to put on her most sympathetic face. "I know you and William had a difficult exchange of words."

That was one way of putting it.

"I am sorry," Mary said.

Ellen nodded, but didn't smile. Mary was obviously uncomfortable, and Ellen was taking great pleasure in seeing it.

"I told him I thought you two should talk."

A flash of irritation. "You and William talked about me?"

Eyes averted. "I hope you don't mind, but I'm concerned about you, Ellen."

Ellen was tempted to go back to her spinning, but she knew she couldn't be that rude. "Thank you for your concern, but I can do all right. I can handle this all myself."

"But you and William were created for each other," Mary said. "I thought that from the first day at the corn shuckin'."

"Don't look that way now. I'm just tryin' to figure a way to avoid talkin' with him at church tomorrow."

Mary looked down at her gloved hands. "Oh."

Ellen didn't like the sound of that. "Whatya mean—'oh'? Whatya done, Mary?"

"Well..." She plucked at the fingertips of her glove. "I brought him here."

Ellen lurched in her chair. "You brought William here?" Her anger rose, and so did the volume of her voice. "Whatya do somethin' like that for?"

"Quiet," Mary whispered. "He'll hear you. He'll think you don't want him here."

"I *don't* want him here. Why on earth did you go and bring him?"

"He says he's got something to say to you."

"And he's afraid to just come here on his own steam? He needed a chaperone?"

Smiling, Mary said, "He thought I could ease you into the idea of you two talkin'. I'm not doin' much of a job, am I?"

Suddenly, Ellen was as nervous as the first time she and William had danced. She smoothed out the apron on her dress, stained in spots by the brown dye. She tried to calm down, to be fair to her cousin. "I know you mean well for me, Mary."

"Will you see him? He'll be awfully upset if you don't talk with him, and I think ya'll will be, too."

Mary was right. She usually was.

"I'll talk to him, I suppose."

Mary smiled as she rose. While she disappeared out the door, Ellen tidied her hair and wished she could have had some warning to make herself presentable. However, Mary probably knew that springing it on her was the only way to make it happen. She knew her like a book.

"Hello, Ellen."

"Mornin', William."

She didn't rise, didn't make a move to give him a kiss. She simply motioned toward an oak chair—a chair that William had made for her. He sat, hat in hand.

"I see you're still spinnin' for Miss Eliza," he said, looking over at the wheel and trying to make idle talk.

"It's what I do." She wasn't going to make this easy for him.

"Listen, Ellen, I found out some things."

"Good. Glad to hear."

"I found out that...well...I learned what happened with you and John Knight when he came to the Collins' place."

"Who told you? Did Mary tell you?"

"Don't matter who told me. I'm sorry 'bout what happened to you, and I'm sorry I stomped outta the shop the other day. I shouldn't a' put you in that spot."

Eyes to the floor. No response from Ellen.

"I understand why you'd want to make sure that somethin' like that don't happen again," he said.

Eyes flashing. "Whatya mean?"

William scratched at the back of his head, as if trying to stir up the right words that wouldn't rile her. That was going to be difficult to do.

"I'm just sayin'...it's gotta be awful for white men to think you're a white woman..."

Ellen stared back, stunned by his audacity. "So you think I'm just usin' you to get married so white men don't come chasin' after me?"

"I don't think that. I just think it might...I think bein' married might protect you from men who might get confused..."

"You mean confused 'bout my skin color? Just say it, William, don't beat around no bushes."

He nodded.

"Besides," she added, "since when does bein' married stop white men from just takin' what they see from black women?"

His eyebrows shot up, and he shook his head. "I'd kill any man who touched you, Ellen."

"And then you'd be killed." Ellen saw that her words stung, so she softened her tone. "I know you'd do anything for me, I do. But don't you see? That's why we can't have children. If we try to protect them, we'd be killed or sold a thousand miles away. That's why we gotta wait."

"I see that, Ellen." He brought his chair a little closer and took one of her hands. "That's why I have come to agree. We'll marry. Then we'll get free. And then we'll have children. In that order."

She jerked her hand back. "I think you're just sayin' that 'cause you pity me for what happened with Knight."

He took her hand again, gently. "It ain't pity. I want you as my wife more than anything. I don't pity you. I love you."

She drew back her hand a second time. "You *really* want to do this—to wait for children?"

"I don't like it, but I'll do it. Why would I lie 'bout somethin' like this?"

"So we could marry."

"I wouldn't say this just to marry."

"So you're sayin' you'd marry me, even if it means bein' more like brother and sister than husband and wife—until we're free?"

"Even if it means all that."

She stared into his eyes, looking for any sign that he didn't mean it.

"You sure 'bout this?"

He didn't hesitate. "I'm sure."

"We'll marry?"

"Yes, we'll marry."

"We'll wait on children?"

"Yes, we'll wait."

"You thought this through?"

William nodded.

She leaned back in her chair and gave him a long, hard stare. No smile. Not yet. He smiled back, but she just glared. He didn't look away. Their eyes connected for a long time, and finally the veneer cracked. She let a smile loose and extended her hand, and he took it in his.

"You already have my heart, you might as well have my hand."

"That's all I want."

"And nothin' more till we're free."

William nodded, and that's all she needed to see.

21

Havre de Grace, Maryland
Sunday Evening, Christmas Eve, 1848

THE SUSQUEHANNA RIVER WAS WILLIAM AND ELLEN'S RED SEA Crossing. Once they crossed this river, the Promised Land was about 60 miles away, with no more transportation changes. They were so close, but William feared an eleventh-hour disaster. It was dark when the train reached the river, and a cold rain spattered against the windows of the car.

The past day's trip from Richmond had been grueling, traveling north through Fredericksburg to the Potomac River, where they took a steamboat to Washington. From Washington, they traveled by yet another train to Baltimore, where they had yet another close call. The Custom Office man stopped William and demanded proof that Ellen—Mister Johnson—was his rightful owner. It was the Charleston scene all over again, except this time the crowd showed considerable sympathy for Ellen and began chanting, "Chit, chit, chit" to the Custom Office man, who was given the job of confirming the identity of Negroes heading north to a free state. When the bell rang for the train to leave Baltimore, as the Good Lord would have it, the man decided he couldn't be bothered and waved them through.

Now here they were, with just one more obstacle standing between them and Philadelphia: a dark river, cold and black as oil, with only a smattering of light coming from the lamps of Havre de

Grace—the Harbor of Grace. They would need all the grace they could get on this final stretch.

No bridge crossed the Susquehanna, and William was astounded to learn that the train's baggage and freight cars were going to be loaded onto a boat and ferried across the cold river. He had never heard of such a thing. It was the next best thing to seeing the waters parted.

The cold rain slapped William's face, every drop a cold pellet, as he stepped out of the train and waited to board the ferry. The white passengers were told to clamber down a covered incline and onto the lower deck of the ferryboat. While the white folk boarded, William and a few other blacks just stood around and watched in the drizzle. Nature was calling, so William wandered off into the dark because he realized this would be his only chance to unburden himself for some time.

Big mistake. He had walked a short way from the landing when a large figure suddenly stepped in front of him, as big as a bear and reeking of alcohol.

"Where ya goin', boy?"

William didn't answer. He made a move to go around, but the man cut him off. They were nearly chest-to-chest. The man had ears that stuck out from his head like big flaps, and his face was a tangle of hair, as if a patch of wild weeds had latched onto his face and wouldn't let go. The man put a hand on William's chest and gave him a shove backward.

"I asked ya, where ya'll goin'?"

"Just answerin' nature's call before boardin' the boat. My master's waitin' for me."

"Why you headin' away from the boat? Looks to me like you're runnin'."

"No, sir. You can ask my master yourself, if you'd come on board with me and talk with him."

"You orderin' me around, boy?"

William looked around for any sign of help, someone to intervene. They were isolated in the dark. "Talk to my master. I need to be on that boat."

"I tell you what I'll do, boy." The large man clamped a hand on William's shoulder and drew him away from the dock and the ferryboat and the trains, and away from the light. William resisted, but the man's grip was steel. He may have been drunk, but the man had full control of his senses.

"Sir, I need to be on that boat."

"I know, I know, and I aim to get you on that boat. But I need to see proof that you're not a runaway."

"Talk to my master. He's proof."

The man let loose of him, but every time William made a move to turn back, the bear stepped in front and forced him backward, deeper into darkness. William could hear the water lapping against the shore, just a few feet away. He could hear the shouts of railroad men working back by the ferryboat, the clanking of chains, and the murmur of voices. The boat seemed so far away by now, and William seriously wondered if the man planned to murder him.

William made a sudden break for the boat, but the man snagged him by the collar. Slapping away the man's hand, he nearly broke loose, but the man tackled him, bringing him crashing to the ground.

The big man let out a growl as William scrambled to his feet, his shoes slipping on the ground. He felt the man's two arms latch onto him with tremendous strength and stop him dead. He resisted the reflexive urge to throw an elbow in the man's face because striking a white man could be a death sentence. He fought to get free, but the man's grip was impossibly strong. The man, roaring with anger, put one hand on William's back and the other hand on his arm, and he heaved—like tossing a bale of hay. Only the man was tossing *William*, hurling him toward the water.

When William hit the frigid water, it felt like someone had clamped his head, neck, and chest in irons forged from ice. He fought the instant urge to breathe in a lung-load of water, and the cold water bit his bare skin in a million places. At first, he managed to get his head above water, taking big, gasping breaths. Then his head submerged, and it felt as if his skull was being crushed; an ache burst behind his forehead. His clothes weighed as much as iron and they dragged him down into darkness, down beneath the freezing, squeezing water, and the river swallowed him.

*****

Ellen searched the boat for any sign of William, but all she saw was a parade of strange faces, a few black but mostly white. Two other slaves traveling on the train with their masters had already boarded, so why not William? Meanwhile, rail workers used hoists to set a floating bridge into position, with the idea of bringing the baggage and freight cars onto the boat. Railroad tracks stretched from the floating bridge, into the boat, and onto the boat's upper deck.

Finding no sign of William on the deck, she entered the boat's saloon, even though she would have been shocked to find him indoors—where the white folk gathered. As she guessed, she found only white faces, except for a couple of black servants.

"Sir, have you seen anything of my slave?" she asked the conductor, who knew William by face.

"No, sir, I haven't seen anything of him for some time. No doubt he has run away and is already in Philadelphia, free as a bird."

The conductor, a northerner with obvious abolitionist tendencies, was teasing Ellen, but Ellen didn't smile, didn't laugh.

"Could you help me find him, please, sir?"

The conductor's grin disappeared, and he snapped, "I ain't your slave hunter," and he stormed off, leaving Ellen lost in the dark with the noise and the smoke of a dozen cigars. She made three more passes around the deck, calling out William's name, but people answered with bemused stares.

She approached a Negro. "You seen my boy? Goes by the name of William."

The black man stared Ellen directly in the eyes—a bold move on his part. Did he sense her lack of confidence? "No, ain't seen him on the boat."

"But he was on the train, wasn't he?"

"Sure, sure, he was on the train, but he got off. I saw him get off."

"But you didn't see him board the ferryboat?"

"No. Haven't seen him since."

Ellen knew that, as a master, she should be angry at the Negro's gruff manner and failure to use the word "sir" even once, but she didn't care at this point. She needed to find her husband. She considered getting off the steamboat, but what would she do without money? William carried all their money because they knew that a slave would never be marked as a target by pickpockets.

"You think your boy run off?"

Ellen turned and saw a white man at her side—a man from the train, with whom she'd not spoken.

"No. He wouldn't run."

"That's what most masters say until they come north with their slave."

"But we ain't north. Maryland's a slave state."

"True. I wouldn't think he'd run until ya'll stepped on Pennsylvania soil. Then where'd he go?"

Ellen spun around, taking yet another scan of the faces on the deck. Then she leaned over the railing and watched the baggage car roll on board, while shadows scrambled in the darkness. She had no answer for the man.

Macon

Knight didn't think Molly and her family would run—not until their master had been put beneath the ground. After that, who knew? It was quite possible they would flee, so he would have to keep an eye on them.

Knight, Slator, and Hughes had discussed these matters at some length at the jail and then departed ways. Hughes was the only one with a family, but he planned to work through Christmas Eve because he seemed to be much more attached to his jail and his guns than to his wife and children.

Knight had no family of his own, so he was alone for Christmas Eve. He still intended to find a wife and break into the wealthy circles

« 180 »

of the city, but he had learned that the rich families were like fortified castles with very deep moats.

It was dark by the time he approached the Collins estate—another one of the Macon castles, fortified by years of tradition. He knew that Christmas Eve was not the time to be talking with Dr. Collins about William and Ellen Craft, but if Knight was anything, he was persistent.

Dismounting, he adjusted his cravat, straightened his top hat, and approached the Collins home. The butler, a middle-aged black man with streaks of gray in his hair, seemed surprised to see him at the door.

"Tell Dr. Collins it's an urgent matter."

"Yes, sir."

The servant directed Knight to take a seat in the gentleman's parlor, where he was left waiting for almost an hour—Dr. Collins' way of telling him that his time was more precious than Knight's. He could hear voices coming from the back of the house, the dining area, and the smell of a roast permeated the entire home. Laughter erupted every now and again.

"What is it that could not wait until after Christmas?" said Dr. Collins when he finally appeared. He swept into the room in full dinner-party dress. "We have dinner guests this evening, and I have no time to spare."

Knight stood and gave a small bow. "I am very sorry to inconvenience you, Dr. Collins, but I had hoped to talk to you prior to this very busy day."

"Make it quick then." Dr. Collins motioned for Knight to take a chair, while he remained standing—a visual reminder that he stood on a much higher plane.

Knight did as commanded, placing his hat on his lap. "It is about William and Ellen Craft, sir. Did Missus Collins tell you of my concerns?"

"You talked to my wife?" Dr. Collins looked like he swallowed something sour.

"Yes. I had hoped to talk with you a couple of days ago, but I discovered you were traveling on business."

"Get to the point. What is your concern about William and our Ellen?"

"I'm concerned that they may not be where they claim to be."

Dr. Collins frowned, his mouth tightening. "You think they have run?"

"It is certainly a possibility, sir. I did not see them at the home of Mister Slator, either yesterday or today. And Ellen's Aunt Molly seemed quite evasive on the matter."

"You were at the Slator estate? Twice?"

"Yes, sir. I was also there when he was shot in the street. A most unfortunate matter, sir."

"Yes, yes." Dr. Collins raised his chin, as if releasing his neck from the grip of his too-tight collar. "You seem strangely obsessed with poor Molly and her niece Ellen."

Knight didn't know what to say, so he simply responded with, "Yes, poor Molly."

"How do you know that William and Ellen were not at the Slator home? Did you check the premises thoroughly?"

"Not thoroughly, sir, but Molly said William and Ellen were with Mister Slator in town. When I tracked down Mister Slator, I found no sign of them."

"Did you talk to Mister Slator and ask him where they were?"

"I tried. But that was...that was when the unfortunate incident occurred."

Dr. Collins strolled over to the bookshelf and stared at the volumes lining the top shelf. He slowly turned.

"Mister Knight, I appreciate your concern, but I do find it odd that you would be so worried about one of my servants."

"It's William I'm worried about. He works in my shop, so his whereabouts affect me greatly, sir."

"I see, it's your shop now. And I suppose you think that I should simply desert my family and friends on Christmas Eve to go looking for them."

Knight ran his hand across the top of his hat. "No, sir. Most defi-nitely not, but I thought you might want someone else to look into the matter more deeply for you."

"By 'someone,' are you referring to yourself?"

"I am certainly willing, sir. But, of course, that is your decision."

"I am glad you think so, Mister Knight." Dr. Collins stroked his chin and then took one step closer. "I will tell you this, Mis-ter Knight. It is Christmas Eve, and I plan to enjoy this night with friends and family. Tomorrow is Christmas, and Ellen is due to re-turn to our fold. I will give the matter some thought, and we will see what Christmas brings."

Or doesn't bring, Knight thought.

Knight stood and they shook hands. "That is most wise, sir."

For the first time, Dr. Collins smiled at him. "It is Christmas, Mister Knight, and we must show charity to our lessers."

Was he referring to William and Ellen Craft, or to *him*?

"Yes, sir. Merry Christmas, Dr. Collins."

"And Merry Christmas to you. Have a good night, Mister Knight."

Dr. Collins laughed, as if he were the first person to make a play on the words "knight" and "night." Knight made his final farewells, put on his top hat, and stalked out into the crisp Christmas air. He kicked at a stone, so sick of the ignorance of fools like Collins.

22

Macon
Summer 1846: Two Years Earlier

"MY HEAVENS, DON'T YOU LOOK BEAUTIFUL," SAID MISS Eliza. "A perfect fit."

Ellen smiled back. She was seated in the parlor, with Mama running a brush through her hair. It brought back the day 9 years ago when Miss Eliza was in the same position and wearing a very similar dress. Miss Eliza had borrowed this white wedding dress from a free black woman in Macon, and it fit Ellen as if it had been made for her. She didn't even have to make a single alteration.

"Here, let me," Miss Eliza said to Mama, holding out her hand for the brush. "Ellen has such beautiful hair."

Mama let out a "hmmff," reluctantly placed the brush in Miss Eliza's hand, and then Eliza began to draw it down through Ellen's long, black locks. As the mistress of the house, no one could tell her she couldn't brush her half-sister's hair.

Ellen and William were being given a full wedding, one benefit for house slaves. When field slaves were given permission to marry, the master simply decreed them married, and that was that. No ceremony, no fuss. For a wedding to be more formal, you not only had to be a house slave but you also had to be a *highly favored* house servant.

Ellen's marriage wouldn't be legally binding, of course, but they could pretend for a day.

"Thank you, ma'am, for givin' me this day," she said, beaming. "You are so generous."

Ellen overflowed with gratefulness. She had long mastered the trick of appearing happy and grateful for everything her benevolent master and mistress had provided. It was a lie, of course. Every moment of this wedding, she was going to be conscious of the fact that she and William could not live as true husband and wife until they got away from this place.

She knew it could be worse, much worse. Some masters forbade marriages to spouses off the plantation—"marrying abroad." And she knew of a nearby plantation where the master lined up the newly purchased slaves, men on one side and women on the other, and told them to choose a mate for life—on the spot. She wasn't facing something like that, but still...

Ellen's dreams leading up to the wedding day had been vivid and shocking. In so many of the nightmares, she was in her wedding dress, giving birth in a cotton field, and there was blood everywhere—blood on the leaves, blood staining the white cotton in the fields. In most of the dreams, she saw John Knight watching her give birth—just waiting for her baby to be born. In most of the dreams, John Knight took her baby away and rode off with it in his arms.

"William is a good man, a hard worker," Miss Eliza said.

"He is."

"And you have always had a special place in my heart, Ellen."

"The same for you, Miss Eliza. I couldn't be happier."

It was a lovely lie.

It was also a lovely day. It was hot, but there was enough breeze for the outdoor wedding to keep the guests from fainting. The sky was clear of clouds and the deepest blue you could imagine. Brother Emmitt played the fiddle for the wedding march, and Ellen made her way across the yard, past the smiling faces of so many other slaves—and a scattering of whites. She felt like she was walking the chalk-line again, balancing a pail on her head as she approached William, looking so fine in his black pigeon-tail coat, black top hat, black pants, and white vest. Mary stood next to Ellen as her bridesmaid, wearing a blue hoop skirt, while Frank was at William's side.

Deacon Miles stood in front of a table covered with a white tablecloth and topped by two gold candlesticks. His stiff white collar rose so high that it nearly touched his ears.

"And the Lord God caused a deep sleep to fall upon Adam, and he slept," Deacon Miles began, reciting Scripture from memory. "And the Lord, he took one a' Adam's ribs, and he closed up the flesh thereof. And with this rib, which the Lord took outta Adam, he formed himself a woman, and brought her unto the man!"

Rubbing his hands together, Deacon Miles gave William and Ellen a wink and went off on a tangent. "Ellen, you got you William's rib, for I firmly believe that the Good Lord took out one of William's ribs and placed it in you back when you were born to the world. And I believe without a single living doubt that the rib protecting your heart is the rib that come outta William."

The deacon shifted his gaze to William. "And William, you gave her your rib 'cause your duty is to love her and protect her, to be a fortress around your wife, a rib around her heart. You will be strong, like a rib, and you will protect her heart and do whatever it takes, *whatever it takes*, to always keep her safe."

Deacon Miles was treading on dangerous ground, for "doing whatever it takes" could be interpreted as something very bold. But he knew how to walk the chalk-line, too; he knew just how far he could go without tipping over the bucket. He also knew when to shift back to the safety of Scripture.

"Therefore shall a man leave his father and his mother, and he shall cleave unto his wife: and they shall be one flesh!" he declared.

When the ceremony reached its "man and wife" pronouncement, Deacon Miles got to kiss the bride first, as tradition dictated. Then Ellen kissed her husband second, followed by Mary and Frank. Having a mother or father or even a half-sister kiss the bride was not typically part of the ritual, but Miss Eliza couldn't help herself. With tears in her eyes, she rushed up and gave Ellen a kiss on the cheek as well.

The wedding supper followed, with tables covered in white tablecloths and loaded down with chickens and sweet potato custards and apple pies and pots of rice. After the feasting and the dancing, as guests began to disperse, William found a moment to draw Ellen off to the side, beneath a shade tree.

"I have somethin' for you," he said, taking her right hand in his.

She smiled. "Wasn't marryin' me enough?"

"It's all the world. But I wanted to find somethin' to show the world you're mine."

A frown crossed Ellen's face. "William, you can't afford no ring. This isn't a white folk wedding, you know. So you shouldn't have—"

William put a finger to her lips. "I didn't spend a penny. But I did have to slip one thing outta your cabin. I don't think Miss Eliza would mind what I did."

Ellen's look became even more worried. "William, what did you go and do? I don't want you gettin' in no trouble."

Digging deep into his pocket, William pulled out something small, something silver. It was a ring.

Ellen bit her lip and worked this over in her mind. "But William, there weren't no rings layin' around in my cabin. So where did you get this from if you didn't spend money? You didn't take this from—"

Once again, William placed a finger on her lips. "Just look at it closely. Take a *really* close look."

Ellen rolled the ring around in her fingers, and she burst out laughing. "You made this from one a' my thimbles! I thought I'd lost one of 'em."

"It's what the Quakers do."

"They do?"

"They don't believe in jewelry for no good purpose, so they make wedding rings from something functional. Here, let me."

Taking her left hand, he slid the ring onto her ring finger, the finger with a vein that led straight to her heart. The ring was beautiful, and Ellen knew why he had crafted it for her. A silver band on her hand would be a sign to the John Knights of the world. It would tell every white man who saw her as a white woman that she was attached. It was his way of protecting her, just as Deacon Miles had exhorted him.

Ellen extended her hand and sized up the ring. From a distance, you'd never know it was made from a thimble. "It fits like a glove."

"So do we—till death us do part."

"Yes. Till death."

23

Havre de Grace, Maryland
Sunday, Christmas Eve, 1848

WILLIAM HIT BOTTOM. HIS FEET TOUCHED THE MUDDY bottom of the Susquehanna River, but he hadn't given in completely to the icy water. He was conscious of the fact that in moments he might have to open his mouth and breathe the river into his lungs. The river around him would strangle him from the inside.

Although disoriented and in complete darkness, he had a vague awareness that he hadn't fallen very deep beneath the surface of the water. It was possible that the river was not much over his head this close to the bank, so he pushed off from the bottom with as much power as he had remaining. His head popped above the water and into the blackness of night. He was not a good swimmer, but he had enough fight left in him to keep his head above water and gulp another mouthful of air. That was a good sign, for his father once told him that drowning was usually a quiet killer—with almost no thrashing.

He was running out of time. He fought to keep his head above water, but he swallowed a mouthful of river and began to cough and gag. The freezing water stung his throat and chest. In the dark, he couldn't tell where the shore was, even though it was probably no more than 5 feet away, but he probably had less than 30 seconds before the river pulled him back under, and his limbs lost their ability to save him. He chose a direction and dog-paddled through the dark. Choose wrong and he died. He reached out, hoping to clutch grass and mud, but he reached into thin air, grasping at darkness. His strength was leaving him, his muscles were aching, and his arms were shutting down. Already, they were feeling heavy and weak, and he knew that very soon they would become nothing more than two heavy anchors, dragging him back below, this time for good.

The fingers of his right hand suddenly touched soil, grass, mud. The cold soil gave way, but he lunged, finding purchase on a tree root sticking above the ground. Something solid. He pulled. His body rose higher above the surface, and he breathed in deeply. Soon his entire chest was on land, he had two hands on the root, and he pulled, dragging his stiff and soaking limbs onto the bank. He wasn't going to drown, but he wasn't safe yet. He was numbingly cold, and he would freeze to death if he didn't find warmth soon. He had to look down to even make sure his feet were still there. His teeth were chattering so hard that he was afraid they would shatter against one another. Every joint in his body had become stiff, like a day-old corpse, and his fingers were no more than five icicles. When he clenched his fist around the root and pulled again, he was afraid his fingers would break off like frozen flesh.

Worst of all, he wanted to sleep. He was so drowsy, but he knew that if he went under, he would never wake up. He had to stand, but he couldn't. His body wanted to remain motionless and prone, and he had a sinking feeling that he was never going to make it back to the ferryboat before it left. His eyes, covered with ice crystals, closed.

*****

Ellen felt the tears building, but she wouldn't let them come, not surrounded by men on a ferryboat. She had found that mimicking the externals of a man was the easy part—the pants, the short hair, even the deeper voice. It was mimicking the internal world that was so difficult. She knew that a white master would not start blubbering if he couldn't find his slave. A master might get angry—red hot angry—but anger was difficult for her to show when she was feeling overwhelmed by the possibility that something had happened to her husband. He might have been taken—or worse.

Unable to locate William on board the ferryboat, she rushed down the plank and moved along the waterfront, calling out for him—in a master's fashion. She pulled her coat tight, as wind whipped the drizzling rain sideways.

"William! William, you rascal, you devil, show yourself! I know you're out here somewhere!"

She injected as much righteous anger as possible into her words, but it seemed feeble in contrast to how a real master would sound. She hurried along the riverbank, not daring to go too far into the dark for fear that the ferryboat would soon leave.

William had told her she should continue to Philadelphia alone if they were ever split apart, but she hated the idea. William wouldn't leave without her, so how could she do it to him? As the "white man," she was his protection; without her, he would be labeled a runaway for sure. She couldn't desert him, even if he had made her promise.

"All aboard that's goin' aboard!" came the shout from the boat.

So confused, Ellen hurried back to the ferryboat, where two men were just preparing to haul the plank back onto the boat. They stopped in their work when they saw her figure emerge from the darkness. They immediately recognized her as the man with all the bandages.

"Just 'bout left without ya, sir," said one of the men.

Ellen came to a halt at the edge of the plank.

"I'm sorry, I just..."

William had told her to go, to keep running. But how could she leave him behind?

"Ain't you comin' aboard, sir?" asked the man.

That was a good question. She didn't move a muscle, and the men stared at her, and then exchanged glances. This must have struck them as very odd behavior.

"*Keep runnin',*" William had said. "*Keep runnin' and don't look back. Don't be Lot's wife. Just keep runnin'.*"

Ellen hurried up the ramp, but she couldn't resist a final look. As she stepped onto the ferryboat, she turned and glanced back, hoping to catch sight of William making a mad dash to the ferryboat. All she saw was darkness and water.

Looking back, she felt herself dissolve, crumble inside, fall to pieces, and just blow away like so much salt.

Macon

Mary's mama sat at the kitchen table, stone-faced, rigid with grief and anger. Frank had been trying to convince her that they needed to leave the house immediately, but it was like talking to a statue. She would not be moved.

Mary put an arm around Mama, who just stared at the center of the table.

"We gotta run," Mary said. "We gotta run north tonight before these men come back."

"I can't. I'm sorry, but I can't leave until I seen your papa buried properly, a good Christian burial."

Frank kissed his mama on the cheek. "But Mama, the Lord would want us to run. The angel told Mary and Joseph to run to avoid Herod's sword."

Mama raised her gaze from the tabletop. "When an angel walks through that wall and tells me to leave my husband before he's buried, then I'll go."

Frank looked away, and Mary wiped away her tears. She felt guilty for even thinking of deserting the man who had raised them and protected them, but that man was gone! Would he want them to sacrifice their lives for his physical remains?

"You two should go," Mama said. "Take the twins with you. No sense in all of us bein' at risk."

"Mama, you know we would never leave you," Frank said. He still had his gun in his hand.

"If you would never leave me, then why would you ever think of leavin' your father?" Mama stared at him fiercely.

Frank blushed and his eyes sagged with shame. "I won't leave my father. I won't."

Mama's gaze softened, and she put a hand on Frank's shoulder. "I'm sorry, Frank. I just...you know, I have to see him again. I have to say goodbye."

"I know."

"I will say goodbye to your father tomorrow, and then we will leave. I promise."

Frank hung his head and nodded. Mary rose from the table, came around the back of Mama, and draped her arms around her. Mama patted her hand and made a shushing sound, the same as when Mary was a child and Mama wanted to assure her that everything would be all right.

24

Crossing the Susquehanna River
Monday Morning, Christmas Day, 1848

I
T WAS TOO LATE TO TURN BACK NOW. IT WAS PAST MIDNIGHT,
making it officially Christmas Day, and the ferryboat had left the
dock; it was steaming its way across the Susquehanna River, carrying
the train cars on board. When they reached the other side, the train
cars would be unloaded from the boat, placed back on the tracks, and
the locomotive would continue on its way to Philadelphia—without
William. Ellen was heading for the Promised Land without a penny
in her pocket and without her husband.

After the rain let up, she made two more passes around the deck
of the boat, on the unlikely chance of coming across William. Fail-
ing to find him, she stood at the railing, staring out on the water and
wondering if she had done the right thing. Laughter erupted from
inside the boat's brightly lit saloon, followed by whooping, but she
nearly jumped out of her shoes when she heard multiple gunshots
coming from somewhere in the distance. Were they coming from
land? From on the water? She wondered if someone was firing at a
runaway slave—firing at William.

"Don't worry. Probably just duck hunters in a coffin boat," said a
man, appearing by her side. It was a white man, drawing on a large
cigar and blowing circles of smoke into the night.

"Duck hunting in the dead of night?"

"Hunters drift up in a coffin boat and catch the ducks sleepin.'"

Ellen brought that image to her mind. "Doesn't seem quite fair," she said.

"It ain't. Give every bird one chance for life. That's my motto when I hunt."

"Ah."

More gunshots sounded, echoing along the river. It was hard to tell how far away the hunters were, but Ellen's curiosity was piqued.

"Coffin boats? Never heard of 'em."

"Nasty things. Some rivers outlaw them. The boats are no more than a box, like a coffin, and the ballast pulls it down deep in the water so the very edge of the boat is pretty near level with the water. The hunter lies down in the bottom of the boat, like a corpse, and he steers the vessel right into the midst of sleeping ducks. Then up he pops, and he starts shooting away with his swivel gun. Bang, bang, bang!"

As if on cue, his imitation of a swivel gun was followed by real gunfire in the distance.

"I love to hunt, but that ain't my way of doin' things," he said. "Coffin boats is not sportin'. Not sportin' at all."

Ellen nodded, but said nothing.

"Say, you're the fellow who lost his slave, ain't you?"

Again, a nod of the head.

"That's a shame. I can get a team together when we reach the other side. We can track him down for ya."

For a price, probably.

"Thanks for the offer, but I have a feeling he'll show up. He always does."

"Ah. Done this before has he?"

Ellen nodded. "Many a time."

The man took a deep puff and exhaled a chimney-load of smoke into the air. Ellen watched it drift away and disappear into the dark. The man chomped down on the cigar with the corner of his mouth and nudged Ellen on the shoulder with the back of his hand.

"Have a good night then, sir. And Merry Christmas!"

"Merry Christmas to you too, sir."

Ellen flinched once again at the sudden burst of gunfire on the water.

Macon

Mary woke to the sound of a single gun blast. At first, she thought it was all a dream. Then she heard shouts and scuffling and bellows of anger, and realized it was coming from down the hall and down the stairs. Hurling aside the blankets, her feet hit the cold wood floor. She dashed out of her bedroom and began to sprint down the hall, not even considering the danger. A man's hands grabbed her around the waist from behind, stopping her dead in her tracks, lifting her feet off the floor, and taking her breath away. She kicked and struggled and screamed.

"I got the oldest girl!" came a voice beside her ear. It was Willis Hughes and his face was only inches from Mary's right ear; she was hit with a blast of sour breath from close range.

On Christmas morning, of all times, Hughes, Knight, and their cohorts had descended like Herod's soldiers. There seemed to be men everywhere, at least a half dozen in the upstairs alone. She heard Emma scream, and then Antoinette screamed, from their bedroom. She saw lanterns swinging in the dark, splashing light on the walls, the strange faces of men caught up in the glow. The sound of the fiercest struggle was coming from downstairs where Frank had said he would keep guard. She heard furniture breaking, one man cussing up a blue storm, and Frank yelling. At least her brother seemed to be alive and kicking. She had been afraid that the gunshot was Frank being shot dead.

Hughes lifted Mary higher off the ground, and she kicked her legs, striking one of the men in front of her. The man wheeled around, and Mary saw that it was the fellow who called himself Simon Slator—her new master. He smiled at her. Their house was overrun by devils.

"You can't do this! This is my house! My husband's house!" The voice was Mama's, and it was coming from downstairs.

Hughes was strong, and he tightened his hold around Mary's waist so she could barely breathe. With her feet kicking air, he kept her in his grip and rushed through the chaotic hallway and down the staircase to the first floor, where two lantern lights showed Mama struggling in the clutches of yet another man. Mama broke loose, her nightgown ripping. She yanked a vase from a nearby table, spun around, and hurled it at two men. They both ducked, but the vase went wide and shattered against the wall.

Before Mama could find something else to throw, the two men were upon her, one grabbing her by the hair and yanking back.

"If you'd a' come peacefully when we asked politely, we wouldn't a' had to do this!" shouted another man—dressed in a black cape and top hat. It was John Knight.

Upstairs, Mary heard breaking glass.

25

On the Train to Philadelphia
Monday Morning, Christmas Day, 1848

WILLIAM OPENED HIS EYES. HIS HEAD FELT THICK, AS IF IT had been packed with cotton. He was so lost, so confused, so sick to his stomach. He fought his way to the surface of consciousness, and it felt like he was swimming back to the surface of the river again. It all came back to him in a rush. He remembered. He had nearly drowned.

But now he was being awakened, being pulled from deep sleep by a white man. A train conductor? The man had both hands on his shoulders and was shaking him and shouting in his face.

"Boy, wake up! Boy, you wake up *now!*"

"What? What's happenin' to me?"

Taking in his surroundings, William was shocked to find that he was sprawled on top of some bulky bags and large trunks, with blunt edges sticking him in the back. No wonder he ached all over: He had been sleeping on top of luggage in the deep recesses of the train's baggage car, and it felt like a hot knife was jabbing him in his lower back. He rose to a sitting position. The train was moving, so he figured they must be on the other side of the Susquehanna by now.

"Boy, your master is half scared to death about you!"

William's next surprise was his clothes. He examined himself and realized he wasn't wearing his own clothes, but someone else's. He plucked at his pants, wondering how...why...

"Boy, you even listenin' to me?"

"What?"

In the lantern light, he noticed that his own clothes were draped over a pipe running along the wall of the train's baggage car. They looked wet and shiny in the yellow glow, and he remembered. After climbing out of the river, he had staggered back to the train, which hadn't yet been loaded onto the ferryboat. He had climbed into the baggage car, his clothes stiff, waterlogged, cold, and heavy. He had found the baggage car deserted because everyone was on the ferryboat, so he stripped off his wet, cold clothing and rummaged around in the dark car, feeling for the latches on trunks, his fingers aching. When he finally managed to get his fingers to work and open one of the trunks, he had put on someone else's clothes—layers and layers of warm, fresh, dry clothing. White man's clothing, but he didn't care. He must have put on three layers before he had collapsed on top of the heap of luggage and fallen fast asleep. He thought he had died, but here he was, still on board and heading for Philadelphia.

"Boy, what you wearin'?"

William, feeling punch-drunk, climbed off the pile of baggage and stood in the middle of the car. The conductor inspected him, running a lantern up and down so he could get a good look at his entire body. He was wearing three shirts, two vests, and one coat.

"Fell in the river, sir. Thought I'd died."

He figured it was no use trying to explain that he had been *thrown* into the river. The conductor wouldn't care about that detail—or even believe it.

The conductor looked over his shoulder, and William noticed that two black men were also in the baggage car. One stared at him in shock, while the other was trying to contain a smile.

"Boy, you got any extra clothes for this fool to wear?" the conductor shouted at one of the Negroes.

"Yes, sir."

The man went to his own sack and pulled out a raggedy pair of pants and a shirt and handed them over.

"Those my only other pair a' clothes, sir."

The conductor stared at the man, and William was surprised to see sympathy in his eyes. The conductor pulled out a coin and tossed it toward the Negro. "Buy yourself a new pair when we get to Philly."

Was this conductor an abolitionist? William wondered.

After William changed into the raggedy clothes—which didn't provide much protection against the northern air—the conductor put away the white man's clothing.

"The owner of these clothes will probably smell the river in them, but not until he's off the train and checked into a hotel," the conductor said. He turned and gave a severe look to William and the other two men. "Not a word of this to anyone. Not to *anyone*. You hear me?"

All three nodded. William would be a fool to tell anyone how he had worn white man's clothes, but he hoped he could trust the other two men to keep silent.

The conductor stared at the other men for a few moments more, as if he was driving his point home with his eyes, and then he motioned for William to follow. "Come with me. Your master will be relieved to see you."

More than you can imagine.

*****

Now that Philadelphia was getting so close, worries mounted for Ellen. She wondered where she would go once she reached the city. How would she be able to locate William, and who could she trust? How would she pick out an abolitionist from the crowd? And how could she get anywhere without a single coin in her pocket?

Gloomily, she stared out the window and gazed into the night. Every so often she caught a glimpse of a single light, but it was like staring into a deep well.

The Philadelphia, Wilmington, and Baltimore train stopped at all kinds of towns strung along the tracks between Baltimore and

Philadelphia. Charlestown. Elkton. Stanton. Ellen had had a bench to herself since crossing the river, but at Stanton, a man boarded, plopped down next her, and tipped his hat. He had a cushion underneath his arm, which Ellen assumed was for his posterior, but instead he placed it on the floor and propped his feet on it. He caught Ellen's curious gaze.

"It's for the vibrations, you know," the man said—an older gentleman, gray beard and all. "My doctors recommended it as a way to keep a train's vibrations from disturbing the equilibrium in my body. Train vibrations can do things to you on the inside, you know."

She didn't know. The man must have seen Ellen's eyes going wide because he amended his comments. "But I wouldn't let it worry you. You probably don't take trains every week like I do."

She smiled back weakly—another thing to worry about. Were the jerks and jolts of the train shaking up her innards and scrambling them, so that her stomach was where her heart should be? She felt a little sick.

The kindly man nudged the cushion closer to Ellen. "We can share if you'd like."

Ellen didn't like the idea of striking up a conversation with another passenger this close to Philadelphia, but she also didn't want her guts scrambled. She scooted a little closer and put her feet on the cushion.

"Thank you, sir. When I get to Philadelphia and see my doctor, I will be sure to get his advice before I travel on another train."

"You do that. Trains are a different beast from horses and coaches."

The gentleman asked about Ellen's rheumatism, as she knew he would, and they talked for some time. Actually, he did most of the talking, but he put her at ease, and the truth was that she had become confident in her disguised voice. She hoped she wouldn't get too comfortable, though, because that was when you slipped up. There was only 30 miles to freedom, and she had to remain on guard.

When the train reached another stop along the way, the man launched into another monologue on the risks of train travel. Hearing a commotion toward the back of the car, Ellen tossed a glance over her shoulder and nearly shrieked out loud. Standing at the back, with the conductor at his side, was William.

She jumped to her feet and stared, unsure how she should react. She knew what she wanted to do—run down the aisle and throw her arms around him—but her legs wisely remained rooted. She also felt like crying, and she had to fight back the tears. Masters do not cry over recovered slaves. *Masters do not cry.* She realized she was smiling, and that wouldn't do either. She needed to stir her anger, so she tried to recall something about William that infuriated her. She thought back to the corn shucking and recovered the feelings she had for William when she first saw him: her self-righteous anger.

"William! Where on earth have you been?"

She knew she was making a scene, but she had to do it. William stared at the floor and mumbled, "Sorry, sir. Fell asleep in the baggage car, sir." He was playing his role well.

She felt like they were on stage. All eyes in the car were upon them.

"I thought you had run off and left me to fend for myself in Philadelphia! I brought you along because I thought I could trust you!"

"Sorry, sir. I was tired, fell asleep."

It also looked as if he had changed clothes, but Ellen knew better than to bring attention to that. He must have had a good reason.

"Just don't let it happen again. You hear?"

"Yes, sir."

Ellen tipped her hat to the conductor. "And thank you for discovering his whereabouts, sir. This devil can't be trusted."

"Happy to do it," the conductor said, nodding, but he wasn't smiling. He looked at Ellen as if she was some sort of monster, and that's when she realized he was the man who had shown abolitionist sympathies back on the ferryboat. She gave him a sickly smile, feeling odd to be seen as an overbearing master.

She went back to staring out the window, and she no longer cared whether the train's vibrations jostled her innards because her heart was back in the right place. William was alive, and they were almost to free soil. The hint of a smile appeared on her face.

26

T HE CONDUCTOR ESCORTED WILLIAM BACK TO THE BAGGAGE car, and William took his seat across from the other two black men. He wished he could be left alone for the last few miles of this trip, but the conductor had other ideas. The man leaned against the door of the baggage car, chewed on a toothpick, and seemed to be sizing William up.

"I never saw a fellow so badly scared about losing his slave in all my life than your master," the conductor said. "He thought you had taken French leave for parts unknown."

Without a word, William nodded.

Spitting out his toothpick, the conductor moved in closer. He looked around the baggage car, as if to make sure there weren't any prying ears, other than the two Negroes.

He leaned down and spoke in hushed tones. "Let me give you a little friendly advice. When you get to Philadelphia, run away and leave that cripple, and have your liberty."

William was stunned. He couldn't believe he was hearing this from a white man. Was it a trick of some sort? A test?

"No, sir," he said. "I can't promise to do that."

The conductor stood up straight, as if he had just been kicked in the behind by a mule. "Why on earth not? Don't you want your liberty?"

William considered his answer carefully. This was a white man he was talking to, after all. "Yes, sir, I do. But I ain't never gonna run away from such a good master as I have at present."

"Whether he's good or not don't matter, boy. He don't own you. *Run.* You may never have the chance again."

William rubbed the palm of his left hand. He felt sick from the lack of food and the forced baptism in freezing water. "Sorry, sir, but I ain't leavin' my master. He's ailin', and he needs me."

The conductor put a hand on William's shoulder, and William flinched instinctively.

"Tell you what, boy. When you get to Philadelphia, find your way to the offices of the Pennsylvania Anti-Slavery Society and look for men by the names of Miller McKim and William Still. They'll help you. Do you hear me?"

William nodded. This was valuable information, but he still wasn't sure if the conductor was trying to trick him into saying something that would implicate him as a possible runaway. He was so confused, so sick to his stomach. His legs ached and his head throbbed.

"The Pennsylvania Anti-Slavery Society is found at 31 North Fifth Street. You got that? North Fifth Street. Miller McKim. William Still. Those are the names. Can you remember all that?"

"I'll try, sir."

"Just down the street from the Anti-Slavery Society, on Fifth Street, is a boardinghouse where the landlord is an abolitionist. He'll keep you safe. His name is Jeremiah Buller."

So many directions, so many names, and William had a hard time keeping them straight in his mind. He repeated them several times before the conductor departed, leaving him mightily confused. The other two Negro men stared at him for almost a minute after the conductor left and the train began rolling again.

"You think you'll do it?" one of them finally asked.

He shook his head. "I can't leave my master. He's ailin' in a bad way. I can't leave him."

"You're a fool then."

One of the men got up and leaned against the grimy window. It was still early morning, but the darkness was beginning to give way to light on the horizon. "I think we might be in Pennsylvania."

"Then we're rollin' on top a' free soil," said the other man. "You just think on that, boy. When you step off this train, reach down and grab you some dirt in your hands. Look at it closely. It might not look any different than southern soil, but it is. It's free soil. You hear me?"

"I hear ya."

Remembering that all of their money was still in the pockets of his stiff, wet, frozen clothes, William retrieved his duds from where they were hanging. The clothes had a lot of drying to do, but he didn't want to make the mistake of leaving them behind, so he folded them up as best as he could. First, he checked the pockets, digging into the cold cloth, and confirmed that their money pouch was still there.

He felt the slap of a cold wind and noticed that one of the other men had pulled down the lone window in the baggage car and was sticking out his head. "Come here," he said to William. "Stick out your head and look over yonder."

William was suspicious of everyone at this point.

"C'mon, the window ain't gonna bite you."

Getting up on tiptoes, William stuck out his head and felt the blast of morning air, and his eyes began to water in the wind. Down the tracks, in the distance, he could see flickering lights. A swarm of sparks flew by, pouring out of the train's smokestack, along with a black cloud, like a genie from a bottle. He could also see a couple of men in other carriages sticking out their heads and staring at the approaching lights.

"This is it, old horse!" one man shouted to the other. "Philadelphia!"

The train bell clanged, startling William so badly that he banged his head while pulling it back inside.

"Philadelphia is comin'," said one of the Negro men, smiling so satisfied. "So's your freedom."

"Elijah here, he bought his freedom 5 years ago, and I was born free in the North," said the other man. "You can be free, too, and it won't cost you a cent."

By the time they pulled into the Philadelphia station, the full light of morning had crept across the land, and William was so afraid that something or someone was going to stop them in the final minutes before freedom. Slave catchers, alerted by telegraph, could be waiting for them. The train came to a sudden, lurching stop, and William was hurled off his seat, much to the amusement of his two companions who had been bracing themselves by holding onto a post.

"That's the train tellin' you somethin', boy," said one of the men. "It's tryin' to shake some sense into that head a' yours. *Run*, it's sayin'. Run and be free."

The other man pulled open the door to the baggage car, and the light poured in. William's legs were shaking when he stood back up, and he wondered if it was just the cold working up and down his body. He stood in the doorway and looked down on the crowd for anyone who might be searching for two runaway slaves from Georgia, but there were just too many faces. He took the plunge and walked into freedom, and the shock was almost like being thrown into cold water again.

Stepping down onto the platform, William noticed a break in the wooden planks, and bare earth showed through. Crouching down, he dug out some free dirt with his fingers, scooped up a handful, and put it in his pocket.

Macon

Eliza's husband was frightening her. It was Christmas Day, but every ounce of good cheer had been drained from him. He snapped at the children whenever they laughed at the breakfast table, and he had hardly touched his eggs or ham. The servant girl, Marabel, served them, and she did a fine job. She wasn't Ellen, though, and Ellen was supposed to be serving them on Christmas Day.

Eliza was afraid to speak what was on her mind—and his.

Had Ellen run away?

It didn't seem possible. It had been only 2 days since the shooting of Mister Slator, so perhaps she was caught up in mourning and the funeral planning. Dr. Collins had already sent a servant to fetch Ellen from the Slator home just outside Macon, and it was obvious he wasn't going to smile until he received word of her whereabouts.

"I have never had a servant run on me—until Joshua. And now Ellen!" Dr. Collins tossed his handkerchief on the table.

"We don't know that she has. There could be a reason."

"I give them 4 days to spend with family, and this is how they pay me back for my generosity!"

The table went deathly quiet. The two children exchanged glances and knew better than to speak. They even tried to chew quietly for fear of setting off their father. When they suddenly heard the back door open, Dr. Collins shot to his feet and glared at the hallway leading to the back of the house. The stable boy, Louis, appeared in the doorway, afraid to step completely into the dining room.

"Well?" Dr. Collins seemed to dare him to give them bad news.

"I'm sorry, sir. The Slator house is empty of peoples."

Eliza could see Dr. Collins' jaw clench as he ground his teeth. "Are you sure? Did you go inside?"

"Yes, sir. I knocked what had to be a dozen times. The door was partway open, so I went in and called out and looked everywhere, up and down, front to back. The place was empty."

"There could be a good reason," Eliza said to her husband.

"On Christmas Day?" Dr. Collins said. "There's only one reason. They ran."

Eliza blinked away tears. Her Ellen wouldn't have done this to her. They were like sisters. They *were* sisters. She put her up in a fine little cabin. She let her make clothing, rather than work in the fields. She gave her the finest wedding a slave could expect to get. She gave her the world. She gave her love.

"Perhaps...they're just lying out."

That had to be it. Many slaves would run away and hide in the woods for a few days, maybe even a few months, but they wouldn't leave the region, some out of attachment, some because they had no idea where to go. Some even wandered back.

Dr. Collins' glare answered his wife's desperate suggestion; he didn't believe for a moment they had remained in the area.

"If they left the area, they must have had help from someone who could read maps and tell them where to go, how to get there," he said.

"You think they are headed for Philadelphia?"

"It's 4 days' travel from here. They might be there today."

Eliza felt a sting of betrayal—and anger and outrage. She suddenly wanted to break something, and she was tempted to slam her glass down so hard on the table that it shattered. Her hand was trembling, and she rubbed her right temple. *Calm, calm, calm.* She stared at her husband across the table.

"John Knight warned us," she said coldly.

Dr. Collins leaned both hands on the table. "Louis, get me my coat!" he bellowed, and the stable boy jumped into action.

"What are you doing?" Eliza asked, trailing him down the hall.

"Sending a telegram to Philadelphia. We still have time."

"On Christmas morning? The telegraph office is closed."

"Then I aim to open it, even if I have to break down its door and send the telegram myself."

Dr. Collins nearly tore the door off its hinges as he threw it open and marched out. The door slammed with a bang.

Philadelphia

Ellen stepped down from the train, in disbelief. She was in Philadelphia. *In Philadelphia.*

As she worked through the crowd, the first thing she noticed was the cold of the North, and she pulled her coat around her tightly. The second thing she noticed was William crouching down and digging in the dirt. When he rose back up, their eyes met, and she had to work to stifle her smile. She was still a white man, still a master—until she shed these men's clothes. *Don't stumble now.*

Glancing around, she saw a white man with a walrus moustache eyeing her from behind a copy of a newspaper, and she tried to hide her alarm. It was probably her imagination working, but she wondered what would happen if anyone asked for proof of her ownership of William. Did she have to show her proof on free soil? She hurried toward William, and she cast another look over her shoulder. The man had tucked the newspaper beneath his arm and was still staring at her intently. That was not good. Slave catchers might have been alerted in Philadelphia.

"Don't smile, don't speak," she whispered to William.

"What's wrong?"

"Just start walking. Find us a carriage."

When William glanced back over his shoulder, she added, "Don't look back, neither."

William had their trunk, and she led him through the crowd, hoping to shake the man with the walrus moustache. She nearly collided with a newsboy hawking papers, books, cigars, soap, and biscuits. A quick look back confirmed her worst fears. The man was still on their tail, his eyes on her as he dodged people on the platform.

Emerging onto the cobblestone streets of Philadelphia, Ellen and William spied a horse-drawn cab and darted for it. Before they could reach the cab, it took off, already packed with paying customers. They continued, in search of transport.

"Stop!"

It was the man shouting, but Ellen whispered, "Keep walking" to William.

"Stop! You with the bandages!"

No doubt about it. The man was definitely talking to them.

"There! There's a cab!" Ellen said.

It was a green cab with an ornate, gold-trimmed window, and it seated only two passengers. Perfect. They reached the cab before anyone else could claim it, and William said, "To the Buller Boardinghouse on Fifth Street."

But the driver didn't seem in much of a hurry. He noticed the gentleman in the walrus moustache, who was running toward them by this time, and he sleepily informed them, "Yonder gentleman seems to want to speak with you."

Ellen contemplated running, but she knew it was useless. The man had them dead to rights. Her heart was beating so hard that it felt like it was going to leap out of her chest and go running down the street on its own steam.

"What's the hurry?" the man said, catching up with them and leaning over to catch his breath.

Ellen looked at William to see what he might do. If the man tried to arrest them on the spot, would William fight back? William was much younger and stronger, but do they string up Negroes who hit white men in the North? Of course they probably did.

The man reached into his coat pocket, and she expected to see either a gun or a badge or both. Instead, the man pulled out a bottle.

"I don't know why you ran like that, mister, when I got something that will soothe what ails ya. It's Whitehead's Essence of Mustard, and it'll take care of your rheumatisms, gouty afflictions, and complaints of the digestive system like nothing you ever seen before. The moment I saw you disembark from the train, I knew this little bottle was your sure savior."

Ellen stared in wonderment at the brown-tinted bottle in the man's hand, and she couldn't help it. She started laughing. She tried to control it because her laugh was too high and squeal-like for a man, and she attracted the oddest stares from passersby, but she was so relieved and so tired and so slaphappy that she couldn't contain herself.

The coach driver scratched at his sideburns. "You got anything for madness?" he asked the man with the brown bottle.

The medicine hawker was struck speechless. Ellen's face was red and twisted by uncontrollable giggles, and tears had come to her eyes.

William tried to explain. "We had a long trip, and my master, he's a little tired and light-headed."

"I can see that, boy. But mister, Essence of Mustard will also prevent your chilblains from bursting."

At those words, the only thing that burst was another peal of laughter from Ellen. She turned, leaned against the cab, and buried her face in her arm. These people probably thought she was as crazy as a crockhead, but she couldn't help herself. As a man, as a master, she couldn't cry, as much as she wanted to, so she let loose with the next best thing—tears of laughter.

The man slid the bottle of Essence of Mustard back in his pocket, buttoned up his jacket, and stuck out his jaw in defiance. "If you don't want to purchase my cure, just say so. No need for rudeness."

Turning on his heels and trying to muster as much dignity as he could, the man stalked back toward the train station to search for more ailing folks. Ellen removed her green spectacles and wiped the tears from her eyes with the sleeve of her coat, careful not to let her laughter slide into a full-blown cry. The cab driver already thought she had lost her mind.

In some ways, she had. Lord, she couldn't take any more of this.

*****

Ellen held it together all of the way to the Buller Boardinghouse on Fifth Street, and after William carried their trunk up the dark wood stairs, and they closed the door to their room, the mask fell and so did she—nearly. Her legs started to give way, but William grabbed her before she could hit the floor.

> Ellen was in a cotton field, wearing the long shirt of a young slave, and she was leaning back against a large stone, straining and screaming, blood everywhere. She was giving birth. Trying to, at least. William was there, and so was Mary, and Ellen felt as if she was going to split in half. Her lower body tightened like a clenched fist, squeezing, squeezing, squeezing. When the constricting pressure seemed unbearable, she let out a shout. Mary leaned over her, encouraging her, telling her that the Lord was with her in her travails, but she preferred the Lord to lift the pain entirely or just kill her. When the squeezing returned, she felt her face going red with the strain. Her hair was long again, wet with perspiration. And when she looked up, there was John Knight, leaning over Mary's shoulder and smiling down on her. He had blood on his hands.

When Ellen came back to consciousness, she was lying in a featherbed, and she wondered for a moment if she was back in

Macon, back in her cousin's bedroom. But there was William, sitting at the edge of the bed and placing a wet cloth on her forehead. And then she realized...

The bandage around her face was gone. The sling on her arm was gone, and her clothes...she was wearing a simple brown housedress. Those infernal pants were gone. The cravat—gone. And the itchy shirt. Gone. She had become a woman again. She looked off to her right and saw the clothes and hat of "Mister Johnson" hanging on a hook on the wall and looking like nothing more than a lifeless scarecrow. Mister Johnson had vanished, and Ellen Craft had returned from the dead.

"Merry Christmas. How you feel?" William asked.

"Like I been run over by a coach—while givin' birth."

He took her hand and prayed the same Psalm that he had on the first day of their escape. "In God I put my trust; I'll not be afraid of what man can do to me. Thy vows are upon me, O God. I give praises unto thee. For thou hast delivered my soul from death, so deliver my feet from falling, so I can walk before God in the light of the living."

"Amen," she said. For 4 days, she had been in the grip of so many fears that it was hard to feel normal. It was difficult to release the tension.

Ellen rested all afternoon, drifting back into sleep, mercifully without the dreams of birth or John Knight. When she awoke, it was evening, and she was famished.

"I can bring up some food to you."

"No. It will do me good to walk. My back is stiff."

"You sure?"

Moving into a sitting position, she waited for the light-headedness to pass, and then her husband helped her to her feet. She caught her reflection in the mirror.

"But my hair."

It saddened her to see her hair chopped short. She could toss away the pants and the man's jacket, but she couldn't grow her hair back in an instant.

"With a bonnet, no one will notice."

William took a brown bonnet from the trunk and helped her on with it. After he retrieved her shawl, she was ready to face the world again; she latched onto his arm, and they stepped through the door.

They hadn't told Jeremiah Buller, the boardinghouse proprietor, anything about their adventure when they had arrived. All the man knew was that a cotton planter and his slave had checked into his boardinghouse. As they came down the staircase, he looked up from the counter—and looked again. Confusion. A white woman on the arm of a Negro was a shocking sight, even to a man with supposed abolitionist sympathies.

"What happened to the young cotton planter?" he asked, eying Ellen with suspicion and probably wondering if she was William's mistress. Entertaining an unattached woman in the rooms was not allowed.

"You're looking at him," said William. "At *her* I mean."

Buller's eyes flicked from William to Ellen, back to William, then back to Ellen. "I don't understand. You went upstairs with your master. You came down with your..."

He didn't speak the word. *Mistress.*

William was quick to squelch any scandal. "Sir, may I introduce you to my wife, Ellen Craft."

"Your wife?"

The poor landlord had to be completely mystified. A white cotton planter suddenly disappears on his premises, and now this Negro man claims to be married to a white woman, who appears out of thin air!

"I know you didn't arrive with your wife," he said.

"Oh, but I did. I arrived with both my wife and the young cotton planter. They're one and the same."

Buller's eyes did a little dance once again, moving from one to the other, before settling on Ellen and staring at her long and hard.

"You're...?"

"I am."

This would not be the last time that William and Ellen shocked someone with their story.

27

Philadelphia
One Week Later

ELLEN WONDERED IF SHE WAS LOSING HER MIND.

She was nervous being around white men, even abolitionists, and a blanket of panic fell over her whenever she was being
questioned about their escape. Word had gotten out about their
escapade, at least in abolitionist circles, and men came to the Buller
Boardinghouse to see this miracle for themselves. A couple of men
even asked if she would put on her disguise, and so she did—because
she was used to obeying white men. But it terrified her, and it made
her feel as if she was on an auction block, being inspected.

Now, though, her mind had taken a turn for the worse. She was
seeing things. She stared out the front parlor window of the Anti-
Slavery Society office, and she saw the flash of a man's face in a
group of people passing by. *John Knight.* She was sure she had seen
John Knight's face, but in the blink of an eye, he was gone, a passing
phantom.

At first, she didn't say anything because she wondered if it was
just a figment of her imagination. William was in an adjoining office
with two abolitionists—William Still and Robert Purvis—mapping
out their next move. Still and Purvis were given the job of handling
William and Ellen because of their color and Ellen's sensitive state of
mind. William Still was a young free black, handsome and intense,

and Purvis was a light-skinned man, the son of a free black woman and white Englishman.

As she stood at the window, she looked down at her own hands. It seemed strange being so afraid of white people—they shared the same shade of skin. It was a good thing that every glance in a mirror didn't strike her with terror, but with her mind slipping, what if it came to that? What if she couldn't even look at her own skin without spiraling into panic?

She looked up from her hands, and there he was! *John Knight.* He was standing directly across the street from the Anti-Slavery Society office, looking down at a piece of paper. She let out a scream, and backpedaled from the window.

William was by her side the next instant, with Still and Purvis right behind. He helped her find a chair.

"Ellen, what's the matter?"

She was shaking so hard, and she couldn't stop. "I saw him. I saw John Knight."

William exchanged glances with the other two men. "John Knight worked with me back in Macon," he explained.

"Where'd you see him?" Purvis asked Ellen, going to the window.

"Directly across the street."

"He's gone now. There's no one there," Purvis said, but Ellen heard the doubt in his tone.

"He was there. I saw him with my own eyes."

"I know, I know," William said, sitting down next to her. His voice sounded skeptical as well.

"William, I saw him! I did!"

"I know you did."

He didn't sound convinced.

"You don't believe me, do you?"

"I think I should get you a cup of coffee," William said, rising from the chair.

"Don't you even think it's possible I saw him?"

"Yes, it's a possibility."

"But just a possibility?"

"Lookin' out a window, it's also possible you saw wrong."

Before Ellen could protest, there was a sudden sound from the foyer. The front door had opened and someone was entering without so much as a knock. Mister Purvis and Mister Still hurried into the foyer to investigate, and Ellen could hear their formalities and greetings. Then a familiar voice reached her, clear as a bell.

"My name is Timothy Thurber, and I am interested in joining the Anti-Slavery movement."

It was John Knight's voice—no doubt about it. Ellen gasped and shot up from the chair; William clamped his arm around her and drew her into the adjoining room—Miller McKim's office. He closed the door, but kept it open just a crack.

"Sir, you can't just walk in there!" they heard Purvis saying.

"Just lookin' 'round at what you got here," came Knight's voice, growing louder. It sounded like he had moved into the parlor. William eased the office door shut, hoping that Knight didn't hear it click. "How do I join up to help?" Knight asked.

"You will have to talk to Mister McKim when he is in the office, but he is not here today."

"Don't be alarmed by my accent, mister. I may be southern born, but I am abolitionist through and through. I wanna help the cause."

"Sir, you cannot just walk in here and stroll from room to room."

"What's in here? Is this Mister McKim's office? You certain he isn't in?"

Footsteps neared. There was no lock on McKim's office door, so William put his weight against the door and squeezed the handle tightly. Ellen could see the handle starting to turn, but William's grip prevented the knob from doing anything more than twitch. She leaned against the door with both hands to help William keep it shut.

"Door seems stuck." Knight's voice was inches away, separated by only a wooden door. Ellen wondered if the man could hear her breathing.

"Mister Thurber, I am going to have to ask you to leave," said Mister Still. There was a scuffling sound on the other side of the door, and Ellen saw the knob twitching again in William's grip.

"All right, all right, but is this how you treat all interested parties?" Knight asked.

"When they walk in here like they own the place, we do."

The voices drifted away, and they heard Knight asking when he could have a meeting with Mister McKim. Mister Still told him to come back tomorrow.

William and Ellen's eyes met. They were both still leaning against the door, each breathing hard.

"I think it's time we leave Philadelphia," William said.

*****

As soon as Knight was gone, they began to pack their few belongings, and Ellen noticed that William even packed her disguise. Did he think she was going to need it again? As he folded up "Mister Johnson's" coat, it was almost as if *she* was being folded up inside the trunk, and she felt the creeping sense of being smothered. Maybe she really was losing her mind. Maybe pretending to be somebody else, even for a few days, had jumbled her mind, the same way that train vibrations can tumble up a person's innards.

Within the hour, they had slipped out the back door and were on a coach heading for the docks along the Delaware River, but Ellen had the strangest sensation that Knight was still on their trail. While the coach traveled through Philadelphia, William warned her not to raise the leather curtains that covered the windows extending from the ceiling to the armrest of the chairs, but Ellen didn't have to be told. She was terrified of looking out any window for fear that Knight would have his face plastered against the glass, tapping it with his fingernails and grinning like a ghoul.

Even after they were on a steamboat, chugging along the Delaware and heading away from Philadelphia, she was afraid of spotting Knight on board. Mercifully, it was a short trip, 25 miles out of the city, and they took a carriage the final stretch toward an isolated farmhouse owned by Barclay and Ida Ivens. They moved through woods, the trees stark and skeletal. The day was overcast and flecks of snow whisked about the carriage, but no real snow.

The ground looked black and bleak, and the carriage rattled and shook, and when it hit a rut, the entire vehicle seemed to lurch forward and backward.

At last, they reached the Ivens home, which was tucked away along a winding path that led to a clearing in the woods. The house was plain. It had no shutters or ornamentation, just a wide front porch that extended the length of the house. Everything was perfectly symmetrical, with a large stone chimney hugging each side of the house and a single window on each side of the perfectly centered front door.

A woman emerged from the front door, and Ellen gripped William's arm.

"She's white," she whispered.

Three daughters, who looked to range from 13 to 16 years old, trailed just behind their mother. They too were as white as cream.

"I thought they would at least be light-skinned blacks—like Mister Purvis."

"It will be all right, Ellen. They're going to protect us."

"But they're *white*."

The woman, Missus Ivens, hiked across the yard, coming toward them and hitching up the hem of her heavy dress. She wore a black dress with a white lace collar, and her hair was parted perfectly in the middle, making her head as symmetrical as her house. Her smile was kind.

Ellen turned to go back to the coach, and William put a hand on her arm.

"Ellen. They're Friends. They're Quakers."

"But they're white. We can't stay here in the woods with them. Alone. Isolated."

"It's all right."

"No, it ain't all right. I got no confidence in white people. I'm leavin.'"

William put his arm around her, stopping her in her tracks. By this time, Missus Ivens was upon them, all smiles. She put a hand on Ellen's arm.

"How art thou, my dear? I am Missus Ivens and thou must be Missus Craft. Please come inside. I dare say thou art cold and hungry after thy journey."

Ellen recoiled at the woman's touch, but she reluctantly let William draw her toward the house.

"Mister Ivens will be home shortly, but we can eat immediately," the woman said.

Missus Ivens acted compassionately, but Ellen couldn't shake the feeling that it was all a trap. She couldn't help but sense that, when she walked through the front door, she would see John Knight standing there waiting for her in the foyer.

The three daughters, Abigail, Rachel, and Hannah, introduced themselves, and stared at Ellen as if she was some exotic creature. Ellen had been getting those kinds of stares all week. After a life of anonymity, it was if she was being pushed out onto a stage every day. If the girls asked her to put on her disguise for them, she would scream.

They didn't. Instead, they did their best to make her feel comfortable, tending to her every need. That, in itself, was novel. Three white girls waiting on her hand and foot?

After a delicious meal of potato soup and bread, she felt better, but when Mister Purvis announced that he would be returning to Philadelphia first thing in the morning, leaving them alone with this white family, the fear landed on her again, heavy as a stone.

She went to sleep early, and they were set up in a room with twin beds packed with goose feathers, as far as she could tell by the faint smell. It was so nice being in a bed, and it brought back memories of the night she spent at Mary's house. She envied Mary, always had. Mary fit into the white world so easily and had it so comfortable.

Ellen slipped away into sleep, her only escape, and this time John Knight didn't follow her there.

Philadelphia

John Knight woke up feeling dirty and miserable. This was his first time in the big city, and he hoped it would be his last. The hotel's flea-trap mattress was nothing more than a crunchy sack of straw that kept him awake for half the night. The rats and mice kept him up the other half, and his body became a pathway for a pair of rodents. He kept his shoes within reach, and at one point during the dismal dark he hurled one of them in the direction of what sounded like a rat or some other vermin. By morning, the blaze in the fireplace was a cold mush of ash, and his fingers were half frozen with the cold, clutching his thin blanket, and he saw his breath in the morning light. How could people live like this in the North?

As if all of that wasn't miserable enough, he had shared the bed with more than just the mice and rats and bedbugs. He had shared it with a lodger from New York, who snored as loud as a cow in labor. Knight climbed out of bed and discovered that the pail of water to wash his face was half frozen. The proprietor of the place had told him that if he needed to relieve himself during the night, he should use the nearest window, but Knight had pilfered a pot from the downstairs kitchen. He didn't care if it was supposed to be used for the day's meals. He would be eating elsewhere.

Sent to Philadelphia by Dr. Collins, Knight had scouted the various locations where he hoped to find William and Ellen Craft—the Pennsylvania Anti-Slavery Society office and the Quaker church hall. Nothing had come of his efforts other than that scuffle with some abolitionists at the Anti-Slavery office, so he had decided to drink away his frustration. He had stumbled into an Irish pub, deep into the night, and that's where he had encountered a talkative slave catcher, who said he had heard about two slaves from Georgia, a husband and wife, being holed up in the Buller Boardinghouse. Knight had vowed to raid the place early in the morning, when no one would be awake, when no one could stop him from yanking William and Ellen Craft out of their beds.

After dressing, he made his way in the dark early morning hours, reaching the boardinghouse just before dawn. The back door was unlocked, hanging off of one hinge, and he slipped inside. From the outside, it didn't look like a very large building, so there couldn't be many rooms upstairs. He crept up the staircase and found four doors leading into bedrooms. This would be easy pickings. With a gun strapped to his hip and a candle in his left hand, he turned the handle to the first door he encountered, held out the candle, stepped inside, and peered around. The room was empty, and the bed was untouched. It looked thick and soft, like a feather mattress, and if he hadn't had a job to do, he would have climbed into it and caught up on lost sleep.

The second door was ajar, so he made no sound as he eased it open. This time, the bed was occupied and he crept across the room, his light leading the way. Hovering over the bed like an angel of death, he held the light closer, and amazingly the people didn't even stir. The sleepers were a husband and wife, both white, portly, and old, and obviously not William and Ellen Craft.

The third door. One of these rooms had to contain the Crafts. He put a hand on his gun, just for assurances. Then he turned the handle with a soft click. He eased open the door, and it creaked. He stuck in his candle, then peeked in his head—and found himself staring at the barrel of a gun. A man in his nightclothes was propped up in bed and taking aim.

Knight dropped the candle to the floor and was out of the room just seconds before the gun exploded. Hearing the man's pursuit, he flung himself down the stairs, slipping and sliding on his back down the final five stairs. Falling on his back might have saved his life because another gunshot went off, splintering the wood just above his head.

The man never had a chance to reload before Knight was out the door and long gone and wishing he had never come to this infernal city.

28

Macon

IMON SLATOR WAS FED UP. HE WAS GETTING AN EARFUL FROM A nosey old lady by the name of Huston, and he wondered whether the rules about striking a woman applied to busybodies like her.

Slator had already sold off Aunt Molly and the twins at the auction block, but he planned on holding on to the other two—Frank and Mary. Frank looked like a strong worker, despite his temper, and Mary was one of the prettiest slaves he'd ever seen. After he had chained the brother and sister in the back of his wagon, he headed toward the auction building to collect his things, but Missus Huston dogged his every step.

"Mary is so delicate," the gray-haired lady said, pointing to the oldest girl in the back of the covered wagon. "She's unaccustomed to hard work and won't be much use to you on the plantation."

Slator grinned. "I don't want her for the field. I want her for another purpose." He hoped those words shocked Missus Huston to the core, and maybe she would clear off.

From the look on her face, the words did shock, for she turned red with embarrassment, but she redoubled her efforts and followed him inside. Already, two more slaves were standing up on the block, and planters were gathered all around, inspecting them before the auction began. Slator picked up his satchel, which carried his liquid lunch. He had stashed it in the far corner and had almost left without it. With this woman giving him such a headache, he would need all the whiskey he could get. The three bottles clinked as he picked up the sack, and he hoped they wouldn't break.

"But Mister Slator, Mary is *your cousin!*" Missus Huston said.

Oh, he wanted so much to haul off and slap the woman across the face.

"The devil she is!" he said. "You see any colored blood in my face?"

"But Mary's father was your uncle, isn't that correct?"

"We don't know for a fact he was her papa. But we do know he was my uncle."

Over the past week, Judge Jeffreys had sided with him and ruled that he was Mister Slator's sole white relation and entitled to all of his uncle's property. The windfall was well worth the taint of being related to a man suspected of treating his slave like his lawfully wedded wife.

Outside again, he headed for his wagon, striding over a small puddle.

"What will you take for the poor girl?" Missus Huston asked.

"Nothin'. The critter ain't for sale I said."

"You must have a price, Mister Slator."

"Not for this one I don't. I ain't gonna sell her, so you can trouble yourself no more."

If Mary and Frank had been dark-skinned mulattos, he knew he wouldn't be having this problem, but some people hated to see nearly white slaves in chains. It hit too close to home.

He had read all about the phony slave auctions that the bothersome preacher, Henry Ward Beecher, was holding in churches up north. Beecher would pretend to auction off young women—*white women*—at his church to raise money to support his abolitionist meddling. The preacher man knew it would stir up people to see white folk on the auction block, even if it was all pretend. Seeing the real thing here in Macon—a light-skinned mulatto being auctioned off— was bound to bring him grief, so he wasn't about to put Mary on the block, and he sure wasn't selling her to Missus Huston. He wished he could put *Missus Huston* on the block and auction her off to the highest bidder.

"Mister Slator, you cannot steal away this young lady," she said, still in his ear. "It is not proper! Let me purchase her. I will pay you handsomely."

"Lady, if I wasn't a gentleman, I would be givin' you the wrath of my open palm."

"If you *were* a gentleman, you would put that young woman in my care. Remember, sir, there is a just God."

Slator had had enough. He climbed into the wagon and shook the reins, and the wagon lurched into motion. The woman, spry for an old lady, had to hop back a step to avoid being sideswiped. He would not have minded if she had been knocked to the ground, except he knew that would draw even more trouble down on his head.

Slator had found all the cash that his late uncle had stashed in his house, including the money that the mama, Molly, was secretly keeping. He still had more belongings to collect back at the house, and then he was traveling far away from the Missus Hustons of the world.

South Carolina was as good a place as any. He opened a bottle of whiskey to celebrate.

*****

Mary stared at Simon Slator's back and wondered how he could keep the wagon on the road. Since leaving Macon, he had been guzzling wine and brandy, pilfered from her father's home. Back at the house, she had overheard Slator debating with himself about whether he should take his uncle's finest carriage, but he was a practical man and knew that the canvas-covered wagon would hold so much more plunder. So he loaded the back of the wagon with whatever property looked appealing—cutlery, jewelry, top hats, a painting, a fishing pole...and Frank and Mary. Both of them were chained at the wrists, and another chain connected their ankles to an eyebolt on the inside of the wagon.

Slator had also taken whatever guns he could find from his uncle's estate, and he stored those up front with him—not anywhere near

Frank. Her brother kept casting his eyes at one particular shotgun, well out of reach.

Mary and Frank said nothing, but they communicated through looks, and she could tell that Frank was watching and waiting for any opening to escape. This terrified Mary, because the man had an arsenal up front with him, and she didn't want Frank to wind up with a face-load of gunshot. She had lost everything in life except Frank. She was afraid she would never lay eyes on Mama or Antoinette and Emma again, and she tried to keep the picture of them alive in her head. The sky to their west was a dark gray and silent lightning broiled inside the cloudbank. The breeze had picked up, snapping the canvas around their heads. Mary hated storms.

Just when she didn't think it could get any worse, Simon Slator began to sing:

> *The sky with clouds was overcast,*
> *The rain began to fall;*
> *My wife, she whipped the children,*
> *And raised a pretty squall;*
> *She bade them with a frowning look,*
> *To get out of her way;*
> *Oh! The deuce a bit of comfort's here,*
> *Upon a washing day!*
> *For 'tis thump, thump, scrub, scrub,*
> *Scold, scold away,*
> *The devil a bit of comfort's here,*
> *Upon a washing day!*

As Slator belted his off-tune song, he directed an imaginary orchestra, waving around a half-empty bottle with his right hand. Seeing that Slator was increasingly preoccupied and sloshed, Frank began to work at his chains, tugging at them gently, hoping to loosen the bolt on the side of the wagon. The last time he had tried fiddling with his chains, Slator had overheard the clinking and threatened to shoot him in the side of the head if he didn't stop. But this time, his singing drowned out the noise of the chains. In the distance, she also heard the first rumble of thunder, and Slator's singing increased in volume.

> My Kate, she is a bonny wife,
> There's none so free from evil
> Unless upon a Washing day,
> And then she is the devil!
> The very kittens on the earth,
> They dare not even play,
> Away they jump with many a bump
> Upon the Washing day.
> For 'tis thump, thump, scrub, scrub,
> Scold, scold away,
> The devil a bit of comfort's here,
> Upon a washing day!

Frank cursed under his breath because the chains held fast. He scooted back, getting into a better position so he could kick at the sideboard with his boots, hoping to break the wood away. He kicked gently at first, just to make sure that Slator didn't hear. Slator seemed to be slumping forward, falling into a groggy stupor.

"I think the drink is putting him to sleep," Frank whispered, and he gave a fiercer kick at the sideboard. The wood made a slight snapping sound, but no visible cracks appeared. The wagon was a sturdy one, made out of hickory. The wind picked up in intensity, and the canvas covering began flapping wildly, as if it was trying to rise up and fly. The sky darkened to a greenish gloom, and the two horses pulling the wagon became agitated, rattling their bridles. Slator slumped farther forward, and Mary wondered if he was even awake. Frank kicked again at the sideboard, this time with more force, for Slator was not responding. Another kick, the wood cracked, and Mary spotted the sliver of a break. This might just work.

But then the sky itself cracked, as if God had given a mighty kick to the clouds, and the black sky burst and splintered; a bolt of lightning broke across the air in a jagged flash of light. The horses panicked and bolted, and the reins fell out of Slator's limp hands. The wagon had been moving down a hill when the lightning lit a spark in the horses, and it lurched forward, hitting ruts and throwing contents in the wagon around like loose objects in a capsizing ship. The horses ran wildly, driven by fear, and the wagon swung crazily behind the two panic-stricken animals. A pan hit Mary squarely in the back, and the stone bust of a Roman senator barely missed bashing her in the head before it hit the canvas and then bounced back for a second attempt at her skull.

The wagon went up on two wheels, briefly, but didn't tip. Hurtling ever downward, it picked up speed, and the horses suddenly pulled them off of the road, heading for the cover of the woods. Awakened, Slator shot up in his seat and gave out a startled yelp, but he was no longer in control. The horses weren't in control either; they were powered by pure panic, and the skies had opened, pouring buckets of rain on their heads. The wagon lurched and tipped and rolled and creaked and cracked like a small boat caught in a typhoon at sea.

Slator screamed and cursed and seemed to be looking for the brakes and reins, but he couldn't do much more than hang on for dear life. Their fate was out of his hands and in the hands of God. The last thing Mary remembered thinking was that she hoped God would pick up the reins Himself and steer them to safety. The last thing she remembered hearing was the scraping sound of tree branches running their stick fingers across the side of the canvas. The last thing she remembered seeing was the wagon making a sharp left turn and then striking against a tree as thick as a rain barrel, with the branches ripping through the canvas and slicing her right cheek. The wagon splintered all around them, and the wooden frame disintegrated in a chaos of sound and fury.

29

The Ivens Farm, Pennsylvania

LLEN. CRAFT.

Ellen stared at the words in wonder. Hannah, the oldest of the Ivens girls, told her that these two words comprised her name. Hannah had scrawled the name across a slate with chalk—white letters on a black background—and she sounded them out.

"I can teach thou how to write and read," she said, adjusting the white soft cap that tied under her chin.

"That would be wonderful," said Ellen, looking for a similar affirmation from William, who sat next to her in the drawing room. It was late morning, another overcast day, but a busting breakfast of eggs and bacon and an abundance of hospitality had begun to break down her defenses.

"Ain't we too old to learn?" said William.

Hannah shook her head and smiled, and she scribbled out another white name on the slate. "And this is thy name, William. This is thy *first* name. And *last* name."

William. Craft.

Ellen tried to memorize how their last name began with a large curving letter, like a scythe, followed by a series of smaller marks that were knitted into strange and perplexing shapes.

"Hast thou ever learned the alphabet?" Hannah asked.

William said he had learned to speak, but not write, the alphabet, and that was as far as he got, while Ellen said that her mistress, Miss Eliza, once tried teaching her how to write the alphabet when they were young. That was many years ago.

"Abigail and Rachel can help on some days, but I am prepared to begin teaching immediately. This morning."

Ellen felt as if Hannah had opened a door and was inviting her inside. For all her life, she had been on the outside of closed doors. When Eliza climbed into her featherbed growing up on the Smith plantation, Ellen had to sleep on a hard pallet outside the bedroom door. Whenever important guests were in the house, she was relegated to the kitchen, separated from the guests by a swinging piece of wood. When it came to the secrets of how the world worked, it was the same. Now this young Quaker girl, at least four years her junior, was inviting her in. Of course she would accept!

"Thank you. I would like that very much."

"And thou, William?"

"Yes, ma'am, I'm prepared to learn."

Hannah crossed the room and picked up one of the many cats that roamed the Ivens house and yard in search of mice. She placed the cat in Ellen's arms; Ellen stroked the soft fur, and the cat let out a contented purr. It was a white cat with tufts of brown around the ears and face.

"Today we shall start with three letters that spell the word 'cat.' C, A, and T. Each day thou will learn three new letters. Thou will learn the sounds of each letter, and will learn to write them with thine own hand."

She explained that by learning the three letters that made up the word "cat," they would also know more than half of the letters that made up their own last name. C as in CAT. C as in CRAFT. Mesmerized, Ellen watched her scrawl the string of letters on the slate, and she felt as if she was being let in on a deep and dangerous secret.

East of Macon

Mary felt her face and touched blood. She was sprawled out in the mud as the heavens emptied. Pushing herself up into a sitting position, she surveyed the damage. The wagon was a shambles, with wreckage spread all around her, like a house leveled by a twister, and she saw no sign of the horses, which had broken free from their bridles.

Not only had the horses broken free—so had Mary. She suddenly realized that the chain on her leg had snapped away from the side of the wagon during the crash. She still had chains clasped on both wrists, but her leg was free. She heard groaning to her right and saw Frank raising himself into a sitting position and holding his head with his two hands, also linked at the wrists. She hurried over, her clothes soaked and heavy, but she saw no sign of blood, no gash in the side of his head.

"We're alive," Mary said. "And we're free."

To prove it, she stood and lifted her right foot, giving it a shake. Frank, however, was not so fortunate, for his leg chain was still attached to the side of the shattered wagon. What about Slator? She hoped he had been hurled face first into the nearest tree and died on contact.

Frank must have had a similar thought because they both looked over to the edge of the woods simultaneously, and they saw the man's body slumped amid the debris, face down in the mud.

"The key, Mary. Hurry. Get the key from his pocket."

Mary took two steps, and the chains dragged behind, clinking like a ghost. Slator stirred. He was alive and moaning, and he turned onto his side. Mary held her pose, not making a move, not a sound. When Slator became motionless once again, she quietly, gently lifted up her leg chain. If she carried it, rather than dragged it, she could move quietly. If Slator roused, she could crack him in the face with her chains.

It seemed to take forever to cross the 20 feet of soggy, muddy ground. Her dripping hair dangled in her eyes, and the rain picked up in intensity. A flash of lightning, followed immediately by thunder, stirred Slator once again, and she paused, frozen in motion. When Slator stopped shifting, she began moving, one small step at a time. He was still lying on his right side. His eyes were shut, and his face was bruised and covered by multiple small cuts. A sliver of wood protruded from the skin along the jawline.

Which pocket held the key? She tried the coat pocket on his left side—the only pocket she could reach with him lying on his right side. He didn't move a muscle as she slipped her hand into the pocket and felt around. It was awkward business since her two hands were still linked. She found a handkerchief, nothing more. Disgusted, she wiped her hand on her dress, and then she began to sob. Her brother, crouching in the rubble, shushed her. She wished Slator was dead, but his coat had a large rip, and through the hole she noticed his rib cage expanding and contracting.

To get at his other coat pocket, she would have to turn the man. Crouching, she put both hands on his back, but he groaned and muttered at her touch, and she pulled back her hands. Perhaps it would be better to yank the edge of his coat out from underneath his body. So she tried, but the fabric was stuck, trapped under the weight of his frame. She wiped another wet strand from her eyes, and the rain let up a little.

Mary tugged again at the coat. This time it came free, and she nearly fell over backward. Her chains clinked, and Slator moaned. When he quieted, she jammed her hand into the pocket and felt her hands wrap around the cold steel of a single key.

"Quickly, quickly," Frank whispered.

Mary inserted the key into the lock chaining Frank's wrists. It was a perfect fit, and moments later Frank was unlocking his leg chains and Mary's wrist shackles. Slator stirred once again, and when they looked over toward the trees, they were horrified to see the man sitting up, scratching his head and looking dazed. The shotgun! It was within Slator's reach! Frank leaped over a piece of the wagon, and Slator's addled eyes seemed to suddenly focus, as if he realized what the young man was doing. Slator looked around for the gun. Frank was fortunate that their tormenter's first instinct was to look to his right, instead of his left.

When Slator looked left, he was staring into the muzzle of the shotgun in Frank's hands.

Slator moaned. "Boy, you sure have a fondness for pointing guns at me."

"I have an even greater fondness for *shooting* people like you."

Slator made a move to get up, but he stopped when he heard the cock of Frank's gun.

"Mary, chain his wrists."

She didn't move. It was as if he had just asked her to chain up a rabid dog.

"I'd do it, Mary, but I can't aim a gun and chain him up at the same time. You'll have to."

Slator smiled. "I always wanted to be handled by this young beauty."

Frank used the butt of the gun to smash the side of Slator's head, and Mary screamed. The man slumped sideways, knocked cold.

"I'll chain him up myself," Frank said.

"If he's still alive. What if you killed him?"

"That's not my worry."

"It should be. Running away is one thing. Murdering a white man is another."

Mary could tell that her words rattled her brother, so she felt for Slator's pulse. "He's alive, thank God."

Frank dragged Slator's body deeper into the woods, and he used all of the chains they had at their disposal. They used both sets of leg chains to connect Slator's legs to two different trees, and they used both sets of wrist shackles. The man was weighted down with chains.

Realizing what they had just done and what kind of danger they faced, Mary's legs gave out and she dropped to her knees in the mud. Her brother knelt beside her and wrapped his arms around her.

"The Lord delivered us," he said.

"We aren't delivered just yet."

Frank helped Mary to her feet, collected two guns, and broke the rest against a tree so Slator wouldn't be armed if he somehow escaped his chains. Then they headed in the direction of Savannah.

*****

Frank carried a shotgun and had given a pistol to Mary, insisting she carry it. It had stopped raining, and it was close to midday, when travel was most dangerous, so they remained hidden in the thick forest. Frank led them on a southeasterly direction. The sky had cleared and Frank could gauge their direction by the sun, visible through the tops of the trees, which were as bare as bones.

Mary felt cold, even though she had changed into dry clothing after the rain had let up. Slator had included a couple of extra dresses in the wagon supplies, probably with an eye for dressing her up in different gowns for his amusement. They carried as much clothing and food as they could in a large sack, along with the money that Slator had pilfered from Mama and Papa. Oddly enough, they were now rich.

As they made their way through the gloom of the forest, they tried not to talk. The silence protected them, but it also spooked Mary. She kept imagining the distant sound of Negro dogs, and the image of Joshua Hamm, torn and bleeding, was stuck in her mind. She heard the snap of a branch off to her right and hoped it was just a deer. Frank held up a hand, and they halted and listened. He spun around, surveying the area. It was nothing but trees, as far as the eye could see. Mary could hear Frank's inhaling and exhaling, and his breath was visible, drifting off like campfire smoke. They moved on, saying nothing. As the day slogged on, the temperatures began to warm, and the mud dried in her tangled hair. They moved into lower ground, where a fog was building. The sun was blotted out.

"You sure we're going the right direction?"

"Pretty certain," said Frank.

The fog would give them a white cover—almost as good as the black cover of night. She had to rely on sound alone as the fog thickened and the moist air left water droplets on her skin.

They heard multiple cracks and snaps, but from which direction? Sound was deceiving. Frank and Mary stopped and listened once again. This time it was not a solitary snap. The crunching and snapping was continuous and seemed to be closing in on them. Whoever or whatever was approaching was coming closer. Frank cocked his gun, and Mary instinctively backed up a step.

Suddenly, a short figure burst through the curtain of fog and came to an abrupt standstill. It was a stocky Negro man running barefoot, his clothes tattered and bare legs streaked with scrapes. Frank and Mary stared at him in stunned silence, and the man breathed heavily as his gaze fell on Frank's gun. He probably expected Frank, a light-skinned man, to aim the barrel at him and tell him to get down on his knees, but Frank just looked at Mary. They were probably thinking the same thing: If this man was a runaway slave, he might be leading slave catchers directly into their path.

"Go," Frank whispered.

The man looked confused.

"Go," he repeated.

The man must have been baffled why two "white folks" were telling him to scat. Was Frank going to shoot him in the back for sport once he started running? Still, the Negro did as he was told and took off. He soon disappeared into the fog, the crash of twigs and branches fading into the distance.

Frank and Mary continued. They didn't speak. Mary couldn't help but see themselves in the eyes of that poor man. She wondered if her own eyes showed the same glow of fear. The presence of the slave probably meant the forest was overrun with slave hunters and dogs. She didn't hear barking, but they hadn't gone more than another 10 minutes before they heard another crashing of underbrush, and a second figure materialized from the fog, this one holding a shotgun. It was a white man.

"Don't try it," the man said, when Frank made a move to raise his own gun.

30

THE MAN TOOK ONE STEP CLOSER, HIS GUN STILL AIMED point-blank at Frank's face. Mary didn't budge, and neither did her brother. Frank just stared at the barrel of the gun, only 2 feet away, knowing it could take his head off with one twitch of the finger. Then a smile broke across the stranger's face, and he mercifully lowered his weapon. The man had the reddest, roundest face that Ellen had ever seen. He was dressed in a long black coat, and his misshapen top hat had a gaping rip in it.

"I beg your pardon, sir and madam, but I can never be sure of what I'm seein' in this here fog. I thought for a moment you mighta been runaways."

Mighta been?

"Farthest thing from it," said Frank. "We broke a wagon wheel and decided to make off by foot."

"Through the forest, instead of the road?"

"With the rain, we wanted to find some cover. But the fog set in, and we got lost."

"I can see that. Say, you ain't seen a runaway, have you— dark-skinned, short man, about 5 feet 2 inches, stocky as a tree stump and strong as a bear? He run off this mornin'."

"No, sir," said Frank.

Frank didn't miss a beat—not a flicker of hesitation. The man let out a soft curse.

It was clear from the conversation that this man took them to be white folk, as white as the fog all around them. It was a good thing

Frank was wearing a wide-brimmed hat or his hair might have been a dead giveaway.

"If you keep on headin' this direction, you'll come outta the forest and run right into the small town a' Pittney." The man moved in closer, uncomfortably close.

Frank took one step back. "Thank you, sir."

"Glad to help. This ain't the kind a day you want to be traipsin' through the woods with a flower of a young lady. Not safe, especially with a runaway on the loose."

The man's eyes settled on Mary and didn't leave her, and she felt herself blush.

"If you see the runaway, fire shots in the air as a signal, and keep him under guard. I'll reward ya'll handsomely. Mordecai likes to lay out in the woods for weeks at a time, and I've a notion to sell him and get him off my hands. You lookin' to buy a slave, mister?"

"No, sir, we don't have the money or the need."

The man tipped his hat and bowed—an exaggerated flourish. "Very well then. And a good day to both of you."

Frank and Mary took off in the direction he had indicated—quickly, before the man changed his mind and decided their skin carried too much color. The encounter, though, gave Frank an idea, as good as gold.

"You know," he said when they emerged from the forest about a mile later, "I think we might be able to pass ourselves off as white folk—as long as I keep my hair covered with my hat."

They came out on a fallow field on higher ground, where the battle-smoke fog had thinned. On the far side of the field was the edge of a town.

"You think so?"

"You saw it. Once he took a look at us, he didn't think for a moment we were runaways."

"I don't know."

"It might be our best chance of escapin'. Let's test it out and head into town and see what we find," Frank said, pointing toward the village.

Mary didn't move. "But why head into town if we don't have to? What if your test fails?"

Frank turned, with his shotgun propped on one shoulder and the sack slung over another. "Sis, we're gonna need to move faster than feet can carry us. Once someone stumbles across Slator and frees him, an army will be after us, so we need transportation, and I hope to find somethin' here. A buggy perhaps."

"You're not aiming to steal one, are you?"

Frank jangled the bag of coins attached to his belt. "We're rich, Mary, if you haven't forgotten. We can buy ourselves two if you'd like. You stay hidden, while I scout out the possibilities. I want you safe—in case my test fails."

"Just keep your hat on," Mary said.

Her brother gave her a long hug, set her on a log, and smiled confidently. He was right. They needed to travel faster than on foot, but just because one old man in a forest mistook them for white folk didn't mean an entire town would be blinded.

The log beneath Mary felt cold, and she hugged herself for warmth. She watched Frank stride across the field and disappear into the whiteness.

The Ivens Farm, Pennsylvania

"Your story must be heard," said William Wells Brown. He was a tall, thin, well-dressed man with light brown skin and heavy eyebrows—a strikingly handsome man, full of energy, with the most intense eyes that Ellen had ever seen. Brown, a leader in the abolitionist movement, also was their first visitor since they had arrived in the Ivens' house. They had all collected in the parlor—Brown, William and Ellen, and Mister and Missus Ivens.

"But we ain't public speakers," said William.

"Your story will do the speaking for you," said Brown. "Just tell the story, plain and simple. I felt the same hesitation after I escaped and was first asked to address a crowd."

William ran his fingers through his beard. "How'd you get away?"

Abigail brought out coffee on a tray as William Wells Brown told how he had been working on a Mississippi steamboat 15 years ago when he up and ran and worked his way to Canada. Since then, he had married, become an abolitionist speaker, learned to write, and published two books, including a narrative of his life.

"You should write a narrative," he said out of the blue.

William laughed. "I could if you don't mind readin' an entire book consistin' of the words CAT, DOG, SUN, and GOD."

"You have to start somewhere," said Brown. "I too started with CAT and DOG." He paused for a sip of coffee and then set down his cup and saucer. "We would like you to come to Boston, and tell your story."

Ellen felt the fear creep back into her bones. For the past few days, the tension had washed away for the most part, and she had begun to feel like she was a part of the Ivens family. She had never experienced such love from a white family, and now they were being asked to give it all up so soon?

"But will it be safe? Shouldn't we remain hidden for a little longer?" William asked.

Brown studied his hands. "I can't say there's no risk at all, but you'll be further north, and Boston is strong in abolitionist spirit. No slave has ever been recaptured from its streets."

"When will these meetings be takin' place?" William asked.

"The end of the month. But please consider this. Your story will travel south and give so many hope."

The words hung there in the silence.

"Perhaps this is all too much, too soon," said Mister Ivens, setting down his cup with a clink.

Mister Ivens had given them an opening to back away from the invitation to move to Boston, but William didn't go for it.

"If we agree, could Ellen remain out of the meetings—for her safety?"

Brown looked over at Ellen, as if gauging how she felt about this idea. She averted her eyes, but she could sense that Brown did not like William's suggestion. He responded carefully.

"People will want to see with their own eyes a woman who passed herself off as a white gentleman," Brown said. "But she don't have to worry. Women don't speak at these events."

"But if people know what she looks like...I just...I don't want to put her in any form of danger."

"We will see to that," said Brown.

"But you can't guarantee it?"

Brown shook his head. "No one can do that, short of the Lord Himself—and even He doesn't usually hand out such guarantees."

In Philadelphia, Ellen had felt like she was being paraded on stage for people to gawk and wonder, but now she was being invited to step onto a real stage. It made her queasy just picturing it.

William didn't answer immediately, but Ellen saw his demeanor change—as if a lantern had just been lit behind his eyes. It was the same look he had had at the corn shucking so long ago. She knew her man, and he couldn't resist any chance to poke his fingers in the eyes of the masters and their overseers.

Ellen knew right then and there what lay ahead. They were going to Boston.

31

Boston,
Wednesday, January 24, 1849

F ANUEIL HALL WAS PACKED TO THE RAFTERS. ELLEN HAD NEVER seen so many black and white folks mingling inside one building. The noise scared her. The size of the city scared her. Even the smiling faces of white people scared her because she couldn't shake the feeling that there was something sinister behind the grins.

It was evening, and an enormous, three-tiered chandelier hung over the heads of the crowd like a celestial being, throwing light in all directions. Running along the sides of the enormous hall were two balconies held up by a double-decker row of white pillars, similar to the front porch of a Macon mansion. The balconies were packed with people, black and white jumbled together, looking down on the stage for the annual meeting of the Massachusetts Anti-Slavery Society. They put William and Ellen in the front row on floor level, and William seemed to be having the time of his life. All smiles. He was a fish in water. Ellen felt more like a cat in water.

It didn't help that there had been incidents since they had arrived in Boston. Just one day earlier, they had been verbally attacked on the street by a man who spotted her latching on to William's arm and assumed they were a black and white couple—not natural, in his eyes. Lewis Hayden stepped in before William could give the man a fist full of knuckles to the eye.

They had been put up on the northern slope of Beacon Hill, a world of haphazard streets, twisting alleys, secret passageways, tumbledown tenements, and so many black people in one place. She had never seen anything like it. Lewis Hayden said the maze of alleys made it much easier to elude any slave catchers who dared to venture this far north. Every time someone spoke the words *slave catchers*, her stomach twisted a little tighter, like tightening a screw in her gut. When she heard words like that, she wondered: Why were they even doing this? Stepping onto a stage was like waving your arms and telling the slave catchers, "We're here! Come and get us if you dare!"

Boston had many sympathetic whites, but that didn't keep the city from being as divided as any place she had seen. The southern side of Beacon Hill was white and rich, with stately mansions—a world of poets, philosophers, politicians, and preachers. However, inside Fanueil Hall on this particular day, the two sides of Beacon Hill had come together.

The proceedings started with a reading of several resolutions that had to do with the Free Soil Party. Ellen had no idea what that was, and she quickly became buried under all the words pouring down on her from the stage in front of them. Then one of the abolitionists moved that the resolutions be tabled so they could introduce everyone to "the Georgia fugitives," as they had become known.

Ellen grabbed William's arm and squeezed it tight. Their new friend, William Wells Brown, took to the stage and began talking about them.

"Ellen, the wife, is so nearly white that, by clothing herself in male attire, she was enabled to pass as a white man, while her husband attended her as her servant," Brown declared to the crowd after reading a New Jersey newspaper's account of their escape. "The husband was a journeyman cabinetmaker, and by industry and prudence had been able to lay by a sum sufficient to meet the expenses of their flight."

Thunderous applause. Ellen was afraid to glance back at all the people reacting to their story.

Then Brown looked down upon the front row, stared directly at William and Ellen, and asked them to take the stage. Ellen froze, but William was on his feet almost before Brown finished making the invitation. He helped her rise, and the applause came down on her again, gusts of cheering. *This is a mistake,* she thought. *This is all a mistake. They're gonna find us and catch us before we even walk out of this building.*

William offered her his arm, and he whispered in her ear, "Just walk straight like we're doin' the cake-line walk again. It's all a matter a' balance."

Walking up and down a field with a pail balanced on your head was easy work compared to walking up the short flight of stairs and onto the stage with so many people staring back at her. She had never been looked at by so many eyes at the same time in her entire life. She couldn't grasp that all of these people were thinking about her, Ellen Craft, at the very same moment. Her name and her face were lodged inside their thoughts. She nearly tripped on the bottom step, but William caught her. Good thing she didn't have a bucket of water on her head, or she would be out of the game already.

The crowd was on its feet, stomping the floor and clapping. Some were shouting. Ellen felt tears coming to her eyes, and she wiped them away with her handkerchief. She began to shake, and she noticed that the massive chandelier was also beginning to shake from the noise. She hoped it didn't all come tumbling down Jericho style.

"I would like to lay three propositions before you tonight in the presence of these Georgia fugitives," Brown shouted, standing to the right of William and holding out his hand to the crowd. Ellen had no idea what he was talking about. Propositions? He didn't say anything about propositions.

"First proposition! All persons present who would help return a slave to his bondage, please say 'yes.'"

What? Why was Brown asking who would return them to bondage? Was this a trick? It made no sense.

But the room had gone deathly quiet. Not one person responded "yes" to the proposition that they would return a slave to bondage.

Ellen's heart was thudding so hard that she thought people in the back row could hear it.

"Second proposition!" Brown shouted. "All who would stand still and do nothing for such a slave, please say 'yes.'"

Again, not a sound. Not a peep. Not even a rustle of paper. Brown let the silence expand and fill the room.

"Third proposition! All who would aid in protecting, rescuing, and saving a slave from going back to slavery, please say 'yes.'"

The room exploded. The crowd leaped to its feet, and hundreds of voices shouted, "Yes!" It was an Everlasting Yes, rolling down on William and Ellen and scaring her half to death. Ellen felt William's arm tighten around her. She realized that tears were streaming down her cheeks and she couldn't stop them. She buried her face on his shoulder and sobbed. When they left Georgia only 1 month ago, she could never imagine this in her wildest dreams. It was terrifying and wonderful all at once, and she wished she could stop crying so she could look down on the crowd from the stage and take it all in, but the tears kept coming and coming, blinding her.

Macon, February 12, 1849

Miss Eliza screamed, and the maid came running. "What's wrong, Miss Eliza?" asked Marabel—Ellen's replacement.

Miss Eliza had been eating her breakfast—a soft-boiled egg and a glass of milk—while she read the *Georgia Telegraph*. The paper was neatly folded and placed just to the left of her plate so she could read and eat, the way Dr. Collins did it.

"Fetch Dr. Collins! Now!"

"Yes, Miss Eliza." Marabel took off like a shot toward the back room, where Dr. Collins was reading one of his many medical journals. He had made it clear he should not be disturbed when he was doing his early morning reading, but this was an exception. This was an awful, horrifying exception.

"What is it, dear?" Dr. Collins entered the room and gave her a warning look, as if to say, "You had better be dying if you're interrupting my reading."

It was almost that bad. She *felt* as if she was dying.

"Here, here, here! Read!" Miss Eliza stabbed the newspaper with her finger.

Snatching up the paper, Dr. Collins read. As he did, his look of slight irritation transformed into a frozen scowl. He didn't shout—didn't even let out a growl. He calmly set the newspaper back down on the table, not saying a word. He looked like he was about to erupt at any second.

The article, a reprint of a New England story, told of the escape of William and Ellen Craft. At the end of the story, the local editor had added, "The Mr. and Mrs. Craft who figure so largely in the above paragraph will be recognized at once by our city readers as the slaves belonging to Dr. Collins and Mr. Ira H. Taylor, of this place, who runaway or were decoyed from their owners on December last."

When William and Ellen didn't show up on Christmas Day, Miss Eliza had hoped that they had simply been delayed by something unforeseen. When they didn't return in 3 days, she hoped they had been "lying out" nearby, as some slaves do. Even when John Knight returned from Philadelphia, claiming to have heard about two escaped Georgia slaves who resembled William and Ellen, she tried to convince herself it wasn't true.

But now this: The truth stared back at her in black and white.

"We have been humiliated," she said. "Publicly humiliated."

They had also been betrayed, Miss Eliza thought. Dr. Collins was known far and wide for the benevolent treatment of his servants, and he even took criticism for it from other plantation owners. But Ellen had thrown his generosity in his face—and hers. Miss Eliza had given Ellen all her love. They were like sisters. *Sisters!* She had brushed Ellen's hair. She had tried to teach her the alphabet. She had once even let her sleep in her bed when Ellen was a small girl and it was storming outside. And this was how she repaid her!

She was mightily tempted to knock the table setting onto the floor and let Marabel clean up the mess. She wanted so badly to break something.

"Shall we send Knight north again?"

Dr. Collins shook his head. "If only Knight had more authority..."

"But the law is on our side."

Every good master was well versed in the Fugitive Slave Act of 1793, which allowed slave owners to recapture escaped slaves from any one of the states. However...

"The law has no teeth," Dr. Collins said. "*It has no teeth.* It needs bite."

For one second, the talk of teeth brought to mind the image of Negro dogs that were bred to run down escaped slaves. Cuban bloodhounds. She pictured the teeth on these monsters, and she saw in her mind the ripped-up body of Joshua Hamm. She had been sick to her stomach when that happened. Now, she thought, *If only the law had teeth like that. Then we could send Knight north again, and he could drag them back—or tear them to pieces.*

32

Six Weeks Later

I am an Abolitionist!
Then urge me not to pause;
For joyfully do I enlist
In Freedom's sacred cause:
A nobler strife the world ne'er saw,
The enslaved to disenthral;
I am a soldier for the war,
Whatever may befall!

Ellen sang out strong and loud, as William Wells Brown led 200 souls in song at yet another gathering of abolitionists, this one in Northborough, almost directly west from Boston. She was growing weary of the traveling, never having gone much farther than the plantation for most of her life, but Brown seemed to have an endless supply of energy. In addition to his speaking and writing, he had created a hymnal of antislavery songs, and he began and ended every meeting with hymns. It was like a church service, except Quakers and Mennonites were not ones to shout to the rafters.

I am an Abolitionist!
Oppression's deadly foe;
In God's great strength will I resist,

And lay the monster low;
In God's great name do I demand,
To all be freedom given,
That peace and joy may fill the land,
And songs go up to heaven!

They had been traveling nonstop since the day in Faneuil Hall when Brown first introduced the Georgia Fugitives to New England. The cities rolled by, day after day after day: Salem and Lowell and New Bedford and Springfield and Brookfield and on and on. The meetings followed the same pattern—antislavery songs followed by speeches followed by resolutions followed by more speeches. William did all of the speaking for them because women did not ordinarily talk in public, and that was fine with her. She was still getting used to all of the attention from New Englanders who had never laid eyes on an escaped female before, let alone a "white slave." Everyone wanted to shake her hand and give her a good looking over. Although the attention was becoming routine, it was quite another thing to step in front of a large crowd and speak. That she could do without.

William was taking questions from the audience when an older woman stood and seemed to be hunting Ellen with her eyes. When her gaze landed on Ellen, the woman spoke. "Would you be so kind, Mister Craft, as to allow us to address your wife directly?"

Ellen's heart dropped. *No, no, no.*

A murmur ran through the crowd, and Ellen was horrified to realize that people were muttering their approval of the woman's suggestion. Her mind raced and she tried to think of a way to graciously decline. William beamed down on her and motioned for her to join him on the stage. She slowly shook her head, but Brown was by her side the next instant, helping her to her feet. She made the death march up the stairs to the platform feeling as if she was being led to the gallows. What could she possibly say to these people?

"My wife has not prepared a statement of any sort, but I am sure she would be glad to answer any questions you might have of her."

You don't know your wife very well then, Ellen thought, giving William the evil eye, but there was no backing off. If she could impersonate a white planter for 4 days, surely she could impersonate a public speaker for the next half hour. This was what she told herself, but she didn't believe a word of it. These were educated people, white people, and they wanted to learn from her?

The first woman's question was how she managed to disguise her voice to sound like a man. Ellen stammered her response.

"I tried...I tried to talk with a deep voice." *What kind of answer is that, woman? Of course, you tried to speak with a deep voice!* She followed this response with a strained smile, but she felt like it was a stupid grin, so she became serious. "I practiced with William, and he suggested...well, he suggested I try not to do too much talking."

This triggered laughter, which shocked Ellen, and she wondered if she had said something foolish, but the expressions on people's faces seemed genuinely friendly. She wondered if that was enough of an answer to satisfy the woman; then she remembered how she pretended to be deaf on the train, so she related the incident when Mister Cray kept trying to draw her into conversation. This drew a murmur of approval and amusement.

The initial shock of talking before a crowd wore off, and she tried to pretend she was speaking to one person at a time. Three questions later, she could almost say it was enjoyable. People paused to clap on two occasions, and both times she wasn't even sure what she had said that triggered such a response.

Then a young woman toward the back of the room stood up and called out her question. "Do you think your mother and cousins back in Macon know you are safe?"

Ellen was slow in responding. "One of the reasons we were willing to give our names in public was so word would get back to my mother, and she would know we were all right," she began. She paused as it slowly dawned on her. A stranger in the audience might be able to guess that she had left a mother back in Macon, but how did this woman know she had cousins there? Ellen stared hard at the figure of the woman at the back of the room. The woman took a few steps closer, and she came into the light. She was smiling. She was Ellen's age, and she was the prettiest person Ellen knew.

"Mary?"

"It is."

Suddenly, Ellen didn't care how she came across in public. Mister Brown leaned over and asked, under his breath, if she knew this woman, but she didn't bother to answer. She hurried down the steps of the platform, and she kept repeating the same words over and over. "My Lord, my Lord, my Lord, my Lord, my Lord!"

She threw herself into Mary's embrace, and they both became a mess of tears and sobs. "Lord, Lord, Lord, it's true. But how? How?"

Mary didn't answer because she was too choked up by tears, so they hugged again, and Ellen breathed in the perfume that her cousin always wore—a perfume she had always envied, but now she loved the scent for all the memories it brought back.

As they continued to embrace, Ellen heard Mister Brown's powerful voice speak out from the stage. "Mister Craft has informed me that the lady whom Missus Craft is embracing is her cousin. They haven't seen each other since the day Mister and Missus Craft left Macon."

At first, the audience didn't seem to know how to respond to such news, but a few moments later there was applause and whistling. Then Ellen spotted Frank, just a few steps behind Mary, and she couldn't help herself. She hugged Frank, and the tears erupted once again. The encore embrace was greeted by another wave of applause.

*****

"But how did you come to be here?" Ellen asked. The meeting had dispersed for the evening, and the two cousins found a moment to talk, while William and Frank conferred on the other side of the meeting hall. Mary and Ellen sat on a bench at the back of the room.

"It started with what happened to Father. Did you hear what befell him?"

Ellen shook her head. Tears pooled in Mary's eyes, and Ellen took her by the hand. She had a hunch what was coming.

"Papa was killed. Shot down on the street by a drunk."

This was what Ellen had always feared for Mister Slator. "I am so sorry."

Mary had difficulty continuing. "But the drunk didn't do it because Papa was white and Mama was black. Mister Slator...Papa... he was trying to protect her. The man had accosted her right on the street."

Mary launched into a retelling of everything—what had happened after Mister Slator had died, how their house had been taken, and how the family had been split apart. She also told how Simon Slator's wagon had broken apart on the road, how they had purchased a buggy in a small town, and how they had raced to Savannah and boarded a steamboat for New York before Slator and his men could track them down.

By the time Mary reached this point of the story, she had regained her composure and even gave Ellen a mischievous grin. "We passed ourselves off as white people."

Ellen cocked her head and laughed lightly, and the cousins embraced again. "I suppose it runs in the family."

"When we reached New York, we heard about the famous 'Georgia fugitives.' Imagine our excitement when we discovered that their names were William and Ellen Craft."

"You heard about us in New York?" Ellen was incredulous.

"Yes. It was in the newspapers. I even heard people talk about it on an omnibus."

Ellen took both of Mary's hands in hers. "I am so happy you are here. You must come and stay with us in Boston. I'm trying to convince William and Mister Brown to let us remain in one place for awhile, so we're not moving around day after day. You and Frank can live with us."

Mary sat up straight and looked surprised by the invitation. Then a slight smile tugged at her lips. "I would love to come to Boston, but there is something holding me in New York."

Ellen was still learning to read, but she had no had trouble reading between the lines of her cousin's sentence. "A man?"

A nod of the head and another mischievous grin. "He's a white man."

"But isn't that...?"

"It's all right because people see me as white. They think I am Mediterranean. But to be honest, I am so confused, I don't know what I am anymore."

"Does it matter?"

The cousins went silent, and Ellen felt old jealousies creep back over her. Mary was going to pass herself off as a white woman courting a white man. So why did Ellen feel a sense of betrayal? Did she think that Mary was taking the easy way? Why should she expect her cousin to choose the more difficult life?

"Does he know?"

"About my mother being a slave? Yes, he knows."

"And he accepts that?"

"He does. He even agreed to perform the ceremony with me."

"You mean marriage?" Ellen asked.

"No, no, we are not even betrothed—yet. But remember the ceremony that my father and mother performed—what we saw that night?"

The image returned: Mister Slator cutting Aunt Molly's hand, releasing a rivulet of blood, and putting it to his mouth. How could she forget?

"You mean the exchange of blood?"

"My intended, Jonathan, he has my blood. One drop makes us one blood."

"You cut your skin?" It was a nonsensical question. How else could it be done?

"Just a few drops mixed with wine. We shared the cup."

"Have you told anyone about this?"

"You're the first."

Ellen took Mary's hand. "You should keep it that way, for I want you to be safe, and being discovered as a mulatto married to a white man could be hard."

It could be as difficult as a "white Negro" married to a black man.

Ellen placed her other hand on top of Mary's. Their skin tone was almost the same, although Mary's was a little browner. "I'm black and you're white," Ellen said. She smiled. "Can't you tell from looking at us?"

They stared at their hands, and then simultaneously looked up and their eyes locked. They broke out laughing.

33

Boston
October 4, 1850: One and a Half Years Later

WHEN ELLEN AND WILLIAM ARRIVED AT FIRST AFRICAN
Baptist Church—or the African Meeting House, as it was
called—they found a mob outside. News had just reached
Boston about the capture of James Hamlet, an escaped
slave in New York, triggering an epidemic of panic across the black
community. There were more than 200 escaped slaves in Boston, and
each one feared being the next victim. In that way, it reminded her
of the fear of the mystery illness that moved from house to house
last year, except the source of this new fear was no mystery at all. It
was the result of a few simple ink marks on paper when President
Fillmore signed the new Fugitive Slave Law.

The African Meeting House was a three-story blocky brick building on Smith Court, just down from Belknap Street. William and
Ellen fought their way inside, but every seat was filled. Most in at-
tendance were black, although several prominent white abolitionists
stood out. Among them, Ellen spotted William Lloyd Garrison, the
bespectacled publisher of *The Liberator*.

She and William stood toward the back of the room, well beyond
the curving, light-brown benches facing the narrow pulpit. A white
railing formed a half-circle in front of the pulpit, like the bow of a

ship, and their friend Lewis Hayden stood at the podium, calling for calm. He might as well ask a storm to settle down, settle down.

"Mister and Missus Craft, whatya plan to do?" asked a voice to their right. Ellen turned and saw one of their neighbors on Southac Street—Henry Brown, no relation to William Wells Brown. Henry had made an equally bold escape just 3 months after them.

"We ain't movin' north, that's for sure. We're gonna fight it out, if we need to," said William.

Ellen didn't realize they had made any such decision. Henry Brown smiled and nodded, and Ellen felt angry that William would make such a decision on his own. She was also angry because they had been trying to have children, at long last, and now this. How could they have a child when they could be snatched back to slavery at any moment?

The Fugitive Slave Law made the threat real. The earlier version of the law said southerners could retrieve escaped slaves from any state, but there had been no real threat because northern authorities rarely cooperated in the hunting down of runaways. The new law remedied that. It *required* police officers in the North to arrest any suspected runaways, and they could be hit with a $2,000 fine if they refused. Any citizen who dared to help a runaway slave could be similarly crushed by jail time and a big fine. As if that wasn't bad enough, a northern black accused of being an escaped slave would not be given a trial by jury and couldn't even testify.

We were sitting ducks, Ellen thought, bringing up the image of the hunter blasting away at sleeping ducks on the water at night. But there was one big difference: Blacks in the city of Boston were not going to be caught sleeping.

When the room finally settled, Lewis began by denouncing the new Fugitive Slave Law and explaining that the stories about James Hamlet were true. This former slave had been nabbed on the streets of New York and sent back to the slave states—all in a matter of hours. The threat seemed so sudden and arbitrary, but that's what made it so frightening.

"And the winepress was trodden without the city, and blood came out of the winepress, even unto the horse bridles, by the space of a thousand and six hundred furlongs!" declared Reverend Monk, standing up in the crowd and reciting from the Book of Revelation. "America is sleeping on a volcano, and we will erupt if these pirates come to steal our lives!"

Joshua Smith leaped to his feet and declared in a booming voice that he had lived long enough, and if he couldn't be a free man in Boston, he would die fighting. Then he pulled out a knife and waved it in the air and encouraged everyone in the room to buy Colt revolvers.

Ellen's eyes drifted down to William's waist, where his revolver was strapped. He had purchased the gun on September 19, the very day after Congress had passed the law. He used what little money they had saved up from her seamstress work and his job at the secondhand furniture store on Federal Street. William never could land a job as a cabinetmaker, because he and other blacks had been barred from skilled trades by Boston whites. They lived with Lewis and Harriet Hayden on Southac Street, but she wondered whether they should move on further north to Canada, as many families had already chosen to do in the wake of the new law. People were calling it a reign of terror.

"Shouldn't we consider Canada?" she said to William later that night as she readied for bed. She trimmed the wick of a tallow candle before lighting it and using it to guide them to their bedroom. It was a sputtering old candle, and it gave out a slightly foul smell.

"You know I can't leave now," William said.

William had just been made vice president of the League of Freedom, and Lewis Hayden had been made president of the new organization, formed this night to resist the Fugitive Slave Law.

"But we could have a child once we reach Canada," she said. "A free child."

"And if they pass a law allowing slave hunters into Canada to snatch us back, what then? Do we keep runnin' to the top of the world until we run outta space? I'm done runnin.'"

Ellen set the candle on the table beside the bed. The floorboards were cold under her feet, so she quickly climbed under the covers. "But we're so well known as escaped slaves, William. We'll be prime targets."

"Our notoriety will protect us. Slave hunters will go for someone lesser known. Trust me."

She wished she could trust his judgment, but William didn't know what Dr. Collins might do—or John Knight. The dreams had returned, the ones in which she is in a field giving birth, blood everywhere, only this time an entire mob of white folks is gathered all around her, waiting to steal away the child once it is born. She had prayed that they could have had a child by now, but the Lord hadn't blessed them with one, and she had become angry at God for her barrenness. Now she knew the reason for it all. The Lord can look down the path of time as easily as a person can look across a field. He had seen this law coming, and she knew now that it was good they had remained childless. She wished so much they could pack up and move to Canada this very evening. She wanted a child, not a fight.

"We gotta stop this now, on the streets of Boston—even if it means dyin'," William said.

"Don't say that!" Ellen shouted, and her anger took William by surprise, from the look on his face.

She was afraid of losing William, in part because of the dreams. When she had had one of the nightmares last week, she woke drenched in sweat and overwhelmed by the sudden realization that in all of her dreams about the birth, never once did she see William's face. He was gone.

Macon

John Knight felt a comforting sense of satisfaction whenever he entered the Collins house. Although this had been the scene of his greatest humiliation—his embarrassing and inadvertent court-ship of a slave woman—the irony was that the woman's escape had reestablished his footing in both the Collins house and the Macon community. After all, he had been right all along. He had suspected the Crafts were on the run, and no one had believed him. Now he had been proven correct, and everyone knew it. He made sure that those who didn't know of his Great Hunch, as he described it, soon learned of it.

He leaned back in the large chair in Dr. Collins' library, surrounded by floor-to-ceiling bookshelves on all sides. Knight had taken to smoking a pipe, and he puffed away contentedly, imagining that this was his own personal study. He hoped to have one like this some day—once he developed a habit of reading more than one book per year, and once he made his fortune. Seated next to him was Willis Hughes, the Macon jailer who also hadn't seen the urgency in Knight's warnings about William and Ellen Craft two Christmases ago. He too had to eat dirt when news of the Crafts' escape emerged.

"Remember, Mister Knight and Mister Hughes, the element of surprise is crucial," lectured Dr. Collins. "Go to Judge Levi Woodbury and obtain an arrest warrant before you do anything, and try not to let your presence in Boston be known. Then swoop down on William and Ellen Craft before they have a chance to prepare their defenses."

Knight sucked too deeply on the pipe and nearly burst into a coughing fit. He resented Dr. Collins' manner—trying to tell them how to do their job. If Collins had believed his story in the first place, the man would not have even found himself in this predicament.

"Are you listening to me?" Dr. Collins said, directing his attention at Knight.

"We both understand, sir," said Hughes. "We know how important surprise is."

Knight didn't answer; he *wouldn't* answer such a condescending question. He just smiled and thought about how Robert Collins' constant coddling of his slaves brought this problem upon his head. But that's a Whig for you. Whigs saw themselves as compromisers, intellectuals, planners, and builders. Knight saw them as weak and muddled. Their political party was unraveling over the issue of slavery, trying to find a compromise that made everyone happy, North and South. Couldn't be done, Knight thought. It was just as useless as

Dr. Collins' attempts to keep his slaves happy with all of these modern notions. Look where that got him.

"If you are asked what you are doing in Boston, what is your cover story?" Dr. Collins asked.

"We're actin' as if we're in Boston for business because we want to establish a bucket factory in Macon," Hughes said.

"It's not just a cover story," Knight said sharply. "I *am* planning on developing a bucket factory."

"You are?" Dr. Collins stared at him as if he couldn't believe he was capable of doing such a thing, as if a monkey had just announced he was building a ladder to heaven.

"Yes. I am developing a factory."

Dr. Collins stared at him for a few moments, sizing him up. "I see. Just don't let your business dealings get in the way of your real job—retrieving the Crafts." He picked up a Boston newspaper, stared at the front page, and then shook it in the air. "The Boston abolitionists are bragging that an escaped slave has never been taken from their streets—ever! Do you hear that?"

Knight had heard the claim, and the Boston mob had to be put in their place. This was something on which he and Dr. Collins could agree.

"One week from now, everyone in Boston will be eating dirt," Knight said.

"I will hold you to that promise." Dr. Collins set down the newspaper, went to his bookshelf, and pulled out a volume. It was his way of saying that the meeting was over. "Just get the job done, and I will pay you handsomely."

On the way out of the door, Knight passed by the lady of the house, and he greeted her with a broad smile and a tip of the hat. "Good day, Missus Collins."

"Good day, Mister Knight," she said coldly. She still didn't seem to like him much, but that would all change when he returned to Macon triumphant with William and Ellen Craft in chains.

34

Boston
Monday, October 21, 1850

OHN KNIGHT WAS HAPPY TO BE OUT AND ABOUT ON THE STREETS of Boston. As he breathed in the fresh morning air, he felt like he had just escaped from prison. It was a cool day, with storm clouds building on the horizon, but at least he was outside.

When he and Willis Hughes had arrived in Boston on Saturday, he had assumed he would live it up on Dr. Collins' expense at the nearest pub, but Hughes would hear nothing of it. He insisted they stay locked up in their room in the United States Hotel, a stylish establishment on Beach Street, just across from the Boston and Worcester Railroad Station.

"If people find out who we are, we're ruined," Hughes had said. "So no leavin' this room till Monday."

"Nonsense! How will anyone know who we are?"

"Because when you open your mouth, words spill out."

Hughes was not a big man, but he was pugnacious and well armed. The man would not hesitate to beat Knight to a pulp if that was the only way he could keep them locked up in their hotel room through the weekend. He was a jailer, after all, and he knew his business.

It had been a long 2 days.

Now it was Monday, at last, and Knight took a carriage north from the hotel to Federal Street, where they had learned from a private detective that William Craft worked at a furniture store. Knight went alone and hadn't even told Hughes what he was up to because he knew his plan might stir the jailer's wrath. He gawked at the enormous, 4- and 5-story buildings rising up on both sides, and he felt as if he was riding through a man-made canyon, hemmed in by these huge white-stone and red-brick buildings. He felt the power and the pulse of the city, and it made him feel powerful as well.

It didn't take him long to find William's furniture restoration shop at 62 Federal Street. Hughes had told him not to let his presence be known until they could descend on his store and make the arrest, but Knight had a much better idea. He would lure William back to their hotel, where it would be easier and safer to make the arrest. He was confident he could work his magic and lure William to the hotel.

He pushed open the door, the bell jangled, and there he was. William Craft had his back to him, and he crouched only about 15 feet away, reattaching the leg on a dark-wood chair. William swung around with a smile on his face.

The smile vanished in an instant.

William Craft hadn't changed a bit. He hadn't even tried to disguise his features in the most basic way by shaving off his beard. His eyes radiated fear, and Knight delighted in his power to make this man feel very much in danger.

"Bill, my friend!" declared Knight, moving within hand-shaking range. He extended his hand, and William just stared at it for a few moments. Then the fugitive took his hand, and they clasped like long-lost friends. Knight beamed back at him, but William did not crack a smile.

Knight surveyed the surroundings. It was a rather dismal shop, nothing like Cubbins' cabinetmaking shop back in Macon.

"I see you are still in the woodworking business, Bill! Good for you."

William seemed disarmed by his jovial approach, but that was his plan. "How is the cabinet shop in Macon?" William finally said. Making conversation clearly pained the man.

"I am still working at the shop," Knight said. "But I have plans, big plans to start my own business. I would like to create a bucket factory."

William glanced toward a door leading into a back room. Was he checking his options for escape? Most likely. Knight needed to reassure him, to get on his side.

"I figure I couldn't go wrong with buckets, Bill. People are always gonna need 'em, and nothin' will ever replace the simple, standard bucket for luggin' water or milk or whatnot. A bucket is a thing a' beauty, and watertight wood is a marvel. Nothing gets out of a well-made bucket. Not a single solitary drop escapes."

William seemed to be getting increasingly alarmed as he spoke, and Knight realized that it probably was not wise to talk about how buckets let nothing escape. William probably thought he was sending a message: Macon was a watertight bucket.

Change the subject, quickly.

Knight found a chair that wasn't broken and tested its sturdiness before settling down. "I just arrived in Boston, and I would love to see the sights. Would you be able to show me around, Bill?"

"I would if I could, sir." William motioned toward the chair he was working on. "But as you can see, I have considerable work before me."

"You always were a conscientious worker. Always admired that about you, Bill. But it will only take a few hours."

For the first time since Knight had stepped through the door, William smiled. It was a forced smile, but a smile nonetheless.

"I wish I could, sir. It would be a real treat showin' you 'round, but customers call." William leaned against his workbench and wiped his hands with a rag. "Did you come alone to Boston, Mister Knight?"

"Oh, yes. That's why I was hopin' for some company."

William didn't respond. He continued to wipe his hands with the rag, working between his fingers.

"Here's an idea then," said Knight. "Why don't you come to the United States Hotel on Beach Street, and I can take a letter back to Macon with me. Would your wife like to send any word back to her mama? Her mama speaks of her often, and I am sure she would like to know how ya'll are doin'."

Surely, William Craft could not resist this idea.

"That is most generous of you, Mister Knight."

"So you'll come to the United States Hotel?"

"Let me talk to my wife about such a letter, and we will be in contact."

He had him. He knew the letter would lure him in.

"Come to the hotel later today, and I will make sure I hand-deliver it to Missus Craft's mama myself."

"Thank you kindly."

Knight stood up and shot out his hand. Once again, William stared at the hand as if he was holding a gun. William eventually shook, but Knight noticed that his palm was moist with sweat. Wiping his hand on his shirt, Knight headed for the door.

"And if you change your mind 'bout that tour of Boston, let me know, Bill!"

"I will."

*****

There was no way that William was going within eight blocks of that hotel. He wasn't a fool. As soon as Knight was out of the shop, William barged out the door and ran all of the way to Southac Street, where they had been lodging with their friends Lewis and Harriet Hayden. He found Lewis at his kitchen table reading a copy of *The Liberator*. His gun sat within reach on the table, just beside a chunk of bread.

William was talking even before he had completely entered the kitchen. "John Knight is in Boston!"

Lewis didn't startle easily, but William could see the shock in his eyes. Lewis set down the newspaper carefully and ran his hand across the table. He sighed, as if drawing himself together for a day that he knew would eventually come. "Where did you see him?"

"He came into my store, invited me to give him a tour of Boston."

Lewis laughed. "A tour of Boston? And he thought you would agree to such a preposterous plan? The man is outta his mind!"

"Evidently. He then suggested I come to the United States Hotel and give him a letter for him to take back to Ellen's mama."

"If he's at the United States Hotel, we'll send someone there to talk with the porter, get information on whether he's in the city alone."

"I asked him if he came with anyone and he denied it, of course. But we need to get Ellen to a safe place."

"Where is she now?" Lewis asked.

"Workin' at Reverend Gray's house on Mount Vernon Street."

"We will send word to her immediately and move her to a place of safety. In the meantime, we gather our lawyers."

"Lawyers? We need guns, not lawyers."

"We need both. And we'll use both, if we need to. But we start with lawyers."

William rubbed his eyes, and he noticed that his right hand was shaking. The reality was setting in. He could very well become the James Hamlet of Boston, with police breaking down this door, putting him in chains, and throwing him into a boat back to the South—all within a matter of hours.

Lewis must have noticed his distress, because his friend came around the table and put a hand on his shoulder. "They aren't taking you, William. They will have to march through a hundred men to get to you."

"I'm more worried 'bout Ellen. She couldn't take goin' back to Macon a slave again."

"They will have to march through *300* men to get to her."

*****

"A good upholsterer is like a good sculptor, giving shape and substance to a chair or a couch," Miss Dean told Ellen. "She is also a good painter, selecting the right colors and right textures. And she is a good craftsman, combining all of the elements into one beautiful piece of furniture."

Ellen had been working as a seamstress since they arrived in Boston, but to ease the financial burdens she thought she would learn the craft of upholstering. It would be the ideal complement to William's struggling furniture repair store.

The furniture in Reverend Gray's home was exquisite, and Miss Dean explained how to get your stitching to follow the curves and whirls of the wood. She was just beginning to tell her how to distribute the horsehair stuffing evenly when a middle-aged white woman, Missus George Hilliard, entered the room, escorted by one of the maids. She seemed agitated, strangely out of breath.

They exchanged greetings and formalities, and Miss Dean and Ellen stared at her, waiting for her to explain the sudden appearance. Missus Hilliard was a lady of high standing, the wife of a U.S. commissioner, and she was a lady of high style, wearing a white crepe hat topped by ostrich feathers and white damask roses encircling the wide brim. She was also an active abolitionist. Ellen had heard that her home was tied into a network of secret passages to convey slaves throughout the neighborhoods whenever slave catchers were reported in the city.

Missus Hilliard may have hidden slaves, but she wasn't very good at hiding her emotions. Ellen could tell that something was upsetting her.

"I...I was wondering, Ellen, if perhaps you would come to our house because we have some important seamstress work for you to do."

Miss Dean and Ellen exchanged looks. Missus Hilliard had come running in, as if the city was on fire, and all she wanted was to hire her out for some seamstress work? Something didn't add up here.

"I am just now teaching Missus Craft how to stuff a chair properly," Miss Dean said.

Missus Hilliard ran her hand across the back of a chair. "But this is...this is quite urgent, Missus Craft."

Missus Hilliard couldn't maintain her gaze, and her eyes drifted to the floor. She was not a very good liar.

"Has something happened to my husband?"

"Oh no, dear, he is perfectly safe. But..."

Missus Hilliard tossed away any pretense of normalcy.

"But there are believed to be slave catchers in the city. One by the name of John Knight."

Stunned, mouth gaping, Ellen slowly lowered herself into one of the plump-cushioned chairs.

"We must get you to our house—immediately," Missus Hilliard said. "They won't dare come to our residence."

Ellen reached out and took her hand. "Oh no, Missus Hilliard, I cannot put you and your husband in such a position."

She was well aware of the penalty for harboring a slave under the new law—6 months in prison and a $2,000 fine. She could never ask her friend to do such a thing.

"Nonsense. I have already talked with Mister Hilliard, and he insists you come to our home."

"But if he were caught, he would have to resign his position."

Ironically, she thought, U.S. commissioners like Mister Hilliard would be the ones issuing warrants for the arrest of escaped southern slaves under the new law. Hiding out in the Hilliards' house would be like hiding from wolves in a wolf den. Who would think of looking there?

"We will not be caught. We have sheltered escapees before you, and we will do it again after you are safe. Please. You must come now because time is of the essence."

Ellen searched the woman's eyes, trying to determine if she was hiding even more information. "Why? Has Mister Knight already obtained a warrant for our arrest?"

"They have tried, but Judge Woodbury denied them. But they haven't given up."

"*They?* John Knight is not alone?"

"Knight is staying at the United States Hotel, and our spies at the hotel say he is accompanied by a man by the name of Hughes."

"Willis Hughes?"

"Yes. I think so."

"He is the Macon jailer."

"Please, Missus Craft. There is no time to lose."

"Will William be with me at your house?" Suddenly, she felt an overwhelming need to be with her husband.

"He is barricaded in the store, guarded by a dozen men. He is safe."

"But will he be coming to me—to your house?"

"He does not want to put you in jeopardy. He thinks they will come to wherever he is."

"But I'm already in jeopardy, and I want to be with my husband. I don't want to be alone when I am caught."

"We won't let you get caught. Your husband knows what is safest, and he believes that his presence would put you in greater danger. He wants to lure them away from you."

"But I need to be with him. Why can't I be with him?"

This time, Missus Hilliard didn't bother answering. There was no good answer, as far as Ellen saw it. Still, she would go along with the plan, and she would go into hiding. Missus Hilliard helped her to her feet, and they exited through the back door.

35

Saturday, October 26, 1850

OHN KNIGHT AND WILLIS HUGHES WERE NO LONGER CLOAKED in anonymity—or so it seemed. As they moved down the street, Knight sensed eyes moving in their direction. People stared. Some glared. He wondered if it was all his imagination because these Bostonians couldn't possibly know who they were. He and Hughes moved past a bakery, and a black man leaned out his head and watched them walk by. He looked at them as if they were invaders from a foreign country, displaying the uniform of a hostile occupation. It didn't make sense. For the past few days, they had been trying to obtain an arrest warrant, so word had leaked out about their presence. What's more, William had probably spread the word about his appearance at the furniture store, but that didn't explain how they could be picked out of a crowd in a city of over 100,000 people.

They had been turned down for an arrest warrant by Judge Levi Woodbury, who sent them to the U.S. Attorney George Lunt, who said he was too busy and sent them to U.S. Commissioner Benjamin Hallett, who turned them down cold. Hughes was ready to shoot somebody until "the Colonel" stepped in—a lawyer named Seth J. Thomas. With his help, they were finally able to wrestle an arrest warrant from George T. Curtis, another U.S. commissioner. That was Friday. It was now Saturday, and they were heading to the marshal's office to find several officers to back up the warrant and arrest the Crafts.

Knight noticed a white man and a black man walking on the opposite side of the street, whispering to each other and glancing over at them. He thought the men had been following them for a couple of blocks. Or was he just being paranoid?

Two buildings down, in front of a cigar shop, a black man swept the sidewalk. He stopped sweeping to watch them pass. As they moved beyond the man, they heard a single word leak out, almost a whisper: "Bloodhounds."

Hughes stopped and turned and glared. "What did you just say?"

The black man stopped sweeping and craned his neck around, as if he thought Hughes was addressing someone standing behind him.

"I'm talkin' to you, boy. What did you just say to me?"

The black man shrugged and said nothing. The door to the cigar shop opened, and two more black men stepped out. One was large, well over 6 feet tall. Hughes was a tough bulldog, but Knight didn't like the idea of tangling with a tree.

"Some problem here?" asked the big fellow.

"This boy here called me an insulting name." Hughes jerked a thumb in the direction of the guy with the broom.

The big fellow had a rag in his hands, and he wiped them clean. "What he call you? Slave catcher?"

Hughes didn't answer, just scowled. Again, the question moved through Knight's mind: How did these people know who they were?

"You don't know the first thing about us, boy," Knight said.

"Colored folk ain't deaf and dumb. We have ears and eyes everywhere, so we know *exactly* who you are."

The big man pointed a finger toward a tree rising out of the sidewalk a short distance down the street. A handbill had been nailed to the tree and fluttered in the breeze. Hughes strode over to it, gave it a hard look, and he ripped it off the bark.

"What's it say?" Knight asked.

Hughes shoved the handbill into his mitts, and Knight scoured the words:

SLAVE HUNTERS IN BOSTON!

Below these bold words, he was shocked to read a complete and very accurate description of himself and Hughes, followed by a quotation from Hughes:

"I am a Jailer, and I catch negroes sometimes. I am here for Wm and Ellen Craft and I will have them if I stay till eternity, and if there are not men enough in Massachusetts to take them I will bring them from the South!"

Below this quote were the words:

MEN OF BOSTON!! SHALL THESE VILLAINS REMAIN HERE?

Snatching back the handbill, Hughes ripped it to pieces and tossed it on the sidewalk. The black man wandered over and swept the handbill into a neat little pile, while the big man disappeared into a store.

"Let's go," Knight said, not wanting trouble. He had noticed that the white man and black man across the street had stopped and were staring at them. They were soon joined by two other black men. Knight and Hughes were outnumbered and out-muscled, from the looks of things, but that didn't matter to Hughes. He folded his arms across his chest and stood his ground. The big man reemerged from the cigar store with a hammer in one hand, and Knight nearly lost his nerve and ran. Was the fellow going to break their skulls?

He also noticed that the big man had another handbill in his hand, and he strode up to the tree and nailed a fresh paper to the bark.

SLAVE HUNTERS IN BOSTON! SHALL THESE VILLAINS REMAIN HERE?

Satisfied, the big man stepped aside, folded his arms against his chest, and stared at Hughes. The two men locked eyes, neither backing down.

"C'mon, Hughes, let's keep on walkin'. We got a job to do."

Hughes didn't answer. He continued his stare-down. The men on the other side of the street crossed over. Then Hughes finally broke away from the locked eyes, strolled back to the tree, ripped off the handbill, wadded it up, and tossed it on the ground to be swept up again. Knight's eyes went to the hammer in the large man's hand. Another black man emerged from the cigar store, and he too carried a hammer. He also had a gun strapped to his waist, and in his other hand was a stack of close to a hundred handbills.

"Leave them be," Knight whispered. "We can't spend all day here tearing down handbills."

The big man grinned and silently pointed across the street. Knight followed the pointed finger and spotted two more men, also carrying handbills, posting them to trees and walls up and down the street. Seeing the handbills sprouting up everywhere told him they needed to find the marshal and make this arrest soon, before every single person in Boston knew who they were. He took Hughes by the arm, but the pug shook loose.

"We've got to do this quickly," Knight whispered.

Hughes was stubborn, but he had a practical core, so surely he would see the futility of ripping down handbills, when more would just sprout up in their place. He finally turned, his anger obvious, and they continued down the street, picking up the pace. They passed another six handbills in the next two blocks, and Hughes ripped each one down, tearing them in half before flinging them to the ground.

Four blocks down, they turned right and encountered a group of four men—white men. Knight cringed inside because so far it seemed they were meeting as much hostility from whites as from black men.

"We heard you were coming, and we're here to help," said one of the men, the one carrying a stick of wood with a protruding nail. Finally: allies.

"Thanks," Hughes said, barely batting an eye at them. He maintained his gaze on the marshal's office located just down the street in the courthouse, and he didn't miss a stride. The four men fell into step with them, two on each side like bodyguards.

A small crowd had gathered in front of the courthouse, and Knight's confidence rose even higher when he saw three policemen. At least they had the law on their side, and no amount of harassment could combat the force of the law.

"Are you John Knight and Willis Hughes?" asked one policeman, stepping forward to meet them. He was flanked by a white man in a black frock coat and top hat—perhaps some Boston authority, here to ensure their safety.

"We are," Hughes said, eying them suspiciously.

The policeman exchanged a glance with the man in the top hat, who slowly nodded his head. Then the officer turned back and faced Hughes squarely.

"Mister Hughes and Mister Knight, I am putting you under arrest."

Knight's jaw dropped as the words barreled into him. Even Hughes was struck mute.

"You must be mistaken, sir," Knight said, trying to sound calm. "We have an arrest warrant in hand to pick up Mister and Missus William Craft. Is that who you mean to arrest?"

"No, sir. You are being charged with slandering Mister and Missus Craft."

Hughes came to life. He moved in on the officer, planting himself only 2 feet away. "Slander? What in the world are you talkin' 'bout?"

"Your slander has damaged William Craft's business, Mister Hughes," said the white man—the one in the frock coat and top hat. "You claim that William Craft stole his clothes and stole *himself* from his master."

"He did steal himself," Knight said. "He's not his own property!"

"Shut up, Knight!" Hughes said, before directing his wrath at the man in the top hat. "And who are you?"

"The name is Wilbur Sutton, and I work with the Boston Vigilance Committee."

"Vigilance Committee! Vigilante is more like it!" Hughes lunged at the man, but another officer hooked him under the arms from behind and held him back. Knight was hoping their four "bodyguards" might step in and help, but they had all melted away into the crowd.

Knight was knocked for a loop, and what happened next was a blur of sickening impressions. Bystanders pointing, smiling, calling them bloodhounds, dumb dogs...being led to a carriage and being pushed inside and Hughes ranting and spitting…being strong-armed by three officers. So many curses rang in his ears and a feeling of nausea rippled across his midsection.

Sunday, October 27, 1850

The moment that William walked through the door of Reverend Parker's home on Beacon Hill, Ellen rushed out of the ladies' parlor and into his arms. She hadn't seen him for 4 days, and she was afraid she might never see him again. For all she knew, he had already been killed, but no one had yet worked up the nerve to tell her. In the past week, the city had become armed to the teeth. She had never seen so many swords and guns, and even Reverend Parker kept a sword close at all times.

Hugging William, she couldn't help but notice that he now had a dirk knife strapped to his waist, on the opposite side from his gun.

"You won't leave me again, will you?" she said, still clutching him. William didn't answer.

After spending some time in the Hilliard home, she had been moved to Reverend Parker's home on Beacon Hill, and she assumed that now that the slave hunters were in jail, they could be together again—and remain together. The danger was gone, wasn't it?

"William? You're coming to stay with the Parkers, aren't you?"

"Let's not discuss this now," he said. He pulled apart and led her into the gentlemen's parlor, where a group of men had gathered: Lewis Hayden and Charles Lenox Remond, both black; and Reverend Parker and Wendell Phillips, both white. The men all stood when she entered the room, and she wondered if they expected her to occupy herself with Reverend Parker's wife Lydia while they talked strategy. But Mister Remond cleared his throat and motioned toward two open chairs.

"Please have a seat," he said, smiling. Mister Remond, a tall, thin man, had a shock of hair that shot up straight from his head. The hair sloped down on one side, but the other side was cut sharply, like the sheer face of a cliff.

Reverend Parker started the meeting by reviewing the arrest of Willis Hughes and John Knight. Ellen had felt such relief when she heard the news, but the men were talking as if the arrest hadn't ended the matter.

"We believe that Hughes and Knight will be released on bail tomorrow," Reverend Parker said, sending shock waves through Ellen. Reverend Parker glanced at her, his brow furrowing, as if gauging the impact of this news.

"Who is posting bail?" asked Mister Redmon.

"We do not know, but it might be Watson Freedman," said Lewis. "He has been calling the arrest of Hughes and Knight a humbug, a sham."

"What's a man like that doing with a name like Freedman?" wondered Reverend Parker.

"It could also be John Pearsons posting bail," said Mister Phillips.

Like Redmon, Phillips had a long, narrow face, but not the same startling tower of hair. In fact, his light hair was making an active retreat, leaving most of his hair on the sides of his head as sideburns. Parker was bald as well, even more so with the top of his head completely devoid of hair.

"What do you recommend as our next move?" asked William. "We might be triggering a war here."

"Sometimes I wonder if a war is just what we need," said Reverend Parker.

That sobering thought brought down a curtain of silence.

"We do have some legal maneuvering at our disposal," said Mister Redmon.

"Such as?" William asked.

"We could have you arrested," Reverend Parker said softly, almost as if he was afraid to let out the words. When William laughed, Reverend Parker added, "I am serious, William."

Ellen wanted to speak, but held her words. *Was Reverend Parker insane? Have us arrested? That is exactly what we are trying to avoid!*

"Our lawyers say that if you are arrested and taken prisoners of Massachusetts, then you cannot be removed from the state."

"What good is that? Either way we will be prisoners," William said.

"Once the slave catchers are gone, state charges will be dropped, and you will be free again."

"I don't understand," William said. "We have done nothing wrong. Are you asking us to commit a crime just so we could be arrested by state authorities?"

Reverend Parker rubbed his hands together, and Ellen noticed a blush creep across his face. Even his smooth-domed head had reddened with embarrassment. "Well...that is just the thing, William. Technically, not morally, you have already broken a law and you could be arrested."

Ellen was baffled. They had broken no laws, except for the Fugitive Slave Law. What was the man talking about?

Reverend Parker continued, treading carefully. "Technically, you and Missus Craft...well, how shall I put this? Technically, you and Missus Craft are not legally married."

It took a moment for the words to sink in, but when they did, it was Ellen's turn to blush. They wanted to arrest them for being in a sinful relationship!

"But we were married by a minister," William said, with an edge to his voice.

"I know, I know. That is why I say you are on solid ground in the eyes of God. But in the eyes of Massachusetts, a slave wedding is not legal."

"I will not have my wife arrested for any reason, but especially not that one," William said. "Absolutely not. That is not an option."

"Even if it means keeping you from being arrested for breaking the Fugitive Slave Law and sent back south?"

"I am proud to have broken the Fugitive Slave Law. That is man's law, not God's. But I would not be proud of breakin' the Lord's laws."

"But you haven't broken the Lord's laws," said Lewis. "You have only broken Massachusetts law."

Ellen stared in shock at Lewis. She could not believe their good friend was in agreement with this horrible scheme.

"That is not how it would seem to our friends—and our family," Ellen said, finally speaking up. She shuddered at the thought of her mother hearing about how they had been arrested for such a crime. The southern papers would play it up for all its worth, and word would reach Mama.

"It may be our best option," said Lewis. "Our only option."

"We can fight," William said. "People are ready. People are armed."

"Actually, there is another option," said Mister Phillips. "We can argue that the Fugitive Slave Law is a civil case, not a criminal one. If it's a civil case, authorities are not allowed to break down the outer door of a house to arrest you."

"Will that distinction be recognized and obeyed by authorities?" asked Reverend Parker.

"It's unlikely," said Mister Redmon. "We have a few policemen on our side, but most of them are willing to enforce the Fugitive Slave Law, even if means breaking down some doors."

"Then we use our guns and swords," said William.

Ellen didn't understand William's attitude. Her husband seemed to be spoiling for a fight.

*****

Daniel Webster, the Massachusetts statesman who had crafted the Fugitive Slave Law, pointed a gun at Ellen's head. She was sitting in a wooden chair in the middle of Reverend Parker's parlor, and Webster pressed the barrel of the gun against her temple. She felt the steel dig into her scalp. She looked up at Webster, and was terrified by his deep-set eyes, like a skull with only the thinnest skin, not completely concealing the bones below.

"I am not a Massachusetts man," he said to her. "I am not a northern man. I am an American, and I will preserve the Union over your dead body."

Then he pulled the trigger.

Ellen woke up sweating. It took a few moments for reality to settle on her, for the dream had seemed so vivid. She was still in Reverend

Parker's home, sleeping in a bed—alone. William had gone back to Lewis Hayden's house, and everyone had insisted that she remain safely tucked away in the Parker residence.

She sat up in bed, feeling alert and tuned in to every sound. She listened to the wind and other night sounds—a dog in the distance, the creaking of the foundation. Then she lay back down, afraid to go back to sleep. It reminded her of the nights sleeping on a pallet outside Miss Eliza's bedroom door. She was separate and alone.

36

Monday, October 28, 1850

JOHN KNIGHT WONDERED IF THEY MIGHT BE SAFER STAYING locked up inside the Leverett Street Jail. They were now at the courthouse, where bail had been posted, and he could hear shouting outside—angry shouting. He and Hughes were being led out a back exit from the courthouse, a long rectangular brick fortress.

"For your own safety," said the young day policeman leading them down the long, echoing hallway.

Knight was all for safety, but Hughes came to a standstill when he realized where the officer was taking them. Hughes looked like a bull pawing the sod.

"I ain't goin' out no back door," he insisted, lacing his language with the foulest possible words. He had been sputtering curses nearly nonstop for 2 days.

"Be reasonable, Mister Hughes," said the policeman.

He stood his ground. "We ain't sneakin' thieves. We're goin' out the front door!"

The officer sighed. "Listen, Mister Hughes, there is a mob out in front of the courthouse, maybe a thousand people. You don't want to walk into that."

Knight's heart was suddenly in his throat. "A thousand? Are the people for or against us?"

DOUG PETERSON

The officer turned and stared at him for a few moments, as if he had never heard such a fool question. "Most of 'em are coloreds, so going out the back is for your own well-being."

Hughes spit his words back at the officer. "It's your job to ensure our safety, whether we choose to go out the front door or the back! We're free American citizens!"

"Don't be a fool. Most of us officers are on your side, so you need to listen to us and let us take you out the back."

"I'm goin' out the front, I tell ya!"

"Willis, stop and think a moment," said Knight. He wasn't about to risk his neck for the principle of going out whatever door they choose. "We're here to arrest William and Ellen Craft. If we go out the front door, the mob might prevent us from doing that job."

The mob might also prevent us from ever walking again, but he didn't say that.

"Sir, your friend is right," said the policeman.

Hughes's face had turned blood red. "I ain't a second-class citizen!"

"No one says you are. We sometimes have to follow this same procedure for the safety of certain dignitaries."

There, Knight thought. *We're like dignitaries.* But Hughes didn't buy the argument. He stared back at the officer as if he were the devil himself.

"Please, Mister Hughes, be reasonable," said another officer, an older man who joined them. He carried the weapon of choice among Boston policemen—a long stick, painted blue and white. It could be used for knocking people on the head, and it was good for holding back crowds. Today, both functions would probably come in handy.

"There ain't a thousand souls out there," Hughes said, making his way for the front door. "You're just tryin' to put the fear a' God in us. But I ain't afraid and neither is Mister Knight." With those words, Hughes strode toward the front door, and Knight just watched him go, too terrified to budge. He felt light-headed and a little nauseous.

"You still want to go out the back, sir?" an officer asked him.

Too late for that. Knight was determined to stick with Hughes, so he headed for the front door and together they stepped out into the glare of day. The roar of the crowd was like a physical force, hitting them in the chest and overwhelming every sense. Boston had about 50 day officers, plus night watchmen, and much of the force appeared to be here, holding back the crowd with their long blue-and-white sticks. Although most in the crowd were black, there must have been some people on their side because men were shouting in each other's faces and shoving each other. It was a roiling riot of a mob. Knight remained rooted at the top of the stone steps flanked by thick pillars on each side; too terrified to take another step forward, he sidled behind a pillar, but Hughes plunged into the frenzy, almost as if he delighted in the threats and anger pouring down on him. The man smiled back at the crowd, soaking up their taunts.

"Slave hunters, go home!"

"Bloodhounds!"

"Apes!"

The policemen cleared a path to the awaiting carriage, which had been brought around from the back, and Hughes took his time strolling toward the vehicle. The two horses pulling the carriage stamped and snorted, their eyes ablaze with fear, but Hughes was calm. He even waved at the crowd, as if mocking them. This riled the mob even more, and someone threw a tomato, hitting one of the policemen instead of Hughes. Knight still hadn't left the protection of the pillars, and a young officer stood at the bottom of the steps shouting up at him to hurry. Within a few moments, Hughes had reached the carriage, and he was looking back at him and shouting. Knight had no idea what he was saying; the noise was too great.

Just run, just run, he told himself. *Get it over with!* With an officer on either side, Knight bolted forward. Hughes was still standing by the carriage, waiting for him, the fool! He was almost daring the crowd to do something violent.

One moment later, someone took him up on the dare. Knight saw it all unfold, as if time had slowed. A white man with a long beard down to his chest extended a hand, and in his hand was a revolver; his arm was fully extended. The gun was aimed directly at the side of Hughes's head. Hughes continued to stand at the open door of the carriage and bellow back at Knight, oblivious to the gun so close. There were screams, and then another white man sprang into action, grabbing the shooter's right arm and pushing it up to the sky as the gun went off, causing Hughes to flinch and duck. For the first time, Hughes looked genuinely afraid, and he scrambled inside the carriage before the shooter could try again. Knight was sure he would be next, and someone else's gun might blast half his head away. Who knew how many hands clutched revolvers in this crowd.

There was a terrible scuffle where the shooter had been standing, and it appeared that the attacker was on the ground, being restrained by police. The last thing Knight saw before throwing himself into the carriage was a huge policeman clubbing the shooter.

The carriage took off, and people had to scatter to avoid being trampled. Knight ducked down low, but Hughes stared out at the mob, with the look of defiance. Faces of protesters flashed by on all sides, and a rock hit the back of the carriage.

"Bloodhounds, go home!"

One man in the mob got close enough to smash his hand against the side window, shattering it into a spiderweb of cracked glass, but Hughes didn't even seem to notice or care. When Knight finally had the courage to sit upright, he looked out the back window and noticed that most of the mob had given up, but some split away and kept chasing the carriage down the street. He didn't feel safe until the carriage had raced three blocks down and made a sharp right turn.

"We've got the warrant and we've got the law on our side," Knight said, as if he had to convince himself they were in the right. "We should lay low until it's safe to get an officer to make the arrest."

Hughes didn't answer. The man had a permanent scowl glued to his face.

They reached the United States Hotel, where Knight hoped they could lock themselves in their room until the storm blew over. He was relieved to see only a scattering of people out front, and most of them were occupied with screaming at each other. Some of the people were clearly on their side, and they were arguing with the ones who would like nothing better than to tar and feather them and run them out of town on a rail.

More policemen were on hand, trying to separate the bickering people with their long, blue-and-white sticks. This time, Knight didn't hesitate to get out of the carriage. All of the officers at the courthouse seemed to be on their side, and he assumed the same would be true at the hotel. If he could survive the mob at the courthouse, he figured he could run this small gauntlet, but his path was blocked by one of the policemen. That's when he spotted him—the lawyer in the slick top hat: Wilbur Sutton, the Vigilance Committee member. An officer was at his side, and not a sympathetic policeman from the looks of him.

Knight knew what was coming.

"Mister Knight and Mister Hughes," said the policeman, "I am arresting you for attempting to kidnap William and Ellen Craft."

Before Hughes could throw his fist, another officer clubbed him in the back of the head with his stick. Knight put up his arms, for he would go willingly—even eagerly. Perhaps, he thought, they would be safer back inside a jail cell.

37

Wednesday, October 30, 1850, 10 P.M.

"I HAVE TO BE WITH WILLIAM," ELLEN SAID.

Reverend Parker's wife Lydia reached out and took her hand. They faced each other in the Parkers' library. "Soon you will be together," she said. "Very soon."

"That is what I was told yesterday."

For the past 2 days, the street drama had continued. The bloodhounds, Hughes and Knight, had been released on bail—another large chunk of money put up by a wealthy slavery sympathizer. However, the Vigilance Committee continued to find new and creative ways of arresting the two slave hunters. They had Hughes and Knight detained for spitting and cursing on the streets and later arrested for driving a carriage too fast. The money mounted up, but they were bailed out again and again.

"My husband has convinced the two men that it is in their best interests to leave Boston and return to Georgia," said Lydia.

Reverend Parker had gone to the United States Hotel that morning to talk with Knight and Hughes, and it appeared that the slave hunters finally saw the futility of staying in Boston. Reverend Parker also told them he would not always be there to save their skin. It was Reverend Parker, after all, who had saved Willis Hughes's life on Monday. When a man in the mob was about to blast the Macon jailer in the temple, Reverend Parker had pushed the shooter's hand into the air just in time before Georgia blood could be spilled on Boston cobblestones.

"The slave hunters have returned to Georgia," Lydia said. "So you will be with William soon."

"But if the slave hunters have left, the threat is over," Ellen said. "Why can't I be with William tonight?"

"We must be absolutely certain it is safe," Lydia explained. "We must be patient."

We. Why does she keep saying "we"? I'm the one who has been separated from her husband, her lifeline, for almost a week. I'm the one who has been cooped up in Reverend Parker's library on the third floor.

"Try to sleep, and you will be united with William in no time," Missus Parker said, patting Ellen's hand and departing.

Ellen couldn't help but feel as if she had become a prisoner—a pampered prisoner, but a prisoner nonetheless. She spent her entire day in this library surrounded by books that she couldn't read. She had learned to read a little bit at the Ivens' house, and Missus Parker was starting to give her additional lessons. But the books in Reverend Parker's library were immense and far beyond her powers. Occasionally, she would take a volume from the shelf and page through it, amazed at the sheer number of words that existed, most of which she couldn't even sound out. She busied herself by picking out the scattering of words that she did know—common words like "the" and "God" and "to" and "up."

It was strange. All week she had felt an odd mixture of boredom and terror, and the combination jangled her nerves. She was tired of running and tired of hiding, and she was lonely for William. That night she decided to act. She would sneak out of Reverend Parker's house and make her way to the Hayden home on Southac Street. The two homes were not far apart, one on the south slope of white Beacon Hill and the other on the north slope of black Beacon Hill. But the two homes seemed worlds apart.

The fireplace was going, but it didn't provide much warmth on this chilly night as Ellen snuggled beneath the heavy quilts. She brought them up to her nose and stared into the darkness, listening for sounds downstairs, willing herself to stay awake. Reverend Parker stayed up reading by candlelight after his wife retired to bed, and his habits ran like clockwork. She knew that the house would go dark in an hour's time, so she would bide her time. It could be dangerous out on the streets at night, but at least there were gas lamps to discourage any robbers. She prayed.

At last, the house descended into silence, and she waited to make sure everyone in the home had fallen asleep. Finally, she cast aside the covers and changed into her dress as quietly as possible; then she crept down the stairs and slipped outside. The night was pitch black, except for a few candles still burning in one or two nearby homes. The gas lamps along the streets burned feebly, like dying stars in a dark sky, but they would guide her way. She took off in the direction of the black neighborhoods, dashing along the cobblestone streets and running as fast as possible in a long skirt.

*****

There were six of them. John Knight, Willis Hughes, and four Boston sympathizers, who wanted to do their part to clean the city of escaped slaves. They were well armed. Knight had a pistol, a sword, and a knife, but he hoped he wouldn't have to use them this night. He had never killed a man, and he wondered what it would feel like to push a blade through human flesh and scrape human bone.

Perhaps it would not come to that. Perhaps the abolitionists would give in to the inevitability of the law and hand over William Craft. Hughes had arranged for a wagon, manned by two constables, to meet them at Lewis Hayden's home. Surely, that would convince Craft to come peacefully.

The streets were dark and desolate. They moved north up Belknap Street, which led to Myrtle Street—the southern border of the black slope of Beacon Hill. They passed several houses, where candles were burning and people were carousing and shouting, and then they moved past a stretch of houses as dark and quiet as gravestones. The tenements on both sides of the streets were a far cry from the bow-front windows and ornamental doors and black-iron railings of the luxurious homes of the southern side of Beacon Hill. They passed boardinghouses and bars shut for the night and side streets so narrow that it was a wonder a carriage could pass through. Knight caught a strong whiff of tar from the nearby ropewalk, where workers laid out long strands of material before twisting it into rope for ships.

Hughes led the way. They were heading for Southac Street, where they had heard from police sources that William Craft was holed up. They did not know the whereabouts of Ellen Craft, so they had decided to settle for arresting him alone. Knight had been all for leaving town, but Hughes was one stubborn man. Hughes had come up with the scheme of pretending to leave for Macon. They even boarded the train going south because they knew spies were watching and wondering if they would really leave town. They had put on a convincing show. They had sympathizers with the railroad, and one of their contacts had sneaked them off the train in a cargo box. When word got out that they had fled the city, guards would be lowered, and William Craft would be ripe for the plucking.

No meddling abolitionist lawyers would be around when they showed up at Lewis Hayden's house in the middle of the night. There would be no more arrests on trumped-up charges like slandering the Crafts. No more days in prison waiting to be bailed out. No more mobs. Just snatch him and go.

They moved west on Myrtle Street, but they paused near the intersection of Myrtle and Garden. Footsteps sounded on cobblestones, coming from behind them in the dark—fast-moving footsteps, clicking on stone.

"Quickly, quickly." Hughes motioned their band off of the sidewalk and into a narrow alley squeezed between two buildings. The footsteps were coming closer, moving down Myrtle Street. Had their ruse been found out? Were they being pursued?

Knight and the others kept their eyes on the nearest gas lamp, hoping to catch a glimpse of their pursuer. One of the men was breathing heavily, and his breath smelled of onions. Hughes thumped him in the chest and told him to stop breathing. The man sucked in his breath, and they crouched low, staring out into the darkness.

There! A figure emerged from the darkness for a split second and raced through the small halo of light from the gas lamp. It appeared to be a woman in a cape! But what would a woman be doing out on the streets in the dead of night, unless she was a prostitute? They paused and listened for the sound of someone chasing her, but they heard nothing else except her footsteps as she rounded the corner onto Garden Street.

Knight scratched his head. "You know...I think the woman...I think she looked to me like Ellen Craft."

"You certain?" asked Hughes.

"Not certain. I only got a quick look. But it's possible."

Hughes smiled. "Let's hope then. Maybe we'll be able to catch ourselves *two* Georgia fugitives tonight after all."

Hughes motioned them out of the hiding spot, and they moved carefully the final block down Myrtle before making a right onto Garden Street. They stopped at the intersection and looked north. They heard noises again, the faint sound of shoes on bricks, moving away from them. It was the woman again, only this time she was hobbling, not running. Must have twisted her ankle somehow. She passed through another pool of light from another gas lamp and then was gone, swallowed by the dark. She was moving north as well—toward Southac Street.

When she was a good distance away, their band of six moved forward like midnight pirates. Knight put his hand on the hilt of his sword, which dangled down and thumped against his leg, as if reminding himself it was there.

*****

D.K. Lucas was sure he had heard something outside his window. He always slept with his window open, even on a nippy night. Good for the lungs. D.K. was a black man—a night soil man, whose job was to empty cesspits and dispose of human waste. It was an oddly fitting job for a man like D.K., who kept the cleanest of apartments and fought filth whenever he could. He was even an advocate of dry brushing, in which he brushed his skin regularly to get rid of lice and open the pores of his skin.

Night soil men did their dirty work at night, of course, and D.K. had just finished his work and settled down to sleep when he thought he heard a grunt and a thump outside his window. He leaned out the window and stared down from his second-story room onto the cobblestones below.

"Who's there?"

He had good night vision, being used to working in the deepest pit of the dark, and he leaned over farther—sure that he saw a figure moving on the ground—but it was hard to make out black against black.

It was worth investigating, so he put on his shoes and picked up a gun. With all that had been going on in the city, he was ever conscious of the threat of slave hunters and suspicious of anyone on the streets at night. William Craft lived with the Haydens just around the corner on Southac Street, so the threat was real. He had told Mister Hayden he would keep his eyes peeled at night for human bloodhounds coming into the north side of Beacon Hill to recapture escaped slaves.

Downstairs, he eased open his front door, but only a crack, and he heard voices coming from down the street. Technically, it was now All Hallow's Eve, October 31, but most of the merrymaking and rowdiness would happen later in the evening, not the early morning hours. But maybe someone was getting an early start.

"How far to Southac?"

"A couple blocks. But shut up."

"Is the woman headin' to Southac?"

"Shut up, I said."

A group of men passed by the door, moving shadows. D.K. caught the glint of a sword. It was just as Hayden had feared. Slave hunters. It had to be. Who else would be heading for Southac Street?

D.K. didn't even stop to think it through. He broke for the back door, which emptied into an alley, and he took off running. He was fast, and he knew every shortcut through the neighborhood. He would warn the Haydens, and he was prepared to fight. He was Paul Revere on foot.

38

Thursday, October 31, 1850, 2:30 A.M.

THEY WERE COMING.

Ellen had run most of the way from Reverend Parker's house to Lewis and Harriet Hayden's boardinghouse on Southac Street, tumbling and twisting her ankle along the way. Her ankle throbbed, and her shoulder ached from the fall.

D.K. Lucas, a black man, had just come barging in bearing the bad news. He said that six slave catchers, armed with swords and guns, were approaching, and Ellen was afraid she might have drawn them to this house. William and Lewis began readying the gunpowder, preparing to blow the house sky high—if it came to that. Lewis rolled the first of two kegs of gunpowder out the front door and into the night, while William went to light two torches.

Ellen was beside herself, and she followed William to a back room. "Let's run, William! We got time before they get here."

"I can't leave Lewis here to face them alone."

"But they're not comin' for Lewis. They're comin' for us. If we're gone, they'll leave 'em be."

"D.K., take Ellen out the back," William said, as if he had no patience for her concerns.

"No, I'm stayin' with you!" She was tired of being shoved out of sight. If William was going to be taken, she would be taken with him. If he was going to be killed, she would be killed alongside him.

D.K. put an arm around her and pulled her toward the back kitchen, gently but firmly. At first, Ellen let him do so, but when she craned her neck around, she saw Lewis rolling the second keg of gunpowder out the front door. She tried to break away, for she had to keep William from being a fool of a hero. She came alive in D.K.'s hands, but he clamped down the moment he felt her resist. He was a thin, short man, but his grip was iron.

"Lemme go!" She pounded on D.K.'s chest and even landed a few blows on his face, but the man locked her down even more firmly. He pulled her out a back door and into an alley. She kicked and screamed and thrashed from side to side, and if she could have sunk her teeth in his hand, she would have bitten hard and deep.

Finally, she went limp in his hands, exhausted from the explosion of energy, so sick of it all. Why hadn't she and William left for Canada when they had the chance? What good was blowing yourself up, along with a handful of slave catchers? It wouldn't stop others from coming.

"That's it, Missus Craft, just calm down now," D.K. said. "Everything's gonna be fine now."

D.K. let her collapse into a heap on the alley ground. Everything was not going to be fine now.

*****

William saw them coming. He counted six, just as D.K. reported. He and Lewis stood at the front door with the two kegs of gunpowder concealed behind their backs. Both he and Lewis held pine-tar torches high above their heads and slightly in front of them. They didn't want a single stray spark to get caught in the wind and land on the powder kegs—at least not yet. Not with the holes open at the top of each keg.

The six men moved into view, caught up in the faint glow of the torches, and William was shocked to see that one of them was John Knight and another was Willis Hughes. Knight must have seen the surprise on his face because he grinned like a jack-o-lantern. "Hello, Bill. Didn't expect to see us?"

"Don't blame your spies at the train station," said Hughes. "They saw us board the train; they just didn't see us get off. Now if ya'll come quietly with us, we can end this right now."

"I ain't takin' one step in your direction."

"That's fine," said Hughes. "We're happy to make the first move."

Before Hughes could approach, William and Lewis stepped aside, like two curtains parting on stage, and behind them stood the main attraction—two kegs of black powder—enough to scatter their body parts up and down the street.

Hughes stopped, and Knight backpedaled two steps. William had never seen eyes go so as wide as Knight's, while Hughes kept his gaze steady and strong. With his compact build and short fuse, William couldn't help but picture him as the human counterpart to the kegs of gunpowder.

"You wouldn't blow yourself up just to avoid goin' back to Macon," Hughes said.

When he took one step forward, Lewis lowered his torch closer to the keg. William noticed a spark flick off the end of the torch and land on the ground, only inches from the keg. William's mouth had gone dry, and sweat beaded on his forehead. Would he have the nerve to jam his torch into the keg's opening? Even if he didn't, Lewis probably would. His friend would have no qualms about going out in a blaze of glory.

Hughes hadn't backed up an inch, but he also hadn't come any closer, while Knight and the other four men retreated two more steps.

"Workin' at the cabinet shop can't be all that bad," said Hughes. "I'm sure your wife would prefer to see you in one piece workin' in Macon than scattered all over the front of this nice home, as if someone been hackin' on you with an axe."

It was a disturbing image, William had to admit. Could he put Ellen through this?

"You have a lot more to lose, Mister Hughes," William said. "You have a secure job; you have your freedom. Step closer and all that goes up in fire and smoke."

Hughes tested him. One step closer. Lewis's hands lowered 6 inches—6 inches closer to sending them up in a geyser of flame. William prayed that their human bonfire would go quickly so he wouldn't feel a thing.

Several of the men had receded into the darkness, but William could still see Knight—his eyes, his mouth, his nose, but not much more. He looked like a disembodied ghoulish mask hanging in space, 6 feet above the ground. Hughes stood much closer—too close.

"I'm not leavin' without you, Craft," said Hughes. "I'm a determined man."

"You'll be determined *and* dead if you come any closer," Lewis said.

Hughes smiled back, and William wondered if the powder kegs really would be enough to deter the jailer. He lowered his hand another couple of inches, and he looked down at his torch, afraid of stray sparks. Perhaps it would be best if he just gave himself up. Would their deaths serve any purpose?

"We have a wagon on its way with two constables," Hughes said. "There's no way out of this."

William wondered if he was bluffing—although he was well aware that most of the city's policemen were willing to enforce the new Fugitive Slave Law, especially if it meant avoiding a stiff fine.

Knight held out a chain in his left hand and jangled them like sleigh bells. "C'mon, be reasonable, William. Wearin' chains ain't as bad as burnin' flesh."

He had a point.

"How do I even know there's powder in them kegs?" Hughes asked.

Lewis handed his torch to William, hefted one of the kegs from the ground, and poured out a small stream of black powder.

"Could be dirt as far as I know." Hughes was looking for fireworks, so Lewis took his torch back, put the flame to the grain, and it went up in a puff of fire and smoke.

"You know of dirt that can do that?" Lewis said with a sly smile. He and Hughes stared each other down, while William wished this could just be over. Waiting to die was worse than dying.

*****

Ellen felt D.K.'s touch on her back.

"You stay right here, Missus Craft. I gotta go, but promise me you ain't moving. Can you do that?"

She raised her head and nodded. She was still on the ground, her dress spread out around her in the filth of the alley. The bricks felt cold, and she wiped her eyes with the back of her sleeve.

"Stay," he repeated. As soon as he took off running down the alley, however, Ellen was on her feet. She was not some dog who could be put out back and told to stay. She had just run a thousand miles from Georgia, and it wasn't going to be in vain.

She made a move to cut through the Hayden home but then realized that they might have the powder kegs set directly at the front door. The last thing she wanted to do was knock over a keg and inadvertently set off an explosion, so she swung around to the east side of the building, where a very narrow alley led from the back to the front. Staring down the alley was like looking down a pitch-black tunnel, so she walked slowly, carefully probing the dark with her hands.

As she neared the end of the short alley, she could distinguish the movement of people directly ahead in the glare of torchlight, and she suddenly realized that one of them was Willis Hughes, only about 20 feet away. Her hand shot to her mouth to contain her instinctive gasp.

But Hughes had seen her. His head snapped in her direction, and she turned to retreat, but he was on her before she could take more than a few steps. She felt a blade against her neck as he dragged her out of the alley and into the open.

39

THE KNIFE PRICKED ELLEN'S SKIN, SHE FELT A GENTLE TRICKLE of blood, and she wondered for one horrifying moment if her throat had been sliced open.

"Another step and I cut her throat." It was Hughes's voice, and it was coming from just behind her right ear. Based on the threat, he must not have cut her very deeply—yet. He probably figured that a live wife would make a better bargaining chip than a dead one.

Hughes was positioned directly behind her, smelling of cigar smoke and sweat, with his left arm wrapped around her and squeezing so hard that her ribs ached. She kept her neck extended as far from his knife as possible. William stood only about 10 feet away, and he held out his torch, like a flaming sword pointed at Hughes. His face was all rage, but he couldn't move any closer without risking her life.

"You hurt her, and I will see you die," William said, taking two steps forward. She felt the knife press against her throat, and William stopped.

"Let us take her, and she'll live," Hughes said. "Try to stop us, and she dies."

Ellen's neck stung and throbbed. She could feel the steel pressing down against her skin. Only a little more pressure and the blade would begin to cut. Out of the corner of her eye, she saw John Knight flanking Hughes on the right, his gun drawn. He looked as frightened as she did.

"Just move back, one step at a time, and you'll live," Hughes whispered into her ear.

"I'm not gonna let you take her," William said.

"Try to stop me and watch her bleed, boy."

Hughes pulled her backward, in more of a hurry now. She was afraid he might trip and the knife would slice deeply. As Hughes moved backward, William and Lewis advanced, careful not to get any closer than 10 feet away. Was he going to drag her all of the way to the white side of town?

The commotion in the streets had awakened people in several nearby buildings, and folks had drifted out in their nightclothes, many of them armed, all of them black. The men encircled the slave catchers, prepared to spill blood, and Hughes placed the knife closer to her skin.

"Tell 'em to stand back, Craft!" Hughes demanded.

William did as he was ordered, and the men gave the slave catchers room to retreat. It didn't seem as if there was any way for this to end well. She was either going to be dragged alive out of Boston or killed on the street like a dog.

*****

William wanted badly to jam this flaming stick down Hughes's throat. He matched the slave catcher's every backward step with a forward step, but he didn't dare move any closer. Lewis made a move to circle around from the side, but Knight and the other four thugs cut him off.

"Take me instead," William said.

Hughes stopped shuffling backward. He stared—a curious look. "You want to take her place?"

"That's what I said." William handed his torch to Lewis and extended his arms. "Free her. Shackle me."

"That's an interesting proposition, William."

He continued to hold out his arms. "I'm more valuable to you than my wife is."

"True. You'd draw more money on the market."

Knight jangled the shackles and made a move toward William. As he did, William stepped back. "Free her first. Then take me."

Knight laughed. "You think we're fools, William?"

William didn't answer that.

"We ain't givin' her up till your wrists are in chains," Hughes said.

"I ain't doin' that. Free her first."

In the distance, they heard the rattling sound of an approaching wagon, which had just turned onto Southac Street.

"You don't have much time, William," said Knight. "The wagon is comin', and when the police arrive, they'll take you both. Give yourself up quickly, right here and now, and your friend Hayden can see that your wife is safely away."

He was right, William thought. Ellen still had a chance if Lewis could whisk her away now. The north slope of Beacon Hill was a network of secret tunnels and hiding places, and the authorities would never find her. But he had to act quickly—before the police arrived. He really had no other choice; it was a gamble he had to take. He looked over at Lewis and said, "Make sure she's safe." Lewis nodded and William stepped forward, arms outstretched.

"William. Don't. William." Those were the only words Ellen could get out before Hughes dug his knife into her skin, just enough to silence her and release a fresh flow of blood.

"Hurry!" William shouted, and Knight was upon him, latching the black iron shackles around each wrist.

"It will be nice havin' you back in Macon, Bill, although don't expect to be there long," Knight said, finishing the job. "Mister Taylor is fixin' to ship you as far south as you can go without winding up in the Gulf."

"Now let her go," William said to Hughes.

Silence—then scuffles, as Ellen squirmed in the grip.

"Let her go."

"We came for two a' you. We're goin' home with two a' you," Hughes said.

William started to lunge forward, but he knew it would be death for Ellen if he attacked. He wanted so badly to hit, rip, tear, slice, and beat Hughes's face.

"You said you'd release her!"

"Don't rightly recall that."

The carriage pulled up, powered by two horses. The authorities had arrived, and if something was going to happen, it had to happen now.

It did.

For one brief moment—the thinnest slice of time—Hughes turned to look at the carriage. William didn't know how it happened, but he and his wife acted perfectly in synch. They sent no signals to each other, but they acted as one force, as one person—something they had been doing since the day they linked arms and balanced two pails going up and down a plantation field. They were linked in every respect, and they moved in unison. Ellen broke loose from Hughes's grip, but not completely. He wasn't entirely off guard, but she squirmed away just enough that his knife was no longer at her neck—but only for a split second. Before Hughes could draw her back in, William was there, behind him, his shackles were around the man's neck, and he was twisting so hard that he wondered if the man's head was going to pop off.

He dragged the slave hunter backward. Hughes jammed his knife down and back in an arcing stab, sinking it into William's thigh. William barely noticed. Hughes pulled out the knife and was attempting to stab again when Lewis grabbed his hand and nearly broke the man's fingers extricating the knife. Then Lewis drew Ellen to safety. Hughes kicked and tried to claw the chain from around his neck, but William was too strong, too enraged.

Knight appeared too shocked to do anything but gape, but one of the other slave catchers made a move to attack with his knife. William yanked Hughes around like a rag doll, making him a human shield, and the slave catcher nearly sank his blade in Hughes's gut by mistake. William was squeezing the life out of the man, Ellen was screaming, and Lewis was next to him, shouting, "Don't kill him! Don't kill him! William! Let up!"

William understood that killing Hughes would be his end, but he didn't let up. His arms were an independent force, squeezing with power, while Lewis tried to pull his hands away from the chains. Men had emerged from the carriage, and pretty soon they would be arresting him, so why not take Hughes with him? Why not finish him off? Put the dog down. If a Cuban bloodhound attacked a plantation owner's wife, the man would shoot him in the head and dump him in a ditch. He should do the same to Hughes.

Even in the dark, William could see that Hughes's face had gone purple. He almost laughed out loud. Hughes was no longer a white man. His face was getting darker by the moment.

Ellen screamed again, and that broke William's trance. He let go, pushed Hughes forward, and the man fell face-forward onto the ground. He was alive. Barely. Gasping for breath, he sounded like a horse that William once heard struggling after being shot in the head. He remained on his knees, gagging and puking.

Ellen latched onto William, but his arms and legs felt as if they were burning, as if a powder keg had gone off inside his body and engulfed him from within.

"Take her to safety!" he shouted at Lewis, but for some odd reason his friend was grinning. "Take Ellen to safety! You hear me?"

"That's not necessary," Lewis said, and he pointed toward the carriage.

William finally saw. The carriage carried two people—D.K. and a Boston constable sympathetic to their cause. D.K. had run for help from the other side of Beacon Hill, and help had arrived. These were not Hughes's constables, here to arrest William or Ellen.

The policeman strode over to Knight and Hughes, who looked up from his knees. They must have known what was coming. The other slave catchers had vanished into the darkness.

"Mister Knight and Mister Hughes, would you please come with me peacefully?"

Knight looked down at Hughes, who was struggling to his feet and coughing so hard that he spattered his shirt with blood. Knight made a move to help his partner up, but he abruptly changed his mind and took off running instead. In disbelief, Hughes watched him disappear into the darkness. Then the jailer looked around, saw he was alone, surrounded, and pretty near dead, so he took off, following Knight into the darkness. D.K. and a few men pursued, but the policeman did not bother. He probably knew that arresting the slave hunters for enforcing the Fugitive Slave Law wouldn't stand a chance in court.

"They're gone," William said, drawing Ellen in tighter.

She pressed her head against his chest. "But how do we know they ain't gonna come back?"

"D.K. and the others will make sure. If they have to chase them across state lines, they'll make sure they're gone for good."

"But slave hunters will just keep comin' back. What's to stop them from comin' back? What's to stop them from takin' our children?"

"Try not to think about that," he said. "Tonight we're walking in the light of the living."

William kissed the top of her head.

"Tonight, you're safe," he added.

"But I want to be safe tomorrow," she said softly.

He understood completely.

40

London, England
Spring 1851: Six Months Later

LLEN LINKED ARMS WITH MARY AND APPROACHED THE MOST magnificent structure she had ever seen. It was a glass palace—the Crystal Palace, people were calling it. It rose up from the grass of Hyde Park in London like something from a dream.

"I cannot believe this was built in less than a year," said Mary.

Ellen didn't say a word. The construction of a magnificent structure within a single year did not shock her nearly as much as the realization of just how far their lives had come in a single year. When it was learned that Dr. Collins had written to President Millard Fillmore, and that there was the real risk of the U.S. Army being sent to Boston to enforce the Fugitive Slave Law, William had finally seen a reason to head farther north. After going through a second wedding, just to make their marriage legally binding, they had fled to Canada. Then, almost exactly 2 years from the day they had reached Philadelphia—around Christmas of 1850—they had taken the steamboat *Cambria* to Liverpool, England, which had once been a bustling port for the shipment of slaves. On that December day, William and Ellen had arrived as free Americans far out of the reach of Knight, Hughes, and any other would-be slave catchers.

Ellen had caught pneumonia on the trip across the Atlantic, but when she finally recovered, she and William had connected with their old friend from America, the former slave William Wells Brown. They had traveled all around England, talking about slavery, and Ellen was always the highlight of the program, dressed up in her disguise: top hat, overcoat, sling, and jaw bandage—and of course her green glasses. To be honest, Ellen quickly had grown weary of repeating their story, putting on the disguise, and parading in front of strangers.

They had become famous in England and were sought after by some of the most prominent people in the country, among them Alfred, Lord Tennyson, and Lady Noel Byron, widow of the great poet Lord Byron. However, nothing could have prepared them for meeting Queen Victoria and Prince Albert at the Great Exhibition of the Works of Industry of All Nations—all of it housed in the magnificent Crystal Palace. They had met the Queen a week ago, and the Prince had been thrilled to meet them, for he was president of the British Anti-Slavery Society.

Imagine that. Prince Albert was thrilled to see *them*! They had come a long way from the cotton fields of central Georgia. There was only one thing missing in their lives, but William didn't like to speak of it, so Ellen mostly stayed quiet on the subject. Today, they would soak up the exhibits in anonymity.

"I want to see everything," Ellen said. "During our previous visit to the Crystal Palace, circumstances did not afford us the opportunity to take everything in." By "circumstances," she meant their visit with the Queen.

"I heard the building is so big that four Saint Paul's cathedrals could fit inside," said Jonathan Scott, Mary's husband, a white businessman—a wealthy man. He and William were walking just a few steps behind. Mary and Jonathan still lived in New York, and they had come across the ocean to see William and Ellen for the first time since Boston.

"Do you think people will recognize you in the crowd?" Mary asked Ellen.

"I don't believe so. I am very good at hiding in plain sight."

The building was like a three-tiered cake of glass with an arching glass roof running down the middle. The Crystal Palace, a hive of activity, was big enough to encompass an entire avenue of elm trees.

Ellen was most interested in seeing Elias Howe's new sewing machine—a prize feature among the American exhibits. They went to that exhibit first, squeezed to the front, and marveled at Howe's remarkable machine, although she noted that it could not sew in as straight a line as her hand.

"Don't worry, a machine could never replace you," said Mary, as they worked their way back through the crowd that had packed around the sewing machine.

While William and Jonathan were occupied with studying Samuel Colt's new guns, also in the American exhibit, Ellen and Mary found a seat to rest a spell. Ellen still tired easily—a side effect of her pneumonia. People passing by probably saw them as just two more white women. How shocked they would be if they knew that only 6 months ago slave hunters were tracking Ellen.

"There's so much here, it's overwhelming," said Ellen. The bustle and the machines were wonderful, but gadgets seemed so trivial compared to the flesh-and-blood people in their lives. She and Mary talked about Ellen's mother, about how they were still making inquiries into purchasing Maria's freedom. Ellen explained that the Major and Missus Smith were still too outraged by their escape to even consider selling Maria.

Ellen leaned her head on her cousin's shoulder, feeling so much like that 11-year-old girl again, being taken from her mama.

"Frank is going back to Georgia," Mary suddenly said, and Ellen sat up straight, as if yanked by puppet strings. "I was waiting for the right time to mention it, and finally realized there is no right time."

"But he'll be captured. He's not—he's not as white as I am."

"White enough. We posed as white going north, you'll remember. And most people in New York see me as white."

"But why go back?"

"He's aiming to get our sisters free."

Ellen couldn't imagine it—the very notion of going back after working so hard to escape.

"He's cultivating whiskers and a moustache, and he cut off his hair and purchased a wig 'cause his hair is the main thing that could give him away," Mary said. "He is probably on the way there as we speak. Pray for him, Ellen."

Ellen nodded. She closed her eyes and placed her head back on Mary's shoulder, and she prayed for Frank—but it was difficult to concentrate with all of the noise. After awhile, they got up and purchased cups of tea—a British tradition that Ellen embraced enthusiastically.

Ellen scanned their surroundings, noticing all of the fine dresses swirling about. She still sewed, and out of habit she couldn't help but examine the finery of the women all around her. Her eyes landed on a case of dresses, but then her gaze drifted to the adjacent exhibit, marked "Horological Instruments." These were some of the most magnificent timepieces she had ever seen. Once again, she couldn't believe how much they had seen in so little time. While in Scotland, they had even been allowed to view the stars and planets through the telescope of astronomer Thomas Dick. At one time, the 12-mile trip from Clinton to Macon had seemed like she was traveling to another world, but now she was looking at other planets.

They had come so far, but something was still missing.

"It seems odd," Ellen said.

Mary stared at her and waited for her to continue. "What's odd, Ellen?"

"I wanted to escape so my children would be free."

"They will be free."

Ellen felt the tears building. She fought them. "But what if I never have children? Was it all for nothing?"

"No, no, Ellen. Your freedom is something. William's freedom is something. Besides, I know you will have a child."

Mary couldn't possibly know that, and the difference in their lives seemed so cruel. Mary already had a child, and once again Ellen felt the knife-stabs of jealousy. Was Mary always going to have the advantages?

"Is the Lord punishing me?"

"For what, Ellen? That makes no sense."

"Then why do I have to wait?"

"Rachel waited a long time to have a child, but He opened her womb."

Ellen smiled. She had used the same Scripture on William long ago when she had reminded him that Jacob had to wait a long time before he could marry Rachel. But Mary was right. Rachel had to wait a long time for children, and she had to stand by and watch Jacob's other wife, Leah, have one child after another. Mary was Ellen's Leah.

"I didn't do this for myself, you know. I escaped for my children, and my children's children," Ellen said once again.

Mary sighed and said nothing. She reached out and took Ellen by the hand, and Ellen was glad her cousin didn't try to speak.

41

Ockham, England
October 22, 1852: One and a Half Years Later

LLEN'S BODY HAD BEEN TAKEN OVER BY ROLLING WAVES OF pain. Each pain started out small, just a ripple, a tightening, but then it built and built and built until the crushing sensation felt like a loaded wagon was rolling across her abdomen. She moaned as the pain subsided, and she braced herself for the next wagon to come crush her.

"You're doing fine," said one of eight women who were taking care of her in the lying-in room. Male physicians tending to women and delivering babies were becoming much more common, and they performed their delicate examinations unsighted—with their eyes on the mother's face—but the idea of a man in the room, even William, was too much. She had decided she would do this with her midwife and the other women who sprang into action whenever a mother was in confinement. It was the female version of the volunteer firemen who leaped to action when the village bell rang out an alarm. Only this fire was inside her belly.

She wished she had her mother by her side—or Mary. Her mother would be rubbing olive oil on her abdomen and applying hot compresses to reduce the pain, and her steady presence would be the finest balm of all.

The next wagon came rolling over her, crushing, crushing, crushing, and for a moment it felt as if the wagon was just sitting there on top of her, going nowhere, pressing down. This time the wagon on top of her abdomen seemed to be carrying a load of iron.

She let out a guttural scream that she couldn't contain.

One woman dabbed her forehead with a sponge.

Another held her hand.

Another talked to her calmly.

One just stared. That would be Missus Damby, a 50-year-old veteran of childbirth, a stone-faced spirit of doom. She was the one who told her, "Childbirth gives you 9 months to prepare for death." She brought hot water into the room, but mostly she just stood off in the corner, a stoic reminder that Ellen might be exiting the world just as her newborn entered it, like passing spirits.

It was coming again. The wave. She felt a rise of panic. She felt trapped inside this body. There was no way to get out of the path of pain. She gripped the edge of the bed so hard that she thought the wood was going to splinter in her fingers.

"Do you think ether would smooth your path?" asked Missus Gladstone, the woman holding her hand, when the latest wagonload had rolled off of her body and she was panting and sweating.

When she was asked earlier in the day, she had refused the ether. "Just one-eighth of an ounce on a handkerchief," Missus Maloney had said, but Ellen dismissed the offer. Missus Damby made it obvious that she did not approve of ether under any circumstances. "Eve didn't use it," she said.

But now, but now...

Here it came, building, building, rolling on, relentlessly cruel. Another wagon, and this one felt heavier than all the rest put together. She was beginning to wonder whether she would survive. Maybe Missus Damby was right. Maybe this was death.

Ellen had started the day on her back, and when the first pains came, she remembered thinking this was not nearly as bad as she had expected. She felt a sense of pride—that she could handle this with much greater ease than other women. She was paying for those thoughts.

Now she was on her left side, and Missus Gladstone was massaging her lower back, which ached with a low-level throb. The next wagon came rolling over, and she tried counting the number of flowers in the pattern of the wallpaper. One, two, three, four, five, six, seven, eight...she closed her eyes and waved off another offer of ether.

Between contractions, she sometimes stood and leaned against the dresser, rocking back and forth. She felt a little nauseous as the pain expanded from beyond her abdomen and assaulted the farthest reaches of her body, like an invading force. It suddenly occurred to her why men were kept out of the lying-in room. If they came anywhere near their wives at this stage, the women would kill them on sight.

The women of Ockham were so nice, but they weren't her mama, and they weren't Mary. William and Ellen had come to this small village, 20 miles outside of London, to attend the Ockham School and finally master the art of reading and writing. They had succeeded, and the letters she wrote to Mary and her mama on a daily basis were her only link to her old life in America.

"Who's Mary?" asked Missus Gladstone, as she gave Ellen's hand a squeeze after another wagon had rolled across her.

"What?"

"You were calling for Mary."

"She is my cousin, my dearest friend."

"She would be proud of you, Ellen."

"She already has two children, and she would think I am weak if she saw me now."

"You are anything but weak."

Ellen suddenly smiled—something she hadn't done for the past 5 hours.

"Right about now, I think I might prefer being Mister Johnson again, rather than Ellen Craft. Maybe being a man wasn't so bad after all."

Missus Gladstone smiled back, but she must have seen the panic in Ellen's face because she squeezed her hand and said soothing words. Ellen had returned to the world of pain.

*****

When Ellen reached the pushing stage, the pain was still there, but her mind was more separated from it. She felt a growing sense of excitement, feeling the baby moving down, moving out, and a stretching, stretching. She was working hard. She was plowing through the pain, getting somewhere, pushing, pushing, straining and stretching and pushing. She felt the head coming through and an intense ring of burning; she could even feel the soft hair of her child's head. Then came the shoulder, rotating as he passed through, and then a sudden rush of relief and completion.

The women were all smiles. Even Missus Damby couldn't contain the flicker of a smile, even though her predictions of doom had not come to pass. Ellen was still alive. In fact, she felt more alive than any other time in her life. It was strangely similar to the feeling she had had when she stepped onto free soil for the first time. Ecstatic. There was no other way to put it.

"It's a boy, Ellen!"

A boy. William will be so happy. They placed him on her chest, and he was so red and alive and squalling. His head was cone-shaped from the delivery, and he had little white spots on his skin, but she had never seen a more beautiful child in her life.

By the time William entered the room, she no longer wanted to murder him.

It was all a fog when she looked back on the hour that followed, but she remembered the tears and William being there by her bedside. "This was what it was all for," she told William before she gave in to the tears. She looked down on their child. His name: Charles Estlin Phillips Craft. So many names for so small a person, but the names were given in honor of the friends who had helped them along the way. If they could have given this child 100 names to honor them all, they would have.

They had come 5,000 miles to reach this point, and they still had a long way to go. Five thousand miles and what seemed like 5,000 labor pains. She wasn't sure if she had ever seen William cry, and she could tell he was working hard to keep the tears at bay. They had come through it all, arm in arm, a chalk-line walk with the world balanced on their backs.

"This was what it was all for," she said again.

William didn't answer. He didn't dare speak or he'd break down. She could tell. So he just nodded his head, and that's all she needed to see.

Epilogue

William and Ellen lived in England for 19 years. Even from such a distance, William tracked down his mother and sister Sarah and bought their freedom, and the mother and daughter reunited in America. The Smiths, angry about Ellen's escape, never did agree to sell her mother Maria to them. However, after the War Between the States, Maria became free, and Ellen sent money to her so her mother could join them in England.

William and Ellen returned to America in 1869, and in 1870 they visited Georgia, where William was reunited with his sister Sarah. They rented a farm, the Hickory Hill plantation in South Carolina, and started a school to teach children from neighboring farms. But in the fall of 1870, the Ku Klux Klan burned down their house, barn, and school, so they salvaged what they could and moved to Savannah, where they ran a hotel and raised money to create a new school. They rented an abandoned farm in Woodville, Georgia, and modeled their new school after the Ockham School in England.

William and Ellen retired in Charleston, South Carolina, where two of their children—Ellen and Charles—lived. Ellen Craft Crum, their daughter, went on to become a prominent civil rights leader, founding the National Federation of Afro-American Women.

Ellen Craft passed away in 1897 at the age of 71 and was buried beneath her favorite pine tree in Woodville, Georgia. William followed her to Glory in 1900.

They had five biological children, three adopted African children, and many descendants. All of one blood.

And He has made from one blood every nation of men to dwell on all the face of the earth. (Acts 17:26)

Author's Notes

When I began researching the remarkable stories of the Underground Railroad, two of them stood out. The first story was that of Henry "Box" Brown, a slave who nailed himself shut in a wooden box and was mailed to freedom, from Richmond to Philadelphia in 27 hours. I tell this story in my first novel, *The Disappearing Man*.

After *The Disappearing Man* came out in 2011, I couldn't help but see that Ellen Craft's story made the ideal companion piece. Both stories focus on couples—Henry and Nancy, and William and Ellen—although *The Disappearing Man* highlights the husband while *The Vanishing Woman* highlights the wife. Both are among the most unusual slave escapes of which I am aware, and both escapes were motivated by the desire for family. Henry decided to escape because he wanted to be reunited with his wife and children; Ellen wanted to escape to have free children. They began their adventures from different starting points, but when Ellen and William reached Richmond, they followed the exact route the rest of the way to Philadelphia as Henry Brown did.

As if that wasn't enough, Henry and Ellen escaped within 3 months of each other.

My primary resource for *The Vanishing Woman* was the first-person narrative *Running a Thousand Miles for Freedom*, published in 1860 and written in William's voice. Most of the incidents in *The Vanishing Woman* are true, including the dramatic confrontation in Boston, where Lewis Hayden and William really did threaten to blow up the house with gunpowder. However, I had to fill in a lot of blanks and expand on events that their narrative covered in a matter of a few paragraphs. For example, the narrative does not tell about the courtship between Ellen and William, so those chapters are fiction. However, I present all of the central events of their escape, with details filled in and embellishments to flesh out the scenes.

The subplot with Ellen's aunt and cousins, Frank and Mary, is also true, for William relates this tale in *Running a Thousand Miles for Freedom*. Relations between whites and blacks in the antebellum South were often more complicated than we think. William says that a wealthy white man treated Ellen's aunt, a slave, as his wife, while the children were treated as free children. William doesn't mention the man by name, but I called him Mister Slator. When Mister Slator died, the family was apprehended and split up by his nephew, as the novel describes, and Frank and Mary made their escape when the nephew became drunk while taking them to South Carolina by wagon. That is all true. Frank and Mary then made their ways north, posing as white people.

However, in telling this story, William does not indicate the year of Mister Slator's death, as well as Frank and Mary's ensuing escape. For drama's sake, I chose to combine Frank and Mary's tale with William and Ellen's story. Also, William does not say how Mister Slator died, so that scene is a fictional version of what might have happened.

I had a chance to visit Macon, Georgia, where William and Ellen lived at the time of their escape. The home of Dr. Robert Collins and his wife Eliza still stands near the corner of Mulberry and New, although it has been converted to offices. Ellen's cabin in the back no longer exists, but a servants' quarters that might have been similar to her lodging can still be found only a couple of houses down from the old Collins Estate behind the famous Cannonball House (the only house in Macon to be hit by a cannonball during the Civil War).

In addition to walking the streets where Ellen and William walked more than 160 years ago, I followed their route to Savannah, Georgia, and saw the spot where the old train station stood— the place where they would have arrived before taking an omnibus to the wharf along the Savannah River. I also traveled to their next destination—Charleston—and I saw where the steamship would have docked. William and Ellen say they went to a hotel during their short time in Charleston, but they do not mention its name. I chose the Planter's Hotel, which would have existed at the time. This hotel is now the beautiful Dock Street Theater on Church Street.

This is the first novel about Ellen Craft of which I am aware, although there are several children's books. I also came across only one nonfiction book entirely devoted to the story of William and Ellen Craft—*5,000 Miles to Freedom*, by Judith Bloom Fradin and Dennis Brindell Fradin, published by National Geographic in 2006. However, numerous nonfiction books devote chapters to William and Ellen Craft, and they made invaluable resources. They include the following:

Black Foremothers: Three Lives, by Dorothy Sterling, the Feminist Press at the City University of New York, 1988.

Forbidden Fruit: Love Stories From the Underground Railroad, by Betty DeRamus, Atria Books, 2005.

Fugitive Slave in the Gold Rush: Life and Adventures of James Williams, by James Williams, University of Nebraska Press, 2002 (first published in 1893).

Georgia Women: Their Lives and Times, Volume 1, edited by Ann Short Chirhart and Betty Wood, the University of Georgia Press, 2009.

Sarah's Long Walk: The Free Blacks of Boston and How Their Struggle for Equality Changed America, by Stephen Kendrick and Paul Kendrick, Beacon Press, 2004.

Shadrach Minkins: From Fugitive Slave to Citizen, by Gary Collison, Harvard University Press, 1997.

Walking on Cotton: Civil War and Emancipation Era Guide to Macon, GA, by Conie Mac Darnell, Center City Press, 2012.

In addition to these books, other important resources include:

Black Bostonians: Family Life and Community Struggle in the Antebellum North, by James Oliver Horton and Lois E. Horton, Holmes and Meier, 2000.

Courage and Conscience: Black and White Abolitionists in Boston, edited by Donald M. Jacobs, Indiana University Press, 1993.

Macon: Georgia's Central City, by Kristina Simms, Windsor Publications, Inc., 1989.

Macon's Treasures Remembered: The Antebellum Years, by Jo Mc-Connel and Sadie Crumbley, Hallmark Publishing Company, Inc., 2002.

Mulatto America, by Stephen Talty, HarperCollins Publishers, 2003.

Railroad Journey: The Industrialization of Time and Space in the 19th Century, by Wolfgang Schivelbusch, the University of California Press, 1977, 1986.

Runaway Slaves: Rebels on the Plantation, by John Hope Franklin and Loren Schweninger, Oxford University Press, 1999.

Stylin': African American Expressive Culture, by Shane White and Graham White, Cornell University Press, 1998.

Discussion Questions

- How did Ellen Craft's story change your perceptions about race in the nineteenth century? What surprised you?
- What unique challenges faced someone like Ellen, who looked white but was classified as being of African descent?
- What were the turning points in Ellen's relationship with her half-sister, Eliza? How did their relationship change throughout the story?
- How was Ellen's path in life different from her cousin Mary's path? How were their paths similar?
- What were Ellen's strengths? What were her weaknesses?
- What did Ellen's hair represent to her?
- What are ways in which the theme of blood comes up in the story?
- In the nineteenth century, the idea arose that one drop of African blood made you African. In what ways did *The Vanishing Woman* grapple with this belief?
- Does the "one drop" rule still hold sway today? Explain why or why not.
- How do people of mixed descent determine whether they are part of a specific race? Has it changed over the years?
- Is the idea of "race" a human creation?
- Are racial categories helpful or harmful? In what ways?
- What was the Fugitive Slave Act of 1850? What would you have done if you had been in William and Ellen's shoes when the Act was passed in 1850? Would you have left Boston for Canada or stayed and fought? Explain.